Allie Spencer is an author with many strings to her bow. She gained a B.A. in English and Related Literature and an M.A. in Medieval Studies before reading for the Bar. She completed pupillage in London with a leading set of family law barristers and then joined a firm of solicitors as a matrimonial specialist.

She is the author of three novels: *Tug of Love*, which won the Romantic Novelists' Association New Writers' Scheme prize for the best debut of 2009 and was shortlisted for the 2010 Melissa Nathan Award for Comedy Romance, *The Not-So-Secret Diary of a City Girl*, and *Summer Loving*.

# ALLIE SPENCER

arrow books

Published by Arrow Books in 2012

2 4 6 8 10 9 7 5 3 1

First published in Great Britain in 2012 by
Arrow Books
Random House, 20 Vauxhall Bridge Road,
London SW1V 2SA

www.randomhouse.co.uk

Addresses for companies within The Random House Group Limited can be
found at: www.randomhouse.co.uk

The Random House Group Limited Reg. No. 954009

A CIP catalogue record for this book is available from the British Library

ISBN 978-0-099-55706-7

The Random House Group Limited supports The Forest Stewardship
Council (FSC®), the leading international forest certification organisation.
Our books carrying the FSC label are printed on FSC® certified paper. FSC is
the only forest certification scheme endorsed by the leading environmental
organisations, including Greenpeace. Our paper procurement policy can be
found at: www.randomhouse.co.uk/environment

Typeset by SX Composing DTP, Rayleigh, Essex
Printed and bound in Great Britain by
CPI Group (UK) Ltd, Croydon, CR0 4TD

To Flora. Thank you for the loan of your name and I hope you approve of what I have done with it once you are old enough to read.

GMA x

# Acknowledgements

As ever, there are a host of wonderful people who were involved in this book and who helped make it as good as it could possibly be and I would like to start by thanking the 'professionals', namely my editor Gillian and my agent Teresa for working so hard to bring it into being. Next I extend humble thanks to my friend Sarah Jane Stratford who dug me out of a hole when I needed it and generally cheered me on from the sidelines. Then come the raft of people from whom I have borrowed names – Flora C, of course, and the Bellas; plus Julie, Nina and Dan. And the REAL, living breathing Melinda who lent herself and her band, the fabulous Madam and the Ants to the book (go and see them if you find yourself in San Francisco – they rock!). Special thanks also to Ali Thomson and Charles who advised on the hospital scenes (anything accurate is down to them, the mistakes are all mine). Then there are the people who were simply there for me – Grace, Caz, Clive, Nancy and my other, wonderful friends – you know who you are. Finally, I need to thank my family – both my immediates (boys, I love you) and my extendeds – especially my own cousins and grandparents, both departed and present. This is a book about families, about how they sometimes drift apart but do their best to hold strong when the chips are down. Precious beyond measure.

It was my birthday.

My thirtieth birthday.

And it was destined to be fabulous.

Amongst other things, it was the first day of a much anticipated romantic fortnight in San Francisco with my boyfriend Barney. We were travelling there separately: I'd arrived three days earlier for a series of meetings with some important clients and, now I was off duty, he was flying in later that afternoon. That left me with a few hours to kill and a serious holiday mood to get into, so I booked myself into 'InSPAration' (the in-house spa – sorry, 'holistic wellness retreat' – at my hotel) for a spot of R and R.

Spas were not my natural habitat. In fact, the only other time I'd been to one a tiny Korean woman who didn't speak any English nearly aromatherapy-massaged me into an early grave. This time, however, I was hoping that the Goddess of Overpriced and Slightly Pointless Beauty Treatments would be on my side. Not only did I want to look my best for the holiday – and Barney, obviously – but I needed to destress from work and, in particular, from my clients, Earl and Sadie McMaster, a couple who had not yet heard that slavery had been abolished.

So there I was, lying on a table in a semi-darkened room, covered in something that smelled like vanilla yogurt, with whale music assailing my ears.

And I was starting to regret my decision.

Azure, my six-foot, ice-blonde Norwegian therapist – sorry, 'wellness facilitator' – dipped her hand into a large silver bowl and sprinkled what looked like large pink flower petals over me. I picked one off the top of my leg and studied it. There were words printed on one side.

My heart sank. Oh God, they were affirmations. No one had said there would be affirmations.

'Repeats after me,' instructed Azure, 'my souls is like a beautifuls dove, soarings upwards on ze vings of tranquuvillities.'

Something in her voice told me I didn't have any choice in the matter.

'Mysoulislikeabeautifuldovesoaringonwingsoftranquu-illity,' I muttered grudgingly, hoping she didn't want me to actually *mean* any of it. Then I turned my mind back to the serious business of relaxation.

*Breathe in – and out. Ignore all references to doves, wings and soaring. Limbs feeling loose and heavy. Good – very good – and—*

Oh crap! Had I emailed the link from the Harrods online furniture catalogue to Mrs McMaster?

I tensed. Instantly.

I'd recently started work at Relocation Wizards, an agency that helped people who were long on money but short on time bring themselves and their unfeasibly large salaries to the United Kingdom. I had some experience in the field already, but the Wizards were pretty much top of the pops as far as the relocation industry were concerned and I was anxious to impress my new boss, Brenda – even if it meant half killing myself to satisfy clients as perennially pernickety as the McMasters.

I made a mental note to check my 'send' box the moment I got back to my room, and then turned my thoughts once more towards relaxation.

*Forget work. Work is over for two whole weeks. Back to the breathing. In and out. In and—*

Bella. Should I try emailing Bella one last time?

Muscles. Tense. Yet again!

Bella was my cousin, although growing up we'd been more like sisters. She'd moved to San Francisco two years earlier to take up a nursing position in a prestigious private hospital, and I was hoping we'd be able to catch up whilst I was in town, but she was proving strangely elusive and I was beginning to wonder if everything was OK.

*Forget Bella, forget the McMasters, forget the doves. You can deal with it all later.*

Azure swept her hands over my face and then my feet, depositing more of the yogurty substance round my toes. I did my best to enjoy the sensation, even if it was a little cold and gooey.

*Breathing. In and out. In and out. In and—*

'My bodies is bloomings with pleasure like ze new - born rose,' she informed me as a second helping of pink paper petal-like nonsense fluttered down on to my body. 'Now you say.'

Arrrrghhh! *How am I supposed to relax with all these interruptions?*

'Look,' I said, feeling decidedly bolshie and unrose-like, 'as far as pleasure is concerned, I think I'd be experiencing a lot more of it if we could lose ze – I mean the – affirmations. What do you say?'

'Affirmations is essential to ze healings process.' She put her hands on her hips. 'Zey detox ze souls while ze nutrients from ze goat placentas detox ze skins.'

I nearly leapt out of my paper knickers.

'*Goat placentas?*'

Azure narrowed her fjord-coloured eyes.

'It is opening ze meridians and making ze chis to circulate,' she said in a manner I considered unnecessarily aggressive for a wellness facilitator, 'and anyways, ze placentas only comes from very small goats.'

*Because the size of the goat made any difference?*

I held up my hand.

'Today is my birthday, Azure, and I am going to do what I want – and what I want does not involve chanting mantras or being wrapped in the reproductive by-products of four-legged mammals and – urgh!'

Something gloopy dripped off the end of my nose and into my open mouth allowing me to tell you with confidence that a goat's placenta face-mask tastes unbelievably rank.

As last straws went, it was pretty much definitive.

I slid off the table with as much dignity as I could

muster whilst wearing spa paper pants and pale creamy yuk. My plan was to grab my robe and then head for the showers as a matter of urgency but, three steps in, I slipped.

Yes, it had to be – on the goat cream.

I cannoned across the marble floor, collided with Azure who was still holding her silver bowl of affirmations and I, a Norwegian wellness facilitator and a blizzard of pink paper strips went flying – straight into the fire alarm: hitting it with such force that it went off.

'You will be going outsides now,' Azure announced, passing me a robe and, I noticed, smiling. 'It is ze rules. We have to go out and wait on ze streets for ze fire brigades.'

I took a moment to appraise my appearance: plastered in yogurty goaty goo, to which a flurry of pink strips was now adhering, and faced with the prospect of a street full of strangers, firemen and, yes, perhaps actual mocking.

I took a deep breath and struggled to my feet.

'My soul is like a dove,' I said, closing my eyes for a moment and trying to feel the chi flowing freely through my meridians and keeping me calm, 'soaring upwards on the wings of tranquillity.'

After I was (eventually) allowed back to my room, where I showered, dressed and did my best to forget about what had just happened, I decided to get away from the hotel for a bit.

Well, the rest of the day, actually.

I hopped on a passing cable car complete with a clanging, old-fashioned bell, and, as it pulled away up the side of one of the unfeasibly steep hills that the city was built upon, watched in awe as a panoramic view of first downtown, then the Bay and finally the shoreline opposite slowly revealed itself, the midday sun glittering on the water.

This is me, I thought.

On my birthday.

In San Francisco.

A shiver of excited anticipation ran down my spine.

The cable car drew to a halt and the bell clanged loudly to indicate the end of the line. The majority of the passengers – including me – scrambled out, and I found myself at the intersection of four busy-looking streets. After considering my options for a moment or two, I decided to turn into the right-hand one, and I made my way along a broad pavement lined with shops. These looked much older than many of the deco structures I'd seen downtown and were timber-built. Like most of the other buildings in this part of town, their frontages were painted a multitude of bright colours. I passed an eclectic mix of businesses plying their trades: smart coffee shops cheek by jowl with kooky-looking vintage clothing emporia, bright and breezy bookstores, yoga studios and – brilliantly – a henna tattoo parlour for dogs rejoicing in the name Doodles on Poodles. A nearby signpost told me that this eclectic thoroughfare was called Hope Street.

I stopped. Bella lived on a road named Hope Heights; was it possible that I'd inadvertently stumbled upon her neighbourhood? I glanced round, searching for a friendly-looking shop or café in which I could make enquiries. A few metres further on I spied what looked like a real American diner: a scarlet awning overhung the pavement and enticing aromas wove their way from an open window making a beeline for my nostrils. My stomach rumbled and I realised I could quite happily have eaten a horse, not to mention the saddle, bridle *and* the whole of the British Olympic Equestrian Squad.

I would have lunch *and* ask directions to Bella's road. Sorted.

I walked over to the door, pushed it open and stepped inside. A woman, probably in her sixties, with greying hair and a slim, elegant figure, stepped out from behind a counter and smiled at me.

'Hi, honey, welcome to the Apple Pie,' she said. 'You look as though you're in the market for a bite to eat.'

I nodded. Although ideally I'd welcome more than just a bite.

'Then you've come to the right place. None of your fast food here, just the old-fashioned slow variety. I'm Sylvie, by the way, and over there is my sister Elvira.'

An almost identical-looking lady, albeit with a slightly rounder face, glanced up from refilling a coffee cup and waved in our direction. They're friendly, I thought, and waved back. Nice to have a bit of good old-fashioned customer service after Azure the Nordic Ice-Maiden and her ridiculous affirmations.

As I waved, however, I felt something tickle the top of my ear. I was about to investigate but found myself needing both hands to take the enormous laminated menu Sylvie was thrusting at me. I'd never seen anything like it: it was so huge you could have gone hang-gliding with it.

'Wow,' I said, wondering if I'd actually have time to read it before Barney's plane landed.

Sylvie laughed a rich, lazy laugh that made me think of golden syrup drizzling onto thickly buttered bread and ushered me towards an empty banquette.

'Our specials today,' Sylvie said, once I'd got myself settled, 'are crayfish and locally grown avocado on organic rye; bagels and sustainably sourced lox with tofu vegetable cream cheese; or papaya, blueberry and pomegranate buckwheat pancakes with maple syrup and crème fraîche. Or I can rustle you up a plate of my signature free-range chicken and spelt waffles with a kumquat compote. Try saying that without your teeth in.'

'Blimey,' I said, thinking I'd have to have a degree in nutrition to understand half of what she'd just told me, 'can I start by ordering a coffee, please?'

'Sure, honey! We have regular, cappuccino, mochachino, chicory, half-caff, decaff, organic, organic fair-trade—'

I held up my hand. My brain was swimming. Probably in fair-trade organic coffee.

'Regular please, full caff, semi-skimmed milk, no sugar.'

I reckoned that probably covered all coffee-related eventualities.

But I was wrong.

'Longe, extra longe, super longe or gigante?'

All I wanted was a cup of ground roasted beans steeped in hot water and topped off with a dash of milk. What, might I ask, was a *gigante*? What scale of weights and measurements did *that* conform to? Were we even still talking about hot beverages?

The mind boggled.

'Longe,' I said, hoping that as it was the first option she had mentioned, it wouldn't be served in a bucket-sized container. 'And may I have the chicken and waffles, please?'

'Sure you can.' Sylvie smiled her lovely smile. 'Coming right up. Slowly.'

With that, she bustled off.

I stared out of the window at the busy street for a moment and then scooped my lovely, technolicious new phone out of my bag. It had been an early birthday present from me to myself and I was almost embarrassingly excited about it. I unlocked it, and the wallpaper image of the little white terraced house I shared with Barney popped on to its screen.

My coffee arrived. I took a sip and, as I did so, I became aware of the tickle at the top of my ear again. I scratched at it impatiently, hoping it wasn't some form of native insect; and then, when the scratching

9

didn't work, shook my head, sending my long red ringletty curls flying across my face.

The tickle persisted.

I was just about to try and find my compact mirror so I could take a proper look at my ear when I felt the weight of a gaze come to rest upon my shoulders. I turned round and there, on the other side of the high leather seat that divided my banquette from the one next door, were a pair of vivid blue eyes, scrutinising me with amused, but intense, interest. The eyes were set into an oval face with a high forehead, from which a mop of thick, dark, hint-of-a-curl hair was swept casually back.

'I am a gift to the world for others to unwrap,' the gazing man announced, his mouth curving naturally into a half-smile.

I looked at him suspiciously. My guidebook had warned me there would be people like this in San Francisco.

He held out a pink strip of paper.

'This is yours, I believe,' he said. 'At least, it fell out of your hair.'

I took it grudgingly and turned it over between my fingers. Azure's revenge: a renegade affirmation.

'Thank you,' I replied awkwardly, fervently hoping he didn't think it was some sort of invitation.

'So,' he continued with a wicked, infectious grin, 'how many times a day does your hair have to repeat it?'

My eyes met his and a strange, shivery feeling

10

zipped through me. Shivery . . . but rather nice.

'Well,' I said, my awkwardness suddenly vanishing, 'first I'd have to teach it to speak.'

'Hey, don't joke; there's a Tibetan herbal shop on the Haight that will give you pills for that,' he returned seamlessly, popping a forkful of food into his mouth. 'Steak and home fries,' he mumbled, 'best meal in the world. But anyhoo, tell me: is your hair here on business or pleasure?'

I tried to look away, vaguely aware that he was flirting with me, but found I couldn't. The Bay-blue eyes refused to let me go and, out of nowhere, my stomach gave a little flip of pleasure.

'Why, what do you do to out-of-towners?' I replied, allowing myself to enjoy a repeat performance of the tummy-flipping. 'Or do I not want to know?'

The man's expression suddenly became very serious.

'Well,' he said, lowering his voice and glancing con - spiratorially round the room, 'round about this time of year, everyone in the neighbourhood gets together and makes this enormous wicker man. Then, as the sun sets, we lure any strangers we can find up the hill to the park, dance round them in wild abandon and . . . what are you doing tonight, by the way?'

A self-conscious warmth spread from my cheeks to my neck and down to my décolletage. I was aware my skin had probably turned the exact same shade as my hair. I, however, didn't care.

'I'll have to check my diary,' I informed him boldly,

my own lips curving into a grin as mischievous as the one beaming from the next banquette. 'I'm not sure if I have a window for frenzied ritual human sacrifices.'

Then, with a start, I remembered. Barney: that was what I was doing tonight. Barney! Birthday stuff! Romance! How could that possibly have slipped my mind?

The spell of the blue eyes was broken. Faster than Usain Bolt leaving the starting blocks, I yanked the smile off my face and glanced at my phone, feeling the blush crash across my skin once more – only this time out of guilt. The little white house blinked accusingly up at me.

I muttered something that could have been an excuse or an apology, or hopefully both. Even though there was no way Barney could know what had just passed between me and the gazing man, I still felt I wanted to make things right between us, so I tapped the message icon on my screen, thinking I'd send him a 'love you' text he could open when he'd landed, but nothing happened. I tapped again, and again, but the screen remained totally and annoyingly frozen.

I let out a low grumble of annoyance. There was a pause and I felt the gaze from the neighbouring banquette come to rest upon me once again.

'Problem?' asked the man at last.

I paused, mid-tap. Conversation with Gazing Man had proven to be dangerous territory and I was wary of going there again, but equally, I couldn't just ignore him.

'I paid for an app that guarantees an international connection,' I told him, staring hard at his chin in an effort to avoid the magnetism of the blue eyes, 'but it's not working.'

'Give it here.'

His tone was cool and professional and for a split second disappointment flashed through me. Then I shook myself and remembered that, even if I *were* available for flirting purposes, I certainly wouldn't set my sights on a man who wore a T-shirt saying 'Have You Tried Turning It Off and Turning It On Again?' across his chest. Fashion sense aside, though, I was technologically desperate and I sensed that this was someone who might be able to help.

The man stared at the handset for a moment or two and rubbed the bridge of his nose. Then he pressed a few icons and typed something on to the keypad.

*Nice hands,* the thought flashed into my brain before I could stop it. *They match his face.*

'There you go,' he said, thrusting the phone in my direction before changing his mind and taking it back again. 'No, wait; if you're in San Francisco, you'll be needing this.'

He tapped the screen a few more times, scrolled down and typed in something else. Then he waited, nodded approvingly and gave the handset back. I again focused my gaze on to his chin. I didn't care if he thought I was peculiar, it was the only safe option under the circumstances.

'Full connection,' he said, his lips curving back

13

upwards into their infectious perma-smile, 'plus a bonus something extra for free.'

'Thanks,' I said, taking the phone and transferring my eyes quickly to the screen.

Result! There *was* a connection. Plus a new icon, one I didn't recognise: a blue circle, containing a yellow diamond with the letters 'S' and 'C' written across it in red.

'I've rerouted your account so that any calls or texts, as well as all your internet access, should only be charged at your normal UK rate,' he explained, 'but check your bill tomorrow and, if anything untoward shows up, there's something else I can hook you on to. The bonus something extra, by the way, is called SuperConnect.'

'It is?' I said.

Then, so that he didn't think I was a complete hick from the sticks:

'It *is*.'

The man grinned modestly, almost as if he'd invented it himself.

'It's new,' he said, 'and it's not available in the UK yet. In fact, it's almost not available over here either, but it's going to help you get the most out of your stay in San Francisco. Look . . .'

He gently took my phone back and, as he did so, his thumb brushed against mine. I don't know if there was an *actual* electric charge that zipped between us, or whether it just felt like it. Whatever it was, we leapt apart as though we'd been Tasered.

Totally forgetting my no-eye-contact policy, I stared at him in horror. My boyfriend – whom I not only loved very much but with whom I had been living for the past two years – was, at this moment, several thousand feet above the Atlantic, being asked if he preferred chicken or beef. No other options were on the table.

The man shook himself.

'So, SuperConnect,' he began. 'OK, um, yes. SuperConnect. You fill out your profile here, and put in all your likes, dislikes, whatever, and join up with your friends who also SuperConnect.'

He used the word 'SuperConnect' as though it was a verb.

'OK,' I said, trying to block out the aftershocks that were still reverberating along my thumb with enough va-va-voom to give the San Andreas Fault some serious competition.

'Anyhoo,' said the man, his eyes focusing on the screen rather than me, 'then you go on to the public area *here*' – he pressed an icon and we whizzed on to another page – 'and the app will automatically link you up with things of interest happening in your area, your town or even nationally. It's one of its USPs: SuperConnect actually *suggests* activities and events based on your profile.'

I permitted myself to be mildly impressed. Even though I had no intention of actually using SuperConnect – I was the only person in the developed world who still picked up the phone rather than using a social networking site – this was free, and free was always my favourite price.

'So,' said the man, 'what are you into?'

I thought for a moment. It suddenly seemed a long time since I'd been 'into' anything on a regular basis. In fact, now I put my mind to it, I couldn't actually remember the last time I had managed to drag Barney any further than his X-Box console.

'OK.' The man tried a different tack. 'What would you *like* to be into?'

'Um . . .'

I thought.

Hard.

'Music,' I said, the thought coming as something of a revelation. Bella and I used to love going to gigs. 'Local bands, venues, that sort of thing.'

'Cool.'

He tapped something else into the phone, then leaned over the top of the banquette to show me the screen.

'SuperConnect calculates your geographical position so that everything of interest in your area pops up automatically. And at the top of your list' – he squinted at the screen – 'is a Battle of the Tribute Bands coming up at the Lizard Lounge. You've gotta go to that. It's totally a gift for the world to unwrap.'

My answering blush was so hot you could have toasted crumpets on it.

'Thanks,' I said, thinking it sounded like fun but knowing Barney would rather eat his own ear wax than spend an evening listening to cover versions of songs he hadn't enjoyed the first time round. 'Great.'

'No problem,' the man said, continuing to stare at me but failing to actually give back my handset.

'Er, the phone?' I said, holding my hand out. 'Could I have the phone back, please?'

'Oh, right,' he said sheepishly. 'Um, here you go.'

At that moment, Sylvie arrived and laid a plate the size of a manhole cover in front of me whilst giving Gazing Man his bill. She glanced from me to him and emitted a discreet, velvety chuckle.

'I have to go now.' The faintest hint of redness crept across his cheeks. 'I'm Josh, by the way, and – ah – I have to go.'

He folded his laptop, picked it up, and went to slide it into its case, his eyes still fixed on me. The laptop, however, missed the case completely and dive-bombed the floor with a heart-stopping crash. I leapt out of my seat and went to pick it up but Josh got there first. He blew on it, dusted it off and this time managed to place it successfully in its case.

'It's tougher than it looks,' he assured me. 'Smoke started coming out of it while I was on a plane last week – I ended up having to grovel to the emergency services of three different states.'

He fired off another grin; this one so dazzling they could probably see it from the International Space Station. My stomach did its biggest flip yet, but then, before I could speak, he glanced at his watch, started visibly and held up his hand in farewell.

'Later,' he said. 'Big meeting. Enjoy San Francisco!'

Sylvie shook her head as the door swung shut.

'Crazy boy,' she said affectionately. 'That machine of his goes ka-blooey ever so often. But I'm thankful for the small mercies: at least this time we didn't need to call out the fire department.'

'Oh, I don't know,' called Elvira from the counter, 'you can't beat a good fireman first thing in the morning. It sets you up for the rest of the day.'

And they both laughed their smooth, treacly laughs.

I had the very odd sensation of suddenly snapping back into my real life. Josh and the unnecessarily exciting sensations he had stirred within me had vanished and normal service was restored. My stomach rumbled and I as good as unhinged my jaws and swallowed the mountain of chicken and waffles whole, polishing off my coffee as I went. It was all delicious: the food; San Francisco; my birthday. In fact, I thought as Elvira refilled my cup and reeled off a list of organic, sustainably produced desserts, my life is pretty much set fair for the future: new job, lovely house, fabby fella.

But life, as always, had other ideas.

And it wasn't long before I found out what they were.

———

# 2

At six thirty that evening, rather than throwing myself into the arms of my much-longed-for boyfriend, I was slumped against the front door of a four-storey pink, white and grey Victorian house that overlooked the city. My eyes were hot and there was an ominous lump in my throat. There were no tears – yet – but they were in the vicinity: lurking, muttering to themselves and waiting for their chance to strike.

Happy birthday, Flora.

I raised my head and scanned the view. In the distance I could see the Golden Gate Bridge, magnificent and untroubled in the summer sun.

I looked away.

I didn't need iconic symbols of the city reminding me of the holiday I should have had; I needed my cousin Bella. Only Bella was not at home.

Deep within the recess of my bag, my phone rang: the opening few bars of 'Holiday' by Madonna, chosen especially for my once-in-a-lifetime trip. I caught my breath. Maybe this was Bella herself returning my slightly hysterical voicemails. Maybe she was, even now, on her way home. Maybe tracking down her address via SuperConnect and randomly pitching up on her doorstep *had* been a sensible move after all.

Rather than sheer desperation.

'Hello?' I said, wrestling the handset out of my bag and against my ear.

'Flora? Is that you? Sadie McMaster here.'

A cry of disappointment stuck in my throat and never made it as far as my mouth.

Which was probably just as well.

'I'm so glad I caught you, Flora. You see, there are a couple problems with the properties we put on our accommodation shortlist.'

The lump in my throat grew bigger. Please God, I prayed silently, don't let me cry in Sadie McMaster's hearing. Anything but that.

'The house in St John's Wood,' Sadie continued, oblivious to my inner turmoil, 'Earl is worried about the street noise. He says that before he signs anything he wants to see the figures for traffic flow at eight a.m., midday and ten p.m.'

I didn't understand. That house stood in an acre of its own grounds off a very minor road: you could hardly *be* more secluded in central London, and last night it had (and I quote) been 'the most perfect little place they had ever seen'.

Sadie hadn't finished yet.

'And as for the one near the centre of town—'

'The apartment on the Embankment? Stunning, isn't it?' Using vast quantities of willpower, I managed to form a coherent, vaguely enthusiastic sentence.

Not that Sadie was about to appreciate my efforts.

'We've been looking at the pictures you left and we don't like the view.'

I almost forgot about trying not to cry and boggled down the telephone at her. What could possibly be wrong with the view? It was the Houses of Parliament, St Paul's and the River Thames: Canaletto, Monet and William Wordsworth all rolled into one. Had she gone mad?

'That wheel thing – the London Whatsit. Earl wants to know if we pay extra whether we could have it moved.'

*Seriously?*

*They wanted to move the London Eye?*

I balled my free hand into a fist and thrust it down into my jacket pocket. I had spent every waking minute of the past three days going through their accommodation options with them in mind-melting detail. I had sat up late into the early hours of the morning and crossed every conceivable 't' and dotted every potential 'i'. If I hadn't been so close to tears, I think I might have screamed with frustration.

But I was new in the job and needed their approval, so I pulled myself together as best I could.

'Thank you for letting me know, Mrs McMaster,' I replied politely. 'I promise I will look into it first thing when I'm back in the office.'

'No, Flora, we want you to do it *now*. Earl wants you to come round as soon as possible to discuss our options. Plus, you can measure up the chaise longue and his model of Mount Rushmore made entirely from toothpicks whilst you're at it.'

I boggled again.

*Now?*

When I'd taken my leave of her the night before I had explained, quite clearly, that I would be spending the next two weeks on annual leave. Had I gone mad and hallucinated our conversation, or was she seriously expecting me to put everything on hold so that I could measure her furniture?

I did my best to tactfully jog her memory.

'Mrs McMaster, I don't know if you remember from yesterday, but I'm going to be on holiday now for the next two weeks and—'

But I might as well have been talking to thin air.

'Don't be silly, Flora. We'll say four thirty tomorrow, then. Goodbye!' And she rang off.

The tears shuffled closer and I pinched the bridge of my nose in a vain attempt to keep them at bay. A large jaggedy breath tore through me and I stared down at the bright red Converse shoes I'd bought especially for my transatlantic jaunt and wished with all my might that I'd never left home. In fact, I was just about to give up on Bella, the McMasters and San Francisco in general and begin the long trudge back to my hotel where I planned to get miserably but spectacularly drunk, when a number of quite unexpected things happened.

The first was that Bella's pink front door suddenly opened behind me and, with a thud that made my teeth rattle, I found myself lying on my back in her hallway blinking up at a dingy, crumbling ceiling rose. Then a male voice that I did not recognise floated down from on high:

'You know, I'm sure I didn't order one of those.'

I turned and found myself gazing up at a handsome, smartly dressed young man with blond hair, who was regarding me with detached – if concerned – amusement.

'Are you OK?' He extended a hand and pulled me to my feet. 'If I'd known my front step was being used as a place of public rest and contemplation I'd have been more careful opening the door. In fact, for future reference, do you think you're going to make a habit of parking yourself here? Are you likely to be joined by friends? Should I be thinking of going the whole hog and putting out scatter cushions and maybe a few snacks?'

For a moment, I couldn't think of anything to say. I wasn't entirely sure if I was confused, upset or just at the end of my rope. Probably all three.

The young man looked at me expectantly and folded his arms.

'I was looking for Bella,' I managed at last. 'Bella Jones. She lives here. Do you know her?'

'I might,' he replied slowly, 'it depends on who's asking.'

'I'm her cousin Flora.' It was all too much and my voice started to tremble. 'And it's really important that I see her. Preferably now. Or soon – whichever you can manage. Soon would be fine but now would be so much better. Do you – do you know where I can find her?'

The man gave a world-weary sigh.

'I don't,' he confessed. 'In fact, I'm looking for her too. She was supposed to be meeting me here, but she's nowhere to be seen and her phone's off. Could you maybe come back later?'

*Later?* I felt as though someone had pulled a giant cosmic plug and my life – together with my ability to cope with it – was rushing in a huge, mad, swirling spiral towards oblivion. I gave the largest jaggedy, hiccoughing gasp to date.

The man looked at me, an expression of thinly veiled horror on his face.

'Don't cry,' he said. 'Please, please don't cry. You see, I don't actually do girls and all this weepy stuff confuses me.'

'I'm not crying,' I replied firmly, more for my benefit than his.

But it was too late. A big, fat tear rolled out over my eyelid and tracked its way down my cheek.

My companion's horror quickly segued into desperation. He began searching through all his avail -able pockets until, finally, he pulled out a tissue.

'Please, Bella's-Cousin-Flora,' he said, 'it'll be all right.'

'How can it be? I can't find Bella, my new clients are working me into the ground and he . . . well, he du – he du – he du – he du—' I did my best to explain, but found I couldn't actually articulate the one key word. 'It w-won't be all right, ever a-again.'

'All right.' The man reached out and patted me limply on the shoulder. 'Have it your way. It *won't* be all right – but enough of the tears, huh? You're looking at a desperate man here.'

I blew my nose loudly on the tissue and then, through my blurry vision, caught sight of a notice-board on the wall beside me. In between a flyer advertising yoga for pets and another announcing 50 per cent discounts on chakra beads was a Post-it written in Bella's unmistakable flowing hand. 'Toby: See you at the Lizard. Laters. X'.

The tiniest ever flame of hope sparked up in my heart.

'Are you T-toby?' I asked, pointing at it. 'B-because if you are, I think she's at the L-lizard.'

The man whirled round, stared at the note, and then whirled back to face me.

'Why didn't you say so before?' he cried, picking up my bag and looping it over my head. 'Come on!'

He went to grab my hand but, catching sight of the tissue it was clutching, thought better of it. Instead, he pointed at my shoes.

'Loving the ruby slippers.' He winked at me. 'Click your heels together and we'll be there in no time.'

Then he was off. Still sniffing and hiccoughing, I followed and together we half ran, half walked (and, in my case, half stumbled) down the hill, crossed at a set of lights and turned left into a road I recognised as Hope Street.

We continued in this fashion for a minute or more before Toby dived through the front door of an anonymous-looking, plum-coloured building. I plunged in after him and, as my eyes accustomed themselves to the lighting levels, I realised that I was in a bar.

A bar, sir, but not as we know it.

To begin with, there was a large Harley-Davidson in the middle of the floor, another one fixed to the wall on my right, whilst pink and blue Vespa scooters adorned the walls above the doors of the ladies and gents respectively. Assorted vintage helmets and motorbike gloves were littered across the rest of the wall-space, together with black-and-white photos of bikes, more bikes and occasionally, just for a bit of variety, people *on* bikes. The floor space was filled with tables, squashy sofas and a collection of moth-eaten velvet armchairs and, along the length of the left-hand side of the room, ran a wooden saloon-style bar com - plete with another wall-mounted Harley. To round it all off, the image of an enormous red-and-orange gecko holding a bottle of beer in its tail cavorted across the ceiling.

'So, this'll be the Lizard Lounge then?' I ventured, remembering Josh's words from earlier in the day.

But Toby didn't have the chance to reply.

'Hey!' cried a high-pitched but undeniably angry voice from the other side of the room. 'You! Yes, you!

Mr-Run-away-from-Work-and-Drop-Me-in-It-Despicable-Human-Chicken-Man! Thanks to you I have had a total bitch of a day. In fact, it has been the mother of the mother of the *mother* of all bitches, and I am so *not happy about it.*'

Despite sounding like Minnie Mouse on helium, the voice bore the undeniable ring of authority. Toby and I spun round, guilty expressions on our faces.

Me, even though I had no idea what I could possibly be guilty *of.*

Advancing towards us across the room was a tiny woman with black hair that framed her face in a series of elegant waves. Her dress, cut from charcoal-grey silk, was nipped in *Mad Men*-style to show off her miniature waist before flowing outwards over a couple of layers of frothy pink petticoats. She was wearing bright-red lipstick and the highest pair of heels imaginable.

'Put your money away,' she commanded me, even though I hadn't even opened my handbag, let alone found my purse. 'Toby's paying.'

Toby opened his mouth to protest, but she was way ahead of him.

'Three glasses of your finest vintage Brut, please, Bill,' she said to the man behind the bar. 'No, make it a bottle. But be sure to stand back while Mr Yellow-Belly here pays, or you'll be knocked out by the cloud of moths escaping from his wallet.'

'Sure thing, Lisa.' Bill nodded and began putting champagne flutes on a tray.

Toby emitted a choking noise but, nonetheless, reached into his jacket pocket and pulled out his wallet. However, the tiny, scary lady hadn't finished yet.

'And we'll need something to soak it up: a portion of nachos please, with all the toppings.' She turned to me. 'You like nachos, don't you?'

I meekly nodded my assent. Even though I was convinced I would never feel like eating again, I wasn't about to disagree with her.

'Good. And put another bottle of champagne on ice – and keep the change,' she concluded airily.

'Thanks, Tobes!' The bartender nodded appre - ciatively as Toby handed over a bundle of cash.

'I'm Lisa,' the woman said, holding out her hand to me. I noticed that her nails were painted the exact blood-red of her lips. 'Lisa Goldberg.'

'Hi,' I said, as the vice-like grip from her fingers threatened to crush mine to Play-Doh. 'I'm Flora.'

'Lisa's from New York,' said Toby glumly, as if this was the source of all his woe.

'And proud of it.' Lisa threw a peanut up into the air and caught it in her perfect white teeth. 'None of this West Coast "raw vegan, what's my mantra" crap, I come out fighting. Speaking of which, if I hadn't covered for him today, this boy would have had his ass whupped all the way to Reno. Next time Dave from Actuarial asks you out, do *not* take it as an excuse to freak out and leave me wiping the noses of your snotty clients.'

Toby's shoulders drooped and he stared miserably down at his shoes.

'Sorry, Lisa,' he muttered.

'So, um,' I said, trying to work out their relationship, 'are you – are you Toby's boss?'

Lisa dissolved into a tinkling shower of delicate laughter and handed me a glass of champagne.

'You are funny,' she said. 'You seriously think I'd have *him* working for *me*? Ha! I'm his assistant, or his secretary or his PA or whatever the hell you want to call me, and Toby's just about to write me a giant bonus cheque.' Then she stopped and stared at me pityingly. 'He was a jerk, sweetie. Don't waste another second thinking about him.'

For a moment I thought we were still talking about Toby. Then I realised we weren't and I almost dropped my glass.

I stared at her in disbelief but Lisa just shrugged modestly.

'Womanly intuition,' she replied. 'Also, your mascara's smudged, your eyes are red and you have icky bits of damp Kleenex sticking to your hands.'

I looked down, horrified: she was right. I picked the soggy fragments of tissue off my person and, unsure what else to do with them, placed them in my skirt pocket.

'Listen, honey' – Lisa reached out and patted my hand sympathetically with her tiny paw – 'it's the First Law of the Universe: All men are pigs, apart from the ones that are rats and the ones that are worms.'

'And the ones that are really superheroes in disguise,' threw in Bill from behind the bar.

Lisa rolled her eyes.

'Yeah, Bill, and when you learn to fly I'll go on a date with you. But until then, it's the same as it always was: a big fat no.'

Bill grinned and went back to polishing glasses.

Lisa settled herself on the bar stool next to mine and clapped her hands with glee as an enormous plate con-taining nachos smothered in sour cream, guacamole, salsa and cheese was placed on the bar between us.

'Eat,' commanded Lisa, pushing the dish of nachos towards me. 'You look like you need it. No, not you, Toby – you get your own.' She slapped down his outstretched hand.

'I thought I had,' he muttered darkly.

I decided against the nachos, but took a tentative sip of champagne. It was cool and dry and creamy and made me feel ever so slightly better.

But not so much better that I forgot the reason I had come here.

'Where do you think Bella is?' I asked Toby, glancing round the room. 'Do you think she got called back to some sort of emergency at the hospital? That could be why she's switched her phone off.'

There was a strange and rather awkward silence.

'You think Bella is working at the hospital?' Toby asked slowly.

'Of course?' I asked. As far as I was concerned, this was a no-brainer. 'She's a nurse at St Peter's. She's worked there since she moved arrived in San Fransisco.'

'No, Bella's here all right,' said Lisa, 'only I don't think she brought any bedpans with her. Come on, guys, let's get downstairs.'

With that, Lisa picked up her glass and ushered me across the room, leaving Toby to juggle the nachos, the champagne and the ice-bucket as well as his own bottle of beer. I picked my way carefully down a twisting set of steps before finding myself in a basement auditorium. At the far end was a stage draped with red velvet curtains, overlooking a floor packed with little round café-style tables and chairs. For a bit of decorative continuity with upstairs, a lone red scooter hung suspended from the ceiling.

'Quickly!' Lisa speed-sashayed through the tables until she managed to locate a free one, a couple of rows from the stage. 'They're about to start.'

'Look,' I said, following on as fast as I could whilst at the same time trying not to trip over any legs (whether appended to chairs, tables or other people), 'I'd love to stay and watch the show, Lisa, really I would, but I'm desperate to see Bella and she's obviously not here and—'

'Put your glass down, honey,' said Lisa firmly, taking it out of my hand and placing it on the table in front of me. 'That's right. Now leave it there. Uh-uh – no touching. Absolutely no touching.'

The house lights were lowered and Bill from behind the bar bounded up a set of steps into a spotlight, and unhooked a microphone from its stand.

'Ladies, gentlemen and' – he flashed a dazzling smile in Lisa's direction – *'goddesses*, welcome to another session of live music at the Lizard Lounge.'

He paused as a frenzied wave of applause swept the room.

'As a warm-up for our Battle of the Tribute Bands, we have invited all of last year's finalists to give us a short set to get us in the rock-and-roll mood. Tonight we have for your delight Blondish' – the crowd went wild once again – 'Madam and the Ants, Love Cats and, without further ado, please welcome, with their show-stopping version of the international number one hit "Voulez-Vous": Abbadabbatastic!'

He trotted back down the steps as the lights dimmed still further and four figures made their way on to the stage. The audience waited expectantly as they lined up in the darkness. Then a guitar riff tore through the air as they leapt in unison into the glare of the spotlight. Two of them – both female, one tall and dark, the other shorter with long blonde hair and wearing a white catsuit with silver platform boots – shimmied up to the front of the stage and began to sing their hearts, lungs and most of their internal organs out.

Holy 'Mamma Mia!' Thank goodness Lisa had taken the glass out of my hand.

There, in front of my disbelieving eyes, was Bella, prancing about on stage in an outfit best described as 'brave' (or possibly even 'inadvisable'), enthusiastically channelling the blonde one from Abba.

Toby put his finger under my chin and levered my gaping mouth shut.

'Self-awareness, Flora,' he whispered, '"the fly-catcher" is so not a good look.'

I tried very hard to be cool, but cool was pretty much impossible given the circs. It wasn't that it was *bad* (in fact, Bella was pretty bloody amazing), and I'd always known she loved Abba when she was little, but seeing her on stage in the full Abba-esque get-up felt somehow out of sync with my picture of grown-up, professional, nursey Bella. It wasn't that it was *wrong*, per se, but just unexpected – like hearing Beethoven piano sonatas being played on the steel drums.

Auntie Stella definitely hadn't mentioned *this* in her Christmas round robin last year.

After one last, ear-splitting 'A-ha!' the music ended and Bella and her fellow Abba-ites bowed and blew kisses to the audience.

'Bella!' Lisa was on her feet, waving madly. 'Over here! Toby's bought champagne.'

Bella paused to pull off her headband and wipe her sweaty forehead with her sleeve before picking her way through the tables towards us.

She stopped abruptly. Her eyes were fixed on me and – for the most fleeting of seconds – something that looked an awful lot like fear scudded across her face. Then she gave herself a little shake and threw herself into my arms.

'Flora! Flora! Flora-bora-bunyip!' she cried. 'What the hell are you doing here?'

33

'Long story.' I hugged her back, the relief of finally finding her making all sorts of unwanted emotions well up inside me once again. 'How are things?'

'Fine,' Bella grinned. 'Or rather, I mean fabulous. Amazing. Loving it. Never been better.'

'Hey, *garçon*!' Lisa snapped her fingers at a passing waitress. 'The singer lady here is in need of the sustenance of the grape. Please bring our second bottle *tout de suite*.'

The waitress flew off on her mission, while Lisa poured the remains of the first bottle into a clean glass and handed it to Bella.

'So, Flora!' Bella still looked as though her brain was having difficulty wrapping itself around the fact that I was there in the flesh beside her. 'You're here! I mean, I know you said ages ago that you were coming . . . but I didn't . . . well, anyway . . . you're here. Hoorah!'

Then she paused and looked at me more closely.

'Something's the matter, isn't it? What's going on?'

I opened my mouth to speak but, as soon as I did, the tears that had previously plagued me (and Toby) threatened to overwhelm me once again. I pawed at the fragments of tissue in my skirt pocket.

'He du – he du – he du—'

'He dumped her, honey,' Lisa translated. 'There. I've said it. Now Flora can fill us in on the rest of the story. Once it's all out in the open it won't seem half so bad.'

I didn't actually believe her, but I took the deepest of deep breaths and began.

34

'I came over three days ago for work,' I was doing my best to keep my voice steady. 'I have clients relocating from San Francisco to London. The husband works for a supermarket firm called ValueMart, and the wife . . . well, she has too much time on her hands if you ask me.'

*Breathe in.*

*Breathing is good.*

*And out again.*

'And Barney was going to fly out and join me for a holiday.'

Bella nodded encouragingly.

'When was he due?' she asked.

I glanced at my watch.

'Two hours, fifteen minutes and thirty-eight seconds ago.'

I made a high-pitched sniffling noise. Toby looked distinctly nervous and Lisa passed me a paper napkin. I blew my nose loudly into it before continuing.

'I was about to pick him up from the airport but my phone rang. It was Barney and I said: Where are you? And he said: Oxford; so I said: Why are you in Oxford when you should be standing in front of a scary-looking man in a customs uniform waiting for him to stamp your passport? And he said: I've changed my mind and I said: What? About the holiday? And he said: No, about our relationship. I told him I didn't understand and he said it was simple, we were over but he really wanted us to still be friends so I told *him* I'd rather be friends with Adolf Hitler and he told *me* to

35

calm down and if it was money I was worried about he would reimburse me for the hotel and the flight and I said money had nothing to do with it and he could shove the entire Boeing 747 up his bum for all I cared and he said there was no point talking to me if I was going to be abusive and I said I'd barely started and then he hung up on me.

I looked up. Three pairs of eyes were dangling out of their sockets and three jaws swung open incredulously.

'He told you *that*?' gasped Bella.

'On the *phone*?' said Toby.

'He's a schmuck,' concluded Lisa.

'And a bastard,' added Bella. 'A schmucky, bastardy bastard from hell.'

'I swear to God,' growled Toby, 'if that son-of-a-bitch was here now, I'd – I'd – I'd – well, I'd do *something*, that's for sure.'

Bella turned as white as her catsuit and gripped my arm.

'Oh my God! It's your birthday! It's your birthday! Oh my God, Flora!'

She threw her arms round me and for a horrible moment I thought *she* was about to burst into tears. But instead she took the napkin from me and ran its edge under my eyes to hoover up my mascara overflow.

'Right.' Bella dabbed at my nose and then threw the napkin into an empty champagne flute. 'We're going to do something about this. We – all of us – are going out for dinner, somewhere really special. You, cousin of mine, are going to have the best bash this fabulous town can muster. I know it's getting late, Lisa, but can you blag us into the Tonga Room?'

'*Pas de problème*.' Lisa pulled out her phone. 'Are we thinking Robert Pattinson or Jennifer Aniston?'

This made no sense to me whatsoever, but Toby obviously received and understood.

'Robby Pattinson,' he said at last. 'Over the past few weeks, Jen's come down with every disease known to Hollywood-kind. Some of the booking staff are beginning to get suspicious.'

My head reeled. I wasn't sure if it was the effects of the champagne, the tears, or whether life had simply become too crazy for me to cope with.

'Poolside table for five with free Mai Tais,' Lisa said, snapping her phone shut. 'We're in.'

'Five?' I queried.

'Yeah – one for Mr Pattinson. But case anyone asks, the story is that he got a headache and decided to call it a night. Poor thing, he really hasn't been well recently.'

Bella seized my arm again and tugged.

'Come on!'

Before I could argue – or, indeed, really understand what was going on – Bella was marching me in the direction of the stairs. Lisa drained her glass and followed us, taking tiny, tottery steps in her high heels.

'You're going to love it, Flo,' beamed Bella as she bounded up the stairs in her glittery seventies costume, 'the Tonga Room is completely bonkers. This is going to be the best birthday ever.'

A thought flashed over her face and she turned to Toby.

'I couldn't get to the bank today,' she said in a low voice that I had difficulty hearing, 'would you – I mean, if you don't mind – I mean—'

Toby gave her a comforting smile.

'It's fine,' he whispered back, 'I've got it. Don't worry.'

Bella grinned with relief.

'Thanks,' she said. 'I'll pay you back, I promise. I'll text Steve and tell him to bring my fee for the gig tonight over to the Tonga Room.'

'Don't stress about it, Bella,' murmured Lisa as we walked out on to the street and Toby hailed a cab. 'Besides, fee or no fee, I think we could all use a good night out – even if Robby is going to cancel on us yet again.'

'Oh, you know Robby,' replied Toby, 'he always comes up with some lame old excuse when we want to go out.'

'Huh,' sniffed Bella, 'I'm beginning to think he doesn't like us.'

'Who could possibly not like *us*?' cried Lisa. 'We are the life and soul of the party. Any party. *Every* party. Even parties that haven't been thought of yet.'

'And we're going to give my gorgeous cousin here a night to remember,' added Bella as a yellow cab drew up and Toby gallantly opened the door for us.

'Put your tissues away, Flora, the good times start here.'

And you know what? She sounded so convincing, I almost believed her.

# 3

I woke the next morning with a clanging headache and absolutely no idea where I was. I had hazy memories of taxis, the Tonga Room (which had turned out to be every bit as bonkers as Bella had predicted: a remarkable bar-cum-restaurant-cum-South-Sea-island complete with a pool, floating band and indoor thunderstorms), an awful lot of Mai Tais, Toby falling backwards off his chair, and Bella and I dancing a hula on top of our table.

Apart from that it was all a bit of a blur.

I lay very still for a minute or two in order to work out whether I was *actually* being hit across the forehead with a hammer or whether it just felt like it; and after I'd finally decided that my agonies were due to the insane amounts of alcohol I'd drunk the night before, I risked opening an eye.

And promptly did a double take.

My neat, clean hotel room had vanished and instead I found myself in the middle of what looked like a municipal tip. Around me were teetering piles of cardboard boxes and black bin bags, and crammed in amongst those were an armchair with no back, a synthesiser with a couple of missing keys and a pair of battered-looking bongos.

Then I opened the other eye and spotted a Tiffany lamp sitting on one of the boxes. It was the spitting image of one that had belonged to my granny and had been proudly displayed on the dining table in her little Cornish cottage. Whoa! I thought, what were the chances of that?

Then my brain crawled a few centimetres further towards lucidity and it clicked: I must have crashed at Bella's.

Very slowly, so as not to disturb my hangover any more than was absolutely necessary, I picked my way across the room and stood in front of the lamp. Gingerly, I lifted my hand and allowed my fingers to trace the wings of the dragonflies that made up its multi-coloured canopy. Then I put my nose up close to the glass and sniffed. A faint, musky odour twisted its way up my nostrils. Could I actually smell the house where Bella and I had spent so many happy summers together, or was it merely the scent of faith?

Then a motorbike roared past outside, and my head almost combusted with pain. I needed painkillers. Painkillers and then water, in that order.

And no alcohol ever, ever, *ever* again.

As speedily as I dared, I made my way into the kitchen where I found Bella up, dressed and looking unfeasibly chipper for someone who had drunk as much as I had.

'Urf,' I said, covering my eyes and staggering towards a chair. Someone had definitely turned up the brightness level on the sun since yesterday.

'Hello, you!' Bella grinned, squeezing a tea bag against the side of a steaming mug. 'I didn't think you'd be up for hours. You didn't half pack it away last night.'

She reached into the pocket of her sweatshirt and threw a blister pack in my direction.

'Nurse Bella did suggest two Ibuprofen and a pint of water *before* you went to sleep – but you were more interested in singing "YMCA" and then passing out on my sofa. Pretty much simultaneously, if I remember correctly.'

I groaned and swallowed a couple of tablets. What else had I done whilst under the influence? Did I even want to know?

'Did I ring Barney?'

Bella's eyes twinkled.

'No. I confiscated your phone during the fourth round of cocktails. It's in the fruit bowl on the table. Although . . .' she paused thoughtfully. '. . . you might want to think about sending him that picture Lisa took of you tangoing with José the waiter. Something along the lines of "It's all here – wish you were wonderful". How are you feeling about him, by the way?'

'Not great,' I replied, feeling her concern curl protectively round me, 'but definitely a little bit better.'

Bella grinned. She lifted a mug down from one of the cupboards and then opened the lid of a canister on the sideboard.

'Bugger. Out of tea. Here, have half of mine.'

She poured some into the mug and handed it to me.

I really, *really* didn't want it, but I took a sip just to show willing.

For a moment, I thought it was going to make a swift return back the way it had gone but, after a few seconds, the pounding in my head lifted slightly and the glare from the morning sun became a smidgeon less dazzling.

'Organic, sustainably produced, ginseng-infused, fairly traded herbal tea,' Bella told me. 'It gets most of San Francisco out of bed in the mornings. You can't beat it after a couple of drinks – or even after a couple of gallons of drink.'

I took another, larger sip. It was true – there was an improvement, although whether it was the tea or the painkillers, I couldn't have said.

'It still feels as though someone is trying to take off the top of my head with a welding torch,' I said. 'Only now they're doing it in a *nice* way.'

'Good,' Bella continued, drawing up the chair opposite and settling herself down at the table. 'Can't have a hangover cramping your style. So tell me, what's the plan, Stan? Do you have anything arranged for today?'

A pang went through me. What I'd had planned for today was a perfect, soppy twenty-four hours spent doing romance with Barney.

Followed by a whole perfect, soppy fortnight doing much the same.

And seeing that I now *couldn't*, maybe the best course of action would be to ring my airline and see if I could get my flights changed. However much it cost, wouldn't it be better to get home, find out what was going on and try and put it right?

Bella was staring at me. Hard. Without my uttering a single syllable, she already knew what was going through my mind.

'Don't,' she said firmly. 'Don't even *think* about it.'

'But—'

'No.'

'But—'

'*No.*'

I stared back for a moment.

'OK,' I sighed, 'you're right. I know you're right. Whatever's going on, it won't be helped by me rushing back on the next plane out of SFO and hurling crockery in his direction. If I stay on, at least for a week, it gives both of us a chance to calm down and get some perspective on things. And you never know, I might actually *enjoy* myself.'

Bella raised her mug and clinked it against mine. The noise made my brain rattle in my skull, but I appreciated her enthusiasm.

'Living well is totally the best revenge,' she said. 'And speaking of living well, I've been thinking: I know I was really crap returning your calls so, to make it up to you, I wondered if you would like us to spend some time together whilst you're here. I'll be a bit tied up in the evenings with the Battle of the Tribute Bands, but we can do stuff during the day. What do you say?'

My spirits crept up another tiny notch. I wouldn't be

44

having a holiday with Barney but I *would* be having one with Bella. As an emergency back-up-holiday Plan B, it sounded good.

'It could be like the old days when we spent our summers with Granny and Grandpa in Cornwall,' coaxed Bella. 'I've missed you, Flo. Maybe this is our chance to recapture some of the magic.'

'Except now we're grown up and we can drink Mai Tais and go to nightclubs – and I could see you win the Battle of the Bands,' I added, faint flickers of excitement beginning to wash over me.

But then a thought struck.

'I'd love to,' I replied, 'but seriously, Belle, will you be able to take any time off? I mean, the last thing I want is to get in the way.'

'Hey, everything at work is fine. Marvellous, in fact.' Bella grinned, even though that wasn't what I'd asked her.

I opened my mouth to ask what shifts she was due to work that week when I heard footsteps in the hall and turned round to see a medium-height, stocky man with short wavy blond hair walk into the kitchen and make his way over to the fridge. He opened the door to be greeted by some empty shelves, a half-eaten pot of mustard and a dehydrated carrot.

'Oh man,' he remarked, letting the door swing shut again, 'my stomach's so empty it thinks my throat's been cut.'

Bella smoothed her platinum hair away from her face and tucked a chunk of it behind one ear.

'Sorry,' she replied good-humouredly, planting a peck on his cheek. 'I was planning on going shopping yesterday but I ran out of cash. Speaking of which, you were supposed to meet us at the Tonga Room and give me my share of the fee from the gig last night.'

I sipped my tea and decided this had to be Steve, Bella's man. All I knew about him was that Auntie Stella had said he worked in management and that she thought he was the best thing since sliced white.

'I had a meeting with Chris.' The man reopened the fridge, as though he expected a pile of food to have magically materialised in the past thirty seconds. 'Sorry, Belles, I thought I'd mentioned it. He's starting up a live music venue in Oakland and he's looking for investors. It's a great opportunity: in fact, he's offered me a fifteen per cent stake for ten thousand bucks. Bargain, eh?'

Bella's good humour evaporated in an instant. She stared at Steve as though he had just offered her shares in a chocolate-teapot factory.

'Ten thousand dollars? You can't – we can't—'

I stared down into my mug of tea, trying to pretend I wasn't there.

'It's cool, Belles,' replied Steve lightly. 'We'll have a lot more cash once you and I are living together. Besides, it's a once-in-a-lifetime offer. Fifteen per cent for—'

'I don't care if it's one hundred per cent for a dollar twenty. Steve, we still can't afford it.'

Gingerly, I lifted my eyes from my mug. I sincerely hoped they weren't going to have a row with me in the room.

Steve, however, didn't respond to Bella's comment. Instead he was systematically working his way through the kitchen cupboards, shutting each one when he saw it was bare and then opening the next. They were so totally devoid of anything even remotely edible, I began to wonder if Bella was sub-letting from Old Mother Hubbard.

'Oh man,' he groaned as he opened yet another, this time containing nothing but a bag of lentils. 'Is there *really* nothing to eat in this place?'

'I'm sorry. I've said I'll go shopping later' – Bella still sounded prickly – '*if* I can get my hands on some cash . . .' She paused. 'So, babe, it would be really great if you could give me that money from the gig last night.'

Steve looked at her and frowned.

'The fee from the Lizard Lounge?' Bella repeated, holding her hand out to receive it. 'I checked with Bill and he said he paid it directly to you.'

She seemed really anxious to get her paws on the money. I didn't understand why – surely she was on a good salary at the hospital?

Steve looked awkward.

'I'm sorry,' he replied. 'I don't have it on me right now.'

'Oh well.' Bella twisted her hair between her fingers and forced a smile. 'When you do, could you drop it round, please?'

'Sure,' he replied. 'Yes, of course.'

Then Bella looked at me as though she'd only just remembered I was in the room.

'Steve,' she said, giving herself a little shake, 'this is Flora, my cousin; she'll be in San Francisco for a couple of weeks. Isn't that great?'

Steve grinned and winked at me.

'Good to meet you, Flora,' he said. 'Anyway, babe, gotta run. If you do make it to the shop, pick up some beers for me, would you?'

And with that, he was gone.

My eyes met Bella's.

'Steve in management?' I asked.

Bella pulled her bathrobe up around her neck and gave a sheepish grin.

'Mmmmm,' she said. 'Only not in the normal sense of the word: Steve manages bands – including Abbadabbatastic. It's sort of how we met.' She paused. 'I suppose you could say I'm sleeping with my boss.'

I drained the last few drops of my herbal tea. My hangover was now little more than a distant – if rather unpleasant – memory and my respect for whacky herbal remedies had increased a hundredfold. If San Francisco could cure a hangover, I wondered, could it do the same for a broken heart?

'Holiday' blared out of Bella's (predictably empty) fruit bowl and we both jumped a clear three feet into the air.

'It's probably my clients,' I explained to Bella. 'I'll fill you in properly later but basically they think the word "employment" is synonymous with "bonded servitude" and – Hello? Flora Fielding speaking, Relocation Wizards—'

'Flora, it's Barney. How are you?'

The truth? I felt as though a passing surgeon had whipped out my vital organs and replaced them with lumps of ice.

But my instincts told me it was really, really important that he didn't know this.

As far as *he* was concerned, I had to be a -OK, fan-bloody-tastic and zippedy-doo-dah all rolled into one.

'I'm fine, Barney,' I replied, checking my voice was free of any lurking wobbles.

'Good,' he said, sounding surprised. 'I mean, yes, good.'

'In fact, I'd go so far as to say I'm great,' I lied. 'And Bella was thrilled to see me. She couldn't contain herself. We have so much to catch up on.'

From across the table, Bella gave me the thumbs-up.

'The pair of us had a wonderful night out with her friends,' I continued in what (I hoped) was a light-hearted and carefree manner, 'then we came back here and I slept like a baby. But enough about me, what can I do for you?'

With each word I spoke, I felt bolder and braver. He had done his worst: he had told me we were over. What else could he possibly throw my way?

Barney cleared his throat. He sounded nervous.

'Or' – I added as a thought struck me – 'are you ringing to apologise for the things you said yesterday?'

'No,' he said, as though nothing could be further from his mind, 'I was – ah – wondering if you would like to pop your key in the post. You know, to save you the trouble of coming round when you get back.'

For a moment, I was sure I hadn't heard him correctly.

'My key?' I queried. 'You want my key? Now? Today?'

Barney cleared his throat.

'Well, obviously I'll have to wait a few days for it to reach me. But as far as your stuff's concerned, you've only got a few clothes and bits back at the house, haven't you? I thought maybe I'd parcel them up and drop them round to your office for when you get back. Then we're done, aren't we? All nice and tidy and no loose ends.'

'A few clothes?' My mouth swung open. 'A few *clothes*? Barney, most of the stuff in the house belongs to me: the sofa, the bed, the telly, the laptop, the table and chairs . . .' I ground, speechless, to a halt.

When I'd moved in, Barney had been big on bachelor minimalism. However, not being a bachelor, I wasn't. So, as well as taking responsibility for the redecorating and renovations (some of which were quite substantial), I'd bought some furniture to make it feel less like somewhere the boys might drop round for pizza and a few games of *Grand Theft Auto* and more like a proper home. However, it seemed that this had slipped his mind.

'Oh.' He sounded surprised. 'So you're wanting to take them with you, then?'

'Of course I want to take them with me!' I cried incredulously. 'I paid for them! Hundreds and hundreds and hundreds of pounds' worth. And all the money I spent on the renovations. Did you honestly think I would just say, "There you are, Barney, thanks for the memories and please have the sofas and the reclaimed fireplaces on me"?'

'Well, I didn't actually think—'

'That's just it, you *didn't* think, did you? Not once in this whole scenario have you once sat down and *thought* about anything. You didn't think when you dumped me five thousand miles away from home; you didn't think that it was my birthday yesterday when you did it; and you didn't think when you rang just now to ask for the key back. You are a big, fat selfish pig and I really wish you were here now so that I could push you into the Bay and you'd get eaten by sea lions.'

There was a pause on the other end of the line.

'So then, what are you saying about the key? Are you going to post it?'

'Arrrggghhhhh!'

In pure frustration, I screamed into the handset before throwing it bodily into the hall. Then I slid down the door frame on to the kitchen floor; Bella came and crouched beside me and slipped an arm round my shoulders.

'I'm sorry,' she said, 'I'm really, really sorry.'

So was I. Even though I'd guessed I would be

51

vacating the little white house at some point in the future, I hadn't in a million years imagined Barney would want shot of me *today*. I'd presumed I'd move into the spare room for a few weeks while we sorted out the furniture and talked things through.

I'd thought it would be *civilised*.

'He wants the key. He's throwing me out.' I rested my cheek on her shoulder.

'Surely he can't do that,' said Bella, shuffling down fully on to the floor beside me. 'Don't you own it together?'

I shook my head miserably.

'He bought it a year before we met and, when we decided to live together, he said it would be crazy to buy a new house when we both loved the old one. And I did, Belle, I *really* loved it.'

Unlike yesterday there were no tears; I was way beyond them. All I could feel was a huge, numbing emptiness that started in my stomach and spread through me, choking everything in its path.

'But he – oh, I don't know the technical gubbins – didn't he put your name on the deeds?'

I tugged at my thick, unruly curls in frustration.

'He promised he would and he kept saying it was as much mine as it was his. But he never got round to doing the paperwork and I never pushed him; some - how the idea we'd split up seemed so unlikely it wasn't worth bothering about. Oh, Belle! How could I have been so *stupid*?'

I put my head in my hands: here I was, a person whose job it was to find homes for people, out on the streets.

The irony of the situation was not lost upon me.

I closed my eyes and thought about my house: the floors I'd varnished; the perfect two period fireplaces I'd hunted down in a reclamation yard; the way the sunlight caught the stained glass in the front door and sent a rainbow of light cascading across the hallway – and the emptiness overwhelmed me.

'Does this mean you'll be flying back to Britain after all?' Bella laid her cheek on the top of my arm.

I opened my mouth to say yes, I probably would, when deep within the numbness something I recognised as defiance began to stir. Going home was what Barney wanted and I wasn't about to give him the satisfaction of thinking he had any control left over me.

'No, it bloody doesn't,' I said, feeling a little of the fight come back to me. 'If I get on a plane now, he's won. I'm staying on in San Francisco for the full two weeks and I'm going to make damn sure I have the most amazing holiday. As for Barney . . . Well, he can go and do something unmentionable to himself. We'll sort this out when *I'm* ready and not before.'

Bella gave me one final squeeze and then released me.

'I've got to pop out for an hour or two,' she said, 'and as for you, you're exhausted. Turn your phone off and go and get half an hour's kip. You'll feel better for it, I promise. I'll see you in the Lizard at two for a late lunch.'

53

I rubbed my eyes with the back of my hand.

'I can't; I need to start thinking about the McMasters' relocation,' I said. 'I've got a meeting with them this afternoon and there's a heck of a lot of work to do first.'

'Give yourself a break,' said Bella firmly, 'you've just had a nasty shock. Go to bed but set your alarm so that you only have half an hour, otherwise you'll be grogged out for the rest of the day.' She shot me a wistful grin. 'You can trust me, I'm a nurse.'

Then she hugged me one last time before scrambling to her feet and walking off into the bathroom, whistling softly to herself.

# 4

In the end, I allowed myself a full hour's kip and – I had to hand it to Bella – it really did help. When the alarm went off and I heaved myself out of bed for the second time that day, I was able to push Barney to the back of my mind and focus on the McMasters' grandiose list of domestic requirements (gold-plated toilet-roll holders, anyone?). Finally, feeling that I had done everything I could apart from build and decorate their new house personally, I made my way back to my hotel to shower and change ahead of lunch at the Lizard.

I decided that the McMasters might be more inclined to believe I was on holiday if I didn't turn up at their house wearing my suit. So I rifled through my clothes and pulled on a sundress I'd bought a couple of summers ago. Scrutinising myself in the mirror (and realising how tired and drawn I looked next to the bright colours of the summer dress) I thought of Lisa and her immaculately tailored vintage clothes. I wonder where she shops, I thought idly, throwing my lipstick into my handbag and slinging the latter over my shoulder. Not that I would ever dare to wear clothes as striking as hers. It took a great deal of chutzpah to dress as Lisa did, and chutzpah was something I had in very short supply at that moment.

I arrived at the Lizard Lounge a little after the others. Even though the sun outside was blazing away in a blue Californian sky, there was a sepulchral gloom inside the bar that meant it could have been any time of day or night you cared to mention.

'Hey! Flora!' Toby's voice came from over at the bar. 'What's your poison?'

I carefully picked my way through the battered sofas and round the Harley towards him.

'Thanks but no thanks,' I said firmly, 'you bought me champagne yesterday. This is my round.'

Toby sighed the sigh of the terminally world-weary and pushed my purse back down into my handbag.

'You've got a lot to learn about the way things work round here,' he informed me in a voice that clearly said he was not the one making the rules. 'What are you having?'

'Coke,' I said, hoping that might ease the burden on Toby's wallet. 'And could you order some food for Bella, please; I don't think she, um, had time for any breakfast today.'

As I spoke, I surreptitiously slid a ten-dollar bill out of my purse and stuffed it into his pocket. Then I wandered over to a table in the middle of the room where I could see Lisa and Bella, engaged in conversation.

'Hey!' I said, seating myself between them. 'How's things?'

Lisa gave me a quick-up-and-down glance.

'Honey,' she said, her eyelashes batting and her perfectly red mouth drawn back into an engaging smile, 'that – that *thing* you have on. What is it exactly?'

She waved her finger up and down in front of me in a quizzical manner and turned up the wattage on her smile until it was positively blinding.

'This?' I looked down. 'It's a sundress. Halter-neck. Cotton. Just a frock really.'

Lisa blinked again and took a sip from her pink cocktail. The colour of her drink exactly matched that of her dress, but it was her skirts which commanded my attention, being even more voluminous than yesterday's grey dress. Had she happened to be jumping out of an aeroplane rather than sipping cocktails in a bar, there was no doubt that she would have made it safely to the ground.

'Is it yours?' she asked, tugging at my hem; her smile still pristine and dazzling. 'I mean, did you pay for it?'

'Yes,' I said, wondering how else she thought it might have come into my possession.

'As in, you went into a store, pulled it off the rail, looked at yourself wearing it *in a mirror* and then handed over your card?'

'Yes,' I said again, wondering how else one went about purchasing halter-neck dresses.

'Oh, honey.' Lisa gave a little hiccoughing laugh and patted me on the arm affectionately. 'You are so funny. I love you.'

Despite the staggering arrogance of that statement, there was not a trace of malice in her voice. Lisa wiped a fingertip under each of her eyes and beamed at me.

'Stand up.'

I did. It was virtually a reflex action.

Lisa put down her drink and turned towards me.

'Now look.' She put both hands on my waist and pulled in my sundress until the excess fabric was ruched behind me like a Victorian bustle. 'You have the teeniest waist and . . . Shoulders back! Stand up tall!'

Again, I stood instantly to attention. I was beginning to understand what life must be like for Toby.

'But,' I said, pointing to my muffin-top, 'look at that. It's horrible.'

'Enough already!' she growled. 'Look at you: a perfect hour-glass. Now keep that spine straight and shove your rack out – believe me, those are two puppies you *don't* want to keep in their kennel.' She laughed her tinkling laugh. *'Voilà!* By the time I've finished with you, you won't be able to keep them off with a stick. Your hotel won't have any carpet left in the lobby because they are going to be beating a path to your *door.'*

'Oh,' I said nervously, not sure whether I was more alarmed by the prospect of a parade of ardent suitors or her use of the word 'puppies'. 'Well, it might not really be *me*; I'm more of a Marks and Spencer girl, really.'

Lisa sighed an enormous sigh and sank back into her chair.

'Honey,' she said, in a very loud, very matter-of-fact voice, 'if I had tits like yours, Toby wouldn't be able to stop me coming to work in a bikini.' Then she flashed me the sweetest smile and took another dainty sip from her cocktail. 'So, how are you today?' she asked. 'Any more news on the Barney front? And I'm talking good news, like he fell in front of a subway train.'

*No such luck.*

At the mention of Barney's name, my earlier feistiness fled. I was no longer coming out fighting and instead felt like I'd just gone ten rounds with Lennox Lewis.

'He wants my key back; he's chucking me out. As of today, I'm technically homeless – and I don't *want* to be homeless.'

Toby handed me my Coke and I sucked it down in one gulp.

'At least he dumped you first,' said Toby gloomily, pulling up a chair. 'When I was seeing Richard he put all my stuff in refuse sacks and left them on the sidewalk along with a note saying he'd been sleeping with the pool cleaner and – ow! Lisa! That hurt!'

'Shuddup, Toby. You are not helping.'

Lisa clicked her fingers and instantly a waitress appeared.

'Honey, another one of these – and make it snappy,' Lisa told her, pointing at the pink cocktail.

'It may not be as bad as it looks,' comforted Bella as the waitress buzzed off to do Lisa's bidding.

'Of course it's as bad as it looks,' I replied mourn -

fully, allowing myself a good wallow, 'unless you are about to tell me that it's actually *even worse* than it looks, in which case I shall borrow a corkscrew from Bill and use it to slowly disembowel myself in a corner.'

The pink cocktail arrived.

'Get outside this, honey,' Lisa commanded. 'It won't make you feel better, it won't even make you *think* you feel better, but it will make you forget that you feel like shit and that's always a good place to start.'

I took a tentative sip. For the first nano-second after the liquid entered my mouth, it felt as though the enamel was being stripped from my teeth. For the second nano-second, I was sure the lining of my throat was being ripped off and, for the third, I thought my stomach might be about to spontaneously combust. However, after that, a muzziness set in which I found quite comforting.

'Why did he do it?' I mumbled. 'Why did he wait until I'd come all the way to San Francisco before dumping me? Why didn't he just tell me before?'

'Because he's a jerk!' Bella and Lisa cried in almost perfect unison.

'Sheesh.' Toby took a sip of beer. 'You ladies. You get stressy when you can't find a guy; stressy when you're dating; stressy as to whether or not it's "going anywhere"; and then super-duper stressy when you break up.'

Lisa's eyes narrowed dangerously. 'When was the last time you went on a date, Toby Bathurst?'

'That's not the point,' sniffed Toby, sounding like

someone who had found a piece of the moral high ground and was not giving it up easily.

'I'd say that was *exactly* the point,' said Lisa, draining her own cocktail. 'Take the words "glass houses", "stones" and "throwing" and use them to make a well-known phrase or saying, Toby. At least Flora here *had* a relationship; at least she was brave enough to try – even if the man she picked was a Grade A loser with a bad case of assholitis. No offence there, Flora.'

'None taken,' I replied ruefully.

'Hey!' Toby rapped his beer mat on the table. 'That's not fair. I *have* dated. I'm just on a dating break. I'm taking some time out to get to know myself and figure out what I really want from a partner. It's completely different.'

'Rubbish,' said Bella, throwing her hat into the ring. 'Richard hurt you, yes, but that was ages ago. You're not dating because you're scared.'

'I am *not* scared.' Toby was aghast. 'This is a "once bitten, twice as likely to avoid emotionally stunted, passive-aggressive co-dependants" thing. Anyway, what about you?'

For a moment there was silence; Lisa shifted uneasily in her seat and I sensed that a very significant line had been crossed, although what that line *was*, I had no idea.

Toby swallowed.

Hard.

But he pressed on.

'OK, I admit it, I've lost my nerve – but you're

hardly one to talk,' he said. 'Instead of sitting at home freaking out about stuff, you could be doing something amazing with those songs you've written. But who even gets to listen to them?'

'Bella, why are you freaking out?' My circuits were being overloaded. 'And what is this about songwriting? And just – well – *what*?'

Bella flushed, red hot on ice-white cheeks.

'P-people . . .' she stammered. 'People have listened to them.'

'Steve, right?' asked Lisa. 'You've played them for him?'

Bella looked down at her feet. This was an awkward manoeuvre given that she was sitting at a table, but she managed it.

'No,' she replied, 'they're not quite there yet.'

'Enough of this crapola!' Toby's views on the subject were clearly pretty uncompromising. 'They are *so* there. Really, really, money-makingly, serious-music-career there.'

'Will someone please tell me what we are talking about?' I cried.

But nobody did.

Instead, Lisa leaned in over the table towards Bella.

'It's true, honey,' she said, 'I steal Toby's downloads when he's at meetings and your stuff almost made me cry. Obviously, I don't believe in public displays of emotion so real tears are a no-no, but you get the idea.'

Bella tugged at the label on her bottle of beer.

'You need to screw your sensible head back on,

Bella,' insisted Toby. 'I'm not saying you're the next Lady GaGa, but you have to admit you've got talent.'

Bella turned even redder and slammed her beer bottle down on the table.

'Stop deflecting, Toby,' she said, 'this isn't about *me*, it's about *you* – specifically about how you need to get real over relationships. Because if you don't, you'll end up crazy with loneliness, buying stuff from the shopping channel in the middle of the night because you haven't got anyone else to talk to!'

'Hey!' said Toby. 'It's not like that!'

'Oh yes it is.' Bella scowled at him. 'You listen to me—'

'I've had enough of listening to you; *you* listen to me—'

'Stop it!' Lisa mountaineered up on to her chair, fluffing out her pink skirts so that it was touch and go as to whether she most resembled an over-inflated ballerina or an enormous stick of candy-floss. 'You are *all* driving me nuts!'

With fire in her eyes, she thrust the swizzle stick from her cocktail in Toby's direction. For a moment I thought she was going to kebab him with it.

'You! Mr Lily-Livered-Bathurst! Listen to me! You need to get your nerve back, get over yourself, and then get *under* someone else.'

Toby opened his mouth to protest. Lisa waggled the stick in front of his lips.

'Excuse me, did I say you were allowed an opinion?'

She turned to Bella, who shrank back into her seat,

her eyes wide in anxious expectation of what was about to be unleashed.

'If you think for one moment that your music is not exceptional, then you really are beyond brainless. There are people out there who would give their *eye teeth* to have the talent you've got in your little finger.'

'Why, what can she do with her little finger?' asked Toby.

Lisa gave him a glare that could have cut through sheet metal at twenty paces.

'Me talking, honey. You so not.'

I sat back and took a sip of my drink, thankful that her fire was not being trained on me.

But – no!

The swizzle stick was out again and pointing uncompromisingly in my direction.

'Me?' I choking on the pink gloopy mixture. 'What have I done? I'm an injured party!'

Toby leaned in towards me.

'Resistance is futile,' he whispered.

Lisa gave him another withering glare before continuing.

'You, young lady, are not giving up; *you* are going home. Only first you need to figure out exactly what that "home" is.'

She had clearly flipped. It was the only possible explanation. Flipped, bonkers, bananas, loopy, cracked. My home was a small, white terraced house in Oxford, only I wasn't going back there any time soon. This thought made my lip wobble dangerously and I turned to face the wall, staring hard at a photo of a leather-clad Chihuahua on a motorbike.

This was Lisa's cue for another demonstration of her freaky mind-reading abilities.

'And before you even think of contradicting me, Flora, the home I'm talking about isn't a "where", it's about finding out who you really are and who you belong to.'

I blinked hard at the Chihuahua.

Why did she need to rub it in? I belonged to no one. As far as I could see, that was pretty much where all my problems started.

'So! People!' Lisa now flourished the swizzle stick less like an offensive weapon and more like a magic wand. 'The lesson today is that all this beating yourselves up ends *here*. Is that clear?'

'Fine.' Toby held up his hands in surrender. 'We promise to look in the mirror every morning and tell ourselves how wonderful we are. Is that enough? Can we go now?'

'News flash, Toby: I'm still talking. Now, each of you is going to do something that scares the hell out of you. It doesn't matter if you succeed and it doesn't matter if you fail – you just have to do it. Toby, you are going to ask someone out on a date.'

Toby looked horrified.

'Who?' he bleated. 'When? How?'

Lisa ignored him. 'Bella, you are going to let someone who isn't me or Toby listen to your music.'

'But it's not—' Bella began.

'Yes it is.'

Lisa trained her sights on me.

'Don't drag me into this!' I cried. 'I don't count. I'm not even going to be in San Francisco that long.'

'Which is why we need to do what we can while you're still within the city limits,' she replied. 'First up, you need to forget about Boring.'

'Barney,' I corrected her.

'That's what I said, honey,' Lisa smiled sweetly. 'You need to forget about Boring and realise how much more you are without him. He was never your home, he was a prison cell and hey, look – hoorah, hoorah! You've just been handed a get-out-of-jail-free card. Second up, you *are* going to have a brilliant holiday. And third up, me, you and Bella are going shopping.'

'Shopping?' I echoed, allowing myself to perk up just a tiny bit.

Shopping couldn't be scary.

Could it?

'Shopping because you are never going to know who you truly are until you can recognise yourself in the mirror. But this is also a humanitarian mission to reclothe you before the fashion police make a well-deserved arrest. Tomorrow. Ten sharp. Drusilla's.' Lisa climbed down from her chair and smoothed out her skirts. 'So from now on, your collective motto is: when the going gets tough, the tough keep going. Deal?'

'Deal,' we muttered into our drinks.

'Hold on a minute.' Bella put her beer back down and leaned in over the table. 'What about you?'

'Me?' Lisa looked genuinely surprised.

'Yes.' Toby was uncharacteristically bold. 'If we all have missions, then you need one too.'

'Please, honey,' she replied, 'my life rocks. What could I possibly be lacking?'

'Well,' I began, remembering Bill's worshipping of the ground she walked on, 'are you in a relationship?'

'No, but I'm good, thanks.' Lisa's smile flickered just for a moment. 'Besides which, people, this isn't about me.'

And she took the last sip from her sickly pink drink, picked up her bag and sashayed as only Lisa knew how out of the door, leaving us feeling as drained as her glass.

# 5

The McMasters' residence was situated on Lombard Street, one of the most iconic and expensive thorough-fares the city possessed, and boasted a commanding view across the Bay. When I rang the doorbell, I had to wait a while for anyone to appear and, when they did, it was a maid complete with frilly apron and white lace cap, who looked as though she had been teleported in straight from the 1930s.

'Mrs McMaster is in the Turquoise Room,' she announced, before leading me down a hallway that would not have looked out of place in an English stately home.

At the end of the hall, she threw open the most enormous set of gilded double doors to reveal a large, sunny salon furnished almost entirely (as one might have supposed) in turquoise. Mrs McMaster, resplen -dent in a colour-co-ordinated kaftan and turban, a pair of turquoise-rimmed spectacles balanced on her nose, was perched on a sofa with the giant, slobbering form of 'little Pugsy', a strapping Doberman with a taste for human blood, sprawled over her knee.

He growled at me as I entered.

'Oh, there you are, Flora.' Mrs McMaster peered at me accusingly over the top of her glasses. 'I was beginning to think you were never coming.'

I checked my watch. I was five minutes early.

'Good afternoon, Mrs McMaster,' I said politely. I lifted my laptop out of its bag and looked for a suitable place to set it up. 'I've done my best to find out about the traffic levels in St John's Wood. It took quite a while and the figures are only provisional but I think—'

I tried to put the computer down on a gilded coffee table directly in front of Mrs M, but Pugsy emitted a low, guttural rumble and opened his mouth to show his fangs off to their best advantage. I took the hint and moved the laptop to another table a little further away and, without waiting for an invitation, sat down in the nearest chair.

Mrs McMaster blinked at me as though she hadn't quite understood.

'St John's Wood, dear?'

'Yes,' I replied. 'The houses in London we had on the shortlist: you'd narrowed it down to one in St John's Wood and another overlooking the Embankment.'

'Oh, I don't think so,' said Mrs McMaster, removing her spectacles and looking at me with uncompre - hending eyes. 'Earl has a weak chest, you know, the traffic fumes in London would not agree with him.'

'I'm sorry.' This didn't make any sense whatsoever. 'I'd understood you wanted to be located as centrally as possible.'

'Oh no, dear, whatever gave you that impression?'

Um – perhaps the form they'd filled out to say that only the Greater London area would suffice? Or maybe even the fifteen emails she'd sent me that morning containing details of Belgravia mansions?

'No, we were thinking more of a country estate. Nothing fancy, you know: a couple hundred acres, a golf course, stables, spa. Just the basics. Somewhere little Pugsy can have a proper run around.'

'Of course,' I said, remembering to breathe deeply and not ruin my professional reputation by screaming loudly and beating my client over the head with my laptop.

Pugsy bared his teeth in what, had he not been a dog, I would have taken to be a gloating smirk. I contented myself with gritting mine and opening up a fresh client-requirement form on my laptop.

'Is there anything else you can give me to work with, Mrs McMaster?' I asked, thinking I might be able to cobble together a long-list of possibilities for her to peruse before I returned to England. 'Number of rooms, preferred area of the country, that sort of thing?'

Maybe, if it was big enough, I could solve my own homeless problems by sleeping in the servants' quarters.

'I've always wanted a title,' said Sadie dreamily. 'Can we get a house that comes with a title? Earl would sound swell with a title in front of his name.'

No, I thought, Earl would sound ridiculous with a title in front of his name. Sir Earl. Lord Earl. Earl Earl.

'Or maybe we should have some peasants. Do people have peasants in England any more?'

70

'Do you mean *pheasants*, Mrs McMaster, for shooting parties?'

'No, dear: peasants. Poor people – bowing and tugging at their hair. It would be *such* a talking point when we had guests over for dinner.'

I felt like tugging at my hair too, only not in the way Mrs McMaster meant it. I had visions of myself being here until the wee small hours whilst Mrs McMaster constructed a life for herself based on *Downton Abbey*.

'I'll see what I can do,' I said pleasantly, making a mental note that I could perhaps hire some out-of-work actors if 'peasants' became a real sticking point. 'Now, are you and Mr McMaster sure that a country house is the direction in which you wish to move?'

I needed to be certain about this. The last thing I wanted was to get to mid-November and have Mrs McMaster suddenly announce that all she'd ever wanted was to live in a yurt, growing potatoes and milking her own goats. Mrs McMaster, however, looked at me as though I was a few blueberries short of a muffin.

'Of course, dear. Earl and I were never keen on the idea of a city. The clean fresh air, the gracious living – we want to experience the *real* England while we are over there.'

I bit back my instinctive reply, which was to say that the real England involved football terraces, chip shops and a number of other things that probably didn't come under Mrs McMaster's idea of 'gracious living'.

'OK,' I replied, deciding it would probably be best

for all concerned if I left them to thrash out their accommodation requirements between themselves, 'if you are sure about London not being the place for you, then I think the best idea would be if I emailed you a fresh client-preference form which you and Mr McMaster can fill out together. Please provide me with as much detail as possible and I'll get on the case when I return to the office.'

Mrs McMaster nodded her consent whilst I pinged the form off into the ether and switched off the laptop. At least that meant there should be a few golden days in which the requirements of the McMasters did not impinge upon my well-being.

'The measuring, Flora. The chaise and Mount Rushmore.'

My spirits sank still further. Damn, I thought I'd got away without the measuring.

'Look, Mrs McMaster, I'm not sure I'm the right person—'

But Mrs McMaster had already rung a bell and the maid had reappeared, holding a silver platter on which sat a large tape measure.

Resistance was useless.

'Ellen, take Flora to the study, please. She's going to measure some furniture.'

Picking up my bags, I trotted obediently in Ellen's wake down the hallway and through another set of ornate double doors. The room I found myself in was considerably smaller than the Turquoise Room, but still resembled the library of a National Trust property more than a working study. Stuffed animals in glass cases stared pleadingly out at me and, in between the bookcases stuffed with leather-bound antique volumes, hung a series of oil paintings depicting Earl himself dressed in tweeds, a shotgun crooked over one arm and an array of deceased wildlife at his feet.

I found myself fearing for the peasants.

Locating the chaise was easy. It was an elaborate affair with an emerald-green damasked cover standing next to the desk. I took the tape-measure off the platter and commenced operations.

As the door closed behind Ellen, I put the end of the tape-measure down on the floor next to one of the legs. My cunning plan was to walk to the other side of the chaise, unwinding tape as I went.

So far, so deceptively simple. However, the tape-measure turned out to be of the self-rewinding variety and insisted on snapping shut as soon as I let go of it, which was unavoidable given that my total arm span was only about half the length of the chaise. To overcome this problem, I stood on one end of the tape and stretched my other leg out splits-style to see if I could reach the far end (answer: no). Then, I lay flat on the floor, the tape-measure pinned beneath my prone body, and tried to unroll the remainder of the tape by pushing it away from me. But the tape was encased in a square container and refused to roll anywhere (another failure). Finally, with despair rising within me, I managed to locate a telephone directory on Mr McMaster's desk and used that to weigh down one end whilst I successfully extended the tape and took my measurement. Relieved, I wrote it down in my notebook, hoping that the McMasters weren't the sort of people who had CCTV installed, and would replay my antics later for the amusement of their friends and relations.

I then looked round the room for Mount Rushmore. When Mrs McMaster had said 'scale' model, I imagined that the scale involved would be quite small. However, hiding behind a floor-to-ceiling bookcase at the back of the study was a structure ten feet high and at least fifteen feet wide.

For a moment I just stared.

It was one of the most pointless and ugliest things I think I had ever seen in my life. Why anyone would want to build it, much less keep it hanging around once they'd finished, was completely beyond me. It didn't even *look* like Mount Rushmore, resembling instead a group of faces suffering the torments of the damned. The faint scent of mouthwash hung in the air.

I moved closer; Mrs McMaster hadn't lied: it *was* made of toothpicks. One or two in my direct line of vision didn't look as though they were unused, either.

Urgh.

I was saved, however, by my slave-mistress bustling into the study in a flurry of turquoise silk.

'Oh, Flora, thank goodness you are still here. There's been an emergency.'

She paused dramatically.

'Yes, a *real* emergency. The lady who does walkies with little Pugsy has just phoned in sick.'

Oh no. Oh nonononono. *Not* dog-walking. Not with sabre-toothed Pugsy!

Think! Think quickly!

'I'm *terribly* sorry, Mrs McMaster,' I began, 'but I couldn't possibly take Pugsy for his walkies. You see, I have this very specific Doberman allergy. I can be *indoors* with them, but the moment I step *outside*—'

'Not walking, Flora dear, I don't trust my baby Pugsy with just anyone, you know.' Mrs McMaster wrung her hands. 'And in any case, he has a little sniffle today – I noticed whilst he was having his fillet steak at breakfast. He is *very* delicate.'

I found the thought of a below-par Pugsy quite a happy one.

'No,' continued Mrs McMaster, 'the dog-walking lady takes his blankets to be cleaned. They need to be done every other day and he's such a sensitive baby he can't bear commercial soap powders next to his skin, can you, Pusgy-Wugsy?'

Pugsy-Wugsy appeared round her legs and growled belligerently. Sadie planted a kiss on top of his head.

'You'll take them to the organic dry-cleaner's, won't you?'

*Organic dry-cleaner's?* Only in San Francisco, I suspected.

'Wouldn't it be better for Ellen to—' I began.

But, yet again, Mrs McMaster was deaf to my words. She thrust a huge laundry bag into my hands.

'Come along, Flora, Pugsy is depending on you.'

I turned to leave the room, relieved to have escaped a closer inspection of Mount Rushmore. As I did so, however, the corner of the laundry bag caught a piece of paper sitting on the edge of Mr McMaster's desk and wafted it on to the floor. I put the bag on the floor and bent down to pick it up, my eye catching the name on the letterhead: 'Stealth Holdings'. However, before I could reach it, Mrs McMaster dived in and grabbed it.

'Really, Flora,' she sighed, placing the letter back on the desk, 'I do wish you'd be more careful.'

I quickly mumbled a half-hearted apology, picked up the laundry and then skedaddled before she changed her mind about the house yet again: *We are thinking of renting a Scottish castle, Flora, preferably with its own private army.*

It simply didn't bear thinking about.

I caught a trolley-bus back to Hope Street where I left Pugsy's blankets at the dry-cleaner's before walking up the hill to Bella's. I was very much hoping she'd be in; partly because I fancied a coffee and a good whinge about the McMasters, but more because I wanted to get to the bottom of what Toby had meant when he'd said she was freaking out. It crossed my mind that it might be something to do with Steve – she had not been happy when he'd talked about investing in the club in Oakland – but whatever the problem, I wanted her to know that if she needed to talk, I'd be more than happy to listen.

My plan, however, was foiled. When I arrived at Hope Heights, I found Bella in a state of extreme agitation – and it had nothing to do with Steve, money or the club. Well, when I say 'found', she wasn't actually anywhere to be seen, but I was able to track down the sound of muffled cursing to a spot under the dining-room table.

'Are you all right?' I asked, lifting up the tablecloth.

Bella shook her head.

'No, I'm bloody well not all right. Bloody Gunnar's only bloody got himself bloody deported, that's all.'

'Gunnar?'

'Bloody Gunnar who is bloody Benny in the bloody band. His visa expired.'

'When?' I asked, innocently thinking it should be a simple matter to ring up the Embassy and sort this out. Surely a few days here or there wouldn't be too much of a problem?

'Nineteen ninety-eight,' wailed Bella. 'They put him on a plane back to Sweden last night and he's just landed. But it's the Battle of the Tribute Bands on Monday – what are we supposed to do?'

'Bella . . .' I tried to crawl in beside her, but caught myself a nasty blow on the corner of the table. 'Bella – ouch – can you come out, please, or I'm going to give myself brain damage trying to talk to you.'

Bella obediently did as she was asked and stood before me, running a harassed hand through her hair.

'Without Gunnar, we don't have a band,' she explained, 'we are an Abba tribute act and you can't be an Abba tribute act with only three people.'

77

'You could hold an audition,' I suggested.

Bella shook her head.

'There's simply not enough time. Just setting up auditions would take days at the very least. God, I'm racking my brains here but I'm just not getting anywhere.'

'Oh, Bella, I am so sorry,' I replied, 'I wish there was something I could do.'

As the words left my lips, a thoughtful expression spread across Bella's face.

'Actually, Flo,' she said slowly, hope once again shining from her blue eyes, 'perhaps there is something.'

'Oh?' I replied, a feeling of unease stirring within me.

Bella nodded earnestly.

'It would only be for one night while Steve advertised for someone else. It would give us the breathing space we need.'

'Oh no.' The penny dropped. 'Oh no you don't.'

But Bella didn't give up that easily.

'Please, Flo, I'm desperate! Besides, you're my family and the thing about families is that they should always stick together and—'

I don't know which appalled me most: the idea of getting up on stage in front of hundreds of people, or doing so wearing glittery spandex. Either way, the answer was the same.

'No one will ever know it's you,' Bella wheedled, 'you can wear a fake beard and—'

*A fake beard?* Just when I thought she couldn't make it any less attractive.

'Listen, Bella, it's simple: if you haven't got a Benny then don't go in for the competition. Do it next year instead when you're back up to quota.'

But Bella wasn't listening.

'Come on, Flo, it'll be *fun!*'

'No it won't,' I protested, 'it'll be excruciating and embarrassing and the stuff of nightmares – and that's just from the audience's perspective.' I paused and took a deep breath. 'I know this is important to you, but, at the end of the day, it's only a band competition, isn't it?'

I paused. My cousin's face told me I had got this very, very wrong.

'Bella,' I said, 'there's something going on, I know there is. Toby said as much in the Lizard earlier today.'

Bella, however, stapled a smile to her face. It wasn't convincing, but it was certainly defiant. It was the sort of smile that said, 'Don't push this one any further.'

'There is nothing', she said slowly and firmly, 'going on. Nothing. I swear, Flora. Toby was talking about some rubbish that got fixed ages ago, and as for Gunnar' – she gave a carefree laugh – 'just forget I ever mentioned it. You know me, I'm horribly competitive; being disqualified from a competition before I've even got to the first round was never going to be my favourite scenario.'

'Well . . .' I hesitated, thinking this was probably not the right moment to press her seeing as she was already in a spin over Gunnar. 'You . . . look, you would tell me if you were in trouble, wouldn't you?'

'I'm sorry, Flo.' My cousin linked her arm through mine. 'You're dealing with enough crapola at the moment without having to worry about me, for goodness' sake. And don't worry about the band either, I'll sort it.'

I decided to let the matter drop – this time, anyway. She knew I was here for her and that would have to do until a more suitable opportunity for a heart-to-heart presented itself.

Bella changed the subject.

'Anyway,' she said, her eyes shining once again, 'enough panicking about the band. It's Saturday night tonight, which means it's party night. Lisa knows this club, the sort that looks like a normal house and you have to give a password to get in. Apparently there's a roof terrace and free drinks and celebs and everything. We're off there in about an hour so you need to go and get your glad rags on. Everything will be fine.'

I nodded reluctantly and picked up my handbag. It would all be fine: the band, Barney, the McMasters; I just didn't have any idea how.

# 6

It was ten o'clock on Sunday morning, the hour
appointed for my make-over by Lisa, and I stood
outside Drusilla's emporium doing my best to summon
up the courage to step over the threshold. It had one
of the most attractive exteriors on Hope Street, and as
well as the gorgeous, dark-clarety-red of its woodwork,
it also boasted elegant line drawings of ladies in period
costumes parading round the edges of its window
frame as well as an original Victorian brass shop bell
over the door.

So far, so tasteful.

However, the contents of the window display were
not as reassuring. Surrounded by a bookcase, a glass
gas lamp and a couple of stuffed birds in wire cages was
a female figure dressed in a cream-coloured crinoline.
She was reclining on a chaise longue (not dissimilar to
the one owned by Mrs McMaster) and holding an
ostrich-feather fan. As a period piece she was absolutely convincing: the silk dress, the lace gloves, the
locket round her neck – even her dark, shiny hair,
which fell in tightly curled ringlets over her ears. The
expression on her face, though, was one of utter terror
and her mouth was open in a soundless scream.

And I didn't blame her, because looming over this

tableau was Nosferatu himself, in full evening dress and an opera hat, all set off with a set of fangs and two trickles of scarlet blood dripping down his chalk-white face.

Bella didn't give this disturbing scene a second glance. Instead, she marched straight up to the door and pushed it open. The bell tinkled merrily and the figure in the crinoline winked at me and then rose up from the chaise.

I screamed very loudly indeed and Lisa, who was waiting for us inside the shop, Bella and the becrinolined girl all burst into laughter.

'Flora . . .' Lisa beckoned me inside and did the introductions. 'This is Drusilla. Drusilla, meet your project for today, Flora Fielding. The girl who needs not only some decent clothes, but a whole new attitude to life.'

'Hi.' I extended a paw in Drusilla's direction. 'You gave me such a shock.'

Drusilla grinned at me.

'So I saw,' she replied in a lilting Dublin accent. 'Did you realise that your feet actually left the floor?'

'It wouldn't surprise me,' I replied. I was still waiting for my heart rate to return to normal. 'Do you often do that to your customers?'

Drusilla shook her head.

'Only when I know I'm going to get a good reaction.' She grinned wickedly. 'When I'm not running the shop, I'm a performance artist – amongst other things – and I like to get in a bit of extra practice when we're slow. Now tell me, what it is that you're after?'

I looked around the interior of the shop. Behind me was a row of fitting rooms screened by thick, red, damasked curtains; to my right was a full-length mirror; and, over to my left, I saw a well-worn velvet sofa upon which Bella and Lisa were already seated. Apart from this, though, the rest of the space was taken up almost entirely by Drusilla's stock. There were clothes on rails, clothes on stands, clothes displayed like works of art on the walls, clothes hanging in dark wooden wardrobes that looked as though they should be bursting with lions and witches rather than dresses and skirts – and that was even before you got to the shoes, bags, belts, gloves, jewellery and fully boned corsets. The smell of the past was all around me.

'I'm not sure,' I said at last. 'Although probably not a crinoline – lovely though yours is, of course.'

'Of course,' Drusilla echoed with a grin. 'Now, let's have a look at you.'

With the hands of an expert, she pinched my T-shirt in around my waist and held it in place with a couple of pins. Then she marched me out to a small space on the floor sandwiched between a hat-stand and a table scattered with gloves and handkerchiefs, and made a full 360 appraisal of me, her lips pursed and her porcelain-like brow furrowed in contemplation.

'I'm thinking 1947 to 1959 . . . what do you say, girls?'

Lisa was helping herself to a flamboyantly iced cupcake, one of a selection sitting on an art-deco cake stand next to the sofa.

'That's gotta be where the smart money is,' she replied. 'It's the waist – not to mention the hips and those bazongas. Wouldn't she have been to die for in Marilyn Monroe's Hollywood?'

'She's to die for now,' said Drusilla, 'and the hair . . . If she didn't have this anti-crinoline thing, wouldn't you be thinking Pre-Raphaelite? Or even Titian or Botticelli?'

I studied my reflection in the mirror opposite: auburn, ringletty hair falling over one shoulder, my pale, freckly skin, a dark, heavy bag under each eye; I certainly didn't feel I bore much resemblance to an oil painting.

'Take a seat, Flora,' said Drusilla. 'I'll bring over a few things for you to try.'

I joined Lisa and Bella on the sofa and helped myself to a cupcake.

'So how's business?' Bella asked Drusilla in between bites.

'Business is great, in fact I think it's probably up on a couple of months ago. Ironic, isn't it? It just goes to show it's true what they say about there being no such thing as bad publicity.'

'Bad publicity?' I echoed, my mouth full of cupcake.

'We're being sold off,' said Drusilla from the other side of the shop, 'or at least, that's what the landlord wants to do. The old guy who owns this parade of shops has had an offer from some sort of con-glomerate; and, from what we can work out, it's the type he'd be crazy to turn down.'

'What will this conglomerate do?' I swallowed my cake and snuck a sip of Bella's tea.

'We don't know,' said Drusilla, 'we're not even sure what they are called. It's all ridiculously hush-hush. However, you can bet your life they won't want to be keeping things as they are.' She sighed. 'I expect it will mean curtains not only for me but the Lizard and the Apple Pie too, plus the Greek baker's and the organic butcher's. I just know it – I can feel it in my water, as my old granny used to say.'

Urgh. *There's no place like home; there's no place like home.*

'And Doodles on Poodles, and the yoga place with the café above it run by nuns who use the profits to subsidise their orphanage in Oakland,' added Bella.

'Plus the independent bookstore that has poetry slams and open-mike nights and the place that does food parcels and lunches on a Tuesday and Friday for homeless people,' concluded Lisa.

I blinked as I tried to take all this information on board.

'But that's awful,' I said, 'especially about the orphans. Can't you campaign about this as a com-munity? Take it to the local papers – the local television station even?'

Drusilla appeared, laden down by an enormous armful of garments.

'The problem is, we have nothing to campaign *against*. If it was a supermarket or a mall or a bypass, we'd have a leg to stand on; but as it stands right now, it's just a change of owner.'

'So what are you worried about then? Maybe nothing *will* happen?'

Drusilla put the clothes down on the arm of the sofa and shook her head.

'It doesn't add up,' she said. 'Why spend all that money if you are just going to keep things as they are? It doesn't make any sense. Anyway, I don't want to think about it more than I have to. I'm lighting candles to every deity I can think of in the hope that the whole thing blows over and I still have a business in six months' time.' She shrugged and then flashed me a grin. 'However, in the meantime I still need to pay the rent so let's see how you go with these.'

She held up a grey-and-black sleeveless dress with tiny red flowers embroidered along the neckline and the shoulder straps. It had a nipped-in waist with a red belt and layer upon layer of frothing net petticoats. I took it into the changing room, removed my denim skirt, shoes and T-shirt (only remembering about the pins after one of them had embedded itself forcefully in my thumb) and clambered in. There was a nasty moment where I thought I was never going to find my way out and instead suffocate quietly in amongst the layers of net, but I persevered and eventually struggled back into daylight once again.

Smoothing down the voluminous skirts, I swung

round to get a look at myself in the changing-room mirror. However, as I did so, a strange feeling began to creep over me. The girl I saw definitely bore a resemblance to me – she had my unruly hair and the chin which always seemed reluctant to separate itself entirely from my neck – but, as I moved and jiggled my way into the dress I found myself looking at someone I did not recognise: a girl with fantastic curves; a girl who stood up straight and showed her figure off to its best advantage; a girl who looked as though she would be perfectly happy on the set of a classic movie. Staring at her gave me a strange – almost itchy – sensation of having stepped inside somebody else's skin. It was bizarre and, before I lost my nerve, I flung open the curtain and stepped out into the shop for the all-important girlfriend appraisal.

Bella gasped and jumped off the sofa with her hands clasped together.

'Oh, Flo, you look *lovely*,' she enthused.

Lisa and Drusilla nodded in agreement, but there was some high-level, professional scrutiny to come too.

'The style is right,' Drusilla helped to shake out my petticoats, 'but not the colour.'

Lisa neatly folded the paper case that had recently surrounded her second cupcake and brushed a few crumbs from her lap on to a china plate.

'You're right,' she said, 'too dark. It drains you, Flora; but it might be just the thing I need to wear to Toby's stupid client drinks thing on Friday. It's an ill wind, as they say. Dru, will you put it on one side for me and I'll try it on later?'

I was hustled back inside the changing room by Drusilla, where I wriggled out of the black-and-grey dress and into a figure-hugging navy-blue number with a mid-calf pencil skirt.

I threw back the curtains.

'No,' said Bella simply, 'no, no, no, no and no. And did I mention no?'

'It's the length,' said Lisa, her critical eye scanning me up and down.

'And the style,' added Drusilla.

'And the *colour*,' chimed in Bella. 'Navy blue makes you look like you work for a building society.'

'Or a budget airline,' said Lisa. 'You look like a cut-price trolley dolly who has had their legs chopped off at the knee and reglued halfway down their shins. Next!'

'Say what you really feel,' I grumbled, pulling the curtain shut behind me and shimmying my way out of the pencil skirt. 'Don't sit on the fence to protect my feelings.'

'Don't worry!' Bella's cheery tones rang out. 'We won't.'

I turned to the next garment: a plain-looking dress fashioned out of orange silk. It had two major things against it: firstly it looked like a limp rag, and secondly it was, as I have mentioned, orange. Bright orange. The sort of shade that not even a colour-blind tangerine would be seen wearing in public.

I decided that Drusilla must have had a moment of madness as she scooped this one off the rails. She might as well have handed me a sandwich-board to try on with the words 'I have no taste, kill me now' written across it.

With a huge sigh of resignation, I undid the orange zip hidden in the seam of the bodice and slipped it over my head. The silk gave a satisfying rustle as it settled over my hips but I didn't bother to look in the mirror. This was obviously a no-go. There was no need to torture myself more than the others would.

I flung back the curtain and stepped out into the shop, bracing myself for a barrage of negativity – and, very possibly, actual mocking.

But there was nothing.

Instead, three faces stared at me, their mouths very slightly open and their eyes wide and unblinking. Without even waiting for their comments, I swung back round towards the changing room – when I caught sight of someone in the mirror.

I stopped.

I did a double take.

It was *me*.

I meant: it was *me*?

I traced the line of my figure down from the sweep of my neck, through the curve of my shoulders to the narrowness of my waist and the perfectly proportioned spread of my hips, from which the elegant silk folds of the dress fell flawlessly.

'Get it,' said Bella. 'Get it and wear it every day. And on the days you *don't* wear it, stay in while it's dry-cleaned and then wear it the next day.'

Lisa gave me a watery smile.

'My baby,' she stammered, 'my baby has grown up!'

'I love it,' I said. 'But I feel . . . I don't know . . . I mean – when would I ever wear anything like this? It's not as though I have wall-to-wall cocktail invitations!'

Drusilla shook her head in exasperation.

'You don't need invitations,' she said. 'You just wake up, think, "Today is a good day to wear an original nineteen fifties silk dress," and you put it on.'

Then she clapped her hand across her mouth and dashed out of her chair across the shop floor, to return holding a pair of golden shoes. She slipped them on to my feet in the manner of Prince Charming claiming his Cinderella.

'Fifteen per cent off if you take the lot,' she said. 'You'll be burying me in a pauper's grave, Flora, but you *have to have that outfit.*'

I did one last twirl with the amazing dress in front of the mirror.

Was this the real me? I was rather impressed – even if I said so myself.

'I'll take it,' I replied, 'but don't feel obliged with the discount, Drusilla, it's your livelihood, after all.'

'No obligation.' Drusilla smiled. 'One of the perks of the job is that sometimes you feel you are reuniting clothes with their true owners. This is your dress; you need to have it.'

'Thanks,' I said and turned back towards the changing room.

'Where do you think you're going?' Bella's voice cut through my thoughts.

'To put my real clothes on, of course.'

Lisa made an impatient clicking sound with her tongue.

'*These* are your real clothes, honey,' she told me. 'Get used to it.'

Reluctantly, I handed over my card while Drusilla parcelled up my old clothes in a brown paper carrier covered with the same drawings of that elegant period ladies who graced the window frame.

'Have fun!' said Drusilla, handing the bag over and preparing to take up her tourist scaring post in the window.

'Oh, don't worry about that,' called Bella cheerfully over her shoulder, 'I'll make sure she does!'

# 7

It was seven o'clock the next evening. I, my vintage shoes and my orange dress were making their way along Hope Street in eager anticipation of the Battle of the Tribute Bands first round at the Lizard Lounge. It had been an uneventful day – which, given recent events, was very much a Good Thing. Bella and I had pottered along Fisherman's Wharf, mooched round Golden Gate Park – oh, and delivered Pugsy-Wugsy's organically dry-cleaned dog blankets back to the McMasters' palatial residence.

I walked into the bar to see Lisa, resplendent in a red, clingy satin dress, perched on a stool next to the bar. There were four cocktail glasses in front of her, each containing a clear liquid and an olive on a cocktail stick. She pushed one of them towards me.

'We're drinking extra-strong martinis,' she said. 'They go with that gorgeous new look of yours, and Toby phoned ahead to say he needs an alcohol über hit to get him through the next couple hours.'

I sipped the martini. It was indeed extra-strong. In fact, it was pretty much like being kicked in the mouth by a Shire horse.

But a bit nicer tasting.

I coughed and blinked.

'Why does Toby need help to get through the next couple of hours?' I asked. 'Has he got himself a date?'

Lisa emitted her tinkle-of-shattering-glass laugh.

'You are funny,' she said. 'No, it's not a date; just stage fright.'

'Stage fright?' I echoed, when the door from the street opened and Toby entered.

I can honestly say that I have never in all my life seen such an unhappy countenance. He wasn't so much a wet weekend as an ongoing monsoon of misery; and he stared at Lisa with huge, tragic eyes, as though he was silently begging her to rescue him from a fate worse than death.

'I don't know why I agreed to do this,' he groaned. 'I don't know how I let you talk me into this.'

'You didn't *agree* to anything,' replied Lisa lightly, 'that would imply there was free will involved. You're doing this firstly because you can sing; secondly because it will be *good* for you – oh, and thirdly because I told you to.'

'Oh yeah.' He looked even more despondent. 'I remember now.'

The sound of footsteps came from behind us and I turned round to see Bella in a pink jumpsuit with a cut-out heart over her perfectly toned tummy walking towards us.

'Come on, Tobes.' Bella handed him something that looked like a large, sequin-encrusted, four-armed starfish. 'Cheer up. Remember you're saving my arse here.'

Toby held the garment (an all-in-one Lycra/ sparkly/silver number) up to the light, rolled his eyes and then let his arms fall limply down by his sides.

'I'm sorry, Bella, but your *arse* is the least of my worries. I am about to put on this . . . this . . .' he was struggling to find words that could adequately describe the depths to which he was about to plunge '. . . this *abomination*, and walk out on stage in front of literally *people,* and entertain them by singing and – God have mercy on me – dancing.'

He put his head in his hands and slumped down on to a nearby chair.

'Yeah, and the Oscar for crying like a baby goes to Toby Bathurst,' said Lisa, pulling him to his feet and leading him over towards the men's room. 'It's your own fault. If you'd done as you were told and asked someone out on a date, then you wouldn't have to do this as a forfeit. Now, go get your costume on.'

By the time he reappeared a couple of minutes later, he looked positively suicidal.

And, to be fair, he had good reason.

Gunnar must have been very tall indeed, because even after Toby had zipped it up, the sleeves of the silver suit drooped limply over the ends of his fingers and the trousers dribbled down over his feet. As my mother would have said, there was plenty of room for growth.

'Put your boots on,' instructed Bella, handing him a pair of white, knee-high platforms. 'You can roll the trousers up and tuck them down inside.'

'There are boots?' wailed Toby. 'Nobody mentioned boots.'

'You're pretending to be a member of Abba,' said Bella sternly, 'of course there are boots.'

'This is an infringement of my human rights,' moaned Toby as Bella and I lifted a leg each, placed his feet in the boots and zipped them up. 'This is cruel and inhuman – and not just for me, but for the poor bastards out in the audience.'

Bella produced an electric guitar from goodness-knows-where.

'You're going to be Bjorn rather than Benny,' she said. 'I negotiated a switch with Randall to save you going ape over the facial hair.'

'You want me to play the guitar?' Toby had moved from despair to incredulity. 'But I've never been near a guitar in my life! Just so as I know, are there any other miracles you want me to perform this evening? Balance the federal budget? Discover the meaning of life? Eradicate world hunger?'

Bella made a tutting noise and zipped up her own vertiginous platform boots.

'Oh, quit kvetching,' cried Lisa, putting her hands over her ears. 'You are a gay man. The lyrics, tune and a dance routine to every Abba song ever written are etched into your DNA. The guitar won't be plugged in – the sound will be coming from the backing track – all you have to do is pretend. Think yourself lucky they're not making you wear the beard, and get out there and win the damn competition already.'

Before he could protest any further, Steve appeared. Toby manfully drew himself up to his full height and thrust back his shoulders. It was a little like watching a silver-backed gorilla square up to a rival on an African mountainside – except that the gorilla in question was wearing a silver lamé catsuit and platform boots. Steve patted Toby on the shoulder.

'Don't fuck up,' he begged. 'We need to win this. Just don't fucking fuck up.'

Toby opened his mouth to reply, but Bella stepped in between them and kissed Steve lightly on the cheek.

'Come on,' she said, ushering us all downstairs, 'we haven't got time. Toby, you need to get into position.'

We only just made it. As Lisa and I settled ourselves at a table (Steve disappeared into a dark corner to talk to a man with a pencil moustache wearing a fedora), the lights went down and Bill bounded up the steps onto the tiny stage.

'Ladies and gentlemen and anyone at any other point in between,' he announced, taking one of the microphones off a stand and twirling into the spotlight with it, 'welcome to the first round of the Lizard Lounge's world-famous Battle of the Tribute Bands. You know the score: three bands perform two songs a night but only one of them can go through to the next round and it is up to you – the audience – to decide who the winner is.'

There was a deafening cacophony of shouting, wolf-whistles, stamping and clapping.

'The line-up tonight, people, is so dazzling you are

going to need your sunglasses. It is so star-studded that members of the University of California Astronomy Faculty will be training their telescopes on it. It is so amazing that the English language struggles to find words that can adequately describe its magnificence. So if you're ready, put your hands together and give a full-on Lizard welcome to our first act tonight: Abbadabbatastic!'

The cheering was so loud, I could feel my eardrums bowing against the force of the noise. Then, as the opening riff of 'Waterloo' rang through the air, Abbadabbatastic were revealed in all their glittery glory. True, Toby's face clearly said that he would rather be having root-canal surgery without anaesthetic than strutting his stuff in front of several hundred people, but as the song got going, his face relaxed; then he smiled and finally even managed a bit of hip-wiggling.

When the song finished, Bella stepped forward to the microphone and did a spiel about how wonderful it was to be lounging with the lizards at the Lizard Lounge (cue another ear-splitting roar from the crowd) and introduced the band members. When it was his turn, Toby grinned and gave an enthusiastic reprise of the hip-wiggling, to the obvious delight of the audience. Then Bella stepped back into line and the soft, opening bars of 'I Had a Dream' wafted over me. I sipped my martini and settled back in my chair, casting a glance over the rest of the audience – only to find myself looking straight into the blue eyes of the man from the diner who was sitting two tables behind me.

I quickly turned away and slipped down as far as I could into my chair. But however far I sank, I could still feel the weight of his gaze resting on the back of my neck.

'You all right, honey?' asked Lisa. 'Or did someone amputate your spine when you weren't looking?'

I took another sip of my martini and stared at my lap. Lisa glanced behind us. 'He's cute,' she said in a voice that could be heard well above the music. 'I wouldn't kick him out of bed for leaving cookie crumbs. Not that I'd give him the chance to *eat* any cookies.'

I became aware of a pounding beat in my ears, which could have been the bass line pumping out of the speakers but could equally have been my heart. I made a super-human effort to focus on Bella's beautiful voice rather than the strange flutterings in my stomach.

But, for some reason, I couldn't.

Hoping that Bella wouldn't mind, I pushed back my chair and stood up. My plan was to make a dart to the bar in order to avoid any awkward interface with blue-eyed men who might fancy me. However, the blue-eyed man in question had obviously been reading my mind because before I had taken a single step he was there, blocking my escape.

'Hi,' I said, trying to strike a balance between making myself heard over the music whilst not disturbing the enjoyment of anyone nearby who wanted to listen.

'Hi,' blue-eyed man replied, an ever-so-slightly-anxious smile crinkling up the corners of his mouth.

The palms of my hands tingled hot and cold.

'So,' he continued, staring at me as if our sight-lines had been superglued together.

'So,' I agreed.

I took a deep breath and tried to transform myself into a girl worthy of my orange silk super-dress; a girl who would smile politely and then simply dodge round any blue-eyed men who happened to be standing between her and the bar.

Only, for some reason, that didn't happen.

'You're Josh,' I informed him, feeling my stomach flip over as I looked into his eyes. (Not that I had any choice in the matter: my eyes were currently refusing to take any orders from my brain that involved looking anywhere else.)

'That's right.' He seemed pleased I'd retained this vital piece of information. 'And you're . . .? I'm sorry, I'm afraid I didn't ask your name when we met.'

At the idea of opening my mouth and uttering the words 'I'm Flora Fielding', my heart began beating so violently that it nearly broke free from my ribcage altogether.

This was ridiculous, I told myself; just because the man had once looked at me in an interested way in a diner did not mean I should automatically turn into a gibbering wreck.

'This is Flora,' a familiar voice from behind me chipped in. 'Flora is from England and is visiting her cousin in San Francisco for a couple of weeks. She likes champagne and martinis; she appears to be house-trained and she's got a great rack. What about you?'

I swung round. Lisa was hanging over the edge of her seat grinning at us. Josh blinked and swallowed, his gaze still firmly fixed on my face.

'I'm Josh Hannigan,' he said, 'and I'm originally from the East Coast, although I now live in San Francisco. And I work in IT.'

'Oh well,' said Lisa, with the air of one forgiving a major transgression, 'I suppose someone has to. Anyhoo, Flora, I know you think he's hotter than a sauna in the Sahara so hurry up and grab him before someone else does.'

Lisa was right; he was painfully cute.

Not that his hotness quotient made any difference to the fact that Barney had just stamped on my heart and smashed it to smithereens.

'Well,' I began, 'you see, Josh, I've only just finished—'

Lisa pulled me to one side. It wasn't subtle, but then again, as I was beginning to realise, that was Lisa all over.

'No,' she hissed, 'nonononono. Stretch those wings, ask him out. Because if you don't, then I will. On your behalf.'

What choice did I realistically have?

I reached behind me, took a large slug of my martini and then said:

'Would you like to go out with me? I mean, would you, *Josh*, like to go out with me? I mean, I don't really want to have dinner with Lisa—'

'Hey, none taken.' Lisa bit the top off her olive.

Josh grinned and ran his fingers through his dark hair.

'Yeah – I mean, yes, I mean . . . That would be awesome. Shall we say Wednesday at seven thirty? I'll pick you up here.'

I nodded.

'And you're sure?' he added with a side glance at Lisa who was busy draining her glass. 'You don't *mind* me taking you out?'

I hesitated. This was my get-out opportunity. The temptation to backtrack was strong, but I resisted.

'As long you mean "taking out" in the sense of a pink, fluffy romcom movie rather than an Al Pacino one.' Lisa swallowed her last mouthful of extra-strong martini as though it was mineral water and smacked her lips together appreciatively.

I nodded my acceptance.

Josh's grin widened to the point that his chin was in danger of falling off, and I found myself smiling back. I wanted to go. I really did – albeit in a scary, knee-shaking, terrifying sort of way.

'I'll see you then,' I said simply.

Josh's eyes shone and he looked completely ecstatic.

'Yeah,' he agreed, his gaze still locked on to mine, 'I'll see you. Wednesday. Seven thirty.'

He took a couple of steps backwards and nearly fell over an empty chair. I stepped forward to help him up but he recovered himself and, with a final, cheery wave, bounded up the stairs two at a time. I fell back down into my seat, my legs giving out on me. 'I Had a Dream' was just coming to an end.

The spell was broken.

'What have I done?' I whispered, half to myself and half to Lisa. 'I've promised to go out with him! *What have I done?*'

'You've done the right thing,' said Lisa firmly. 'Listen to me: you don't ever, *ever* pass up an oppor-tunity like this. Everything about *you* says that you think he's the dog's boxer shorts, and if *he* thought you were any hotter, he'd have had to order a flame-proof suit.'

'But dinner?' I twisted the stem of my glass nervously between my fingers. 'What about starting low-key? Why didn't I suggest coffee – or even lunch?'

Lisa drew her breath in sharply between her teeth, and made a little whistling sound.

'Coffee isn't even on the scale, and you know what lunch means?'

I stared blankly at her.

'Er . . . sandwiches? A light salad?'

Lisa rolled her eyes.

'Don't they teach you anything in England? Lunch means "I *should* ask you out, but as I don't actually like you, I'm going to suggest lunch instead." This guy deserves dinner. And a walk along a beach at sunrise. And a side order of moonlight and nightingales.' She grinned wickedly. 'Frankly, if I see you again before Thursday afternoon, I'll be surprised.'

Before I could reply, the lights on the stage went down and the crowd around us erupted into a thunder of applause. Bella and Toby rushed – or rather tottered on their platform soles – down the steps of the stage and towards our table. It was difficult to work out which one of them was squealing harder.

'You were *amazing*!' I took Bella in my arms and gave her the most enormous hug. 'You were better than the real thing! You too, Tobes. You were fantastic.'

'Oh, stop it!' Toby grinned modestly, towering over us in his enormous footwear. 'Although on second thoughts, don't stop it. Keep it coming with the love. Let me feel the love!'

'Wonderful!' I hugged him too. 'Beyond awesome.'

Toby broke free from my embrace and pointed towards Lisa.

'You two,' he said. 'I was watching you. What was going on here?'

'Goldberg's Dating Service at *your* service,' explained Lisa, giving Toby and Bella 'mwah, mwah' kisses on both cheeks. 'Flora just needed a little push to do the right thing where a very cute man was concerned – unlike some people I could mention, *Toby*. Hey! Bill! More martinis over here before we die of thirst.'

'Say you'll come dancing with me at the Tonga Room on Friday and they're on the house!' called Bill from the table next to ours.

'In your dreams,' retorted Lisa.

Bill grinned broadly and passed the order on to one of his waitresses.

'You already are!' he called back. 'Every night!'

'So who was that guy?' Bella settled down into a seat and took a long slug of my drink. 'He was *gorgeous*!'

'Josh Hannigan,' I replied warily. 'He works in IT.' I pulled my mobile out of my bag and showed them the SuperConnect icon. 'He put this on my phone. I'm not entirely sure, but I think he must work for them.'

Toby took the handset and played around with it for a moment or two.

'Oh man,' he breathed, 'this is cool. This is amazing. How do I get it on my cell?'

'I'm not sure,' I said, taking the phone back and squinting at the screen. 'He downloaded it for me when I met him in the Apple Pie on Friday morning.'

'You met him on Friday?' asked Bella, her eyebrows shooting upwards. 'You met a man-god like that and you didn't tell me?'

'It was all a bit weird. And before Barney dumped me.'

'And you're going out with him When?'

I pulled a face. My doubts and uncertainties about going on a date with Josh redoubled their clamouring.

'Actually, I don't know if that would be a good idea. I mean, after everything that's happened.'

Bella looked at me.

'You're scared,' she said, half-teasingly, half-accusingly.

Out of nowhere, an image of Josh all dark floppy hair and big blue eyes, flashed into my brain. My knees instantly turned to mush.

'Yup,' I replied, 'I think I probably am.'

'Look!' Toby was still enraptured by SuperConnect. 'I know how to do this. You send me the link, then I mail everyone in my address book and get them joined up, and then *they* mail everyone in *their* address book and bingo! The whole world comes on board. And why not? It's genius.'

He pressed a button on my phone.

'There,' he said, 'that's sent it to me, Bella and Lisa. We're all SuperConnected!'

Bless him! He was genuinely excited at the prospect.

'Flora,' said Bella softly, 'I know what happened with Boring the Bastard but you have to go out with Josh. Your instincts are telling you he's a contender and you need to trust them.'

'But what if they're wrong?' I replied, grabbing my martini back before she polished off the lot. 'After all, my instincts told me to move in with Barney. Maybe what I should actually be doing is going home and seeing if I can sort things out there.'

'Home isn't a place,' Bella continued earnestly, 'it's the people in your life. Until you find your tribe, you're never going to feel truly at home anywhere. 'She squeezed my hand. 'Don't give up on Josh. He might not be a date – he might be far more important than that.'

The idea that I would run into someone of life-changing importance in a random diner on the other side of the world was so ridiculous that there was simply no point in arguing about it. Besides, the next round of drinks had arrived.

'Yeah,' I said, taking a sip of freshly delivered martini. 'Of course he could.'

I looked round and saw Steve standing a little way off. Bella waved him over and he took a seat next to her.

'Who was that guy?' she asked, pushing her martini towards him so that he could have a sip. 'The one with the hat.'

'Chris,' he replied. 'He wanted to update me on the club.'

Bella narrowed her eyes.

'Yeah,' Steve continued, twisting the stem of the glass between his chubby fingers, 'it seems there's been a lot of interest. In fact, he might have to put his prices up.'

'Which doesn't matter to you because you're not buying into it anyway, are you, Steve?' replied Bella pointedly.

Steve looked away. His smug expression had evaporated.

'I said *are you?*' Bella repeated.

However, before he could reply, the house lights dimmed and Bill bounded back on to the stage.

'And now,' he said, 'after you've all had a chance to refresh your glasses, please put your hands together and give a huge Lizard welcome to Madam and the Ants!'

The crowd, including us, erupted.

'These guys are good,' whispered Bella, 'very, very good.'

'Yeah, but they don't have me shaking my tushie for them,' Toby announced modestly. 'I'd say they're pretty much doomed.'

Bella rolled her eyes.

'No, but they've got Melinda and she's worth about a hundred of your tushies,' she replied.

Toby sniffed sulkily and gave me back my phone. It emitted a little trill and the name 'Josh Hannigan' appeared on the screen with a little red box beside it. Inside the box was a single word: 'accept?'

I hesitated.

What, exactly, was I accepting? A virtual friend? A dinner date? I really had no idea.

'Put the phone away, Flo,' whispered Bella, 'the glow of the screen is distracting if you're up on stage.'

Obediently, I slipped it back into my bag: the perfect excuse not to make a decision. I'd sort it out tomorrow instead. Or the day after.

No, really, I would.

# 8

I stayed over at Bella's again that night. However, despite the best efforts of the martinis, I didn't sleep well. I was disturbed by alarming dreams, including one where I was out on my date with Josh and he began to tug at his face, only to pull off a rubber mask and reveal himself as Barney. I awoke and lay in Bella's spare bed for a moment or two, trying to banish the image from my mind before heaving back the covers, pulling on some clothes and making my way into the kitchen in search of coffee and some reassurance that the real world was less frightening than my subconscious.

'Hey,' Bella called out as I entered, 'don't look so worried. Nothing terrible can happen on such a beautiful day. Besides, Bill's been round and delivered my share of the takings from last night so I can afford to make like a tourist and do some more sights with you. How about a boat trip round the Bay?'

I glanced out of the window. It was a truly gorgeous morning: the sun shone down from a clear blue sky, making the water in the Bay shimmer seductively.

'Absolutely,' I turned back to face her. 'You're on.'

I'd been worried about Bella ever since Toby's blurt-out in the Lizard earlier that week but the right moment for a heart-to-heart had so far eluded me. Out in the middle of the Bay, however, we could talk uninterrupted; plus we would be surrounded on all sides by very deep water: as a location for trapping cousins where they couldn't run away from difficult questions, it was pretty much perfect.

I dressed and Bella grabbed a giant pair of sunglasses before we made our way down Hope Heights towards the trolley bus stop. As we waited a waft of savoury odours assailed our nostrils from a certain diner further along the road.

'Breakfast?' I suggested, nodding towards the red awning of the Apple Pie as my stomach loudly voiced its feelings about the lack of sustenance so far that morning.

Bella nodded.

'How about a takeaway? I woke up feeling a bit off – but I bet I'll be starving before we get down to the quay.'

'Well, hello, ladies!' trilled Elvira from behind the counter as we entered. 'Are you here for a victory celebration?'

'We heard about last night,' Sylvie called from the kitchen, her voice rising above the sound of eggs and bacon hissing and popping in a pan. 'Apparently it was a close thing between you and the Ants.'

'I was gutted that they were double-booked for the night of the quarter-finals,' Bella-the-ever-generous replied, 'and it was sweet of them to allow us to go through on the nod. I love Melinda, she's a star.'

Sylvie appeared in the kitchen doorway. Elvira took

a step towards her and, in perfect, spontaneous harmony, they sang the opening few bars of 'I Had a Dream'. The diner rang with applause and the ladies bowed and laughed.

'Wow,' I said, my gob pretty much smacked by their impromptu cabaret. 'That was fantastic. Do you sing? I mean: did you sing? I mean . . . that was amazing.'

The sisters laughed heartily and slapped each other on the back.

'Why thank you, Flora,' said Sylvie, 'nice to know we've still got it in us.'

Elvira wiped her hands on a tea towel. 'Now, what can we get you? The specials today are—'

Before we fell headlong into the organic-sustainably-produced vortex of the Apple Pie's menu, I took control.

'We're off on a boat trip this morning, so just a couple of your finest coffees to-go and – oooh – croissants, I think.'

'Is there any news about the lease?' asked Bella as the coffee machine spat and hissed and the pastries were bagged up for us.

Elvira shook her head.

'Still negotiating,' she replied, 'but I don't have a good feeling about it. I reckon in cases like this, no news is definitely bad news. But we trust in the good Lord that it will all work out for the best.'

'Something will turn up,' agreed Bella, 'and if it doesn't – then we'll have to *make* it turn up.'

Elvira laughed and patted her on the hand.

'Quite right, Bella Jones, quite right. We don't go down without a fight. Now, you girls go and make the most of this lovely Californian sunshine, you hear?'

Loaded up with our spoils, we caught the trolley bus from the Hope Street/Hope Heights intersection and swept down the hill towards Fisherman's Wharf, where we walked along the quayside, munching our croissants and perusing the various itineraries on offer.

'Blue and White are the best,' said Bella, pointing at a two-tone vessel that looked a little like an Isle of Wight ferry. 'I did a trip with them when I first moved here. Look: they go out to the Golden Gate, round Alcatraz and head back in time for lunch. Only we'll need to hurry, because it looks like they're just about to cast off.'

The wind tugged at our hair as I bought our tickets (and brushed aside Bella's protests that we should go Dutch). Then we walked up the gangplank and made our way out on to the deck. The perfect place for a cousinly chat.

Assuming, of course, that Bella actually did *chat*, rather than yell, sulk or throw me overboard to play with the sea lions.

'You know, I really admire you for your Abbadabbatastic bit,' I said, folding my arms on the railings and feeling the chug-chug-chug of the engines reverberate up through my ribcage, 'we all do. And Steve was positively ecstatic when you won.'

Bella grinned modestly and took a sip of her coffee.

'Tell me about you and him,' I said, glad that

relations between them appeared to be on the up. 'You mentioned you met through the music but haven't given me any of the gory details.'

A dreamy look came into Bella's eyes.

'They are quite literally gory – unless you're an A and E nurse like me. Someone from another of Steve's bands got a microphone stuck up his left nostril – don't ask – and Steve brought him into the emergency room where I was on duty. It turned out he'd seen me singing at an open-mike night a couple of weeks earlier and, over the alcohol swabs and the dissolvable stitches, he asked me if I'd be interested in joining an Abba tribute act he was setting up. I thought, "Hello, he's nice; why not?" and it all started from there.'

'Oooh,' I cooed, 'I love a good medical romance.'

Bella laughed. 'I suppose it was. And I'm pleased to report that the microphone went on to make a full recovery.'

We stood in companionable silence as the boat pulled out across the Bay. The wind whipped up little white crests on the waves and the skyline of the city shrank down to doll's house size.

'When you were doing open-mike nights,' I said, 'was that with your own songs?'

Bella looked very ill at ease.

'No,' she replied, 'I was performing covers. One step up from karaoke really. You need to understand that the songs I write are purely for myself, not per - formance. I could have killed Toby when he started going on about them the other night.'

'Has Steve heard any of them?' I sipped my coffee. 'After all, he's in the business – he'd be able to give you some proper feedback.'

Bella looked even more uncomfortable and shook her head.

'No,' she replied in a very quiet voice, 'and I don't want him to either. It's hard to explain, Flo, but the stuff I write is very personal – it's incredibly close to my heart – and if Steve turned round and said my songs weren't any good, I don't think I could bear it. Does that make sense?'

I nodded. It did make sense – of a sort. But it also told me that Bella's self-confidence was at complete rock-bottom. She didn't *do* timid and reluctant – she did big, decisive and life-changing.

Now I was really worried.

'I understand what you're saying,' I began to probe further, 'but the thing is, Belle, I—' I stopped, mid-sentence. 'Oh. My. Goodness,' I breathed.

My mouth was open but nothing coherent was coming out of it. I glanced across at Bella and saw that her jaw, too, was similarly slack.

'Awesome,' she breathed. 'Bloody freaking awesome.'

We had reached the first stop on our voyage: the Golden Gate Bridge. There was a tour guide's com - mentary coming from a nearby speaker but neither of us was listening. With our necks leaning back so far it hurt, we gazed up at the towering structure as the little boat rounded one of the pillars that anchored the bridge to the floor of the Bay. The reddy-bronze of its metalwork arched away over our heads and the wind wuthered eerily through the struts and cables. I pulled my phone out of my bag and did my best to take a picture, but it was so enormous that I couldn't fit anything recognisable into the shot. So I settled instead for a pic of Bella with her mouth hanging open, which pretty much summed up the impact of the view.

'You know,' Bella said wistfully, sliding her giant sunglasses down from the top of her head to cover her eyes, 'however bad things are, the Golden Gate never fails to pick you up. Never ever ever.'

The sense of *things being bad* hovered ominously in the air between us. I decided this was my cue to continue my questioning.

'Belle,' I said, 'I know something's wrong. Will you tell me what it is?'

The boat finished its circuit of the giant pillar and we swung back to face the city.

'Nothing,' Bella replied, staring hard at the view, her voice just a tad too defiant to sound truly convincing. '*Nothing* is the matter. I've told you before. Look, can you see the Transamerica building? It's the one there with the—'

'I know,' I pressed on regardless, 'it looks great. But no deflecting, please. If you won't tell me, Bella, then I'm just going to have to guess – and let me remind you that I know you well enough to be able to tell from your face when I hit the nail on the head.' I took a deep breath. 'It's to do with the hospital, isn't it?' I said.

'Specifically the fact that you haven't been there once since I arrived.'

Bella didn't say anything for a long time. She looked down at her coffee cup and picked at the lid. Then, after a silence that seemed to last for ever, she spoke.

'Something's happened, Flo,' she murmured. 'Something I don't have any control over.'

I stared at her, my bravado gone, very afraid indeed of what she was about to say.

'Good God, Bella, are you ill? Have you been diagnosed with something serious? Is that it?'

Bella shook her head and the weakest, wateriest ghost of a smile crept over her lips.

'No,' she said, 'I'm fine. I'm a little tired and my coffee tastes weird, but I think that's just stress.'

'So what's wrong?'

She turned to face me, her sunglasses shielding much of the expression on her face.

'I've been suspended, Flo. Three months ago. Since then, all I've had coming in is what I earn with the band. I have bills I don't know how I'm going to pay, I'm borrowing Toby's spare mobile because mine's broken – which is why I didn't get your voicemails – and I can only afford the apartment because I'm house-sitting for a friend of Toby's. If he hadn't been trans - ferred to Tokyo for eighteen months, I'd be living next to the freeway in a cardboard box or – at best – in some filthy bedsit with hot and cold running cockroaches.'

My troubles with Barney shrank down to a fraction of their former size.

'But . . .' I stammered, my brain struggling to adjust to this new information, 'that's impossible. You're brilliant at your job – you even won the Nurse of the Year award before you moved out here. I mean . . . you got to meet Jonathan Ross and go to a posh dinner and, well, *everything*! What on earth happened?'

Bella pushed her glasses back on top of her head and stared at me. There was something in her eyes that looked very much like fear.

'That's the thing,' she said, her voice even quieter than before. 'That's the ten-million-dollar question, Flo – I don't remember what *did* happen. I was on shift in the middle of the night and my patient, Mrs Hampton, was in a lot of pain and asking for sleeping tablets. I *must* have checked her chart to see that she hadn't been given any meds that would react with them, but I was tired and it was such a routine thing to do that somehow I don't remember the actual details. I *do* recall giving her the sleeping pills and then waiting to see that she was OK before another patient needed me and I had to leave her. About twenty minutes later, all hell broke lose: buzzers and pagers started going off and I saw a bloody crash team heading into Mrs Hampton's room. She had some sort of fit and, although she's survived, she still can't work and no one quite knows what the prognosis is. There's an ongoing inquiry and I've been suspended pending its outcome – hence, no work and no cash.'

Her eyes flashed up at me. I could see the old, feisty

Bella lurking in there somewhere, but I had no idea of how to reach her.

'Toby and Lisa know,' she said at last, 'and Steve, of course, but I haven't mentioned it to anyone else. Not even Mum. I mean to, but I keep putting it off. As far as she's concerned, I've always been Bella the Great, Bella the Magnificent. I don't know how she'd take something like this.'

She paused and tucked her hair behind her ears, only for the wind to immediately un-tuck it and send it lashing back across her face.

'In fact,' she continued, 'I've dug myself a bit of a hole where Mum is concerned. You see, to try and cover up the real situation, I told a whopper and said I was moving to a different hospital.'

'Oh?' I asked, trying to remember if I'd heard anything about Bella's 'new job' on the family grapevine.

Bella looked sheepish.

'Mum asked which one and I panicked and said I was going to work at a place called Sacred Heart where I was on a team with a couple of really great doctors called J.D. and Turk.'

We looked at each other – before both bursting into gulping, cathartic laughter.

'Oh Bella,' I gasped. 'What are you like?'

Bella threw her hands up in the air. 'Well, I suppose if I have to have a fake job, it might as well be in an award-winning sitcom. Jeez, talk about humour being the flip side of tragedy.'

'It's not a tragedy,' I told her firmly, 'and at least you

117

didn't tell her you'd gone to work at Holby City – or, heaven forbid, County General in Chicago.

Bella groaned.

'Lord, you're right! I hadn't thought of that. Mum's devotion to all things Clooney borders on the insane. I think she harbours a secret hope that *ER* was actually a documentary.'

I reached over and squeezed her hand.

'It's OK,' I promised, 'I won't spill the beans. Who hears it and when is up to you. But I'd put my life on the fact you didn't do anything wrong. You'd have done your best and your best is never anything less than perfect. Have faith – that's what Granny would say if she was here.'

Bella nodded.

'Have faith,' she murmured. 'I can almost hear her saying it: *have faith*. It's just, right now, I don't see how it can ever come good.'

We paused as the boat drew close to Alcatraz. A bunch of sea lions basking on a nearby rocky outcrop blinked lazily up at us.

'When's the inquiry due to report back?' I asked at last.

'The week after next.' Bella raised her eyes to meet mine. 'But I'm running out of time. In fact, the more I try to remember what actually happened, the more uncertain I get – now I don't know if I'm remembering things or simply making stuff up because I'm desperate.'

I took a picture of two sea lions fighting over a pathetically small fish.

118

'Maybe you need to stop trying so hard,' I suggested. 'Or find a trigger – something that will kick-start your memory.'

'Such as?'

However I was clean out of ideas. For the time being at least.

'Do you want me to stay on until the inquiry reports back?' I offered instead. 'I can ring work and see if they can manage without me for another week. In fact, the way things are going with the McMasters, they might well *pay* for me to spend an extra seven days pandering to their over-privileged needs.'

Bella shook her head.

'You don't have to,' she said, 'I'm sure I'll be fine.'

'I know I don't have to,' I replied. That wasn't what I asked.'

Bella managed a smile.

'I'll see how I go,' she said, 'but for now, well, if you wanted to move out of your hotel and come and stay with me for a few days, I'd be really happy. It would be lovely to have you around the place. It can get a bit lonely, even with Toby downstairs and Steve popping round. No one knows me quite like you do.'

I shuffled along the railing and put my arms round her.

'I'd love that,' I replied. 'And we'll get you through this, you'll see.'

Bella nodded and then smiled again. It was as though some of her burden had been lifted simply by sharing it.

'Anyway' – she gave herself a little shake – 'let's change the subject. What about Josh? Are you going on this date or not?'

It took me a while to wrench my mind out of the gear marked 'Bella and the hospital' and shift it into the one labelled 'Josh: do I date him?'

'This isn't supposed to be about me,' I said.

Bella managed a grin. 'Sauce for the goose, cousin.'

I took another snap of the sea lions, this time a trio lolling on their backs with their mouths open. I noted that one of them bore more than a passing resemblance to Mr McMaster.

'I just feel it's a bit soon to be rushing into something else. Barney and I only broke up on Friday.'

Bella looked me dead in the eye.

'You're not rushing anywhere. All you have to do is go out with him and have a nice time. It's not serious or anything.' She paused. 'Unless you think it *might* be serious?'

My stomach flipped and my face lit up like Blackpool Illuminations.

'No – I mean, I don't know – I mean, how can it be serious? I've spent less than half an hour in the man's company, for goodness' sake. I barely even know his name.'

Bella's eyes glittered.

'Don't give me that. When you know, you know, Flora. Now, is it serious?'

My tummy did a complete loop-the-loop. I did my best to ignore it.

You know, you can really hate your tummy sometimes.

'To be honest, Belle, I don't feel I *can* move on yet,' I confessed. 'I still have no idea why Barney dumped me. Talk about out of the blue. And then there's the house . . . it's beautiful. It breaks my heart to know I'm going to have to move out. There's so much of me in it.'

'Hey!' Bella elbowed me in the ribs. 'None of that. It hurts, yes, but it's not the end of the world. Believe me.'

I bit my lip. Given what she had to put up with, I had no business mithering on at her. She would have happily mortgaged Granny to be able to trade in her troubles for mine.

'Now,' she continued, 'the way I see it is, yes, you should talk to Barney and get closure – of course you should; but in the meanwhile, you are also *single*, and if a gorgeous guy and a single girl want to go on a date, then why shouldn't they?'

'I suppose so.' There was an undeniable logic to her argument.

'Then you suppose right,' Bella replied triumphantly.

'OK. I will not back out of my date. And I will also – God help me – ring Barney and see if I can find out what he's playing at. But—'

'But what?'

I took her date with Josh, and I raised her Lisa's music challenge.

'I want to listen to your songs in return.'

Bella shook her head.

'No can do. The songs are non-negotiable.'

It was my turn to get tough.

'Bella,' I said in a warning voice, 'you promised Lisa you'd let someone else hear them – and if it's not going to be Steve, then it will have to be me.'

Bella threw her takeaway cup into a nearby bin.

'I need another coffee,' she said, moving away from the railing. 'I wonder if they've got a café on board?'

I grabbed her arm.

'No,' I said, 'no running away. Not this time. Not from me. It's all linked – don't you see? The hospital, your music – *your lack of confidence*. If we can sort one out, the others will follow. It's at least worth a try, isn't it?'

Bella narrowed her eyes, but she knew when she was beaten. She reached into her bag and pulled out her iPod. I hadn't actually meant I needed to hear the songs *now*, whilst we were out on the high seas, but hey, strike while the iron is hot and all that.

'Go on then,' she muttered, 'only don't be too hard on me. They're rough, they haven't been worked on properly, they're—'

But I'd heard enough of her excuses and wanted to make up my own mind. I plugged the earphones in and selected a track called 'Respect Me'. It was just Bella and a piano, but it was Bella as I had never heard her before. Her voice was low and bluesy, with a richness that took my breath away. The song started slowly and then built in tone and tempo until it became an out-and-out Motown number – all it lacked were the backing singers and the horn section.

It was fantastic!

Actually, it was *beyond* fantastic. It was, to use Toby's phrase, really, really, money-makingly, serious-music-career *there*.

The song ended on a big thumping high that made me want to whoop and punch the air. The rhythm thumped through me and the lyrics – *Show me what you owe me, only don't ya do me wrong. Lift me higher, light that fire, give my heart its own true song* – got in under my skin and made me want to sing them out loud. It took me a while to realise that Bella was staring at me, her eyes wide and her mouth open in anxious anticipation.

I pulled the earphones out and handed the iPod back. 'Bella, you have to do something with this. If all your songs are that amazing . . . well, it's a crime against people with ears not to let them listen to you!'

For a moment, Bella looked as though she didn't believe me.

'You mean that? You *really* mean that?'

I nodded.

'And if you *don't*, then I will steal your iPod and upload the damn things straight on to the internet – and then you'll be sorry.' I paused. 'Face your dragons – that's another thing Granny always said. Maybe we should face them together? Not that I'm saying Josh is a dragon.'

Bella grinned.

'Or Steve for that matter.'

'Well then,' I replied, holding up my hand for a high five. 'Have we got a deal? I'll date Josh, you let Steve hear the music.'

There was a slight pause, then Bella's hand hit mine.

'Deal,' she said, the grin holding firm. 'Here's to you and me and our brave new existence.'

# 9

It was Wednesday evening. I slipped on the orange super-dress and golden shoes and watched myself in the mirror as the silk skirts swirled around me. It was still a bit of a shock to see my reflection – and tonight even more so. Bella had texted me and asked me to meet her at Doodles on Poodles, where the owner, Brandi, turned out to be a hairdresser for humans as well as a tattooer of pooches. She gave me a much-needed trim and then pulled my unruly red locks into such a magnificent up-do that it was all I could do to pay attention to crossing the road on the way home, rather than sneaking glances at myself in the wing-mirrors of passing cars and getting run over.

'So it's all going ahead tonight is it, Flo?' asked Bella excitedly as the last curl was tamed and the final bobby pin inserted. 'You look amazing. Although, to be fair, you could turn up wearing a Macy's bag and he'd still fall at your feet.'

'I'm still not sure, Belle,' I said, linking my arm through hers as we made our way back along Hope Street. 'In my heart of hearts, all I want to do is to go home to Oxford.'

We crossed at the intersection and began walking up the hill.

'Well, maybe Josh will change that. Or maybe he won't – but either way, you'll find out a little more about what you want. And that's got to be a good thing.'

'And you?' I turned towards her. 'Have you let Steve listen to that song yet?'

Bella shook her head.

'He's been out of town for a couple of days trying to get us some gigs on campuses nearby. He should be back tonight, although I thought I might wait until the Battle of the Tribute Bands is over so that he can give it his undivided attention. You know, when things are a little less frantic.'

'Well, don't wait too long,' I told her. 'That stuff is dynamite. And besides, you don't want Lisa exacting some sort of hideous forfeit from you like she did to Toby.'

Bella grinned.

'Indeed. Although I think where Toby is concerned she may have tapped into something that was already there – his spandex seventies alter ego perhaps. Scary thought.'

We arrived back at Bella's and had a happy half-hour doing our make-up together, before she went out to pick up a costume Drusilla had altered altering for her. With the coast clear and quiet, I locked the front door, picked up my phone and sat down on the sofa. I would fulfil my promise to Bella to go out with Josh, yes; but, as I'd told her at the Apple Pie, I also needed to know why Barney had dumped me. Maybe there was even some way I could stay at his house for a bit so, when my plane landed at the end of next week, it would be my little white terraced house I returned to, rather than creeping sorrowfully back to my mum's until I found somewhere else to live.

I looked across at the bookshelf on the far side of the room and found myself staring at a picture I'd never noticed before. There, in a sparkly frame, was a photo of me (aged about ten), Bella (wearing pink jelly shoes) and Granny, all standing outside the cottage on a bright summer's day; Granny had an arm round each of us and was smiling into the camera. As my eyes skittered across her much-missed face, I realised that my breathing had slowed and the edge had disappeared from my anxiety. It will be fine, I found myself thinking; one way or another it will work out for the best.

As I sat there, psyching myself up, the phone in my hand leapt into life, making me jump.

'Hello?' I said, thrusting it to my ear, realising it was upside down, and then rearranging it. 'Who's this?'

'It's Sadie McMaster. I need to talk to you, Flora – urgently.'

My heart sank. I couldn't possibly deal with her now.

'I'm sorry, Mrs McMaster,' I said, as politely as I could, 'but I'm terribly busy at the moment. Could I ring you back tomorrow?'

'I'm not the least bit busy, Flora,' trilled Mrs McMaster, magnificently misunderstanding my words, 'which is why I thought I'd ring now. Earl and I have filled out your little form for the second time, although

I have to say, it was a rather tedious task and we *will* be making a formal complaint to your superior about it in due course . . .'

Using huge amounts of self-control, I managed to hold my tongue.

'. . . anyhow, it was returned by email to yourself at nine o'clock prompt this morning. I was ringing to ask why we hadn't yet been sent any fresh property specifications?'

I decided it was time for a bit of plain speaking.

'Mrs McMaster,' I began pleasantly, 'just so that you are fully aware of the situation, I am currently on holiday. I am also dealing with some personal issues and I have, so far, not had time to check my in-box.'

Actually, I'd spent the day with Bella sightseeing downtown, but she didn't need to know that.

'As a special favour,' I continued, 'I will read your form and do some preliminary research over the next few days, but I won't be back in the office until Monday week.'

'Holiday? Don't be silly, dear! What do you need a vacation for? Earl's been in business for forty years and he's never once taken a day off.'

Probably to avoid spending any time with *you*, I thought uncharitably.

'Anyway,' she continued, oblivious, 'we were watching a documentary about England last night and this quaint little place was featured. Near Oxford. Something beginning with "b".'

My heart sank.

'Blenheim Palace?' I asked, fearing the worst.

'Yes, dear, that's it! Do you know it?'

'I don't think Blenheim is available to let,' I said as tactfully as I could. 'It's . . . well, it's a little bit special. But if you like north Oxfordshire—'

'I like Blenheim Palace,' said Mrs McMaster firmly.

I had to dig my nails into my palm to stop myself screaming out loud.

'I'll ask,' I said brightly, thinking that she would probably have changed her mind in a day or so anyway, and be eyeing up Sandringham or Balmoral. 'Leave it with me.'

I rang off quickly and took a few deep breaths to centre myself before turning my mind once again to Barney. Just the thought of speaking to him made a horrible sick feeling lodge itself in the bottom of my tummy, but I glanced back at the photograph and did my best to ignore it. If Bella could cope with the threat of a major investigation into her professional conduct hanging over her, I could ring my ex and find out what the hell was going on. All I needed to do was stay calm and reasonable. This time there would be no shouting, screaming or throwing the phone into the hallway.

I looked at my watch. Allowing for the time difference, it would be the middle of the night in Britain. Obviously, this was a far from ideal time for a soul-searching chat but, on the plus side, it meant Barney was pretty much guaranteed to be in. I decided to give it a go.

The phone purred three times and was picked up.

I took a deep breath and swallowed. There was an awful lot riding on the next few minutes. If I really wanted to go home, then I needed to handle this perfectly. However, on the bright side, after dealing with the McMasters, surely a little thing like speaking to Barney would be a piece of cake?

Fingers crossed, anyway.

'Hi, Barney, it's me.'

'Oh, hello. Hello, Flora.' He sounded fully awake, although anxious, but then again, why shouldn't he be? Our last couple of exchanges hadn't been particularly friendly and he was probably wondering when the yelling was about to start.

I took another deep breath. *I could do this; I could do this.*

'Hi,' I said again, 'I know it's late but I think we need to talk. I was wondering whether now would be OK.'

'Oh?' he said. The anxiety in his voice was increasing tenfold. 'Um, well, yes, I suppose so. I haven't actually been to sleep yet.'

'Good.' I gave a nervous laugh, which I turned into a cough. I couldn't be nervous; I needed to be dignified and calm. I drew as much strength as I could from my magic orange dress and beautiful hair and continued.

'I think,' I said, choosing my words very carefully indeed, 'now we've had a bit of time to calm down and get our heads together, we are in a position to approach things in a mature and adult manner.'

Mature and adult – that sounded good. *Keep channelling mature and adult.*

'Yes,' said Barney, 'I totally agree.'

*Keep going, Flora; keep going.*

'I've been doing a lot of thinking, Barney, and one of the things I've realised is that these few days apart have actually been good for us. I mean, we lived together for the best part of two years and we didn't have the opportunity to get any perspective on our relationship.'

'No,' said Barney thoughtfully, 'I suppose we didn't.'

'And I also realise that we left things to fester. You were busy with your work, I was *frantic* with mine and we simply didn't invest enough in our relationship. The most important thing in the world – us – was left to look after itself. It's no wonder things reached breaking point.'

*Excellent. Don't blame him; spread the responsibility and keep the tone neutral.*

'Flora,' Barney began, 'about your birthday. I am sorry. I am really, genuinely sorry how it worked out.'

'Oh,' I said.

This took me by surprise and, out of nowhere, the lump in my throat reappeared: he genuinely wanted to apologise. He felt *bad*.

And there was more to come.

'And the phone call about the key. I realise now how insensitive I was.'

The lump in my throat swelled and relief swept over me like a tidal wave.

We were singing from the same hymn sheet. He wanted to talk things through as much as I did. Maybe – maybe we could even sort things out and everything could go back to how it was! All it had needed was a bit of maturity, and the chutzpah to take that first step.

'I've thought about moving my flight home,' I said, wiping my fingers under my eyes to check for mascara-leakage, 'so we can sort things out face to face, but Bella is having problems and I want to be here for her.'

'That's fine,' Barney replied. 'I think I can wait ten days.'

I took another deep breath.

I was about to ask if it would be OK for me to stay on for a while in the little white house after I returned when, in the background, I heard a sound.

It was a sound which, if I had heard it in any other context, wouldn't even have registered. But it was a noise I had lived with these past two years and I knew exactly what it meant: someone had stepped on the creaky floorboard in our bedroom. Someone who wasn't Barney.

'Barney,' I demanded, 'what was that?'

'No one,' he said, far too quickly.

This was the wrong answer. In fact, it was wronger than the wrongest thing ever with a bit of extra wrongness on the side for good measure.

'Actually,' I replied, 'I said "what" not "who".'

'I . . .' replied Barney. 'It's just – I mean, it's just – you see . . .'

My skin turned icy-cold and the little hairs on the back of my neck stood up.

I knew. With a horrible, stomach-churning certainty, I knew.

'Who is she?' I asked, hoping that the tremor I could feel in my voice wasn't audible at the other end of the phone line.

'Susan,' he said. 'I've known her for a while. Since uni, in fact. We bumped into each other a few months ago and one thing led to another. It wasn't planned, I swear. Like I said, I *am* sorry. I wanted to tell you – I really did – but I kept putting it off and putting it off because the moment was never right.'

'So you saved it for my birthday? Was *that* the right moment?'

Even though he was five thousand miles away I felt him cringe.

'Well, it's like you just said: we were both so busy with work we barely saw each other.'

'Bloody *hell*, Barney! And if you hadn't done it when I was expecting you to join me for a romantic holiday, when would you? At the funeral of a close friend? Written it in my Christmas card: "Seasons greetings, darling, and by the way you're dumped"? You are un-fucking-believable!'

I sensed him cringing even further.

'But I didn't want to hurt you, Flora. I really didn't. Not at all . . .'

He trailed off into unhappy silence.

I couldn't believe it. I couldn't actually believe it!

He'd been having an affair. An *affair*.

For a moment or two I simply sat frozen on the sofa.

'Flora? Flora? Are you there? Why aren't you talking to me?'

But I could barely breathe, let alone speak. Then I looked down at my hands and saw they were shaking.

Thanks for that, Barney.

It was the final straw. I'd been through the shock and heartbreak thing once already this week; I drew the line at giving a repeat performance.

I removed the handset from my ear and placed it on the dining table.

'Flora?' pleaded Barney's tinny little voice. 'Don't hang up on me! We need to sort things out. Will you be coming to get your stuff as soon as you get back? Flora?'

But I ignored it.

With as much dignity as I could muster, I rose from the sofa, picked up my handbag and a shrug Lisa had lent me for the evening, and walked out of the apartment, leaving my phone lying on the table.

Apparently I wasn't going home after all.

I made my way down the road towards the Lizard with my heart thumping.

How could he do this to me? How *could* he?

Bastardbastardwankerpigtoadrat.

Urggh!

Living in the same house; breathing my air; even doing, well, you know *what* with me – when all the time he had this Susan floozie on the go. No wonder he was away a lot. No wonder he needed to take 'important' phone calls in the bedroom. No wonder he was 'working late at the office'.

And I had been stupid enough to believe he had been telling the truth?

Bastardbastardbastard*bastard*.

Oh God – another, hideous, thought struck me – was this why he wanted me out so quickly? So she could move in and enjoy my Farrow and Ball paints and newly sanded floorboards?

Rat. Pig. Rat. Pig. Ratpigratpigratpig.

Lisa was right: he was a pig. The piggiest, fattest, cheatingest pig in Pigdom. Whereas I had obviously had my brain amputated at some point during the past two years, because this vital fact had passed me by.

I stepped out to cross the road without waiting for the signal, causing a cacophony of car horns, a massed screeching of brakes and one or two 'whatcha think ya doin', lady?'s, but I was so wound up it barely registered.

Had he – I gasped out loud as a truly awful idea flew into my head – had he actually – urgh! – *that* – with *her* in our bed?

Or should I say *my* bed, seeing as I was still paying it off on my credit card? Argghhhhh!

I was so angry that, with a cry of pent-up rage and frustration, I swung my handbag against a nearby lamp-post. The catch opened and the contents were flung across the pavement. Needless to say, this did not improve my mood. And, as I scrambled around on the ground, trying to retrieve my lipstick, mirror, hairbrush and purse, I was aware of one or two of my carefully coiffured curls flopping free of their bobby pins.

Feeling lower that I'd ever done in my life before – and more than a little bit crazy – I looked around, desperately hoping to spot something which would ease the pain.

Directly opposite the lamp-post was a bright, shiny ATM – and it gave me an idea.

In fact, it was such a brilliant idea that I wouldn't have been surprised if an *actual light bulb* had appeared above my head.

I stuffed my things back into my handbag and then, as fast as I could given the fact that the tremors from my hands had spread to my knees, I went over and put in my joint account cash card.

With fingers shaking, I typed in my PIN and selected the option for cash withdrawal. The machine hummed and whirred and presented me with a choice of amounts. Knowing just how much Barney would hate me for doing it, I hit the button for the maximum allowed. The machine hummed a bit more and then spat out a sheaf of notes.

I felt a tiny glimmer of triumph. He might have taken away my home, but I could hit him where it would really hurt: in his wallet.

Glancing a little further down the road, I saw another bank.

Good.

Putting my haul safely away, I made my way over, inserted my card, typed in my PIN and waited. Would it register that I'd just taken a great fat wadge from its friend next door and spit my card back?

I crossed my fingers and waited.

The machine hummed and whirred just like the last one and – yesssss! I was in.

Remembering bitterly just how much money I had donated to Barney in the form of bills, renovations and mortgage payments, I once again selected the maximum withdrawal figure.

There was a pause – then a sheaf of notes appeared in the mouth of the dispenser.

*Thank you very much!*

I took my card back from the machine and did a short but triumphant dance on the pavement.

Now, where next?

Three doors down was yet another ATM. Without thinking twice, I walked across and shoved my card in.

*Maximum amount?* I don't mind if I do.

With a growing sense of power, I pocketed the dosh and assessed the neighbourhood for my next port of call. Could I keep going all night? At what point would my bank realise there was something funny going on?

Did I even care? (Answer: no.)

By now I was on a manic high. On the other side of the street I spotted another cashpoint. I made my way over the road and inserted my card. I may even have rubbed my hands together avariciously.

'Take that, scumbag,' I muttered. 'I hope it chokes you.'

Bastardbastardbastard. Git.

'Hi,' said a familiar voice behind me, 'are you all right?'

I froze, mid-PIN.

It was Josh.

Shit – Josh – the date. He must have spotted me on his way to the Lizard.

Bloody *hell*!

'I've been watching you,' he said. 'Now – are you OK, or is there something going on I don't know about? Is the world going to run out of cash and you're stockpiling against a global catastrophe?'

My breath caught in my throat. It was worse than I'd thought: he had been *watching me*?

I glanced at myself in the shiny metal surround of the ATM. Several more tendrils of hair had escaped from their bobby pins and were hanging down over my ears, whilst the rest of my up-do had slumped alarmingly to one side. My eyes were red-rimmed and a smudge of mascara had made its way down my left cheek. I looked as though I was verging on the insane.

Which, to be fair, was probably true.

Josh leaned nonchalantly against the wall of the bank. He seemed interested – even mildly amused – in what I was doing.

'No,' I muttered angrily, fixing my gaze on the screen and hitting the button for the maximum payout.

'Is that "no" to you being OK or "no" to an impending Armageddon?' he asked pleasantly. 'Although I guess you could count Armageddon as being the ultimate definition of not being OK and cover both bases at once.'

'I am *fine*,' I replied, my teeth more gritted than a motorway in a snowstorm. 'Everything is normal and totally and completely *fine*.'

I took my money and, as I did so, looked him directly in the eye. It was always going to be a risky move. As I did so, he grinned and, immediately, my cheeks flamed so hot you could have grilled a couple of burgers on them.

Go away, I pleaded silently (in case he happened to have passed his mindreading exams that year). *Buzz off; sling your hook; make yourself scarce. I don't want you to see me like this.*

But he didn't.

Out of the corner of my eye, I spotted another bank. One block down, three doors in. I hesitated – but only for a moment. Even though I knew it made me look sectionable, the desire to go and raid it for cash was literally overwhelming.

'I'll just . . .' I said, 'I'll just . . . Excuse me—'

As I walked, I noticed that the shaking in my legs was getting worse. I also noticed that someone was following me. Footsteps that sounded very much as though they belonged to a young man with dark hair.

'Flora, what's going on?'

What I wanted to do at that moment – what I really,

*really* wanted to do – was to press one of the buttons in front of me and have Josh vanish into thin air. But sadly San Franciscan ATMs do not provide this particular service.

'Like I said,' I replied, as yet more adrenalin vacated my body, and I found it hard to type my PIN and talk at the same time, 'everything is cool. Everything is just as it always is. Nothing to see here. Boringly normal.'

'So,' he continued, 'if you're not preparing for a financial meltdown, are you perhaps in the process of a cumulative, slow-motion bank robbery where you end up owning all the money in the world by withdrawing cash from every ATM on the planet?'

The shaking in my hands was worse than ever and I was having real difficulty pressing the buttons on the screen. There was also a searing pain in my chest just where I always imagined my heart to be. *Barney has broken my heart. He has literally broken my heart.*

'Why do you need so much cash?' asked Josh.

'I don't,' I snapped, realising that the shaking had now transferred to my voice-box.

I reached down to put my money in my bag but found my hands were trembling so much I couldn't undo the clasp.

'Flora,' he asked, 'Flora, seriously, tell me what the hell is happening.'

Something brushed against my hand. I looked down and saw that the tips of his fingers were curled around mine. His skin was warm and smooth and comforting and, to my utter astonishment, my tremors subsided.

'Sorry,' he said awkwardly, taking his hand away.

The memory of my conversation with Barney cut through me like a knife.

'I don't want to be here, Josh,' I cried, 'I don't want to be standing in the middle of a street in San Francisco with my hands shaking and my hair looking like it was coiffed by bats and my life falling to pieces. I *don't want it* – do you hear?'

Josh looked me dead in the eye.

'Well,' he said, as though he was issuing a challenge, 'where do you want to be?'

Like a live thing, instinct took over my despairing, angry mind. Where had I always been happy? Where had I always felt safe?

'The sea,' I blurted, the words out of my mouth before I even knew they'd been forming in my brain. 'I want to see the sea.'

Josh looked at me, his gaze inscrutable.

'When I was little,' I was babbling now, 'Bella and I – that's my cousin, the one who sings in the Abba band – used to stay with our grandparents during the school holidays. It was amazing. They lived in a tiny cottage on top of a cliff near Porth Pirran in Cornwall. It was called "The Lavenders" and there were steps that led down the cliff on to the sand and at night you could hear the waves on the beach below as you went to sleep. I loved it, Josh; I was safe there . . . and I need to see the sea.'

'That's good,' he said calmly, 'the sea I can do.'

'*You* can do?' Bewilderment rose within me, adding

to the toxic mix of emotions already sloshing round down there. 'No, really, I wasn't suggesting – I mean, I wasn't asking – I mean, you don't have to—'

One of Josh's quicksilver grins zipped over his face. 'I know I don't have to, but do *you* know where the sea is?'

'No, but—'

'Well then.' He waved at an approaching yellow cab. '*Taxi!*'

'This is madness,' I replied. 'You can't just go round calling taxis and whisking people off to the beach.'

'I think I just did.' The grin widened. 'And whilst we're on the subject, I'm not picking up a whole lot of sanity right now. Maybe we should just take the madness and run with it?'

'But look at me,' I wailed, 'I am not fit to go on a date. I don't even *want* to go on one. That's right – I'm upset and crazy and I don't want to go on a date!'

The cab pulled over with a screech of brakes.

*But the sea; I need to see the sea.*

'OK,' said Josh evenly, 'this is not a date. There will be no fancy restaurants, no flowers, no questions about what you do in your spare time and . . .' His eyes glit-tered gleefully. '. . . absolutely one hundred per cent no remarks about how lovely your hair is looking tonight.'

I had a split second in which to make the decision.

Could it really be any worse than going home and crying myself to sleep in Bella's spare room?

'Be careful,' I growled. 'Or you won't be looking at the sea, you'll be in it.'

'Sounds like my sort of challenge.' The grin flashed up again and he opened the door of the cab. 'Now hurry up or we're going to miss the tide.'

# 10

We whizzed along busy streets; past bars and restaurants, cafés and shops. I looked down at my hands, clenched into tight little balls, the knuckles white and the shakes still zipping through them.

Was this what madness felt like? I wondered and then stopped. Wasn't one of the defining character - istics of madness the fact that you didn't think you *were* mad? So, therefore, if I thought I had cracked, wasn't that proof that I hadn't?

I had no idea.

My head began to spin and I glanced out of the window. We left the main drag of the city behind us and headed west along a freeway (or so I guessed because in front of us the sun was hovering low over the horizon). Then suddenly, in a thin, glittering line sandwiched between the lanes of traffic and the sky, I saw the sea! My heart turned over and my spirits edged up a smidge from rock-bottom.

As we drove, the line grew thicker and wider, taking on the unmistakable gleam of the sea. White horses crashed on to the sand and gulls wheeled overhead.

'Here,' said Josh to the driver, 'here would be great.'

The cab turned off the highway and into a gravelled parking area facing a low sea wall. I opened the door and took an enormous lungful of the salty air.

'Ocean Beach,' announced Josh, with an air of pride, almost as though he'd designed it himself. 'You've got the ocean – and you've got the beach. It pretty much does what it says on the can.'

Beyond the car park was a wide path paved with slabs and beyond that a sea wall. I wandered over and leant against it, staring out half-hypnotised at the waves.

My spirits inched up another tiny notch.

Josh paid the cabbie and came and stood next to me.

'The craziness continues,' I said. 'I'm here, in the middle of nowhere, with a man I barely know from Adam and not a soul in sight—'

Josh solemnly pointed to a couple walking their dog further down the sands.

'All right,' I qualified, 'two souls in sight, but in the company of an almost complete stranger. This is the sort of thing that ends up on crime programme reconstructions, you know; it's what we tell small children to avoid doing at all costs.'

Josh skipped down a set of steps and jumped, two-footed, on to the sand.

'You know what?' he said. 'You're right, we don't know each other. So, these are the rules: you have twenty seconds to tell me all about yourself. However, you can only use words beginning with the letter "W". Then we'll swap, and you can pick my letter,' he added graciously.

Out of nowhere, a bubble of excitement rose inside me and popped in my brain. It was only a tiny bubble, but the difference it made to me was quite profound.

'And this is sane – how?' I asked teasingly.

'I never said it was sane.' The grin flashed across his face like a beam from a lighthouse. 'Oh, and you have to run backwards across the sand whilst you're doing it.'

I looked down doubtfully at my beautiful vintage shoes.

'You might wanna go barefoot. The last I heard they weren't recommending stilettos for the beach.'

I hesitated some more.

'It'll be fun,' he cried. 'When was the last time you had fun?'

'That's easy,' I retorted, 'it was . . .'

Oh. Ah. I ground to a halt.

It appeared, to my surprise, that my adult existence was pretty much fun-averse.

Well, that was going to change.

'All right,' I replied, slipping off my silk footwear and placing my bare toes gingerly on to the sand-covered path, 'you're on.'

The stone steps were still warm from the afternoon sun and the layer of sand on top of them slid underneath my feet and squeezed its way up between my toes.

Pop! Another bubble pinged deep within my brain.

I jumped down on to the sand.

'My name is Flora Fielding—'

'Beginning with "W", remember – and you've for - gotten, you're going backwards.'

I turned and began to pace solemnly in the direction requested.

'I'm a *wizard*,' I said, 'at *work*. Well, the company's called Relocation Wizards.'

'Hurry up,' Josh was jogging along a couple of paces in front. 'You're not running.'

I picked up the pace.

'I like *watercress* and *wasabi* and *wearing pyjamas*! Ha!'

'Nice,' nodded Josh approvingly, 'I like what you did there!'

'And my favourite book is *Wuthering Heights*! And my time's up! Hooray! Your go – and your letter is "A".'

Josh began running backwards and I, relieved that I hadn't tripped over any flotsam or jetsam and gone flying face-down into the sand, spun round to face the direction of travel. The wind blew hard and wound its fingers into my hair, pulling out curl after curl after curl.

'I have a brother called Ashleigh and a sister called Antonia,' he began, 'no really, I do – and I grew up in Amersham – but the one on the East Coast, not the one in England, although we did go there once when I was eight and I cut my leg and had to have stitches at the local hospital.'

'Poor you,' I sympathised.

'My favourite food is apple pie.'

I spotted a blatant lie.

'No it's not, it's steak and home fries!' I pointed out, an edge of glee in my voice.

Josh, panting, held up his hands in mock surrender.

'Actually, it's cheesecake but I couldn't see a way of getting that past you. And my favourite classic movie is *Annie Hall* – that's true, by the way. Your turn, letter "D".'

I span round and the wind whipped my now-nearly-free hair across my face. Yet more bubbles exploded: Pop! Pop! Pop!

'When I was growing up, I wanted a *dog* but we only ever had a rabbit,' I said. 'My favourite *Disney* film is *One Hundred and One Dalmatians* – oh, and I *don't like* computers.'

Josh stopped in his tracks and stared at me.

'How can you not like computers?' he said. 'That's impossible.'

'It's not,' I retorted, continuing my backwards trajectory, 'I have to use them for work, but all this Tweetbook stuff is not for me. I'd rather have a real conversation with someone.'

'No.' Josh shook his head. It was obvious he was deep in denial. 'You grew up in a world run by com - puters. You cannot remember a time before the World Wide Web. You are the IT generation!'

'Yes,' I said, 'and, like I said, the best days of my childhood were spent in a tiny pink cottage on top of a Cornish cliff that couldn't even get a decent TV reception. You don't need computers to make you happy. In fact, sometimes I think the fountain pen was a technological development too far.'

Josh stared at me, mouth open. However, before he could reply, we were engulfed by a tsunami of people.

Running, sweaty people with numbers pinned to their T-shirts, and most of them with large cut-out foam feet strapped beneath their own.

'What the—?' I span round, looking for Josh who had been pulled away from me by a current of fast-moving bodies.

'It's the Big Foot Race!' he yelled from the other side of the crowd, 'it's an annual fun run along the ocean beaches in aid of the orphanage over in Oakland. I'd totally forgotten. Come on!'

To be honest it didn't look as though I had any choice. We were swept up in the rip-tide of runners, children and even dogs. A spaniel with a cut-out foam foot strapped to its head bounded past and barked happily up at me. On a one-to-ten scale of bonkersness it rated about fifteen and a half – but this, as I now knew, was just *so* San Francisco.

I mean, where else would it be considered normal to strap on a pair of enormous feet and run along a beach on a summer's evening?

Picking up my voluminous silk skirts, I sprinted along the sand; my shakes gone and a sense of excite - ment rising within me. Barney might still be a bastard, but he was being one five thousand miles away – *and I was having fun*.

Through the river of bodies, I saw Josh. From snatches of conversation blown over to me by the wind, he seemed to be telling people about SuperConnect. He was clearly obsessed.

'Do you work for them?' I yelled over the panting

and the barking and the shouting and the wind. 'SuperConnect, I mean.'

Josh's grin widened.

'You *could* put it like that,' he shouted back, his voice tugged and buffeted by the wind, 'although, actually, I own it.'

Despite my self-confessed technophobia I was impressed.

'You own it?' I echoed incredulously. 'As in, all by yourself?'

I stared at him, remembering the faded jeans and the tatty hoody he'd been wearing the day I first met him. He didn't look as though he could organise a bun fight in a custard-pie factory, let alone run a software company. Did he spend Friday nights hanging out with Mark Zuckerberg and Steve Wozniak, talking about gigabytes and arguing over who made the most money?

Josh shrugged modestly.

'I wrote it,' he said, 'but, so far, SuperConnect is just me – apart from every other Saturday when my friend Marty comes round to help me with the marketing. The site only went live a couple months ago and I don't have enough cash to pay a company to do publicity for me.'

That would be a no, then.

Although strangely, I found his impoverished enthusiasm rather sweet.

'Hey!' A young male runner pulled up alongside Josh. 'Could we put a fundraising page up on this site of yours?'

'Sure!' Josh looked as though nothing would make

him happier. 'Just link that part of your page to the "community" section – and don't forget to email every-one you know so they can load it up and send it on to *their* friends.'

'Cool!' The young man looked impressed. 'Hey! Zach!' he yelled to another runner a few paces ahead. 'You need to get SuperConnect on your phone.'

'SuperConnect?' queried Zach. 'What's that?'

Josh pulled back and ran next to me.

'Most of the problems in the world are caused by people *not* communicating. In fact, it's a scientific fact: the better connected you are and the more diverse the range of people you know, the longer you live. Our lives depend upon connections. And for a lot of people, seeing their friends in the flesh isn't an option. People move around more now than they've ever done before and they want to stay in touch. What I want to do is help them to communicate and feel loved, not make a pile of bucks.'

A woman wearing a Snow White costume and hold - ing a charity bucket ran up alongside me. Her foam feet were stapled on to her shoulders like wings and she trailed cardboard cut-outs of the Seven Dwarfs behind her.

'Donation for the orphans?' she asked. 'It's not looking good for them – the shop in Hope Street that raises money for their children's home might be about to close.'

I dug into my purse and pulled out a couple of hundred-dollar bills.

'Here,' I said, stuffing them into the bucket, 'with my love. The orphans need it more than me.'

The woman looked astonished.

'Are you sure?' she asked. 'Most people only put in loose change.'

'It's from both of us,' I said, pointing to Josh, 'but he's broke. To be honest, I'm glad it will be doing some good, rather than just sitting in an account gathering dust.'

I made a mental note to find the donations page for the fun run on SuperConnect and email it to everyone I knew in San Francisco. All three of them. Hey – great oaks and little acorns.

Just as I was wondering whether Bill would be interested in using SuperConnect to publicise the plight of Hope Street, two Labradors arguing over a frisbee barged past, knocking me off course. As I struggled to regain a vertical position, I plunged my foot into a pothole in the sand. With my body moving forward but my left foot remaining stationary, some of the less elegant law of physics came into play and I began to fall. Suddenly, a strong and unexpectedly muscular arm came out of nowhere and slid itself round my waist, whilst another wrapped itself across my shoulders.

'Careful.' I could feel Josh's breath on my cheek. 'Maybe we'd better keep the hundred-metre sprint for another day.'

'You're right,' I gasped, trying hard to catch my breath – and my balance, 'that was close.'

We came to a halt and stood, panting, on the sand as

the crowd of runners and barking dogs streamed past and receded into the distance. My sides ached and the skin round my neck and shoulders tingled where he had touched me.

Josh waited for a moment or two, until he had caught his breath, and then undid the laces on his trainers. He slipped them off and wandered down to the water's edge.

'Man!' he cried. 'That's cold!'

He wasn't wrong. I followed, squealing as the lacy edges of the waves skittered over my feet and luxuriating in the feel of the damp sand squidging up between my toes.

'I can't believe you kept quiet about owning SuperConnect,' I said.

'Not much to tell . . .' Josh's voice was carried off by a gust of wind whipping in off the sea.

The heat of the day had gone: the sun was hugging the horizon and the western sky flamed pink and orange. I shivered and clutched my shrug across my chest; but it was useless in the teeth of a chill Pacific breeze.

'Here.' Josh slithered out of his jumper – a soft, blue number that nearly matched his eyes – and placed it gallantly round my shoulders. 'I don't want you getting cold.'

As he did so, the fingers of his right hand grazed my arm and my knees, which had been doing a sterling job of not shaking for a while now, turned into something resembling chocolate mousse.

But in a good way.

I pulled the jumper over my head and buried my nose in the collar. It smelled of the seaside, toast and Josh and it was utterly delicious.

Then I pointed out over the water.

'So,' I said, indicating the horizon, 'what's over there?'

Josh shrugged.

'Sea, I guess. Then some more sea. Then maybe a bit of ocean. Then Hawaii. Then, I don't know – China?'

I shivered again, but this time not because of the cold.

'Big, isn't it?' I gestured to the sea, the sky and the mountains. 'All this.'

'And we're not.' Josh's voice was low and barely audible above the murmur of the waves. 'Flora, it might just be me, but do you ever do that thing where you focus on yourself, then you imagine yourself next to the expanse of the beach, then you compare yourself to the vastness of the earth, then the planets, then the whole hugeness of the universe – all out there, right now, going on for ever and ever and ever?'

I nodded. 'And you feel as if at any moment you might float away into space and disappear?'

'That's the one,' said Josh.

On the off chance that gravity might stop working for a moment or two and this eventuality come to pass, I held out my hand. His was waiting: warm and safe and solid.

'If we go, we go together,' I said.

Josh's thumb sneaked inside mine and traced a lazy circle on my palm.

I wasn't expecting this and, for a moment, it felt as though the world stopped – as though someone had pressed a giant cosmic 'pause' button.

We stood in silence as the sun finally slid beneath the horizon. The ocean gave one last flamboyant inky hoorah of colour before fading into inky darkness. Above it, rose the clear, crisp crescent of a new moon: as thin and brittle as the last sliver of a Polo mint.

'It's beautiful,' I murmured, sensing fresh starts and new beginnings in the twilight air.

'Yes, you are,' he replied, absolutely deadpan.

My stomach gave a lurch but, despite that and the tingling presence of his hand in mine, I decided to keep things light.

'This isn't a date, remember?' I nudged him in the ribs.

Josh nudged me back.

'I wouldn't use a line like that on a date,' he replied, 'allow me a bit of class. No, if we were on a date, I'd probably ask you if it hurts.'

'What hurts?' He had lost me.

'When you fell out of heaven, of course.'

'That's bad.' I gripped his hand tighter. 'Really bad.'

'Or I might want to know if you've ever been arrested?'

'Go on,' I replied.

'Because it must be illegal to be that beautiful!'

155

'Cheese!' I cried. 'Serious cheese alert going down here!'

'Um . . .' Josh paused to consider yet more terrible chat-up lines. 'What about the fact that I need a map because I keep getting lost in your eyes?'

As he spoke, his thumb stroked the back of my hand experimentally.

This time, my stomach didn't just flip, it wrapped itself round my lungs and made me gasp for breath.

'I'm getting cold,' he said, tugging at my hand, 'it's time to go.'

We turned and walked back up the beach, our toes sinking into the wet sand and our eyes, which had acclimatised to the twilight, dazzled by the lights ahead on the highway.

Another shiver zipped through me and, only half consciously, I moved my arm so that his hand brushed against the top of my thigh.

By now, we were nearly back at the car park, half-hidden from the road behind a wooden kiosk. Josh stopped and I, with my heart beating like a heavy-metal bass line, manoeuvred one of my feet in between his.

We were dangerously close; I could just feel the rise and fall of his chest brushing against mine. His free hand was hovering just above the small of my back. I leant backwards against it, feeling the warmth of his palm radiate through the silk of my dress.

'Remember,' murmured Josh, a warning note in his voice, 'this is not a date.'

'You're right,' I said, finding the breathing/talking combo absurdly difficult to do. 'Not a date.'

Strangely, that made me feel better. It wasn't a date; it was something else; unspecified. No rules, no expectations.

I lifted his hand and gently placed it just under my right breast. It felt an audacious, almost scandalous act; and it made my heart beat so loudly, it drowned out the drone of the cars zipping past us on the highway.

Josh showed no signs of objecting. Without averting his gaze from mine, he lifted his thumb and traced it experimentally along the underwire of my bra. I think he was lucky I didn't explode on the spot.

'Hey! You guys! Why don't you get a room?' The shout came from a passing motorist.

I looked at Josh and we both burst into a fit of giggles. The whole situation was ridiculous.

'If I said you had a beautiful body, would you hold it against me?' he whispered, pulling me in tighter.

'Do you have a plaster? Because I think I hurt my knee when I fell for you,' I murmured back.

With a surge of something that could have been excitement or could have been fear, I reached up.

'I don't,' I said, my mouth almost brushing his as I spoke, 'I don't want to go home.'

'Then don't,' Josh murmured back, his lips tantalisingly within reach. 'We'll get a cab; I'll make a call, I'll just—'

'It's not a date,' I mumbled, pressing my lips lightly against his.

'Not . . . date . . . no . . . date . . . not,' he agreed, breaking away to pull out his phone and make the call. 'Ten minutes.'

As he spoke, he planted his mouth back on to mine, before breaking off to run his lips up and down my jawline. I didn't know if I could last ten minutes or whether I would spontaneously combust there and then and leave Josh with a lot of explaining to do to the California Highway Patrol.

But I reckoned it was worth the risk.

The cab dropped us next to a courtyard surrounded by a fence and heavy gates. Josh, his arm round my waist, slid a card into a slot and punched a series of numbers into a keypad. There was a clicking sound and a smaller gate within the large one swung open. We walked across an immaculate brick-paved court-yard towards a large, well-lit front door where he inserted a different card into another slot and punched more numbers into a different keypad before pushing the door open.

'It's hell when you forget to buy the milk,' he grinned. 'Getting back out on the street can take hours.'

We bundled ourselves into the lift and, as the doors closed behind us, he pulled me in close, kissing not just my mouth, but my ears, my throat and my eyes (*my eyes!*) and, after the doors pinged open, we half walked, half snogged our way down a corridor lined with identikit chrome doors, until we reached one that meant something to Josh, because he (with one arm still round me) reached into his pocket and produced yet another swipe card.

The door swung open and we fell inside.

After the well-lit communal hallway outside, it was very dark inside the flat; however, our purposes did not require any light. I leaned against the wall, put my arms round his neck and pulled him in against me. His mouth was on my lips, my neck and in my hair; his hands on my waist, my back, my breasts.

'Ow!'

Something dug itself into my shoulder blade. We were immediately illuminated, blinking and breathless, and I realised it must have been the light switch.

Josh pulled away. He ran his hands through his ever-unruly hair and looked at me. 'Coffee?' he said. 'Or tea?'

'What?' I said, trying to smooth down my unsmoothable hair and wondering if I'd heard him correctly.

'Coffee,' he repeated. 'Or tea.'

I stared at him.

'This isn't a date,' he said, his voice a little hoarse, 'remember?'

Then the penny dropped: he wasn't offering me a beverage, he was offering me an out; if I wanted, it could all end here with two sugars and a splash of milk.

I put my shoes down by the front door and looked him in the eye.

'Do you want me to have a coffee?' I asked.

Josh ran his tongue round his upper lip. What I

159

would have given to have swapped places with that lip.

'No,' he said at last, 'but I want to make sure you have the choice.'

I took a very deep breath.

I thought about Barney, about my house, and about Susan.

Then I took two steps forward and slid my hand into the front pocket of his jeans.

Josh's eyes closed.

'Don't do that,' he told me. 'Well actually, I mean *do* do that. If you don't want the coffee. I mean – oh, *man*!'

He abandoned speech and kissed me – hard – before wrapping his arms around me and bundling me next door into a room that turned out to be the kitchen. As we came up for air, I noticed that his eyes remained closed and he seemed to be focusing on something else.

'Josh,' I whispered, 'are you all right?'

He looked at me and then buried his face in my hair.

'I'm fine,' he said, 'this just feels weird.'

I hesitated: not what I would have expected from a man in the throes of passion – date or no date.

'Good weird,' said Josh quickly, 'definitely very good weird.'

A slight panicky feeling rose up in my chest. I needed tonight; I needed it very much indeed – and not just because Josh was so unutterably gorgeous I would willingly have had my body superglued to his for the rest of eternity.

Deliberately and in what I hoped was a confident

and sexy manner, I put both my arms round the back of his neck and kissed him. Then I ran one hand through his hair and the other across his back, sliding it in underneath his T-shirt. With the show back on the road, I pulled it over his head and then threw it, with a flourish, over the toaster. Then I ran my lips down the line between his pecs and his tummy button before stopping abruptly.

'Your turn,' I informed him.

The brilliant, lop-sided Josh-grin spread over his face.

'So,' he murmured, his mouth on my jaw, then my eyelid, then my collar-bone, 'it's like that, is it?'

'Yes,' I replied, running my hand over his belt and fingering the buckle, 'it is, actually.'

With one deft movement, he slid Lisa's spider-web shrug over my shoulders and sent it flying across the room: it landed on the metallic pendant light-fitting, causing the lamp shade to sway wildly and send beams of light skittering round the walls.

'Excellent,' I said approvingly, 'my turn now!'

With a single tug, I whipped off his belt. I chucked it over my shoulder and it landed with a clatter on the draining board, just missing a couple of coffee cups and a wine glass.

I felt amazingly bold. This was something splendid, something daring – something I never would have thought in a million years I would be doing. And I was loving every minute.

'Now me!' cried Josh.

His eyes gleamed with wicked anticipation as he ran them up and down my body, assessing my clothing for points of access.

'You girls don't make it easy,' he said, pausing in his assessment of my ensemble to run his lips down my neck and deep into the dip of my cleavage. 'I'm beginning to think they used dresses like this as a form of contraceptive. How anyone ever procreated when they had to get through this lot first is beyond me.'

'But you're going to have to,' I said, locking my gaze on to his and undoing the top button on the fly of his jeans, 'if you want me.'

I held my breath. I needed him to want me – or possibly wanted him to need me. I really didn't care which.

'Do you want me?' I asked.

'Yup.' He slipped his hand in under my voluminous skirts and ran the tip of his finger inside my knicker elastic. 'Pretty much *now*, if that's OK.'

'All right,' I said graciously, pushing him away, 'seeing as you asked nicely.'

Very slowly and deliberately, I twisted round and unzipped the dress. Then I slipped my arms out through the shoulder straps and paused.

'Come here,' I ordered. 'You do the rest.'

He didn't need to be asked twice. With his mouth on mine, he slid my skirt down over my hips and, without breaking lip contact, I stepped out and left it in a puddle of silk on the floor. We backed our way across the kitchen and into a living room beyond. So

162

engrossed was I that I managed to trip over a coffee table and fall backwards on to the sofa, sending an avalanche of scatter cushions and computing magazines plummeting floorwards and my miles and miles of thick net petticoats flapping up round my chin.

Josh tumbled down on top of me.

His hands were on my back; on my thighs; in my hair; slipping the straps of my bra down over my shoulders. Words like 'awesome', 'fantastic' and 'beautiful' were murmured into various parts of my anatomy whilst I tugged at his jeans. They slithered off easily and I dumped them on the coffee table.

With his mouth on mine, Josh lowered me back down on to the sofa and gently pushed his knee in between my legs. I felt his hand making its way up my thigh, tugging at my knickers and—

At that moment, a number of things happened.

In fact, they happened so fast and I was so unprepared for any of them that I am not entirely sure about the order in which they occurred.

The first was that Josh stopped murmuring compliments and began muttering the word 'condoms'. However, before either of us had the chance to find any, we heard a noise that sounded exactly like someone opening the front door.

Which was probably because someone had.

Then there were six footsteps – more than enough to bring whoever-it-was down the hallway into the kitchen – and a rather shocked voice said:

'Oh goodness! I didn't—! I mean – I wanted to give this back! You left it at my place.'

From my incredibly inelegant position underneath Josh, I looked up. The first thing that caught my attention was the fact that my erstwhile lover was staring at the doorway as though he'd seen a ghost. His face had gone whiter than a polar bear in a bucket of bleach and his mouth was hanging open, giving him a rather gormless expression.

Using powers of movement that would have impressed an experienced contortionist, I managed to move my neck and saw, leaning against the doorjamb, a petite, dark-haired woman wearing a neat, buttoned-up macintosh and a disbelieving expression. She was holding a neatly folded T-shirt with the slogan 'I'm Not a Geek, I'm a Level Twelve Dragon Master' written across its chest.

Under any other circumstance I might have found that particular choice of words amusing.

But I didn't.

Every tiny hair on my body which, up until now, had been standing on end with pure excitement and pleasure, now stood to attention for very different reasons.

With cat-like grace she bent down and scooped my dress up from its resting place at her feet and stared at it as though it was some sort of deadly weapon.

*It was Flora Fielding, in the hallway, with the vintage evening clothes.*

Josh struggled upright and I took the opportunity to

slither free from his grasp and stand up. I hoiked the straps of my bra back into place and smoothed down the flounces on my petticoats.

I had no reason to feel ashamed, I told myself. I had every right to be in this flat fondling this man. It was *she* who ought to be feeling guilty – she who had gatecrashed my party and rained on my parade (and made me mix my metaphors into the bargain).

'I'm Marty,' said the woman, although no one had asked her to introduce herself. 'Josh and I . . . well, me and Josh . . . we . . . um . . . well, I thought we . . .'

Her voice trailed off into silence; her face was bright red with embarrassment and shock. She was obviously finding the situation excruciating.

As I digested this – and adjusted to the idea that Marty, rather than being one of Josh's male buddies as I had assumed, was actually a woman – my bravado vanished. In fact, I felt as though I had been slapped very hard across the face and found myself literally gasping for breath. Although no one had actually spoken the word 'relationship', everything about Marty's demeanour was screaming that she and Josh went way beyond a bit of marketing.

Behind me, I heard Josh clamber off the sofa.

'I'm sorry,' he said – presumably to both of us at once. 'I am so sorry.'

I felt his hand touch my shoulder. It broke the spell over frozen horror and I flinched away.

'You're right,' I hissed, 'you should be.'

I marched over to Marty, took my dress from her

165

unresisting hand and barged out into the hall. Then, with my self-esteem in tatters, I shoved my feet into my shoes, struggled as best I could into my dress and, without even doing it up, ran across the hall and out the front door, letting it slam heavily behind me.

## 11

'No,' said Lisa sagely, shaking her head, 'that's not the worst thing that could have happened.'

We were sitting at a stage-side table in the downstairs room at the Lizard Lounge. It was the next round – technically the quarter-finals – of the Battle of the Tribute Bands, and Lisa and I were helping Bella get ready ahead of an evening of stiff competition. On the bill tonight were the to-be-underrated-at-your-peril Duran Duran Duran Duran and the formidable Blondish – a Blondie tribute who had last year pipped Abbadabbatastic at the post. As Blondish had got there early and grabbed the only dressing room available, we were performing Bella's *toilette* out in the open with the help of a few glasses of wine – or, in Bella's case, as she had a thumping headache, a large tumbler of iced water and some painkillers.

Toby, arrayed in white trousers, silver boots and a white top with big, flappy, bat-wing sleeves, stared at Lisa in amazement.

'Good grief,' he said, 'I'm glad I haven't been on any of your dates.'

'Oh, Flo's experience was bad,' said Lisa, taking a sip of wine, 'I'm not saying it wasn't but it could have been worse. Nobody died, for instance – that's always a passion-killer.'

'Whoa!' cried Bella in horror. 'You are joking, aren't you?'

Lisa gave her little high-pitched laugh but didn't actually deny it.

'And nobody vomited *in flagrante*,' she continued. 'Oh, and it didn't break.'

'It?' echoed Toby, horrified. '*It*?'

'Yeah,' continued Lisa evenly, applying Bella's eye - liner with a practised and steady hand, '*it* can, you know.'

'Ow-ow-ow!' said Toby. 'And this happened to *you*?'

'Not *to me*, honey, I don't have the necessary equip-ment but yes, let's just say it happened on my watch.'

Toby crossed his legs and put his hands over his crotch.

'Well, I'd have slapped him,' said Bella, leaning into the little mirror she'd propped up on the table and slathering mascara on to her lashes. 'Cheeky bastard, running two women at once. Who the hell does he think he is?'

I topped up my wineglass from the bottle standing in the middle of the table.

'Oh, I don't know,' I said, 'Barney perhaps?'

Bella bit her lip.

'Sorry,' she said, 'I wasn't referring to . . . well you know what I wasn't referring to.'

'I can't believe I was so stupid,' I cried. 'How could I have been so stupid? Tell me?'

Bella squeezed my hand.

'You weren't stupid,' she said. 'He was a git who did a very good impersonation of being a lovely, normal guy. Unfortunately they don't come with the words "emotional arsewit" written on their foreheads.'

'Well they should,' I replied, having strong views on the subject. 'Brandi should add it as one of the tattooing options at Doodles on Poodles. All men who treat women badly should get a health warning scrawled across them so they can be avoided in future.'

'*All men who treat women badly?*' asked Lisa, rouging Bella's cheeks. 'Honey, there isn't enough tattoo ink in the world.'

'At least you remembered to pick up the dress,' said Bella, 'and Lisa's shrug.'

I put my head in my hands. Oh shit, the shrug.

'I'll go and get it,' I mumbled, 'I'll ring him up and go and get it.'

Lisa patted my arm.

'I wouldn't bother, sugar. She's probably already burned it.' She sat back in her chair and a faraway look came into her eyes. 'She'll have doused it with half a bottle of vodka, thrown on a lit cigarette and danced round the pyre, cackling manically as the flames grew higher.'

'You know, Lisa,' said Bella, demonstrating the highly skilled female art of speaking whilst simul - taneously applying lipstick, 'you really scare me sometimes.'

Lisa gave a little sigh and nodded happily.

'Hey,' hissed Toby, leaning in across the table and nearly sending the bottle of wine flying, 'isn't that Mickey Ramirez?'

Bella's eyes flashed over in the direction Toby was looking and then flashed back again.

'It is,' she replied. 'So what?'

'Well, it's been all over SuperConnect – sorry, Flo, I mean a brand-new, technologically advanced, social, community and personal networking site – that he's scouting for one of the major record labels. You need to send him your stuff, Belle.'

'No I don't,' replied Bella. 'And you need to keep your mouth shut – all of you – until I've let Steve hear them.'

'Who's Mickey Ramirez?' I asked.

'Who's Mickey Ramirez?' echoed Toby. 'Who's Mickey Ramirez? You mean you've *never* heard of Mickey Ramirez?'

'Shut up, Toby,' said Bella. 'Of course she hasn't. When I first moved here, Mickey was managing a couple of really good bands in the Bay area. One of them had a nearly breakthrough single and they all disappeared off to New York. He comes back now and again to check out the scene here, but I didn't know he was scouting.'

'But Bella,' hissed Toby. 'You've got to tell him about these recordings of yours. This could be your ticket to the big time. You're insane if you pass on this one.'

Bella flashed him a truly frightening look.

170

'I've said no, Toby, and I mean it. And if you go opening your big fat mouth I will personally fill your pockets with rocks and throw you off the Golden Gate Bridge and – oh, hi Mickey.'

'Hey Bella!' Mickey, a cheerful-looking man wearing a Yankees baseball cap, rocked up to our table. 'I just wanted to say good luck for tonight. I'm rooting for you guys to win the title this year – your sound just gets better and better.'

'Thanks, Mickey. How're things?'

'Great,' he replied, shoving his hands deep into his trouser pockets and rocking back on his heels. 'Lots going on, lots of new ideas. In fact, Bella, I've been wondering what you would say if—'

But we never found out what she would say because, from across the room, the other female singer from Abbadabbatastic called Bella's name and Bella (looking mightily relieved) turned tail and vanished. Then, before you could say 'secret music recordings that she hadn't yet mentioned to her boyfriend' Steve was upon us.

'Hey, Ramirez!' he called jovially. 'What's up?'

The two of them performed a manly back-slapping ritual.

'Hey!' echoed Mickey. 'Good call, buddy, you're just the guy I'm looking for. I'm with Archipelago now, in New York, and I was wondering if you had any heads-ups for me on the scene here in SF. Of course, they'd have to go a long way to beat that Bella of yours. Man, her voice is a killer.'

Steve puffed himself up proudly.

'She's the best, Ramirez. You don't have to tell me.'

Mickey nodded and smoothed an invisible speck of dust from his immaculate trousers.

'Yeah, she's awesome. Someone with her vocals could really hit it big. In fact, it's something I was hoping to talk to the pair of you about whilst I'm in town: Bella's sound is just what we're looking for right now.'

Steve stared at Mickey.

'You mean record? With you guys? In New York? Oh man . . . like, well, I mean, oh *man*.'

Steve was totally blown away by the idea. For a moment I wondered if I could see dollar signs in his eyes as a whole new road out of his financial pre - dicament opened up before him, but I told myself not to be so cynical: Bella loved Steve and I had to trust her judgement, not my own. After all, my track record was hardly a glittering monument to happy relationships.

'Yeah,' continued Mickey enthusiastically. 'Although what I'm really after is someone who writes their own material – you know, so we can market the whole package. I wondered if songwriting was something Bella ever got into?'

Steve's face fell.

'At the moment she only does tribute – but, look, buddy, with the right song and the right marketing, we both know she could go a hell of a way.'

'The problem is, we have singers coming out of our pores, man – I'm on the hunt for an all-rounder.' Mickey looked genuinely disappointed.

Toby opened his mouth – presumably to set the record straight about Bella's songwriting prowess – but Lisa elbowed him hard in the ribs.

'Shh!' she commanded, and Toby sank back despondently into his chair.

'But' – Steve wasn't giving up – 'she's amazing, you know she is. And she could always *learn* songwriting—'

Mickey shook his head sadly and slid a business card out of his wallet.

'Well, in case you hear of anyone,' he said, 'will you let me know? I'm in town for a couple more weeks.'

Then he melted away into the crowd.

Steve picked up the card, turned it over in his fingers then rubbed his face with his hands. He looked exhausted.

'Shit,' he murmured.

Then, shoulders slumped, he walked off in the direction of the stairs and almost collided with Bill coming the other way, a harassed expression on his face.

Lisa sighed.

'The answer is no, Bill. And please, no more flowers. My apartment is like a tropical rainforest. I have monkeys swinging round the kitchen on actual vines.'

Bill pulled up a chair and sat down.

'This isn't about you and me,' he said. 'Is Bella around? Any of the others from the band?'

'I think Steve went out for a breath of fresh air,' I said, beckoning to Bella who was hovering out of earshot behind the stage. 'He's not a happy camper.'

'That may be for the best,' said Bill, looking uneasy, 'because this isn't going to cheer him up. Simon Le Bon-Bon from Duran Duran Duran Duran has filed a complaint about the line-up of your group.'

Bella rejoined us. She looked puzzled.

'Well, it's me, Tobes here, Julie and Randall – just like last time.'

Bill looked even more uneasy.

'I know, Bella, but I need to confirm that this is now your official line-up for the rest of the competition. You see, the names on your entry form need to match the individuals on stage. It says in Rule Six, subsection—'

'Oh, for goodness' sake, William,' snapped Lisa, 'this is the Lizard Lounge Battle of the Tribute Bands, not a United Nations Security Council resolution. They're just jealous because they know they don't stand a hope in hell unless Abbadabbatastic are out of the running. Can't you tell Simon Le Jerk to take his complaint and stick it up his—'

'I can't, I'm afraid,' said Bill, 'but if you fill out another entry form *now*, I might just make sure it gets switched over with the original one so that no one is any the wiser.'

'Fine.' Bella took the proffered sheet and pen from Bill and scribbled furiously. 'There we go. If you want a second entry fee, you'll need to speak to Steve. I'm broke.'

Bill shook his head.

'I'll let it ride,' he said, 'seeing as it's you. But don't go having any more members of your band deported.

Abbadabbatastic are good for business and if you guys make it to the final, it pays both of us.'

And he went off to placate an extremely youthful-looking Simon Le Bon-Bon.

Toby whistled through his teeth. 'That was close.'

'Tell me about it.' Bella took a long drink of iced water. 'We were very nearly toast. Good job Bill fancies you, Lisa.'

'Men have their uses,' replied Lisa sagely.

'If we'd been unable to perform, I don't think my public would ever have forgiven me,' Toby continued.

'Excuse me,' I said, 'you have *a public* now?'

'Of course.' Toby waved his hand with a flourish, nearly spilling the contents of his glass over Bella. 'They adore me: I walk amongst them like a god. They call out to me, "Toby! Toby! Give us more! Give us more!"'

'Tobes,' said Bella, 'are you ill, or did spandex-wearing space aliens invade your body while you were up on stage last time?'

Toby shook his head and gulped down a large mouthful of wine.

'No, it's me, Toby: professional yellow-belly and all-round scaredy-cat. But this . . . it's amazing! I love the roar of the greasepaint, the smell of the crowd; I love the applause; I love holding the audience in the palm of my hand and playing with their emotions through the power of seventies-inspired camp Euro-disco; and I love you, Lisa, for giving all this to me. I love you! I love you!'

Lisa shook her head in disbelief.

'I've created a monster, so help me,' she muttered.

Bella took a last sip of water and tugged Toby's bat-wings.

'Come on, Liberace,' she said, 'I can see Randall and Julie over there. Let's go and warn them about the change-in-line-up issues. Make sure nobody mentions Gunnar. As far as we're concerned, it's always been you up there. You've just shrunk six inches and forgotten how to speak Swedish.'

'How's your headache?' I asked.

Bella waved her hand dismissively.

'Fine,' she said, pulling a grin from her boundless reserves of good humour and stapling it to her face. 'Nerves, a couple of late nights, that's all. I'm fine. Just a bit wiped-out.'

I nodded and let it go. Knowing Bella, an opportunity to strut her stuff in front of an adoring crowd would be the best tonic she could ever have. It would have been much worse if Abbadabbatastic's Battle of the Tribute Bands campaign had ground to an untimely halt.

'Lisa!' Bill called from the bottom of the stairs. 'Can I borrow you for a moment?'

With a heavy sigh, Lisa heaved herself up from her chair and walked over to the staircase. I topped up my wineglass and rubbed my exhausted face. I felt as though I'd been buried, dug up and then gnawed by cheating, scumbag badgers. I had never felt so low.

Then I heard someone speak my name.

I turned round and saw Josh, his hair ruffled,

wearing the same T-shirt I'd pulled off in a frenzy of passion the night before.

My stomach clenched and I wondered if I was actually going to be sick.

'Bugger off, Josh,' I growled, trying to keep my lurching intestines in order.

Josh, however, did not do as he was told. In fact, he looked as though he was here for the duration and settled himself in Lisa's empty seat.

'I said,' I repeated, pushing my own chair back and standing up, 'bugger off. And if you won't, then I will.'

With a face – and a mind – like thunder, I stomped up the stairs, through the door and out into the street beyond.

Flora Fielding has left the building.

As fast as I could – without actually breaking into a run – I strode past Drusilla's, Doodles on Poodles, the yoga café and along the pavement to the next road junction.

Josh, however, was hot on my trail.

'Flora! Flo! Stop.'

Er, no. I don't think so.

Not waiting for the lights, I dodged the traffic and made my way up the hill along a road I guessed ran parallel to Hope Heights. I had no idea where I was going, but above me, I could see trees and railings that indicated a park. Good, I would lose him in amongst the flower beds and the t'ai-chi classes.

A blast of car horns told me that Josh had followed

my jaywalking lead. I ignored the beginnings of a stitch, and increased my speed.

'Flora! I said *wait.*'

Cursing my unused gym membership, I pushed on through a set of iron gates, nearly colliding with a roller-skating aerobics group and a couple of dog-walkers.

'Flora, about last night—'

My face flared bright red. How dare he? How dare he broadcast last night's humiliating events for the whole world to hear? Some of the roller-skating aerobics students had already stopped and were looking at us with interest.

'I have nothing to say to you,' I shouted and continued to walk.

'We need to talk,' he shouted back.

'No we don't,' I yelled, pulling off the path and making my way over the grass towards the brow of the hill.

Josh sprinted ahead and began to walk backwards in front of me. I shut out all memories of the day before's get-to-know-you session on the beach and kept my eyes fixed on the ground, praying that he would fall over a tree root and break his leg.

Or possibly his arm. I was willing to be flexible.

'Flora – last night – I am sorry. I am so, so sorry.'

As if that made any difference. Josh was sorry, Barney had been sorry; everybody was damn well sorry – it didn't make me feel any better.

'I had no idea Marty was going to turn up,' he continued earnestly. 'You have to believe me!'

This brought me up short. In fact, I'm pretty sure I heard the thud my jaw made as it hit the floor.

We had reached the top of the hill. Before us – or rather, before me but behind Josh – was a large and very tranquil boating lake. It was lined on the far side by trees and had a small, leafy island in the middle. Ducks and seagulls were fooling around near the edges and, further out, one or two rowing boats were making leisurely progress across the water.

The tranquillity, however, was totally lost on me.

'And you think that is the *worst* part of what happened?' I cried, waving my hands around in disbelief and sending a nearby duck scuttling into the water in fright. 'Are you seriously trying to say that if she hadn't arrived until after I'd gone, that it would have been all right?'

'Yes – I mean – no – I mean – Flora, listen!'

He reached out and tried to put his hands on my shoulders. Angrily, I shrugged them off. Josh, standing near the edge of the lake, wobbled dangerously for a second or two but managed to recover his balance.

Unfortunately.

'It's not like that,' he cried. 'Look at me, Flora. Look at me and tell me that last night didn't mean anything. Go on, straight between the eyes. Tell me.'

I opened my mouth to deny the sensations that had surrounded every encounter I'd ever had with Josh – but I couldn't.

To make up for this, I stamped my foot hard with frustration. It hurt, but not as much as Josh's betrayal.

'It doesn't matter what I felt. From where I'm standing, the pair of you look pretty much like an item. Reason one: she was genuinely upset to see me in your apartment doing, well, *that*. Reason two: she brought you your T-shirt back from her place, neatly folded. Reason three: she doesn't think it's in the least bit odd to let herself in, late at night, to your apartment. Bloody hell, Josh: what else am I supposed to think?'

Josh took a very deep breath indeed.

'I don't deny that there is more to Marty and me than a bit of marketing, but it's not what you might call a conventional arrangement.'

Did he really think I was that stupid?

'Josh, I don't care if it's an "open" relationship, where you both shag all and sundry; or whether she's "away a lot" and you think it's OK to take a bit of skirt "on the side" to relieve your "manly urges", or if you are cheating on her. Whatever the case, I do not want to be involved in it.'

I find people who make quotation mark signs with their fingers unbelievably annoying so I made sure I vigorously mimed all my punctuation.

'And do you know what?' I continued. 'At the end of next week I shall be getting on a plane and leaving San Francisco. So whatever you might want me to think, however much you protest that I mean something to you, the fact is that you and I were only ever going to be a holiday romance – a meaningless dalliance. Have you got that, Josh? We are *nothing*.'

I sounded pretty convincing. In fact, I might even

have believed my own propaganda had not every atom in my body been screaming at me that he was right: it *had* been something very special.

I looked at Josh.

He had turned pale and seemed to be having problems getting any sort of coherent speech past his lips.

'You . . . mean th-that? You really mean that?'

I stared out over the lake. Right in the middle were a couple in a rowing boat. The man had the oars and was doing his best to manoeuvre their little craft over to the island. He wasn't, however, making a particularly good fist of it and the pair of them collapsed into gales of helpless laughter.

Josh reached out and grabbed my hand. It felt as though I'd run my fingers under a tap and then shoved them into an electric socket.

I snatched it back and turned away. Josh rocked dangerously on the edge of the lake for a second time.

'Flora,' he said, righting himself just in time, 'Marty isn't my girlfriend.'

Now he was talking rubbish. Hadn't he just admitted there was more to the pair of them than a bit of paper - work and a shared commitment to SuperConnect?

'Well, maybe you should let her know that,' I replied archly, 'because from what I saw, I think she's under a different impression.'

Josh shook his head vigorously.

'No, really, we both know where we stand. She's a friend – a friend with benefits, I admit, but nothing more than that.'

I hesitated.

I knew I shouldn't – all the evidence was stacked against him, but deep in the very core of my being I wanted to believe him.

'She and I . . . well, it wasn't planned,' Josh replied, 'we sort of just fell into it. But that's not the point. The point is— Oh, God, what if you're right? What if she – Oh, God, no. No she can't.'

I'd had enough.

'Go and sort things out with Marty,' I told him. 'Because I can tell you now you're wasting your time with me. And if you still want to know if I hurt myself when I fell out of heaven, yes I did. Obviously it damaged my brain because otherwise I'd have run a mile the minute I saw you coming.'

And, in sheer frustration, I pushed him to one side and stalked back off down the hill, ignoring the splash as he joined the ducks and the seagulls in the shallow end.

# 12

I was calm, I was in control, I was confident.

I knew this because I kept repeating the words under my breath. This was not the New Age woo-woo of Azure-at-InSPAration's affirmations, but something I really needed to believe.

It was late afternoon the next day and I was dressed in my business suit, my briefcase and laptop bag in hand, waiting outside the library of the McMasters' house for a meeting requested earlier that day by Mrs M.

I was Flora Fielding, relocation wizard extraordinaire, and there wasn't anything I couldn't do.

(I was also repeating this, and it seemed to be working.)

The first thing I had done after leaving Josh had been to return to the Lizard, drink half a bottle of wine and cheer Abbadabbatastic on to victory. I had then returned home, booted up my laptop and got to work locating the choicest and most exclusive country houses I could find. My plan was to present the McMasters with a breathtaking array of irresistible housing options that would have them falling at my feet and worshipping me as the goddess of the trans - atlantic home-search (so they would get off my back and I could enjoy the rest of my holiday).

What I was *not* going to do was worry about Josh, Barney or anyone else with a male appendage who thought they could treat me badly and get away with it.

My mobile bleeped discreetly in my bag.

I, equally discreetly, pulled it out – and then nearly dropped it straight back in again.

Monkeychucklebuggerfuck: it was Barney.

And he seemed to be having trouble speaking.

'What the—' he began. 'What the bloody – Flora – you – me – you – for the life of me, why? – Flora – what have you – what the bloody hell?'

'Barney?' I asked, glancing nervously at the library door. 'Is everything all right?'

'Of course it's not bloody all right,' he choked from all the way across the Atlantic. 'You took my fucking money.'

*Calm, controlled, confident.*

'No, I didn't,' I replied.

Barney made a noise that sounded like a hyper - ventilating hyena.

'Don't try and deny it, Flora. It was *your* card and the money was withdrawn in San Francisco where *you* are currently staying. You took my money and I want it back.'

'No, I didn't, Barney,' I replied.

'Will you *stop* saying that!'

There was a hysterical edge to his voice which, for some reason, I found mildly amusing.

'You went to five different cashpoints and took out

three hundred dollars each time. I've got the state-
ments here to prove it!'

'I know,' I replied. *Calm, calm.*

'Ah-ha, so you admit it!' He now sounded
triumphant. 'And what do you propose doing about
it?'

A lady carrying a sheaf of papers walked down the
hallway and looked at me.

I covered the mouth of the handset.

'Important business call,' I explained, 'I'll take it
somewhere else.'

I walked further down the hallway and removed my
hand.

'Nothing,' I said, 'I'm not going to do anything.'

'Well then,' he cried, 'I'll make you. I'll call the
police; I'll have your card taken off you. I'll—'

'Barney!' I snapped. 'Shut up.'

'But—'

'Barney!' I repeated firmly. 'Clamp it.'

There was silence. I made a mental note to
remember that particular combination of words: it
seemed to work.

'Thank you,' I said. 'I did take some money from the
joint account, but it belonged to me.'

My ex emitted a small, strangulated whine.

'Mine,' he whimpered, 'mine.'

'No,' I explained, 'it was a *joint* account. Half of the
money that went into it was mine.'

'But there's only two hundred quid left,' he bleated.
'You've cleaned it out. Half doesn't even come into it.'

'I want *my* money,' I said. 'Not yours, *mine*. Every month, my salary goes in there and every month you pay the mortgage from the same account. That means, every month *I* have paid half the mortgage and, now that my services as a live-in lover are no longer required, I decided it was time to redress the financial balance and I want my money back – all of it. *Comprende?*'

'You can't do that,' Barney spluttered down the transatlantic phone link. 'It's theft. It's money with menaces. It's daylight bloody robbery.'

I examined my fingernails and removed an almost imperceptible scrap of dirt from one of them.

'And in order to ensure that this is dealt with properly on my return and *no one* ends up with any more than their fair share, I spoke to the bank manager just now and had the account frozen. There's a letter in the post. You should get it tomorrow. When I get home, we will sort out a fair and equitable redistribution of funds; but until then you're just going to have to sit on it.'

'But I – but you – but we—'

'Now, Barney, I would ask you to do the decent thing but, as that is obviously beyond you, I will content myself by telling you to bugger off. There, even you should be able to understand that. Now, goodbye, and if you feel like ringing me again – unless it is to offer me an awful lot of cash – don't bother.'

And to the sound of further spluttering and more than a few choice expletives, I hung up and returned to my seat. My legs felt shaky, but nowhere near as bad as they had done during previous phone calls. Revenge was indeed sweet.

The lady I'd seen earlier was sitting at a desk across the hallway from the double doors that led into the library, collating her sheaf of papers into four neat piles. She smiled as I approached.

'Bad day at the office?' she asked sympathetically.

I shook my head and stuffed my phone into my pocket.

'Just a little local difficulty with – ah – one of my staff,' I informed her. 'All sorted now.'

'Can I get you a cup of coffee?' the lady offered. 'You look flustered.'

I pulled my jacket down and smoothed out my skirt. I wasn't flustered – I was Flora Fielding, relocation wizard.

'No, thank you,' I replied, 'I'm fine. Excuse me for asking but are you Mona, Mr McMaster's secretary? I'm Flora Fielding; I don't think we've been properly introduced.'

I had spoken with Mona many, many times on the phone. We were practically old pals, but I had never met her and didn't have a clue what she looked like.

'No,' replied the lady, 'she's off having a hysterectomy and a scrape.'

*OK, too much information.*

'I'm the temp, Jessie. Only' – she lowered her voice conspiratorially – 'I'm quite nervous. Mr McMaster has a bit of a reputation. I'm hoping I make it through OK.'

As I watched, she reached into her handbag and pulled out a little brown bottle. She undid the cap, shook a couple of pills into her hand and swallowed them with the help of a sip from a bottle of mineral water.

'Herbal tranquillisers,' she said. 'Don't know what I'd do without them. Want one?'

To be honest, I was tempted, but I declined. You never knew what was in that stuff.

'I love them,' Jessie continued. 'Nature is wonderful.'

I smiled in a way that I hoped conveyed my deepest respect for nature and all her works, before the doors to the library were thrown open and Mr McMaster yelled:

'Hey! You!'

I jumped clean off my seat and Jessie knocked her water all over the collated papers.

'Sorrysorrysorrysorry!' She leapt at the spillage and began dabbing at it with a tissue.

'Sooner we get Mona back the better,' he muttered. 'Don't know why she had to take all this time off. When I had my gall bladder out, I was back in the saddle two days later. Malingerers, the lot of you.'

Jessie went bright red and muttered something grovellingly apologetic. She seemed genuinely distressed but Mr McMaster had moved on and trained his sights on me.

'You,' he said, 'you'd better come in. Only don't go taking up too much of my time.'

I allowed the words 'the feeling is mutual' to roll round my head before smiling, picking up my brief-case and stepping into the library. Pugsy, reclining on the chaise longue, delivered his customary greeting of a snarl and a set of bared teeth.

'Ah, shuddup,' said Mr McMaster.

Pugsy gave a whimper and covered his nose with his front paw.

'So,' said Mr McMaster, seating himself behind the desk covered with papers and picking up a letter, 'what do you want?'

'I emailed you a shortlist of properties this morning,' I said, 'and Mrs McMaster rang me requesting an urgent meeting to move matters forward.'

Mr McMaster focused on his letter. He gave no sign of having heard what I'd said.

I cleared my throat and tried again.

'Your wife requested a meeting here to discuss your accommodation,' I said.

Mr McMaster put down the first letter and picked up a second.

'I want to talk about houses,' I said.

Mr McMaster looked over the top of his letter. He seemed annoyed by my continuing presence in the room.

'My wife deals with that and she's not here,' he growled, and went on reading.

I shifted in my chair. For a while, there was silence, broken only by the tick-tock of a huge grandfather clock in the corner.

'When do you think she will be back?' I asked politely.

Mr McMaster put down the second letter and selected a third.

'Mr McMaster,' I said, 'at what time do you expect your wife to return so that we can commence our meeting?'

Mr McMaster slammed his letter down on to the table with an ill-disguised show of annoyance.

'I cannot work with all these interruptions,' he cried.

I reckoned I had three options. I could do nothing, and possibly sit here until it was time to catch my plane home; I could make an excuse and leave; or I could assert myself politely, which, given Mr McMaster's demeanour, would be rather scary.

I took a deep breath.

'Mr McMaster,' I said pleasantly but firmly, 'I am currently on a much-needed vacation. And I am giving up some of that vacation to help two of my clients – namely you and Mrs McMaster – at Mrs McMaster's insistent request. I researched a shortlist of properties for you between two and four o'clock this morning, and ensured they were on your desk waiting for you when you came into the office at eight thirty. I then cancelled an important engagement . . .'

It had been with Brandi at Doodles on Poodles, who had offered to put some highlights in my hair, but he didn't need to know that.

'. . . so that I could be here this afternoon. Now, I have demonstrated a great deal of commitment to you

190

and your wife and I expect, in return, to be shown some respect. That includes being able to have our meetings at the appointed time.'

'Ah, shuddup,' said Mr McMaster.

For a moment, I thought he was talking to the dog. But no.

I was beginning to realise why the McMasters had been dumped on me by Brenda – and it had nothing to do with my wizardly abilities to relocate them.

'In that case,' I said, picking up my bags, 'maybe you would be so good as to contact me once I have returned to the UK office. Good day.'

Mr McMaster stared at me for a moment. He went pink, then he went puce, then he went red, then he thundered:

'Siddown!'

Instinctively, I did as I was told. Pugsy whimpered again, and put his other paw over his muzzle.

'I pay you,' growled Mr McMaster, 'and if I want you to sit there in silence and wait for my wife, then you will sit there and wait for my wife.'

I thought of the McMasters' account (which I had also been looking at between two and four that morning), where unpaid bill after unpaid bill lurked on the balance sheet. He hadn't paid a penny.

'I'll give you five more minutes,' I said, hoping I didn't sound as nervous as I felt.

'You will give me as long as it takes,' said Mr McMaster.

He gave me a glare that, had I not been spending

time in Lisa's company, might have really frightened me. Then he lifted the phone on his desk.

'Jessie, ring Mrs McMaster and find out where the hell she is.'

There was a pause during which he returned to reading his letter. The door opened and Jessie entered.

'Mrs McMaster says she is staying at the spa for an extra aromatherapy facial, followed by a volcanic hot-stone massage and a wheatgrass juice intestinal cleanser,' she announced nervously. 'She won't be back till gone eight.'

'Jeez!' Mr McMaster threw his hands up in despair. 'Six hours at a spa and she'll *still* look like a trolley-car ran over her head. Is this what I sweat my ass off for?'

'Mr McMaster,' I said pleasantly, 'I am more than happy to conduct the meeting with you by yourself. If you have had a chance to look at the housing options I sent over this morning we could—'

'Do I look like I have the time to consider housing options?' cried Mr McMaster. 'I have three businesses to run; a wife who thinks that if she spends enough of my money she'll look like she did when she was sixteen; a goddamn lazy secretary at home with her feet up eating chocolates and a flea-bitten mutt shedding hairs on my furniture.'

Jessie reappeared clutching her brown bottle.

'Would you like to try one of these, Mr McMaster?' she asked, offering him the herbal tranquillisers. 'They make you feel ever so calm and relaxed.'

'I *am* calm and relaxed, dammit!' cried Mr McMaster, the puce colour returning to his cheeks. 'My problem is that I am surrounded by imbecile females!'

Jessie squeaked and popped two of the tablets into her own mouth.

Just then, a mighty through-draught blew from one of the windows across to the open door, scattering the papers on Mr McMaster's desk to the four corners of the earth. Jessie squeaked again and leapt upon the flying sheets, helped by me.

For a moment, chaos reigned supreme: the wind blew, papers flew, Pugsy barked and Mr McMaster raged. Then, a sheaf of captured letters under my arm, I reached up and closed the window. Calm. Calm, calm.

Only, as it turned out, it was the sort that came before the storm.

I was just about to return the scattered paperwork to the desk and resume my seat when I noticed another sheet lying on the floor. I bent down to pick it up, clipped the side of my head on the desk – and then stopped dead.

In front of my very eyes, right in the middle of Mr McMaster's letter, were the words 'Hope Street'.

And they were not alone. The phrases 'proposed purchase of properties', 'long-term holding', 'land-bank' and, most sinister of all, 'shopping mall', leapt off the page and all but slapped me round the face. The Stealth Holdings logo was plastered across the top.

'That' – Mr McMaster snatched the paper out of my hands – 'is confidential.'

'I know,' I dissembled, 'I wasn't reading it – I banged my head and didn't know quite where I was for a minute. I was – ah – concussed. Yes, concussion; that's the one.'

I rubbed the back of my bonce in what I hoped was a convincing manner.

'Ouch,' I added.

'Would you like—' Jessie had stepped forward, proffering her bottle of pills.

'No she *would not*,' yelled Mr McMaster. 'Now get out, both of you. It's going to take me hours to get this lot back in the right order.'

Jessie and I looked at each other and then scuttled for the door. As it closed behind me, I could hear Mr McMaster on the phone.

'What do you mean "doctor's orders"?' he was saying. 'Goddammit, Mona, what are you? A man or a mouse? Well, you've got two more days, is that clear? Two days or I'll come round and march you back here myself.'

'Good luck,' I said to Jessie as I prepared to leave. 'At least the end is in sight.'

Jessie shuddered.

'I don't know that I'll last two more days,' she replied. 'There's a job coming up tomorrow in an accountants' firm. I might ask for a transfer.'

'Good idea,' I said, checking my watch.

'Shall I leave a note for Mrs McMaster asking her to call you and reschedule?'

I shook my head. 'No, it's fine. I am supposed to be on holiday after all.'

And, with a final wave over my shoulder, I picked up my bags and disappeared before anyone else shouted at me, asked me to measure anything or pick up their dry-cleaning.

# 13

Lisa shook her head in a world-weary way.

'I'll have a Jackie Daniel's on the rocks. Oh and, Bill?'

'Yes?' Bill's face was a study in love lorn anticipation.

'That thing that you keep doing round me – that thing with your mouth . . .'

'You mean talking?' Bill sounded puzzled.

'Yeah, that – well, don't. It's getting on my nerves.'

Instead of crumpling at this latest put-down, Bill grinned, placed a dish of pistachios on the table in front of us and headed off whistling towards the bar.

'You are *so* mean,' Toby said, half in awe, half reprimanding.

'But he loves it,' Bella replied. 'Look at him.'

We all turned round to see Bill happily taking the lid off Toby's beer and throwing ice cubes in Lisa's glass with gleeful abandon.

It was forty-eight hours after my run-in with Mr McMaster. I'd had a chilled couple of days lying in the sun in Golden Gate Park and generally flexing my relaxation muscles. As the afternoon shadows began to lengthen, I'd joined the others in the Lizard – where else? – for an Abbadabbatastic sound check.

Not that there was any tapping of microphones and

muttering 'one two, one two' going on.

Bella was still not feeling well: she was very tired and off her food, complaining that things 'tasted funny' and, as far as I was aware, had eaten little more than a couple of Rich Teas (purchased at huge expense from an English shop called Queen and Country which was run by the campest couple imaginable) all day.

'You know,' said Toby thoughtfully, 'you and Bill would be a match made in heaven: you enjoy expensive drinks, and Bill can get them at wholesale prices; you love being rude to people, Bill loves being insulted *by* you. What's not to like?'

'Oh no. Oh no, no, no, no, no.' Lisa shook her head vigorously. 'No. Not in a million years. Believe me, if we were the last man and woman left on earth, I would be texting the gorillas in the zoo.' She gave a shudder. 'He wears *T-shirts with slogans on them*. Urgh. And trainers – I mean, really!' Then her face brightened, 'But speaking of true love, Toby, I forgot to tell you that you have an admirer.'

Lisa nodded in the direction of the door through which a slightly nervous-looking young man wearing expensive-looking skinny chinos and a checked shirt had just appeared. He was scanning the room, obviously on the lookout for someone.

Toby went a curious pink colour and then put his head in his hands.

'Noooooo!' His voice dropped to a horrified whisper. 'Not Robbie Smith!'

Lisa gave a private smile of triumph.

197

'The very same, sweetie. He was in the audience when you gave your barnstorming best with Abbadabbatastic, and he called into the office yesterday while you were in that meeting and asked if I could pass on a message.'

Toby groaned but Lisa carried on relentlessly:

'Yeah, he wanted you to know how much he'd enjoyed watching you shaking that cute little tushie of yours.'

Toby opened his fingers a crack and, even though less than a quarter of his face was visible, regarded her with a look of unadulterated horror.

'He said *that*?' he hissed. 'Robbie Smith thinks I've got a cute little tushie?'

Lisa grinned and nodded her thanks to a waitress who had stopped to deliver our drinks.

'It might have been a butt,' she replied, 'but whatever it was, it was cute and he loved it.'

'Who's Robbie Smith?' I asked.

Toby's fingers opened again.

'Only the most important client I have on my books,' he said. 'Only the man with more money than God and twice the personal influence. And he was *here* – and he saw me in that white suit with the huge arm flaps! My life is over.'

Bella nudged him. 'He thinks you're cute.'

'Cooo-eeee!' trilled Lisa. 'Over here!'

'Nooooo,' cried Toby, 'noooooo!'

Slowly, almost imperceptibly, he began to slide down the faux leather seat of the banquette.

'Oh no you don't, mister!' Lisa stood up and grabbed him by the arm. 'You face this one like a man.'

'But I'm not a man.' Toby was almost in full-blown panic mode. 'Really I'm not. I'm a pathetic, wimpy sociophobe and – Oh, hi, Robbie; what's up?'

'Hi, Toby.' Robbie looked almost as awkward as Toby.

Which was a pretty tough call right then.

Toby slithered back up on to the banquette.

'I was just . . .' he began, his face turning pinker than a builder's bum cleavage in a heat wave, 'I was just – I was just fixing the wobble on the table leg. There!'

He gave the table a push, almost sending my bottle of beer toppling over and precious fluid ounces sloshing out of Lisa's glass.

'It's fine now. But you've got to – ah – keep on top of these things, haven't you?'

'Are you saying I have rickety tables?' Bill called from over at the bar.

Toby's face was so hot you could have grilled bacon on it.

'No, Bill. No, your tables are swell. It's – um – well, anyway, Robbie: how the hell are you?'

'I'm good. You?'

'Yeah.' Toby ran an anxious hand through his hair. 'I'm good too. The – er – the figures on the new account, it's looking good.'

'Excellent.' Robbie nodded enthusiastically.

'Yeah, really good.' Toby studied the label on his beer.

'Excellent,' said Robbie again.

This was painful stuff. The temptation to leap up and yell 'My friend fancies you' and knock their heads together was almost overwhelming.

'I – ah – didn't know you were in town,' mumbled Toby.

Lisa kicked him under the table. I knew this because she missed and got me instead.

'Yes you did,' she said loudly enough for Robbie to hear.

Toby smiled a truly ghastly smile.

'Oh, you mean *this* Robbie Smith,' he said, his voice taking on a strange strangulated quality, 'I thought you meant the *other* Robbie Smith – the one who lives in Alaska. The one who never ever comes to California.'

'I thought you were quite something,' Robbie said bashfully. 'I'm a huge Abba fan. Love their stuff.'

'Me too – although obviously it's not something I talk about at work,' Toby stammered. 'In fact, Abba tribute isn't something I get involved with on a day-to-day basis. I was – ah – stepping in to help a friend. Silver jumpsuits aren't really my thing.'

'Oh, that's a shame.' Robbie took a self-conscious swig of beer. 'I saw that *Mamma Mia* is showing at two of the movie theatres downtown and I was wondering if you – ah – if you would like to come with me?'

'I think I might be busy.' Toby shook his head in faux regret. 'In fact, I think I'm real busy – you know, with your account. Late nights and everything.'

'No you're not,' Lisa interjected, 'you're free every evening apart from your Abbadabbatastic commitments.'

This time it was Toby trying to kick Lisa under the table. However, once again I got caught in the crossfire.

'Owwww!' I cried. 'Will you two stop that?'

'Oh.' Robbie looked deflated but slid a business card out of his wallet and put it on the table in front of Toby. 'Well, if you change your mind, give me a call.'

Then he gave a sad little smile and walked back to the bar.

'What did you think you were doing, you muppet?' Bella hissed. 'He was *begging* you to go out with him.'

'He couldn't have been any keener if he'd thrown a dozen red roses in your face and serenaded you to the accompaniment of gypsy violins,' I added. 'What are you like?'

'He's a client!' cried Toby. 'What part of "you must not date the clients" do you guys not understand?'

'That's only your own clients,' said Lisa. 'Technically he belongs to Colin in Account Management. You can do what you like to him.' She paused. 'By the way, what would you *like* to do to him?'

Toby went even redder and picked at the label on his beer.

'OK,' Lisa continued, 'put it this way. If you don't ring him, then I will. And I'll tell him how much you like him. And I might need to mention it at work – or even change the departmental screen savers: how

201

about "Toby heart Robbie" surrounded by a couple of big old fat cherubs and—'

'OK, I'll do it!' Toby cried. 'I'll do it – just no screen savers. Not this time. Please, Lisa.'

Bella and I opened our mouths to ask about the *other* time the screen savers had been hijacked, but were distracted by the door from the street being flung open theatrically.

'Hey!'

Steve walked in and sauntered up to our table looking like a cat that has just found some very superior cream.

'What are you drinking, people?' he asked. 'The good times are back.'

Bella turned round and smiled at him. He put his arms round her and kissed her passionately on the lips.

'What's happened, baby?'

'That club, the one in Oakland. Chris backed down and said we could go in at the original rate. Just us. As a favour.' His smile became even wider. 'It's gonna be big, Bella; and when I say big, I mean *huge*.'

Bella's brows pulled together in a frown.

'Steve, I'm not being negative, really I'm not, but we've been through this a bazillion and one times: there are hundreds of venues closing every day. People are simply not going out like they used to. And where the heck do you think you're going to get the cash to pay for this? I know for a fact you're broke because you've been scabbing money off me for weeks.'

The smile vanished from Steve's lips and he looked rattled.

'It's cool, Bella, we can afford it. Look, I took yours and my share of the winnings from the quarter-finals and added it to my next month's rent money – after all, I'll be living with you, won't I? And I've promised Chris the rest when I've spoken to the bank.'

Bella was on her feet. Her face was ashen and her hands, where she gripped the back of her chair, were white.

'You gave him my money? Steve, I *needed* that! Are you mental?'

Steve glanced round nervously.

'It's an investment, Bella, honey. It's safe. We're going to get it back tenfold – probably more. I'm telling you this place is a gold mine.'

'It hasn't even opened yet, Steve. You don't know if it's a gold mine or a bloody bottomless pit – and you had *no right* to take my money.'

Steve looked as though she had just slapped him across the face.

'It was *our* money,' he replied slowly. 'I invested it on behalf of us. For *our* future.'

'No it wasn't.' Bella looked as though she was almost in tears. 'It was mine. And what the hell are you doing "investing" it anyway? You need to pay Eric for the advertising you took out last month, you owe for the repairs on your car, and then there's the credit cards – we can't afford it. *You can't afford it.*'

Steve was silent. He regarded Bella with an almost expressionless face. Then he took a note out of his wallet and waved it at us.

'So anyway, who's up for a drink? Toby?'

Toby raised his beer awkwardly and glanced at Bella.

'I'm good thanks, Steve.'

'Lisa then. Go on, Lisa, you'll have a drink with me.'

'Maybe not the best time, Steve; I think you'll agree with me on that.'

Steve crackled the banknote impatiently.

'Steve,' said Bella, 'if you've spent the Battle of the Tribute Bands money, you can't afford to be standing rounds.'

Then, with an awful lot more dignity than I think I could have managed under the circumstances, she turned away and walked down the stairs towards the performance area.

'Excuse me,' I said.

I caught up with her in the tiny ladies' room. She was staring down into the sink and holding on to the edge of the wash-hand basin as though she was about to collapse.

'Are you all right?' I asked.

Stupid Questions of Our Time.

'He isn't a bad person,' she said, 'he really isn't a bad person – it's just sometimes he doesn't have a fucking clue. I love him, Flo, but I'm not his mum; I can't make decisions for him, doling out a bit of pocket money when he wants it. I need a man who will take respon-

204

sibility for himself – and right now, Steve doesn't seem capable of doing that.'

'So you won't be moving in with him?'

Bella turned away from me and stared at her reflection in the mirror.

'I don't know,' she said. 'I just don't know. If I don't, does that mean we break up? And if we break up, will I lose the band? Right now, the band is all I have.'

I tried to slip my arm round her shoulders, but she flinched and shrugged it off.

'No it's not,' I told her, 'you have us.'

'You're going back to England,' she reminded me, 'and Toby and Lisa have done enough. I rely on them far too much.'

She grimaced and gasped for breath. Her knuckles were white where they gripped the edge of the sink.

'Belle,' I was concerned, 'are you feeling poorly?'

'Mmmm' – she rubbed her stomach – 'it's just my period. I've had these grumbling pains for a couple of days now.'

'Are you going to be all right for later?' I asked, thinking about the semi-finals.

Bella nodded.

'Course,' she said in a tight little voice, 'Dr Theatre, you know. I'll be fine the moment the spotlight hits me. That plus a couple of paracetamol – I'll be grand.'

'If you're sure,' I said, not feeling entirely convinced.

'Really,' she insisted. 'God, I hope we win tonight. I don't know what I'm going to do for money if we don't – only I'm going to have to speak to Bill and make sure he gives me my share of any takings directly; I don't want Steve investing them in any more dodgy night-clubs, thank you very much. Life doesn't get any easier, does it?'

No, I thought sadly, it certainly doesn't.

# 14

Toby persuaded Bella to let him drive her home so that she could put her feet up before the show and I, deciding that she'd be more likely to nap if I was out of the way, made my way from Hope Street up and down the various hills (mostly down) until I reached the waterfront. Once there, I wandered along Fisherman's Wharf, waved at the sea lions and bought myself an ice-cream sandwich called an It's-It. Then I sat on the quay, dangled my legs over the edge and enjoyed the soothing warmth of the afternoon sun on my back. Finally I pulled out my phone and did what I had wanted to do since leaving the McMasters' house.

Logging on to the most powerful search engine I could find, I typed in 'Stealth Holdings' and 'Earl McMaster' and waited for the wonders of technology to do the rest.

*Your search has produced 500,863,113 results*

I allowed myself a small 'hoorah'.

I clicked on the first link, which turned out to be a long, yawntastic spiel from the ValueMart publicity machine about their planned expansion into the United Kingdom. Honestly, you'd think no one in Britain had ever *heard* of supermarkets before, let alone shopped in one. However, I quickly got bored with all the corporate back-slapping and tried the next suggestion.

This was no better. It was an unashamedly schmaltzy number – again pumped out by the ValueMart publicity people – featuring Mr and Mrs McMaster at a local animal shelter. Mrs McMaster was cuddling a border collie while Mr McMaster tolerated a small Yorkshire terrier on his knee. Next to them was Pugsy, staring at the terrier as though he had just decided where his next meal was coming from. According to the article that accompanied the picture, being papped with the pooches meant that Mr and Mrs M. were 'caring' and 'benevolent' human beings whose 'philanthropic good works' meant they loved nothing better than ensuring their stray animal chums were well looked after.

Shame he didn't think about directing some of his benevolence in the direction of his fellow humans, I thought grimly.

The next few links were equally uninspiring until there, at the bottom of the page, I saw the name 'Stealth Holdings'.

I was directed to an article in an online financial journal from several months back. It was a piece about a new shopping mall that had been built on a brown-field site in Texas. Apparently, the land was owned by Stealth Holdings who had bought it well over a decade earlier. Almost as a throwaway in its very last line, the article mentioned that Stealth Holdings seemed to be buying up pockets of land all over the States and had recently purchased a small terrace of apartment buildings in Manhattan which, just like Hope Street, had no hope of ever being developed.

I wondered why.

Why would Earl McMaster invest hundreds of thousands – probably even millions – of dollars in tracts of land that then sat about doing nothing? Was he so rich that he didn't care? Or was he playing some sort of long game?

I looked at my watch. Time to get moving.

I put my phone back in my bag, threw my It's-It wrapper into the bin and began the long pull up the hill towards Hope Street. About halfway, my phone bleeped. Glad of the excuse to pause and get my breath back, I pulled it out and looked at my emails. Oh crap – it was from Josh.

Despite my better judgement, I opened it. There was an attachment of some sort and a two-word message:

*Plan B?*

My annoyance levels, which had been nicely soothed by the sun, sea and ice-cream, once again spiked skyward. How dare he? How very dare he email me – let alone have the gall to suggest plans.

With trembling fingers, I typed:

*Go away and leave me alone. I don't want any plans from you, B or otherwise*

I pressed 'send', then I deleted the email and its attachment and put my phone back in my bag.

Almost immediately a reply, together with the exact same attachment, pinged back. I opened it.

*Yes you do. You really, really do. This is important*

Almost screaming with frustration, I threw the phone back into my bag and ignored the next two 'pings' of incoming emails, hoping he would get bored and give up.

Thankfully he did.

It took me longer than I'd anticipated to pull myself up the enormous slope of the hill that was downtown San Francisco and arrive back at the Lizard Lounge. Hot and very much bothered by Josh's attempts at electronic contact, I bought myself a bottle of Coke at the bar and went to make my way down the stairs. As I hit the second step, however, I became aware of raised voices filtering up through the air towards me. I stopped and peered over the banister. There, right in the middle of the (thankfully almost empty) room, were Bella and Steve. Bella was still in her day clothes and had one arm wrapped round her stomach. As I watched, she moved it across her tummy as though she was in severe discomfort.

'Come on, Bella, be reasonable,' Steve was saying, 'you know it makes sense: why should we both be throwing money away on rent when we can economise and live in the same place?'

Bella glanced round unhappily. She was obviously trying to keep the discussion private – and failing miserably.

'Look, Steve, it's not just about cutting costs. I think

there are other things, other issues in our relationship, that we need to look at. I need to know that it's right for us as a couple to move in together.'

Steve looked as though someone had just taken his security blanket away. There was real fear on his face.

'What are you saying, babe? I don't want to lose you. Are we good? Tell me we're good!'

Bella bit her lip and looked down at her shoes.

'I don't know, Steve, I really don't know. Things haven't been working well for a few months now. We need to talk but now really isn't the time or the place—'

'Bella' – Steve took her face in his hands – 'Bella, listen to me, I love you.'

Bella's eyes closed.

'I know you do,' she said, her voice barely audible, 'I know you do. It's just . . .'

'Just what? You love me, I love you—'

'Maybe love's not enough, Steve.'

As she spoke, she ran her hand over her tummy and gasped, as though in pain.

'Hey! Bella! Are you OK?'

I ran down the stairs, Coke in hand. My cousin seemed to be having difficulty speaking.

'Bloody hell, Steve,' I cried, 'what's wrong? What's happened to her?'

I put my hand on top of Bella's, but she pulled away; her eyes red and watery – but whether because of pain or emotion, I couldn't tell. Steve glared at me.

'Bella and I were having a private conversation,' he said.

I turned to him. 'Steve, I don't care. She's not well.'

'I'm fine,' replied Bella emphatically.

'Yeah, and monkeys might fly out my butt.' Toby clattered down the stairs and walked over to join in the debate. 'Bella, go home. It doesn't matter about the show. If you're ill, just go.'

'Don't be ridiculous,' Bella snapped back at him, 'of course I'm going on stage.'

'Bella?' Steve looked alarmed. 'You told me you were fine. What's up?'

He put his arm round her shoulders but Bella grimaced in pain and wriggled out of his grasp.

'Isn't it obvious?' replied Bella, rubbing her stomach. 'You and I have had a row, Steve. I'm about as far from OK as I could possibly be.'

'What about your stomach?' I asked. 'You keep rubbing it. Do you think you have a bug or something?'

Bella looked at the floor. 'No, it's probably just indigestion – or my period.'

'Are you sure?'

Bella rolled her eyes.

'Well, I've got blood coming out of me so yeah, unless I'm haemorrhaging to death, I think that's probably it.'

Toby put his hands over his ears and grimaced.

'Please, ladies!' he cried. 'This is *beyond* too much information.'

I ignored him and turned my attention back to Bella.

'Have you taken anything for it?' I asked gently.

'Yes.' Bella's face contorted as another spasm racked her. 'Paracetamol. And aspirin. And ibuprofen.'

'Jeepers, Bella-baby,' cried Steve in alarm, 'you'll be as high as a fucking kite.'

'And have they helped?' I asked, my concern growing.

'They haven't even touched it,' admitted Bella.

'Right,' said Steve, 'we're taking you to a doctor. If it's that bad, you need to get it checked out.'

'I'm *fine*,' Bella protested. 'I'm really, really *fine*.'

She gave a little gasp and grabbed her stomach with both hands.

'If you're fine, then I'm a football-playing, bear-shooting friend of Sarah Palin,' said Toby. 'The big guy is right. You need to see a quack.'

Steve ran a harassed hand through his hair.

'Come on, Toby, get her upstairs and we'll call a cab. There's a walk-in place a couple of blocks away.'

I put my arm round her shoulders, but, with a strength that belied her tiny frame, Bella wrenched away from me.

'That *hurt*!' she howled. 'For the last time, Flora, Steve, Toby and anyone else who feels like sticking their fricking nose in, I *do not* need to see a doctor. I'll take some more pills. I'll be OK. I need the money!'

'If you take any more pills you're going to pass out,' Toby informed her. 'Hell-*lo*! You may not realise this but you are not Janis Joplin. Drug-induced comas and untimely deaths are not on my wish-list for my friends.'

'I tell you I am *fine*.'

To prove how fine she really was, Bella got up from the table she had been leaning against and staggered two steps across the room before collapsing down on to a chair with her arms wrapped round her midriff and her face screwed up in pain.

I'd seen enough.

'Toby,' I said. 'Get a cab. Now. Actually – scrub the cab, make it an ambulance. She could have appendicitis.'

'Appendicitis?' Steve sounded shocked, 'Surely it's not that bad? I mean, you can, like, die, from that.'

'That's right,' I told him, wondering what part of the whole scenario he wasn't getting. 'And that's exactly why she needs an ambulance. Steve, she's been ignoring it for ages; by now it could literally be life or death.'

Bella put her head down in her lap and groaned.

'I can't afford it,' she mumbled.

I got down on my knees and put my head as close as I could to hers.

'You're in acute pain,' said Toby, getting out his mobile, 'you need to get to the hospital. Steve – tell her she needs to get to the hospital.'

'I . . .' Steve managed to look terrified and confused more or less simultaneously. 'I don't know – I – oh, shit, Bella. Please don't be sick. Please.'

'I can't afford to be ill,' muttered Bella into her lap.

'It's medical treatment,' I told her, 'not a new pair of shoes. Money doesn't come into it.'

'Yes it does,' Bella replied, 'I don't have any health insurance.'

I rocked back on my heels as the implications of her statement hit me with the force of a ten-tonne truck.

'But you're a *nurse*,' were the first words out of my mouth.

Bella rolled her eyes and groaned. Although whether this was a commentary on me or another spasm hitting her hard, I couldn't tell.

'And this week's prize for stating the bleeding obvious goes to Flora Fielding,' she cried. 'What do you expect, Flo? I'm suspended – and it's not just my pay they cut.'

I looked at her and, as my eyes scanned her face, I saw one of the tears that had been threatening earlier squeeze itself out of the corner of her eye and trickle down her cheek.

'Ambulance here in five,' Toby snapped his phone shut.

'I'm not—' Bella began again.

'You are going to hospital,' I said firmly. 'And they will make you better and we will worry about the money later. Steve will go with you and hold your hand, won't you, Steve?'

I looked round but I couldn't see him.

'Steve? Toby, where's Steve?'

But the room was entirely empty of people we knew whose names began with the letter 'S'.

'Bastard,' muttered Toby mutinously, 'the fucking *fucking* bastard.'

'Toby,' I said sharply, 'he could have gone to get her a glass of water – or call his own insurance company.

215

Just because he's not here doesn't make him a bastard.'

Toby made a noise like steam escaping from a pipe, which I understood to be a wordless refutation of my excuses for Steve's absence.

I looked round the room again. We were about fifty minutes away from the kick-off of the semi-finals of the Battle of the Tribute Bands and people had started to filter down from the bar upstairs. I didn't want Bella and her tummy ache to become the unofficial warm-up act.

'Toby,' I said, 'can you carry her? We'll wait for the paramedics upstairs.'

'But the band!' More tears had joined the first and were streaking down Bella's face. 'What about the band?'

'Oh, bugger the band – as you English people say.' Toby shoved his phone into his back pocket and scooped Bella up into his arms. 'See? I can do bilingual, Bella.'

I looked at the perfect line of his shoulders, the muscles in his arms and – without warning – a picture of Josh, smiling and with not too many clothes on, flashed across my consciousness. With enormous effort, I pushed it into the darkest corner of my brain. Josh was an irrelevance. He and I were more over than the sequinned spandex Abbadabbatastic decked themselves out in. It was Bella I needed to focus on.

As we gained the head of the stairs, Lisa rushed up to us looking flustered. She had no lipstick on and only one hand's worth of nails painted.

'I came as quickly as I could,' she panted. 'What the hell—?'

We all started gabbling at once.

'Bella's poorly—'

'I'm *fine*!'

'And she's going to the hospital—'

'I can't afford hospital.'

'And we're pulling out of the gig—'

'Over my dead body!'

'If we don't get you to hospital it *will* be over your dead body!'

Lisa held up her hands and hollered in a voice that could have started earthquakes and reduced whole mountain ranges to rubble: 'Quiet!'

We did as we were told – along with the rest of the Lizard's clientele.

Once she had regained order, Lisa snapped into dictator mode.

'On a scale of one to ten,' she asked Bella, 'how bad is it?'

Bella bit her lip.

'And I want the truth,' Lisa added.

'About twenty-five,' Bella muttered, 'out of ten.'

Lisa gave a brisk nod of her head.

'The hospital,' she informed us, 'no arguments.'

'But—'

'Shh!'

'But—'

'Shhhhhhhhhh!'

'ButifIgowelosetheBattleoftheTributeBandsandI

217

don'teatforaweekandStevealreadyhatesmeandIjustwan
tto*dieeeeeeeeeee*!'

Bella finally broke down and howled uncontrollably
into Toby's collar.

'No one is going to die,' I said firmly, 'especially not
you, Bella. Your ambulance is here.'

Bella grabbed hold of the back of a chair to try and
stop us carrying her out of the bar. I unwrapped her
fingers, but she promptly rewound them. Toby took a
step in the direction of the door and the chair bumped
noisily along in his wake.

'Fine,' I said to her, 'if we have to take the chair with
us, we will. But you're still going to hospital.'

As the paramedics reached us, another spasm
overtook Bella. She screwed up her face with the pain
and gasped.

'Suspected appendicitis,' I told them. 'Severe
abdominal pain, referred pain in the shoulders and
light-headedness.'

'You're in a bad way,' one of the paramedics
remarked. 'Looks like we got here just in time.'

The spasm passed and Bella relaxed a little.

But only a little.

A stretcher clattered its way through the door and
into the bar. Toby lifted Bella on to it and she was
covered with a blanket and strapped in.

'Has she taken anything?' asked one of the
paramedics.

Toby shrugged. 'Just most of the over-the-counter
analgesics known to man.'

'Which hospital?'

'St Peter's,' I said.

Toby and Lisa looked at me.

'We'll find the money,' I said.

Then she was trundled outside, I climbed into the ambulance after her and the doors were closed. As we drove away, I looked out of the window until Toby and Lisa turned into tiny dots in the middle of a busy street full of other tiny dots, before finally disappearing from view altogether.

I closed my eyes and sent a quick prayer up to Granny in the hope that she would do what she could for us, before turning my attention once again to my stricken cousin.

# 15

The time I spent in the back of that ambulance probably only took a few minutes but, from my point of view, it felt more like a week.

'Are you feeling any better?' I smoothed Bella's hair away from her face. My cousin's skin was damp and clammy, but it felt as hot as a furnace. I didn't need any medical qualifications to see that she was a long way from feeling better. A drip attached to a bag on the wall was depositing a clear fluid into her veins and she was breathing in gas and air via a mask placed over her mouth and nose.

'It's good stuff,' she murmured, her voice a bit on the slurry side, 'I wish I could get hold of this in an off-licence.' Then she grabbed my hand, any pretence at levity vanishing into the air. 'Flo,' she said, so quietly I had to strain to hear her, 'Flo, I don't want to die.'

'Rubbish,' I said, squeezing her hand and kissing her lightly on her burning forehead, 'nobody is going to die.'

'Don't go.' Her eyelids drooped. 'Don't go. Stay here with me.'

'I'll stay for as long as you need me,' I said, patting her hand and putting on a ridiculously upbeat voice, 'and when you're home again, we'll go for that slap-up brunch in Sausalito you were talking about yesterday. And go shopping. And do the labyrinths. And . . .'

As I spoke, Bella's eyelids fluttered down on to her cheeks. In any other context it would have looked peaceful; but right now, in the back of an ambulance blue-lighting its way through the San Francisco streets, it was my cue to freak out and panic.

'Bella!' I said, patting her on the hand and trying to bring her back to the land of the living. 'Bella, wake up!'

I looked round at the paramedic who was radioing ahead to the hospital.

'Help!' I cried.

He threw down the receiver and leapt across to us.

'Bella!' he said in a gentle but firm tone. 'Bella, we are nearly there. You need to wake up. Stay with me, Bella!' Then he yelled to the driver: 'Hey! Louis! Hit the gas!'

I don't think I have ever been so frightened in my life. The ambulance, in a great spurt of speed, took a corner so violently that I was thrown out of my seat. Bella's eyelids flickered open for a second or two – and then promptly closed once again.

'Crash team!' the paramedic yelled into the radio. 'Crash team on standby.'

'Come on, Bella!' I urged as the paramedic fiddled with the various bits of equipment that were attached to her. 'Bella, don't you DARE do this to me.'

The ambulance screeched to a halt, almost cata-pulting me and the paramedic through the doors. Out

221

of the tinted windows I could see a host of people wearing scrubs running towards us. There was a general scramble over Bella's supine form and, surrounded by an almost unfeasible amount of doctors, nurses and goodness only knew who else, she was wheeled into the hospital. Not wanting to be left behind, I scrambled down from the ambulance and followed the pack of medics into a vast reception area.

'I've got a pulse,' shouted one of the bescrubbed individuals. 'Crash team: stay on standby but we're OK for now.'

'Theatre number two one three!' called someone else. 'Take her straight down – the anaesthesiologist is waiting.'

I was about to go too, but someone grabbed me by the hand.

'Are you with this patient?' asked a lady wearing blue scrubs and holding a clipboard. 'I need to confirm her symptoms.'

'Abdominal pain,' I said, watching helplessly as Bella disappeared through a set of double doors, 'dizziness, light-headedness.'

The woman scribbled this down on her clipboard.

'Anything else?' she prompted. 'Any sickness or vomiting? Bleeding?'

'No vomiting,' I said, trying very hard to remember everything that Bella had told me, 'but she said her shoulders hurt and she has her period – although it's a few days late.'

'Uh-huh.' The lady nodded. 'And how long has she had these symptoms?'

'Low-level pain for a day or so,' I said as something flashed into my mind, 'and she said things tasted weird: like she had a metallic taste in her mouth. And she's gone off alcohol.'

The expression on the woman's face changed from focused intensity to real concern.

'And you said she had pain in her shoulders?' she asked again.

'Yes,' I replied, wondering what link there could possibly be between that and an aversion to alcohol.

'Right,' said the woman, putting the pen in her pocket and running to the reception desk a few metres away.

'Is that bad?' I called after her. 'I mean, what are we talking about here?'

But the woman didn't respond. Instead, she picked up the telephone, dialled rapidly, said something (even more rapidly) into the mouthpiece and then ran off down the corridor and through the same double doors that had swallowed up my cousin, leaving me alone and bewildered in the bustling, disinfectant-scented foyer.

My solitude, however, did not last long.

A large, imposing woman holding yet another clip - board wandered over from the reception desk.

'Insurance,' she said, holding the board out. 'Please fill this in, miss.'

I hesitated. I had been so concerned about Bella

that, since we'd left the Lizard, I hadn't given a thought to the fact that she had no insurance.

'We don't have any,' I said, with no real idea what this would mean in terms of Bella's treatment.

I mean, surely they wouldn't turn the trolley round and start wheeling her out into the street, would they?

The woman looked at me over the tops of her rimless glasses.

'So how are you going to pay?' she asked, folding her arms in a no-nonsense manner.

It took a lot of effort on my part to remember that she wasn't being unkind, she was just doing her job.

Although I got the feeling that she was very, very good at doing her job.

'Um . . .'

My brain was rapidly clicking through all the available options: should we have a whip round? Take out insurance NOW and hope it was retrospective? See if they needed any kidneys on the transplant ward – I could manage with just one, surely?

I swallowed hard.

'Let's just make sure we're clear here,' I said, trying to make my voice sound casual and conversational, 'you need insurance – or what?'

'Or cash,' said the woman. 'You need to tell me how you're gonna pay. Or we transfer her.'

'Transfer her?' This sounded hopeful.

'To the County hospital,' she replied. 'And believe me, unless you really don't have any other option, you don't want to be going to County.'

'I have some cash at home,' I said. 'About a thousand dollars. I can bring that in as a down payment – and I'll get the rest somehow. I'll get a loan or something.' A terrible thought struck me. 'You don't want it up front, do you?'

Something that might have almost been a smile rippled over the woman's face.

'No,' she informed me, 'we're not quite that bad. Patient's name, please?'

'Bella,' I said, 'I mean Isobel. Isobel Jones. Address 113 Hope Heights, San Francisco, date of birth—'

The woman stopped writing and stared at me.

'Bella Jones?' she said. 'You mean the nurse?'

I nodded and wished with all my might that I'd had the presence of mind not to bring Bella to her own hospital.

'You OK?' asked the clipboard lady.

I shook my head, feeling not OK in the least.

'I just want her to be all right,' I said, my voice hoarse.

The receptionist's expression softened.

'I can't promise you that, honey, but I *can* tell you that this is the best hospital in the area and we will do all we can for her.'

She went back over to the desk and began putting Bella's details into the computer.

So long as I keep the money coming in, I thought grimly.

The printer made a groaning noise and regurgitated a couple of sheets of paper. 'Sign here.' The

225

receptionist attached them to the clipboard and thrust it at me once again.

I signed with a wobbly signature that was barely recognisable as my own.

'You feelin' all right?' she asked again. 'You want to see a doctor?'

The thought of paying for two medical bills made me pull myself together.

'No,' I said firmly. 'No thanks. I'll be fine.'

'Good,' the receptionist nodded, 'because I think you're wanted.'

I looked up and saw a nurse (at least I found out later she was a nurse) in pink scrubs hurrying towards me.

'Are you Flora?' she said. 'We need to talk. Would you mind coming with me?'

The nurse, who had a badge with Joy-Anne written on it, beckoned me through the same double doors that had recently swallowed up my cousin, holding one open for me as she did so. It revealed one of those seemingly endless hospital corridors containing a constant stream of medical professionals, people on trolleys and more sets of double doors. The tem - perature – already high – felt positively stifling, and the all-pervasive smell of disinfectant wound its way up my nose and down into the back of my throat, making me feel vaguely nauseous. I prayed that all she wanted was to tell me that Bella was fine and could go home.

No harm done.

*Please God, please, let there be no harm done.*

'In here, please.' The nurse opened the door on to an anonymous little waiting room and ushered me in. 'Can I get you anything? Tea? Coffee?'

I shook my head. Given my state of heightened tension and the icky smell of the disinfectant, it would not have been a good moment to attempt a cup of coffee.

'Right, Flora.' The nurse put the clipboard she had been carrying – there seemed to be an awful lot of clipboards in this hospital – down on the table. 'There is some good news and then some bad news.'

I nodded and crossed my fingers for luck underneath the table where she couldn't see them. If I wished *really* hard, perhaps I could make the bad news go away?

'The good news is that we know what's wrong with Bella,' the nurse continued.

I bit my lip and crossed the fingers on the other hand. If a diagnosis was the *good* news, that didn't say much about the rest of it.

'She's suffering from an ectopic pregnancy,' the nurse said, her face intent but kindly, 'she's in theatre now.'

I was so shocked, I think I stopped breathing for a moment or two.

'She's *pregnant*?' I gasped.

The nurse wore a worried expression.

'Are you her next of kin?' she asked.

'No,' I said, shaking my head. 'I'm only her cousin.'

Joy-Anne looked as though she was deciding whether or not to tell me something.

'I know Bella,' she said at last. 'Actually, I'm her line manager. I wasn't aware she had any blood relations over here.'

'She doesn't. I'm only visiting. Her mother lives in England too . . .' My voice trailed off.

'And she's not married, is she?'

I shook my head.

'She was in a relationship,' I said. 'Is in a relationship. I'm not sure. Why?'

'Flora.' The nurse reached out and touched me lightly on the arm. It was a simple gesture, but one that reassured me. Whatever Bella was going through, she had people like this who cared about her. 'She's really very, very poorly.'

My head swam just a little bit more.

'But you said she was pregnant,' I protested. 'Pregnancy's not a disease.'

'I said she was suffering from an ectopic pregnancy,' said the nurse, slowly and calmly, matching the pace of her speech expertly to the processing ability of my brain. 'It's when the egg gets stuck in the fallopian tubes. If it's not caught early it can prove fatal.'

My brain was crawling along at the speed of an arthritic snail, and only some of the more dramatic words from Joy-Anne's last sentence registered.

'Fatal?' I cried, jumping up in panic. 'But you did catch it, didn't you? I mean, she's going to be fine?'

The nurse put her arms round me and, very gently, pushed me back into my seat.

'We're going to do our best,' she said.

I looked at her.

'That's not what I asked,' I said.

The nurse held my gaze.

'I know,' she replied.

'I need to ring some people,' I said, feeling my stomach-churning returning with a vengeance.

Goodness, I'd have been the crappest doctor in the world. I couldn't deal with this sort of thing at all.

'Feel free to make any calls you need on the landline.' The nurse gestured to a phone on the wall. 'You're not supposed to use your cell in the hospital, I'm afraid.'

I nodded and then swallowed.

Hard.

'So, just so that I know, what's the plan?'

'The plan is that we operate and do everything we can for her. And then we wait. Now, if you don't feel up to speaking to her family in England, I can arrange for someone to do it for you.'

'No,' I said, thinking that Auntie Stella would take it better coming from me. 'I will do it. Just tell me that she's going to be OK?'

The nurse smiled sadly.

'You know I can't do that,' she replied, 'but I promise we will do everything we can. Now can I get you anything before I go? If you do want a drink, there's a vending machine just over here.'

I shook my head. I needed some time alone with my thoughts; then some more time alone with the telephone.

'It's hard for us too.' Joy-Anne fixed me with a sad smile. 'We miss her very much. She is a truly gifted nurse.'

She hesitated again and something hovered in the air between us. I decided to be bold. 'I know about Mrs Hampton,' I said slowly. 'Do you have any idea what went wrong?'

Joy-Anne glanced in the direction of the door and then leaned in towards me.

'I don't know,' she whispered, 'but I'd put money on the fact it wasn't Bella. She's too good, too con-scientious. And I checked the chart – everything was written down as it should have been.'

There was a bleeping sound and the nurse looked down at her belt.

'I'm being paged,' she said, 'I'll have to go. I'll let you know when there's some news.'

I gestured in the general direction of the door to indicate that this was OK. At that moment, speech was beyond me.

For quite a while I sat alone in the little room, the muffled sounds of hospital life in the corridor outside only vaguely registering.

*Bella might die. Bella might die. She might die five thousand miles away from home and with the accusation of negligence hanging over her head.*

I put my head in my hands and forced air into my

lungs. Gradually, my thoughts became less frenetic and my heartbeat slowed from a heavy pounding to a regular, steady beat.

I reached into Bella's bag (I had brought it with me from the Lizard) and pulled out her – or rather Toby's – phone. Deciding to ignore the injunction from the nurse about mobiles, I went into her contacts list and found Steve's number. He needed to know – presumably the baby that had nearly killed Bella was his.

With a heavy heart, I pressed the number and listened to it ring.

Steve didn't pick up.

I looked at my watch and wondered if he was in the thick of it at the Battle of the Tribute Bands.

I tried again.

There was still no answer.

'Hi, Steve,' I said as the call clicked on to voicemail, 'it's Flo, Bella's cousin. She's in hospital being operated on at the moment and they are not sure if she's going to make it.' I took a deep breath. 'It's an ectopic pregnancy – a pregnancy that has gone wrong. It can sometimes be fatal and, although they are trying their best for her, I can't guarantee Bella will pull through. Please call as soon as you get this, or come to St Peter's Hospital and ask for me at the desk.'

I rang off and let the phone drop back into Bella's bag. Steve had, ironically, been the easy call to make. I now needed to ring Auntie Stella and tell her that her only daughter was fighting for her life in an operating theatre on the other side of the world.

I felt for Auntie Stella. Uncle Mike had died a few years ago and she was on her own. She would be worried sick, but I could do nothing else for her other than pass on the news together with a few kind words. I couldn't make her sit down and have a cup of sweet tea; I couldn't put my arm round her; I couldn't drive her to the airport and put her on a plane.

I needed someone else to do that.

I picked up the hospital phone and rang another number entirely. Unlike Steve's, this one was picked up almost immediately.

'Mum,' I said, 'I'm sorry to wake you but there's been an emergency and I need you to help.'

Three hours later, I was walking up the hill towards Bella's flat. The city spread out below me like a spider's web of illuminated threads, with the opposite shore of the Bay sending back an answering gleam of light. Above this intricate interlacing of man-made lumines - cence hung the moon; the same moon that Josh and I had seen as a fine, white sliver suspended over the ocean, now ripened into a shapely crescent with a deep orange glow.

It was a stunning scene but, for once, the magic of San Francisco was lost upon me. I was tired, anxious and had had an exhausting evening. After I spoke to Mum, Toby and Lisa arrived and we sat together in the little room, drinking foul vending machine coffee and not saying very much. I tried Steve's phone several more times, but got no further than the voicemail.

Then, after much protesting, Lisa and Toby sent me home for some sleep whilst they took on the night shift.

I turned away from the electric panorama of the illuminated city to make my final ascent of the hill, and almost collided with a familiar figure wearing a full crinoline and an awful lot of eye make-up.

'Flora?' Drusilla squinted at me through her layers of kohl. 'What are you doing? It's the middle of the night.'

'It's Bella,' I said. 'Ectopic pregnancy. St Peter's.'

Drusilla clapped a hand over her red mouth.

'Shit,' she mumbled.

'Oh and indeed shit,' I responded.

Drusilla's eyes flashed over me.

'You OK?' she said. 'You look like you've been mauled by racoons, chewed by possums and hounded by coyotes.'

'Thanks,' I said, 'that pretty much sums up how I feel – and no, I'm not OK. But I'll live.'

Which, I remembered sadly, is more than Bella might do.

She put an arm round me and clutched me to her musty-smelling bosom.

'I wish I'd known. I was at the hospital earlier,' she said, 'I'm running rebirthing classes in the antenatal department.'

This was so incongruous, so well meant and so totally San Franciscan that I found myself smiling.

'Oh, Dru,' I said, 'you are just fabulous, you know? Everyone here is amazing and I love you all.'

233

'You gotta find your tribe, remember?' Drusilla nodded sagely. 'And maybe this is where yours hang out, in good old Frisco?'

Maybe they do, I wondered. Maybe my tribe are a lady wearing a hundred-year-old dress, a bossy PA with a borderline drink problem, a cowardly-lion-turned-disco-diva and my cousin, currently fighting for her life in an operating theatre down the road.

Drusilla gave me another squeeze and then let me go.

'I'll go get some reiki organised for her,' she informed me, 'and a bit of Buddhist chanting down at the temple. My gay Catholic priest best friend will light some candles for her in the cathedral and I'm sure the nuns at the orphanage would be good for a few Hail Marys. We need to bring in the big guns here. Unless . . .' She paused. 'Unless you fancy doing a bit of re birthing while I'm here? It can be very cathartic.'

I guessed that the residents of Hope Heights would not be thrilled by the sound of us moaning and groaning like a pair of strangulated sheep.

'I think I'll pass for the moment,' I said, 'but it was a kind offer.'

Drusilla pressed me once again against the rustling silk of her bodice.

'Now, you – stay strong,' she said. 'We're all here for you.'

And she disappeared back into the night.

I walked the last few paces to Bella's house. I made

my way up the stairs, opened the door to her flat and stepped into the darkened interior. Even though this wasn't the first time I had been home alone at Bella's, there was a deathly hush about it now that sent a shiver up my spine. The curtains had not been drawn and feeble orange light from the street lamps was washing in over the interior, throwing up strange, unnerving shadows and making the normally friendly rooms feel borderline creepy. Even the traffic on the road outside had lost its comforting purr and sounded hushed and muted.

I shivered again and made my way into the kitchen.

I didn't bother to switch the lights on. Somehow it felt safer in the dark; as though Fate, looking for its next victim, might not notice me hiding out in the shadows. One minute you could be healthy and hungry and *alive*, and the next you could be dead.

And the journey from one state to the other might take only seconds.

I sat down at the kitchen table and put my head in my hands.

I thought about Bella and the life she might now never have. Then I thought about me and Barney and all the energy I had invested in his house, then the break-up, and then being distraught over Susan, and slowly – very slowly – I began to realise how futile my tears had actually been. He didn't love me, he had *never* loved me, and no matter how I wept and railed and wished it wasn't so, there was nothing I could have done to change any of it.

Suddenly, I was aware of a new emotion. I homed in on it and, to my astonishment, realised it was relief, as though someone had taken a heavy weight from my shoulders and thrown it into the sea.

Did this mean *I* had never really loved *him*?

One thing was for sure, though; I would never again waste precious time crying over what might have been. Revenge was all very well, but what I needed wasn't payback, it was to walk away from him, and live my life – a better life – with people who really cared about me.

In the darkness, I could make out a shadowy lump on the table in front of me. I reached out my hand and my fingers closed around the shell of Bella's iPod. Pulling out the headphones and fumbling for the 'play' button, I sent Bella's deep, bluesy voice flooding out into the kitchen; filling the empty gloom with sound and vitality, life and optimism.

All I could do, I reasoned, was hope: hope that she would recover, hope that we would both eventually pull our lives around, and hope that there was the strength within us for the fight.

Hope.

It wasn't much, but it was a start.

All I needed to do now was find some.

Out of nowhere, a knock at the front door cut through my thoughts.

I pressed the 'stop' button on the iPod, plunging the kitchen again into sepulchral silence. It was past midnight; who the hell made house calls at this time?

I had no idea, but whoever-they-were knocked again.

My already spooked brain was set to overload.

Without a sound, I rose and made my way over to one of the kitchen cupboards where I helped myself to the heaviest, most threatening-looking frying pan I could find. Then I walked over to the front door and slowly drew back the bolt.

'I am about to open the door,' I announced, 'it's important you understand that I am armed and bordering on the psychotic. Any sudden moves and I will whack first and ask questions later – is that clear?'

With that, I flung the door open and a familiar voice said:

'Watch what you're doing with that thing, it might go off.'

It was Josh.

I stood staring at him, the frying pan frozen in mid-air and the adrenalin trickling slowly out of my body. I was pleased it was Josh on the other side of the door rather than a six-foot gangster waving an Uzi – but once you'd said that, you'd pretty much said everything.

'The door downstairs wasn't locked,' he explained sheepishly. 'I kind of let myself in.'

'Even so – I mean – what the *hell*?' I managed at last.

It wasn't the most articulate of sentences but it was the best I could do given the circumstances.

'I could say the same about you,' he observed pleasantly, gesturing towards the frying pan. 'Is this how you normally greet callers, or were you making a special effort just for me?'

'It's just . . .' I shrugged, lowering the pan and catching myself a blow on the knee as I did so. 'It's, well . . . let's say that today has been a complete shitting nightmare. Yes, "shitting nightmare". I quite like that; it pretty much sums things up.'

Josh gave me a sympathetic smile.

'Then it's your lucky day,' he replied, 'because I am here in my complete-shitting-nightmare-clean-up capacity, to save the day and restore order to your troubled world. Do you want to tell me what happened?'

Something in the tone of his voice told me that he was genuinely concerned.

'It's Bella,' I said, the words out of my mouth before I could stop them. 'Bella's in hospital and I don't know if she's going to live or die.'

The smile vanished from Josh's face.

'Oh man,' he said. 'That's terrible. I'm sorry, Flora; really, really sorry. Is there anything I can do to help? Anything at all?'

As he spoke, a wave of total exhaustion washed over me. I leaned against the door frame and allowed myself to slither down on to the floor. For a moment, silence ensued. An awkward, toe-curling, stomach-clenching silence. Then Josh sat down at right-angles to me; his back against the wall, his shoulder almost touching mine.

'I don't want to intrude,' he said softly. 'There is a

fine line between shitting-nightmare territory and other people interfering. I only came round to give you this.'

He delved into the pocket of his hoodie bag and pulled out Lisa's gossamer-like shrug.

'I was going to leave it behind one of the flower pots outside but when I saw the street door open, I became concerned. I wanted to check you were OK.'

'No,' I said, 'I think I can categorically say that I am *not* OK.'

Out on the street there was a noise – a bang; probably just a car backfiring but it made me cry out. I covered my face with my hands.

'Flora' – Josh swung round and crouched down next to me – 'I'm worried. Seriously. You're not in any fit state to be on your own. Is there someone I can call – someone who would stay here with you tonight and look after you?'

I shook my head.

'There is no one, Josh,' I said, 'I'm on my own with this one.'

Even though we weren't touching, I could sense his body close to mine. I knew exactly where he was, even without looking.

'It may be the last thing you want – after what hap - pened – but, well, would you consider letting me stay with you?'

The word 'no' hung unspoken on my lips as the universe unfolded around me, a cold and unforgiving place.

'Just as a friend,' he added. 'Absolutely no benefits. I promise.'

He held out his hand towards me and wiggled his fingers, just visible in the orange twilight. I thought of Bella lying in a bed at St Peter's hooked up to goodness only knew how many different bleeping machines – and took it. It felt warm and solid and the connection with another human being gave me the tiniest ray of hope for the future.

Hope.

I had found some.

Josh squeezed my fingers.

'This matters to me, Flora. *You* matter to me. This is the least I can do.'

'Thank you,' I said quietly. 'It would be wonderful if you could just stay for a couple of hours so that I can get some sleep. I'm so freaked out I don't think I'd drop off on my own.'

Josh pulled me in towards him and put his arm round my shoulders. I was so exhausted I didn't try and pull away. Instead, I allowed myself to fall against the warmth of his body and, slowly, I drifted off into a dreamless slumber.

# 16

I woke up with a crick in my neck and my head pounding. For a second or two, I had no idea where I was. I sat up and pushed a raft of unruly bed-hair out of my face and blinked. Then a door opened, ushering in a shaft of sunlight – and Josh.

'Coffee,' he said, offering me one of the two mugs he held in his hand. 'I hate to disturb you but your phone has been ringing and I thought you'd want to take it.'

'Thanks,' I said, realising with a jolt that I was in Bella's bed. 'How on earth did I get here?'

Josh perched on the edge of the duvet, took my phone out of his pocket and handed it to me.

'You were beyond exhausted,' he said. 'You fell asleep on me in the hall with the front door open and the frying pan still in your hand. I didn't think it was the most comfortable way to spend the night so I carried you in here.'

As he spoke, the events of the day before swung into unhappy focus. A big, swirling vortex of fear welled up in my stomach and all I wanted to do was throw the duvet back over my head and hide until someone else had cleared up the mess. *Make the scary stuff go away, Mummy.*

But that wasn't going to happen: I needed to get up,

look the scary stuff in the face and deal with it myself. Josh took a sip of coffee.

'I slept on the couch, by the way.' As he spoke Josh did not meet my eye.

'Thanks,' I said. 'I mean, good. I mean, I hope it was comfortable.'

The juxtaposition of the ideas of 'Josh' and 'couch', after our living-room escapades on Wednesday night, was highly inflammatory.

I looked down at my phone and pressed the 'last caller redial' button as Josh slipped discreetly out of the room.

'Where have you been?' Lisa's Minnie Mouse voice ripped through the ether and bounced off my eardrums. 'I called at least a minute ago.'

'Sorry,' I said, pulling myself up into a sitting position in bed and realising with a flood of relief that I was still fully clothed, 'my phone was in the living room and I didn't hear it. Josh just brought it in.'

'Josh?' Lisa switched seamlessly into FBI interrogator mode. 'What's Josh doing there?'

'No,' I quickly corrected her, 'it's not like that. It's—'

'Fine. I'll get the truth out of you later,' interrupted Lisa. 'Right now you need to know that Bella's awake and asking for you.'

'Yes,' I said, scrambling out of the covers. 'Yes, of course. I'll be with you ASAP. I'll bring in some stuff for her.'

'Good thinking, Batgirl,' Lisa said approvingly. 'We'll see you in fifteen.'

I put the phone down and pulled an overnight bag out of Bella's wardrobe. Into it I threw a couple of pairs of clean pyjamas, her dressing-gown, some socks and a few toiletries.

'Bella's come round!' I called out to Josh, whom I could hear messing about in the kitchen. 'I'm needed back at the hospital. Would you be able to find a cab firm on that SuperConnect interweb thingie of yours?'

'Excellent news, but you won't need a cab.' Josh came back into the bedroom and handed me a plate with a slice of buttered toast on it. 'My car's out front; I'll drive you.'

I hesitated. Josh in my darkest hour was one thing; Josh on a bright, sunny morning, after Bella had come round from the anaesthetic and the universe felt a decidedly less menacing place, was something else.

'You're still exhausted,' he said firmly, correctly reading my hesitation as a likely refusal, 'and before you say it, it's no trouble at all.'

I straightened up and pushed my unruly mop of hair out of my face.

'No, really,' I replied, 'it's fine.'

Josh gave me a funny look.

'I hate to say it,' he began, 'I really, really hate to bring this up . . .'

A feeling of dread zoomed in and hovered over me.

'But?' I threw three pairs of pants into the bag and zipped it up. 'Go on, Josh, spit it out.'

'Is this about Marty? Or . . .' He paused. '. . . should I say *still* about Marty?'

I carried the bag into the hall and dumped it by the front door.

'Of course not,' I replied as lightly as I could, despite the fact I felt as though foxes were gnawing at my innards. 'Who you sleep with is none of my business.'

*Let it go. Life's too short to get hung up on men, be they Barney or Josh.*

'Really?' He raised a single eyebrow. 'Then why won't you accept my offer of a lift to the hospital?'

It wasn't a question I trusted myself to answer, so instead I walked into my bedroom to find myself some clean clothes. Josh followed. And he wasn't about to take my silence for an answer.

'Marty is not my girlfriend,' he said. 'What happened on Wednesday was unpleasant and embarrassing but I was not cheating on anyone. Friends. Benefits. That's all.'

I looked up from my chest of drawers, T-shirt in hand. Despite my best efforts, the foxes gnawed even harder.

'And she knows that, does she? Because from the look on her face, I don't reckon she thought of herself as just your friend, no matter what the benefits were. Have you spoken to her?'

'No.' He looked down at his shoes. 'Perhaps I should have done, but I wanted to talk to you first.'

'Hedging your bets?' I hadn't meant to sound so cynical and I could have kicked myself as the words left my lips.

Josh threw up his hands in exasperation.

'Why are you so determined to think the worst of me, Flora? No, I am not hedging my bets, as you put it, I wanted to see if we could salvage something from this – this – mess first.'

I took my clothes into the bathroom, shut the door and picked up my toothbrush. Josh parked himself directly outside.

'Do you believe me?' he called through the woodwork.

I paused, mid-tooth clean. I wanted very much to believe that Josh was one of the good guys; he had given me hope and that meant a lot.

But hope was only the start. I would need more than that before I trusted my heart to anyone else.

'It doesn't make any difference if I believe you or not,' I said, throwing on my clothes and wiping cleanser across my unwashed face. 'None of it matters.'

'It matters to me,' Josh replied.

I threw open the door and picked up the overnight bag.

'Josh, go and talk to Marty. Go and sort things out with her. Please. She's part of your life here; she's part of SuperConnect. I'm not.'

'But you *could* be, Flora; if you wanted to.'

I looked down at my feet. Why did this have to be so hard?

Josh took the bag from my hands.

'All right, maybe now isn't the best time for us to be

having this discussion,' he said. 'Just get your ass in gear or Bella will be wondering if you've left the country.'

Toby was waiting for me in reception.

'Good news,' he said, 'she's fully conscious and the doctor has just checked her over and it looks as though she's going to be fine.'

'Yesssssssss!' Toby and I punched the air in a display of synchronised celebration and high fived.

'She's been asking for you,' he continued, regaining his composure, 'and the nurse says we can see her, but only for five minutes – she's still very weak.'

Toby led me back down the now-familiar corridor. When we reached the little waiting room I looked through the glass in the door and saw Lisa trying to get comfortable in one of the easy chairs (which, I'd decided after my own experience of them, probably contravened the Trade Descriptions Act by its use of the word 'easy').

Toby opened the door and Lisa flashed me something that wanted very much to be a cheery, laid-back smile – only it wasn't.

'Hi,' I said, 'how are you?'

'Oh' – Lisa waved her hand vaguely – 'as well as can be expected. No sleep, the world's most disgusting coffee pumping round my system and only the make-up I carry in my purse to do the emergency repairs this morning. What's happening?'

Her eyes looked from me to Toby and back again.

'Apart from Josh, of course.'

I ignored her.

'Steve,' I said. 'I've left messages for him on his voicemail but he's not rung back. I don't suppose by any chance he's been in to see Bella, has he?'

Toby shook his head.

'Do we say anything?' he asked.

'No,' sighed Lisa, 'not yet. She's not in any fit state. And you never know, he may show today. No point in making trouble where there isn't any.'

'Yet,' added Toby darkly.

There was a tap on the door and a tiny, dark-haired nurse put her head into the room.

'I'll take you down now,' she said. 'Follow me.'

Toby and I walked towards the door.

'C'mon, Lisa,' Toby called, 'you heard what the lady said: we can go and see her.'

But Lisa didn't move.

I took a step over towards her.

'Lisa?' I asked softly. 'Are you OK?'

'Yes,' she replied in a tight little voice, 'of course I'm OK. When am I ever not OK?'

'When your best friend collapses and almost dies and then pulls through against the odds?' I replied. 'It's just a hunch, but it would be enough to make me cry.'

'I am not crying,' said Lisa defiantly, still staring at her lap. 'I told you, I am fine. I have to be fine. It's my *job* to be fine – otherwise who would pick up the pieces for you lot?'

'Come on, Lisa.' Toby slid down beside her and slipped his arm round her shoulders. 'It's nothing to be ashamed of. And Bella's going to be absolutely one hundred per cent A-OK.'

Lisa looked up: her eyes were red and swollen and a single tear was tracking a path through her otherwise flawless make-up.

'But she might *not* have been.' She gave a short, rasping breath. 'It's so shitty; it's so, so shitty. You live this life and you always think it's going to get better; that all the crap will disappear; that this year will be better than the one before. Then bang: one day you wake up and you're dead.'

Toby looked at her doubtfully.

'I don't think you *can* wake up dead,' he said, 'I think the point with the whole death fadoodle is that you don't wake up at all.'

'Oh, wake up, schmake up – whatever!' snapped Lisa. 'The point is you can be perfectly healthy one minute then – bang – you're six feet under with every - one standing round your grave saying what a wonderful, warm, caring person you were.'

'Oh, Lisa.' Toby hugged her. 'You know no one would ever say that about you.'

'Toby!' I cut in. 'You are not helping here.'

I pulled a tissue out of a box sitting on the side and handed it to her. Lisa took it gratefully and dabbed at her eyes.

'Well, all right then,' he tried again, 'we love you, Lisa. We love you now, here, whilst you're alive.'

248

Lisa looked up at him and her bottom lip trembled ominously.

'No, you don't,' she said, 'not really. We all go round saying it, "Oh I just *love* you; you are my *best* friend." But you don't. You're fond of me – you're probably quite scared of me – but you don't love me. Not really. And before I die, I want to be loved.'

The nurse tapped gently on the door.

'Hey! You guys! She's waiting for you.'

Lisa gave a tremendous sniff, pinched the bridge of her nose and then stood up.

'But so what? Forget it. Forget I said any of it. It doesn't matter.'

Her voice was brittle and had the tiniest edge of a wobble to it.

I gave her arm a squeeze. 'Yes it does.'

She looked at me and there, just for the splittest of split seconds, was real loneliness deep in her big brown eyes.

Then she pulled her red mouth (fresh lipstick courtesy of the supplies in her handbag) back into a bright, carefree smile. Normal Lisa service had been resumed.

Or so she wanted us to think.

And I almost – *almost* – believed it.

'Now's your chance to do something about it,' I whispered as we walked down the corridor behind the nurse. 'You're still living and breathing. Any day you are up on the surface walking around is a day you can change your life for the better.'

Lisa gave an almost imperceptible shake of her head and looked away.

I was about to suggest she gave Bill and his undying devotion a go when the nurse opened the door into an airy little bedroom. As we entered, Bella turned her head towards us and managed to summon up the faintest ghost of a smile.

'Hey!' she said. 'What's up?'

'Oh, same old same old.' Toby leant over and kissed her on the forehead. 'Some crazy girl got sick at the Lizard and had to be rushed to the Emergency Room. Beyond boring, really.'

Bella nearly laughed but winced instead.

'Stitches,' she said, 'not good.'

'So.' Lisa, her public face stapled back on, pulled one of the chairs up to the bedside and settled herself on it. 'Are you going to quit scaring the hell out of your friends or do you have anything else up your sleeve – appendicitis, perhaps? Or maybe a heart murmur?' She took Bella's drip-free hand and gave it an affectionate squeeze.

'Are you feeling OK?' I asked, perching on the other side of the bed.

Bella shifted slightly under the covers.

'Better than I was,' she said, 'but still a bit groggy. Major operations suck.'

'You're not wrong there,' I said, stroking her hair away from her face. 'Have they . . . I mean, did they tell you what was wrong?'

Bella nodded and her eyes closed, briefly.

'I'm sorry,' I said, 'I'm so, so sorry. I wish it could have been almost anything else.'

'Me too,' Bella replied, 'me too. I had no idea. Really, I had no idea.' She leaned her cheek against my hand. 'Something was alive and now it's not,' she said softly. 'It makes you think.'

What it made me think about was Steve – and the fact he seemed totally indifferent to Bella's plight. My stomach twisted nauseatingly.

'I told your mum,' I said, 'or rather, I rang my mum and told her to go round and tell yours. I realise you might not have wanted her to know, but when we arrived here last night I didn't know if you were going to make it. I decided that if it was me, I'd want my mother to be in the loop. I didn't tell her anything else, though.'

Bella went very, very still. I was glad I could see her blinking and the sheets moving as she breathed or I'd have been leaping up to ring the emergency buzzer.

Lisa squeezed Bella's hand. 'She did the right thing, sweetie, and you *know* it was the right thing. Besides, you mustn't get mad or you'll burst your stitches and there's no way I want that happening when I'm around to witness it.'

Bella looked up at me.

OK, I thought; here we go.

But – no.

'Thanks, Flo,' she said. 'Is she coming over?'

'The plan is for us to speak again today,' I said. 'What do you want me to say to her?'

251

Bella stared up at the ceiling and bit her lip.

'It's fine,' she said, 'I'll call her. This rubbish about my suspension has gone on long enough and besides, it really is true, when things get rough, all a girl really wants is her mum to help make it better.'

'Are you sure?' I asked. 'Are you *surety-sure*?'

Hearing the words Granny always used when she needed us to make a final decision, Bella's face relaxed. She nodded at me.

'Yup, I'm surety-sure,' she said with a watery smile and squeezed my hand. Then: 'Steve. Did you call Steve?'

I looked at Lisa. We were heading for difficult territory.

'Don't go silent on me, Flora.' Bella looked pale, but her chin was jutting out in that determined fashion I remembered from childhood. She wasn't about to be fobbed off. 'Did you ring Steve? Does he know I'm here?'

'I – ah – I rang him last night, Bella; but I couldn't get through. I left messages. I guess he may not have got them yet.'

My phone buzzed with an incoming text message. For one wild, hopeful minute, I thought it might be Steve. After all, who else could it be? Virtually all the people I knew in San Francisco were in the room with me – and none of them had their phones out. I slipped my mobile out of my bag and my heart sank: it was Josh.

'Flo?' Bella's voice was insistent and hopeful. 'Who was the text from?'

I dropped the handset back into my bag. Josh knew I was busy; he would have to wait.

'Not Steve, I'm afraid. I'm sorry.'

Bella sank back on to her pillows.

'So tell me. Last night. What happened? Who went through?'

'We did,' said Toby.

Bella sat bolt upright in bed, her eyes wide.

'No way!' she cried.

'Way!' replied Toby, a grin creeping across his face. 'The Elvis impersonator guy pulled out after he won a trip to Vegas in an internet poker game and The What – that's a Who tribute,' he added for my benefit, 'had a fight in the men's room so Bill barred them; and because we didn't formally withdraw, it meant Abbadabbatastic were technically the only group left and went through by default.' He gave Bella a sad little smile. 'But no money, though, seeing as there was no music.'

Bella looked out of the window for a moment or two and then turned back to face us. It clearly wasn't the lack of cash that was on her mind.

'He's not coming, is he? Steve isn't coming to see me.'

We all spoke at once:

'We don't know that—'

'He's probably busy—'

'He might well be along later—'

Bella shook her head.

'He's not coming.' This was said as a statement of fact. 'If he was, he'd have been here by now.'

Lisa examined her nails; Toby looked at his feet; I stared at the bedcovers.

'I tried,' I said at last. 'I've rung four times. His phone seems to be switched off.'

This was half the truth, but it was the most palatable half.

Bella put her hand out. 'Can I have my mobile please.'

'Well, I'm not sure if you're allowed—' Lisa interjected.

'I don't care,' replied Bella. 'Please give me my phone.'

I handed over her bag and she pulled out the handset and pressed a couple of things on the screen.

'Hi Steve,' she said, 'it's Bella. I'm in St Peter's, but you know that already. You also know that I've lost the baby but it may be news to you that I'm going to be OK. If you want to see me, you know where I am. Otherwise, have a nice life. Your choice.'

And she hung up and put the phone back in her bag.

For a while there was silence. Bella's eyes glittered suspiciously, but her face remained resolute. Then there was a knock on the door and Joy-Anne's face appeared through the glass.

'You guys have had far longer than you should,' she chided us. 'Bella here needs her rest. You can all come back at six tonight.'

The short little nurse with the dark bob bustled into the room and began to take blood-pressure equipment out of a box, winding the band round Bella's arm.

We shuffled out into the corridor.

'She's going to be fine,' said Joy-Anne, 'she didn't lose too much blood so we don't need a transfusion, it's just a case of letting her convalesce. And as for the bill . . .' She shrugged awkwardly. 'We all know the situation with regards to Mrs Hampton. All the staff here are giving their care for free – even the surgical team. She'll only be charged for the room and the drugs and some of the other fixed costs. It won't write the bill off, but it should help. Bella is still a highly valued colleague – whatever else might be affecting her career.'

'Thank you,' I said, genuinely touched, 'that means a lot. Look, can I ask you about the inquiry?'

Joy-Anne looked uncomfortable.

'Not really,' she said, 'it's all supposed to be confidential. But, as I said before, no one here can believe Bella would be responsible for anything like that; she was always so careful.'

'But presumably there were toxicology reports?' I said. 'I mean, they must be basing their case on *something*.'

'The reports so far have been inconclusive' – Joy-Anne looked round to make sure nobody could hear her – 'and I only know that because I have a friend in pathology. But the Hamptons seem pretty determined to pursue the case. I don't know why – maybe they think if they cry foul for loud enough, the hospital will pay them to shut up and go away.'

Her pager bleeped.

'Sorry,' she said, 'I've got to run. I'll let you know if there's any news on Belle – I promise.'

And away she went.

Lisa smothered a delicate yawn.

'Come on, I'll give you both a lift home.' Toby pulled his car keys out of his pocket and jangled them as we began to walk down the corridor towards the reception area.

'So,' said Lisa, 'does this mean you and Mr SuperConnect are reconnecting?'

I shook my head. Lisa sighed.

'That's a shame,' she said, 'I don't know what it was, but there was something rather sweet about the pair of you.'

'And on the down side,' I said, 'we live five thousand miles apart, he's an IT genius with a brain the size of a planet and our time together has pretty much been an unmitigated disaster.'

'But?' said Lisa. 'I sense a great big "but" hanging around at the end of that sentence. And I'm not talking about Fat-Boy Bathurst's here, either.'

'Hey!' Toby patted the back pocket of his jeans. 'That's one hundred per cent muscle, I'll have you know.'

'Is it Barney?' she asked.

'Barney?' I echoed.

'Yes, Barney. The schmuck who dumped you on

256

your birthday. Barney. Is he – or your feelings for him – stopping you getting it on with Josh?'

I paused.

'I was thinking about Barney last night and you know what? If I'd loved him, I'd never even have looked twice at Josh.'

'So what did you love?'

I hesitated. This wasn't easy for me to admit.

'I think it was the house – or at least, it was what the house stood for. I thought it would mean security and stability and a firm foundation to build the rest of my life upon. But more fool me, but it turns out it didn't. God, does that make me sound really shallow?'

Lisa shook her head.

'The first important thing is that you're not still trapped in that rut. And the *other* important thing is that you connected – excuse the pun – with Josh. Now be honest, Flora, how do you feel about him?'

An image of Josh, a grin the size of the Great Wall of China plastered across his face, tugging at my hand as we ran on to Ocean Beach flashed into my brain and my heart promptly turned over.

I looked away so that Lisa wouldn't be able to read my expression.

It didn't matter what I felt about Josh, or even what he felt about Marty. In a few days I would get on an aeroplane and fly out of his life for ever. That was the real point.

'How long it lasts is up to you,' Lisa replied, her scary-mind-reader abilities coming into play. 'It's got nothing to do with geography or what happened on Wednesday or anything else. Remember what Bella told you: you gotta find your tribe. If Josh is part of your tribe, you'll stick together somehow.'

We all three stepped out, blinking, into the morning sun.

'Maybe,' I said, 'and thanks for the offer of the lift, Toby, but I fancy a walk. I think I'll call in at the Apple Pie for some breakfast. It's not far.'

Then, before Lisa could pester me further about Josh, I waved and strode off across the hospital car park.

# 17

I had to walk right past Bella's house in order to get to the Apple Pie and, as I hadn't showered that day, I decided to pop in and freshen up. After all, I was fond of Elvira and Sylvie and didn't want to put off any of their customers with my bodily aromas. I zipped into the shower, zipped out again and was just borrowing one of Bella's lipsticks when I saw something looking at me from her bedside table.

Tentatively I picked it up. It was a business card with a picture of a microphone on it and the words: 'Steve Morgan. Impresario and Band Manager'.

There was a mobile number, a landline and a business address. I pulled my phone out and tried the landline: just like the mobile it rang and rang and rang.

Steve was proving remarkably difficult to get hold of.

I shrugged and put the card in my purse, thinking it might come in useful. Then, realising I was very hungry indeed and it was past lunchtime, I got dressed and hurried out of the flat.

'Hi, honey!' Elvira lifted her hand in greeting from behind the counter. 'He's already here.'

'Who?' I asked, not unreasonably.

'Your Josh,' replied Elvira and, before I had time to

protest about her choice of pronouns, she beckoned me towards the counter and lowered her voice.

'You know,' Elvira continued, 'this ain't none of my business, but he's a sweet boy. Been coming in here ever since he first moved to San Francisco. He went through a rough time too, not long ago.'

I looked at her.

'How do you know that?' I asked. 'Did he tell you?'

She shook her head.

'I just know,' she said. 'I've been in this business long enough to read people's faces and he's been lacklustre for a while. But this last week, he was like a different man. I thought it might have been something to do with you.'

'No' – I shrugged – 'we barely know each other. Must be something else. Maybe your steak and eggs without eggs just got better.'

Elvira gave a howl of laughter.

'I don't think so, honey,' she said. 'Like I said, sometimes you just *know*. So go easy on him, yeah? I reckon his heart is in your hands.'

Maybe I don't want his heart in my hands, I thought. I'm not even sure if I can be trusted to look after my own, let alone take responsibility for someone else's.

Elvira grinned.

'Take a seat and I'll bring you your coffee. Usual?'

'Yes, please,' I said, strangely buoyed-up to think I now had a 'usual'. 'Is there any more news on the leases?'

260

Elvira shook her head and sighed.

'Sylvie is at a meeting with the landlord just now,' she said, 'but I don't hold out much hope. At the end of the day, he's an old man and it's going to be in his interests to sell up rather than keep taking our rents. It's not personal, it's business.'

'Even though it feels pretty personal,' I added.

'Drusilla had some idea that it might be connected to a company called "Stealth Holdings".'

I thought about Mr McMaster and the letter I'd inadvertently cast my eye over and my cheeks grew hot.

'Really?' I asked, hoping that Elvira couldn't read minds as well as faces. 'And why does she think that?'

Elvira shrugged.

'She said she read something in a newspaper about this company that buys up land, sits on it for goodness only knows how long, and then builds shopping malls or supermarkets.'

'Really?' I said again, trying again to sound surprised.

*Once more with feeling.*

'Of course, the development regulations here in San Francisco are pretty tight, but you never know what's going to happen in the future. This diner has been in our family for fifty years, I would cry if it was bulldozed to make room for a shopping mall. And it's not just the Apple Pie – this whole area of the city would die if Hope Street went.'

'It won't,' I said bravely, my distaste for Mr

McMaster and all his works growing stronger by the second. 'We'll think of something.'

'Like what?' Elvira turned round to attend to the coffee machine, which was hissing and spitting like an angry tom cat.

'I don't know,' I replied, taking comfort in a circular argument, 'because we haven't thought of it yet. But nil desperandum. Where there's life, there's hope.'

'If you say so, honey.' Elvira sounded weary. 'Anyway, your man's over there waiting for you.'

I glanced over at Josh.

He was certainly not my 'man'. However, he'd been good to me last night. I at least owed him a cup of coffee and a thank you.

'Hey!' He flashed one of his zillion-watt grins in my direction as I sat down.

My stomach immediately did one of its loop-the-loop performances but I took a deep breath and waited for it to subside. As I'd said to Lisa, there was simply no point.

'Hey,' I echoed back, leaning over to catch a glimpse of his screen.

It was lines of text made out of a random collection of letters, numbers and symbols. Programming code, I assumed.

Either that or he visited some really weird websites.

'I need to thank you,' I replied. 'For looking after me last night and the lift to the hospital. I've been at a bit of a low ebb.'

Josh's eyes flickered over my face.

'I did notice,' he said. 'My low-ebb radar isn't too bad – for a guy, that is.'

'You didn't have to,' I continued. 'It was above the call of duty.'

'I know I didn't have to' – a smile flickered round the corners of his mouth – 'but I wanted to.'

The smile made me feel a bit funny, so I took Steve's card out of my wallet and put it on the table in front of him.

'I found this,' I said, 'it belongs to Bella's boyfriend. I was thinking I might pay him a visit at work.'

Josh tapped the address on the card. He had lovely wrists, I noted, shapely and slender and just the right tone of olive brown.

'That's not a nice part of town,' he said. 'I don't recommend dropping in.'

'Thanks for the local knowledge,' I said, 'but I don't know what else to try. I've rung his home number and no one answers and I've rung his cell phone and still no one answers. I'm running out of options.'

Josh fixed his gaze on me.

'Flo,' he said, 'I really, really hate to have to say this, but maybe he doesn't want to be contacted.'

He was right; of course he was. All of us: me, Toby, Lisa, Bella and now Josh had all had the same thought at various points during the last few hours.

'I know,' I replied, 'but I need to hear him say that with my own ears.'

Josh nodded, then pressed a couple of keys on his

laptop and a new document appeared. He typed the words: *STEVE: WHAT WE KNOW* at the top.

'So,' he said, 'let's see what the magic of the internet can throw up. What have we got on him?'

I pointed at the card.

'He's called Steve Morgan; he's an impresario and band manager; he works from 131A Delaney Street and he's not answering his phone.'

'OK.' Josh tapped the keyboard, waited, typed something in and scanned the screen. 'So, these are the voting resisters, but his name isn't on them – not the San Francisco area ones, anyway. However, this might prove more fruitful.'

Josh tapped another few keys and we were transported to a well-known social networking site; and the face grinning out at me from the screen was – Steve!

'Brilliant.' I allowed myself a small cheer and jiggled a bit on my seat with jubilation. 'How did you do that?'

Josh shook his head sadly, as though dismayed by the depths of my ignorance.

'Steve hasn't taken any security measures,' he replied, 'it's all open to the public.'

He keyed in something else and suddenly there was a picture of me, my arms round Barney's neck, grinning like a mad person into the camera. My breath caught in my throat: that photo had been taken at Barney's sister's wedding; I'd been the bridesmaid and caught the bouquet and everyone had cheered and Barney's mother had kept hinting how much she loved going to weddings and—

264

I stopped and a little shiver ran down my spine.

I realised I was more upset by the fact the photo was in the public domain than the fact it involved Barney. To be honest, the idea that his mum had wanted us to get married struck me as mildly creepy.

'But . . . I – I don't even *do* social networking,' I protested. 'I am the only person in the whole world who doesn't. How the hell did *that* get there?'

'You were tagged in a photo that was uploaded by someone else. I just put your name in and *bingo*! Three hundred and twenty-five thousand results for Flora Fielding. Look.'

He clicked again and all my details popped up on the screen: name, date of birth, email and mobile number. There was even a photo of me (pre-Barney) on a night out at university wearing a Snow White costume and downing vodka shots. It was all in full view on the internet for my mum, Brenda, the McMasters and anyone else who wanted to gawp at, copy, or use for their own nefarious purposes.

'Oh shit,' I murmured.

'You're welcome.' Josh grinned and, with a couple of clicks, we were back to Steve.

'So we can get to Steve via his social network page?' I asked, hopeful that he would be freely advertising his home address.

Josh shook his head.

'He barely uses it,' he said, 'it's got gig dates and some work-related stuff but nothing personal; not even an email contact.'

'Oh.' My heart sank. 'But I thought there was something called an internet footprint that you could use to track people down.'

'Sort of. In theory you can track someone through the websites they have visited.'

'Great,' I said, 'so what are we waiting for?'

'Well,' replied Josh, 'first we'd need his IP address – that's the address of the company he uses to access the web – then we'd have to ask them to hand over all the data.'

'Really?' My eyes were like saucers. 'And they would? Just like that?'

Josh made a tutting sound with his tongue.

'No, of course not,' he said. 'They'd say no, then we'd have to go to court and . . .'

I flopped back, disappointed, into my seat. Court – lawyers – more expense and time. It was a no-go.

'Although . . .' Josh hesitated. 'I have this friend.' His eyes flashed round the room and he lowered his voice. 'He owns a storage facility.'

Storage? As in lock-up? What was he on about? And why was he looking so shifty?

'A data-storage facility. Where lots of internet companies keep their customer information. If I asked nicely he might let me in to rummage around.'

'Josh,' I said firmly, 'is that legal?'

Josh rubbed the bridge of his nose thoughtfully.

'Well,' he said slowly, 'I suppose it depends on your definition of the word "legal".'

'Forget it,' I said, 'it's a kind offer, but Steve isn't worth getting a criminal record over.'

Elvira appeared at our table and Josh closed the lid of his laptop.

'Coffees,' she said. 'Sorry about the delay.'

Her face looked even more drawn and tired than it had when I'd arrived and, although she was obviously trying to hide it, she wasn't doing a terribly good job.

'Goodness!' I said. 'What's happened?'

Elvira's shoulders sagged and she stared out of the window for a moment or two to regain her composure.

'I had a call from Sylvie,' she whispered. 'The landlord is going to sell. This is it; it is officially the end of the road.'

Josh looked up at me blankly.

'Really, Josh,' I chided, 'where have you *been*? A land-holding company wants to take over the leases on the Hope Street shops.'

'Sylvie says Drusilla asked if it was Stealth Holdings behind the offer but the landlord wouldn't tell her.' She looked grey with stress. 'I guess it doesn't really matter. Either they'll tear the place down eventually or they won't. There's not a lot we can do about it apart from keep on praying.'

Feeling utterly helpless, I patted her hand. Even if I'd had the presence of mind to *read* the letter in Earl's study, I couldn't have told anyone about its contents: it would have been career suicide (and goodness only knew what else besides).

'Sit down,' I said, shuffling up on the banquette. 'Please. Before you fall down.'

Elvira shook her head.

'If I stop now, honey, you won't get me going again. If these people could just see how their decisions affect the little folks like us – well . . .'

Josh meanwhile had flipped the lid of the laptop back open and was typing furiously.

'Look' – he turned the screen round so that Elvira and I could see – 'these are the sites Stealth Holdings have bought in the past ten years. And these are the ones where they have built malls or sold them on to supermarkets. I bet that's their game plan: buy up a site, hold on to it for however long they need to, then sell it on to someone who wants to develop it.'

The picture was a map of the States with hundreds of little red dots on it.

'Malls? Supermarkets? This makes me so *mad*.' Elvira threw her tea towel on the table. 'These boys with their big bucks think they can buy up a community like Hope Street and then rip the heart out of it. You know, there simply ain't no justice in this world. We are hard-working Americans and we don't get no respect no more.'

The diner erupted in a wave of rapturous applause. Cries of agreement echoed round the room.

'Respect, that's where it's at,' called out one of the customers from over by the counter. 'You respect me, and I'll respect you. But there ain't enough of it about.'

The words 'respect me' ricocheted through my mind

and then suddenly, like a bolt of lightning from a clear blue sky, an idea exploded in my brain. It was a pretty crazy idea, but from what I knew of the residents of Hope Street, that was exactly the sort of idea they liked best.

'Elvira!' I was up on my feet, my helplessness and frustration evaporating. 'You and Sylvie sing, don't you?'

I was remembering their Abba impersonation when Bella and I had dropped in for takeaway coffees.

'Well, we used to do a bit professionally,' she replied.

This was even better than I'd hoped.

'How much of a bit?' I asked.

'Oh,' Elvira shrugged. 'Just a bit. Couple of hits in the sixties. When we was younger. Motown. Nothing too big.'

*Motown? Nothing too big? Er, excuse me!*

'They were on *The Ed Sullivan Show* once,' piped up one of the customers seated at the counter, 'and they've got a gold disc.'

I looked up at the wall behind me and, sure enough, there in its glass case was a gold disc with the name 'The Chantilly Sisters' emblazoned across it.

With every new piece of information, the idea in my head was growing.

'And we still sing every Sunday at church with the choir,' Elvira continued. 'And in the shower; and the kitchen – in fact, pretty much anywhere else we can get away with it.'

She stood up, thrust her tea towel in her belt and

opened her mouth. As before, the voice that emerged was deep and rich; it might have matured over the years but had clearly lost none of its original power. The diner broke into rapturous applause once again. A few of the customers even mustered a standing ovation. Elvira smiled, bowed and flourished her tea towel theatrically at her audience.

'But singing ain't going to get us anywhere, honey. Singing is for young people. That Simon Cowell of yours doesn't want two grey old birds on his *Idol* programme.'

'This has got nothing to do with Simon Cowell.' I could barely contain the excitement rising inside me. 'Do you think you could get the choir together for a special performance?'

Elvira shrugged.

'Well, yes, I suppose so.'

'Good. Be here on Tuesday at six please. And all of you' – I gestured to the customers – 'can you be here too? And bring your friends – *all* your friends? It's to save Hope Street.'

They nodded and murmured their assent. I turned to Josh. My stomach was flipping and diving, but whether this was excitement about my brainwave or the effect of those Bay-blue eyes, I had no idea.

'And you,' I said, 'can you do live streaming?'

Josh frowned.

'Well, yes, but—'

'No buts, Josh; this is important. And SuperConnect, can anyone download it?'

'Well, again, yes, but—'

'Great. And the instant messaging – as a group thing?'

'I suppose so, but I don't see why—'

'You will. I need you here on Tuesday ready to go live on the internet. Can you do that?'

'But—'

'Great, I'll be in touch about the details later.'

I stood up.

'Who here has got a smart phone?'

About half the customers put their hands in the air.

'OK. Right. I want you to go to your app store or your internet search engine and find SuperConnect – all one word – got it?'

There were murmurs of assent from the customers.

'OK, it's a free download so if you wouldn't mind' – I cringed at how stereotypically English I sounded but pressed on nonetheless – 'please put it on your phones – your cells – and then send the link to everyone in your address book? All of them. I'd be really grateful. Thanks. Really kind of you. Jolly good.'

I smiled awkwardly and then slid off my seat.

Josh grabbed my hand.

'Flora,' he said, 'what the heck is going on?'

'We're getting SuperConnect up and running,' I said, 'and we're going to save Hope Street while we're at it. Or maybe it's the other way round; I'm not quite sure. The details are still a little woolly, but don't worry, I'll get them firmed up.'

Poor Josh looked as though someone had hit him

271

across the back of the head with a stuffed sock. He stared in delighted disbelief at people busily down-loading his app, then turned back to me.

'Tell me what you're doing with SuperConnect,' he said, his voice low and serious. 'And then tell me when we can talk – I mean, really talk.'

The tapping on the phones gradually stopped and everyone in the diner fell silent. Fifty pairs of eyes were trained on me and fifty pairs of ears strained to hear my answer.

'I was thinking about our conversation this morning,' he continued. 'I decided you were right and I spoke to Marty.'

I closed my eyes and took a deep breath. *He was about to tell me what he and Marty had decided to do about their relationship.*

'Oh?' I said, trying to sound nonchalant.

For something that shouldn't matter to me either way, it was having a profound effect upon my equilibrium.

'Yes.' He rubbed his nose as though he felt uneasy about what he was going to say next. 'You were right, Flora. She hadn't been seeing things in quite the same way as I had.'

My heart was beating so loudly, you could have used it as the bass line for one of Elvira's Motown hits. *Marty loved him – I knew it!*

'Right,' I said, feeling very peculiar indeed. 'Good. I mean, good for you.'

'And now that she and I have spoken, I think that you and I need to talk.'

'No, really, Josh, it's fine. You don't need to tell me anything. I'm pleased for you. Really pleased.'

*Certainly not here, in the middle of a packed diner with everyone looking at me.*

And, before he could say another word, I left. A stunned silence followed me out of the door and back on to the street.

# 18

Pushing Josh and Marty and how unhappy they made me feel out of my mind, I reached the end of the road and took out my phone. I typed Steve's business address into the SuperConnect map app and waited for the internet to work its magic. The location didn't seem to be too far away, so I memorised the route, put my phone back in my bag and set off on foot. It only took about ten minutes to leave the jolly, brightly coloured shop-fronts of Hope Street behind, turn a couple of corners and find myself in a run-down and neglected neighbourhood.

As I walked further, and the streets started to fill with litter, the paintwork began to peel from the buildings and the graffiti became more frequent and more offensive. Of course, I knew that districts like this had to exist even in a town as magical, beautiful and generally together as San Francisco, it's just that I hadn't planned to be visiting them on my holidays.

Or, indeed, at all.

I turned one final corner and there it was: 131A Delaney Street: a brick building with steel bars on the windows and a large, spray-painted message from an individual called LeeRoi, announcing that he had previously graced that particular location with his presence. I stepped up to the door and knocked. However, just as with the phone calls, there was no response. Two teenagers wearing hoodies, over-sized trainers and track pants watched me with the sort of bored interest that only adolescents can muster.

'Whatcha doin'?'

I turned round.

'Hi,' I said, wondering if they would be able to shed some light on Steve's whereabouts.

The boys stared at me, their faces impassive.

'I'm looking for someone,' I told them. 'A guy called Steve Morgan. This is his work address.'

The first two boys were now joined by a third dressed in identikit clothing. He was holding a dog that looked as though it had numbered a couple of velociraptors and maybe a sabre-toothed tiger among its recent ancestors.

'Are you the cops?' he asked.

'No,' I said, 'I'm English.'

The boys digested this information.

'So what's this Steve guy to you?' asked one.

It was a reasonable question and, I decided, there was no reason why they shouldn't know the truth.

'He got my cousin pregnant and she nearly died and he's run off. This is his work address.'

The boys shook their heads and the dog scratched its ear with its back leg.

'Man, that's *low*.'

'That's lower than low.'

'You want us to find him for you?'

'Um, no,' I said quickly, not entirely certain what their definition of "finding" might involve. 'It's – ah – very kind of you, but I think I'll do it by myself if that's OK. So – would you know where I could find him?'

They shook their heads collectively.

'Sorry,' one said apologetically. 'Never heard of anyone called Steve.'

I sighed.

'Oh well,' I said, 'thanks, guys. See you around.'

I turned and began to walk back despondently the way I had come. Then, suddenly:

'Hey, are you Flora?' asked the one with the dog.

I stopped dead in my tracks. How on earth did he know my name?

'Yes,' I admitted, wondering where this was going to lead.

'You've been going to the diner on Hope.'

For the first time, I began to feel rather apprehensive. Had they had me under some sort of surveillance?

'Yeeees,' I admitted slowly.

'Elvira's my godmother. She said she'd had an English girl called Flora in. She likes you.'

'I like her,' I replied, relief washing over me. 'And I'm going to be doing what I can to help her keep the diner open.'

The boys all shook their heads sadly.

'That business with their landlord – it's the pits, man.'

'They shouldn't treat decent people like that. It's disrespectful.'

'You know what' – I agreed 100 per cent with their analysis – 'I think you're right.' Then a thought struck me. 'You guys, you don't sing, do you?'

They stared at me as though I'd just suggested we charter the Space Shuttle and hop over to Jupiter for an inter-planetary rave.

'Yeah, *course* we sing, man,' said the guy with the dog, 'we're in the church choir.'

'And we do beat box,' said one of the others.

Then, before I knew it, they had all begun making various 'chu-dum, chu-dum', 'du-du-du-du', 'boom-boom' type noises.

They were pretty good.

'Do you know SuperConnect?' I asked.

They shook their heads.

'Download it on to your phones,' I said, 'and keep checking it for alerts. Godmother Elvira's going to need you.'

'Awesome, man.' They grinned and I turned, waved and hot-footed it back to civilisation – or at least to the hospital. I needed to see how Bella was doing.

I made my way down the interminable corridor towards Bella's room. By now, I should have known the route blindfolded; but as I turned a corner, I found myself in a part of the hospital I'd never seen before. It seemed to be an administrative area full of offices and secretaries scurrying around with clipboards and folders. I was just about to turn round and retrace my steps when I heard voices.

'I can assure you, Mrs Hampton, that we are conducting our investigations in the most thorough manner possible.'

I stopped dead in my tracks. *Mrs Hampton?*

About three doors ahead of me was a grey-haired doctor wearing the traditional white coat, another man and a woman with her back towards me.

The doctor continued:

'Miss Jones is a very experienced nurse. She has extensive training and experience and I am not pre-pared to be drawn on anything which might prejudice the inquiry. However, I can assure you that St Peter's Hospital is doing everything it can to get to the bottom of the matter.'

'But I'm not well,' protested the woman, 'I haven't been able to work since the incident and it's having a bad effect on our family finances.'

I ducked back round a corner into a waiting area and held my breath.

I knew that voice. I *knew it*. But I couldn't place it.

'I'm genuinely sorry to hear that, Mrs Hampton,' said the doctor, 'and I sincerely hope that after the hearing next week, everyone will be able to move on. However, in the meantime, I do not feel the circum-stances of the case allow me to discuss matters any further with you. I'm sorry.'

'But—' protested the woman.

'I'm sorry,' said the doctor firmly, 'this is no longer in my hands. Good day to you.'

As she went to walk back down the corridor, the

woman turned round to face me – and I got the shock of my life: it was Jessie. The herbal pill-popping temp I'd met at the McMasters' only a few days previously. What the hell was she doing saying she couldn't work?

Jessie and the man made their way in my direction. I threw myself into a chair, held a magazine up to cover my face and hoped they couldn't hear my heart (which was beating so loudly I'd have thought it was audible back in England).

'I'm not sure about this, Hal,' Jessie said under her breath. 'What do you say we just drop the claim?'

'Oh come on, Jessie, you were really sick. At the end of the day, the only person who gets stung is the insurance company and God knows we need the money.'

'I don't know, Hal. Oh – hold on a minute, would you.'

She stopped less than a foot away from me. I watched over the top of my magazine as she opened her handbag, undid the lid of a bottle and popped a couple of her herbal tablets into her mouth. She swallowed and then they went on their way out of the waiting room.

When I finally arrived in Bella's room, she was sitting up in bed reading a novel. She lifted her head as I opened the door to her room and smiled. I smiled back – at least she was going to be all right. That part of the nightmare was over.

'Hi,' I said, leaning over and kissing her, 'how are you feeling?'

Bella pulled a face.

'Pretty pants,' she said. 'In fact, beyond pants. I feel like a tyre that has had a puncture lost all its air and is bumping along on rock-bottom.'

I squeezed her arm.

'You've been pregnant,' I said, 'even though you didn't know; you've had masses of hormones charging round your body and now they're trailing off. You're bound to feel low.'

'I suppose so.' Bella shrugged. 'I still find it almost impossible to get my head round the idea that there was something living and growing inside me and now it's gone.'

'Oh, Belle,' I said, 'it had to go. It would have killed you otherwise.'

Bella's head dropped.

'I know. But it was still there.' She looked up and smiled, but it was a smile that contained no joy whatsoever. 'Steve,' she said, in a voice that contained the tiniest flicker of hope, 'has he called?'

I paused for a moment.

'I'm sorry,' I said, 'I am really, really sorry.'

She looked down at her lap.

'It's fine,' she said. 'Well, maybe not actually fine, but it's something I need to come to terms with. At first I pretended he was trying to ring me, only he couldn't get through because my mobile was off. Then I kidded myself that he really wanted to visit, but his work commitments meant that he was too busy. But, actually, he doesn't give a damn, does he?'

I looked at her and saw the pain in her face. I couldn't say anything.

'It's OK, Flora. You don't have to reply. I know. Things haven't been good between us for a while, but I thought we could sort it.'

'Maybe he just needs time,' I said, even though I knew neither of us would believe it, 'perhaps it's harder than we think for him to come to terms with what's happened to you?'

'Perhaps,' said Bella. 'But I also think it's time I had a bit of a reality check.' She took a deep breath. Then her eyes glittered with something that looked very much like determination. 'It's at times like these you find out who your real friends are. Anyway, enough about Steve – tell me what's been going on in the big, bad world outside.'

I paused. What I had to say wasn't going to be the easiest topic of conversation either.

'I've just seen Jessie Hampton,' I said.

Bella's mouth gaped open and she dropped her novel onto the floor.

'You mean you *spoke* to her?'

I shook my head.

'No, but I overheard a conversation between her, one of the doctors and another man, who I presume is her husband. Now, Bella, am I correct in thinking that she can't work?'

Bella nodded.

'Yes. Apparently she's better than she was physically, but she's prone to panic attacks and can't cope with the pressures of being in the workplace.'

'Right. Because I met her last week temping for Mr McMaster.'

Bella's mouth opened even wider and her eyes were like saucers.

'You're joking?'

'Luckily for you, no. So it should be pretty straight-forward to find out which agency she's with and get them to confirm she's fit for work.'

Bella slumped back against her pillows, a dazed expression on her face.

'I can't believe this,' she said. 'I literally can't believe this.'

'And there's something else,' I said, 'only it's just a hunch, so don't get too excited, but she carries these herbal tranquillisers round with her and pops them like Smarties. Now, is there any way that herbal tablets could have interfered with her medication whilst she was in here?'

Bella considered this.

'Well, it's possible,' she said. 'Certainly patients are warned not to take anything that might interact with their prescribed drugs – and that includes herbal stuff. A lot of people don't seem to under-stand that herbal preparations can be really strong indeed.'

'Do you remember seeing anything on her bedside table?' I asked, taking care not to describe the bottle I'd seen in case I put ideas into Bella's head.

This could be the key she needed to unlock her

memories: I couldn't jeopardise that by planting suggestions in her mind.

Bella closed her eyes and furrowed her brow in concentration.

'There was a vase of flowers,' she said, 'a copy of *Cosmopolitan* and . . . and a brown bottle, about eight centimetres high. Definitely a bottle.'

She looked at me, not quite daring to believe she was right.

I nodded.

'Right,' said Bella, sounding animated for the first time in ages, 'next time I see Joy-Anne, I'll tell her. Thank you, Flo. This is it – this is the breakthrough I needed. I can see it – I can see the bottle – and I can remember walking in and reading the chart and getting the dose ready – and *everything*! Oh, goodness, it's all there!'

A grin danced round her mouth. I threw my arms round her; I was almost too choked up for words.

'Face—'

'—your dragons,' I finished her sentence for her. 'That's right. You faced them and you bloody beat them!'

'Well, you know dragons' – Bella's grin was posi- tively beaming – 'you've got to show them who's boss.'

'Atta girl,' I said, giving her one last squeeze. 'And speaking of dragons – musical ones at any rate – I need to ask you a bit of a favour. You remember that Lisa said you had to let someone else listen to your songs? Well, how about we start thinking big . . .'

# 19

I spent the next two days in a whirl of hospital visits, emails and SuperConnect.

To my astonishment, Bella agreed readily to my suggestion; but her agreement was only the start. As well as her piece of the jigsaw, I needed to track down some musical specialists. Bella suggested a few names and Bill put me in touch with some more. Then, when I had the experts in place, I began the hunt for the huge numbers of walk-on extras vital to the venture. Everyone I spoke to was eager to help, and even rope in their friends and relations, but I still couldn't quite believe that on the day they would turn up in the numbers necessary to make it work.

To say it kept me busy was probably the understatement of the year, but I was grateful for the distraction. Even though Josh and his techie knowledge were integral to the success of my über-cunning plan, I tried to keep our conversations as short as possible – and certainly free from any mention of Marty and what might or might not be happening between them. As much as I hated to admit it, the idea of the pair of them officially becoming an item was painful, not least because somewhere deep inside still lurked a tiny bit of twisted hope that he was in love with me. So long as I didn't know for sure that he had chosen Marty, I could continue to indulge myself.

Irrational and pointless, I know – but frankly, isn't that love all over?

Anyway, at a quarter to six on Tuesday, I made my way down the hill towards Hope Street, carrying a stack of sheet music. I couldn't quite manage a smile but I had a song (literally) in my hand – if not in my heart.

As I rounded the corner on to the parade of shops, however, I nearly dropped the lot. Waiting for me outside the Apple Pie was what I can only describe as a throng: not just customers from the diner, but also regulars from the Lizard and – magnificently turned out in immaculate vintage attire – a huge crowd of Drusilla's clientele and many, many more besides.

It quite literally took my breath away.

Women in crinolines mixed with Elvira and Sylvie's church choir (all wearing red robes with starched white collars) whilst a brass ensemble tuned up nearby. I also spotted a number of people with well-groomed henna-tattooed dogs, whom I took to be Brandi's customers; ten smiley nuns; and a man tinkling away on a battered upright piano. In amongst the throng I also picked out Elvira and Sylvie wearing beautiful 1960s couture dresses (donated for the occasion, I suspected, by Drusilla) and distributing glasses of iced tea; and Bill, who was handing out free bottles of beer.

My legs wobbled and my heart stopped.

It was happening. It was *actually* happening.

Thanks to Elvira, Sylvie, Bill, Drusilla, Josh and

everyone else who had thrown themselves behind the project SuperConnect, my germ of an idea had grown beyond my wildest imaginings. As I stood and watched, a gang of young men shuffled disconsolately round the corner: it was my friends, the Hoodies of Delaney Street. With a squeal, Elvira and Sylvie put down their trays and ran over to the boys, kissing and hugging them as though they hadn't seen them for years, and the boys – like teenagers the whole world over – shrugged and wiped the kisses from their cheeks with resigned good humour.

As the moments passed, my eyes began to pick out more, and still more, familiar faces. However, there was one vitally important person who remained conspicuous by his absence.

Josh.

I bit my lip and thought back to the various moments in the past day or so when I'd dodged his pleas to talk.

Surely he wouldn't leave me in the lurch because of that?

Come on, Josh, I prayed inwardly, this is not the time for arsewittage. Please get yourself into gear and turn up. You know I can't do this without you.

I looked at my watch: five to six.

Josh had told me he only needed two minutes to set up the live streaming. In theory this meant he still had time to spare; I just didn't think my nerves would take it if he left it much longer before making his appearance.

Just to check my respiratory system was still working, I took a deep breath. Then I walked over to the crowd and put my pile of sheet music down on to the ground.

Four minutes and thirty seconds to six.

I stared back along Hope Heights and down the road, hoping to see a familiar dark brown head weaving its way along the pavement towards me. But the scene remained free of dark brown heads – familiar or otherwise.

With my stomach twisting nervously, I made a decision. There was nothing else for it: I was going to have to make a start by myself and hope he turned up in time to do his tech bit.

With a nasty sick feeling creeping over me, I picked up the heavy wooden beer-crate that Bill had donated in lieu of a conductor's podium and climbed up on to it.

'Hello, Hope Street!' I shouted, rather surprised at how well my voice carried above the general hullaballoo.

There was an instant reduction in the general hubbub, as well as a lot of nudging and 'shhhing' and a sea of expectant faces turned towards me.

My knees wobbled ominously.

I forced myself to take another deep breath and I scanned the crowd.

Right in the middle of the throng, I could see Melinda from Madam and the Ants, smiling and waving and looking unreasonably glamorous for six o'clock in the evening. I spied Mickey Ramirez saluting me with his bottle of beer, his baseball cap at a jaunty angle. Elvira and Sylvie were grinning and clapping their hands together in glee, whilst the Hoodie Boys gave a little burst of beat box and then smiled self-consciously. At the sound of footsteps, I looked round and saw Lisa and Toby – Lisa wearing a truly fabulous purple lace concoction, and Toby dressed up to the nines in the most outrageously sequinned Abba costume I'd ever seen – making their way along the street. Lisa came over and squeezed my trembling arm.

'Relax, honey, you're among friends,' she whispered, before taking her place in the mob next to Mickey and helping herself to a bottle of beer.

It was just what I needed to hear. This was *not* all resting on my shoulders. This was a collective effort: my tribe had turned out to support me – just as I, in turn, was supporting them.

A warm, fuzzy feeling settled in my tummy and I realised, for the first time in ages, that I was part of something.

Something big.

Something that, with luck, was about to get *even* bigger.

'OK, people,' I said, feeling my confidence slowly start to grow with every syllable that came out of my mouth, 'this is flash-mob time. In forty minutes we are going live on the internet. If any of you need to email the SuperConnect link to friends and colleagues so that they can then pass the link on to *their* connections, could you do it now, please. We need as many people as possible to see this. We are going for maximum impact.'

There was a murmur of excitement followed by much rustling in bags and pockets as handsets were located. I gave people time to access their phones and then waved my hands around in a manner I hoped would be recognised as a request for silence.

'We have' – I checked my watch again. *Shiiiiiiit!* – 'we have *thirty-eight* minutes now to rehearse. This is a brand-new song but I know you are all more than capable of getting up to speed in the time available.'

'Have you got any music?' yelled the Piano Man.

'Yes,' I said, handing out my photocopied sheets to the people nearest to me, 'take one and pass them on. There may not be enough for everyone, so get as close to a sheet as you can. And many, many thanks to Mickey over there for turning a vocal track on an MP3 player into a readable score.'

While everyone helped themselves to a copy of the song, I glanced round again for Josh.

I swallowed hard. There was still no sign.

He was cutting it fine – assuming, of course, that my nightmare scenario was not about to come true and he had decided to stay at home and forget about us.

'OK, anyone fancy themselves as a conductor?' I called, ignoring the feeling of Josh-related unease that was creeping up my spine.

'You know the song,' yelled back Melinda, 'you conduct!'

'You've got to be joking,' I replied, 'I don't know anything about music.'

'Don't be so defeatist!' Elvira admonished. 'You can do anything once you set your mind to it. Don't you remember telling me that not so long ago?'

Well, yes, I did, but I didn't mean it; I was just trying to make you feel better! I thought.

Out loud, I said: 'I'm sure there is someone else out there who would make a better job of it than me. Mickey?'

Mickey shook his head and fanned himself with his baseball cap.

'This is your baby,' he told me, 'you go for it.'

'But I—'

'Your baby,' chorused the crowd.

There was no escape. I manoeuvred my face into something I hoped would be interpreted as a brave smile and then sneaked another glance at my watch.

A bad move.

*Half an hour!*

'Here.' Drusilla shoved something long and thin at me. 'It's an antique lacquered chopstick I put in my hair when I'm being a geisha. Use it as a baton.'

And why not?

'OK,' I said, raising it hopefully in the air, 'can everyone see the music?'

'This is good stuff,' yelled the Piano Man. 'Did you write it?'

'No,' I yelled back, 'but my cousin Bella did.'

'Then I hope she's going professional,' replied the

Piano Man. 'I'd pay good money for this.'

'I'm working on her,' I replied. 'If she sees what a success this is, she might come round to our way of thinking. Right, people, we'll start with Elvira for the first line, then Sylvie, can you come in? Then the choir, then Madam and the Ants and then everyone else. Keep it rocking, keep it loud and you guys with the instruments, feel free to improvise. OK? One, two, three, and—'

'Actually,' yelled Mickey, 'it's in four-four time. So you need to count "one, two, three, *four*" and move the baton like this —'

'Mickey,' Drusilla growled, 'you want the other chopstick up your ass?'

Mickey shook his head.

'Then keep your mouth shut and do what the nice lady tells you.'

I hadn't thought I would ever find anyone as scary as Lisa, but now I wasn't sure. Maybe they practised on each other?

'OK,' I tried again, 'one, two, three, four and . . .'

The deep, rich voice of Elvira rose up from the throng and cut across the roar of the San Francisco rush hour. Bella's blues-cum-rock-and-roll-cum-soul number suited her down to a tee. The sound was so beautiful, it almost went beyond music and became a physical sensation, soothing my frazzled brain and calming the tensions I'd been carrying with me for days. Then Sylvie joined in, right on cue, her voice lending a dusky sweetness to the melody. I closed my eyes for a moment and listened as the harmonies wound round each other, ebbing and flowing like the tide.

*You genius, Bella, I thought.*

After that, there was a dramatic change of tempo and Piano Man belted out a few up-beat chords before the choir, clapping and swaying from side to side, began to sing. Then the horns threw their magic into the mix, followed by the drums and, before I knew it, there was a whole, magnificent spectrum of sound growing and curling and budding and flowering right in front of me. The song was like a living thing: everyone reacting instinctively to the music, giving it complexities and nuances that I could not have dreamed of in a million years. With my baton/chopstick waving in time to the music almost of its own volition, I was carried along on a wave of pure, amazing melody; rising higher and higher and growing ever more intense and beautiful until—

'Hey, lady! You in charge here?'

I looked up and saw a patrol car parked at the side of the kerb. A policeman was looking out of the driver's window, and the expression on his face was not saying, 'I'm a music fan.' The singing melted away into silence and the instruments ground to a cacophonous halt, whilst a hundred or so expectant pairs of eyes turned towards me.

I looked round nervously, hoping that someone was going to step forward and deal with this, but it seemed as though the buck was stopping with me.

*Dear God, Josh, hurry uuuuuuuuuup!*

'Yes,' I said, trying to sound more in control than I felt, 'I am.'

'Well, this is a violation.' The policeman got out of the car and walked towards me, taking his notebook out of his pocket as he did so. 'You're blocking the sidewalk and causing a bottleneck in the traffic. In fact, these here are multiple violations. *In the plural*,' he added, in case I didn't understand the word 'multiple'.

I looked down the road. It was full of cars – but none of them were moving. People had simply stopped where they were to watch our performance, leaving a chaotic trail of snarled-up vehicles behind them. It was just as bad on the pavement where a huge crowd had gathered on either side of the singers and musicians so that passers-by were being forced out into the traffic.

I looked at my watch.

Fifteen minutes to go. Oh crikey.

'Well, officer,' I began, hoping to appeal to the policeman's better nature, 'it's like this—'

'Hey, lady!' the policeman cut me off. 'Did you hear what I said? Did my lips move and words come out? Clear outta here or I'll arrest you. All of you, if I have to. These are violations of the law.'

Maybe he didn't *have* a better nature.

'No they're not,' said a voice that sounded like mine but couldn't possibly have because I'd never contradicted an authority figure in my life. 'It's an act of solidarity. Do you want a row of beautiful old shops or a shopping mall that will suck the lifeblood from the area and destroy the local community?'

'Especially a row of beautiful old shops that do the best cherry pie à la mode in the whole of Frisco,' added Elvira.

'And the best local beers,' chipped in Bill.

'And give discounts for repeat purchasers of ladies' vintage hosiery,' threw in Drusilla.

The policeman looked flustered.

'Those stockings were for my *wife*,' he growled. 'I told you: she has unusually large feet.'

'Whatever,' Drusilla grinned happily. 'Your secret's safe with me – I mean us.'

She gestured to the crowd, who all nodded in agreement.

There was a long silence from the policeman. Then he stuck his head through the open window of his patrol car and held a whispered conversation with his partner.

I went hot and cold with fear. Would we be moved on? Would Drusilla's jibe about the stockings backfire and have the lot of us thrown into jail?

'Here.' Drusilla handed a card to the person in front of her. 'Pass this over to the officer. It's a Drusilla's Loyalty Card – I'll give him fifteen per cent off his next visit.'

The policeman thought for a moment, his face softening.

Then he looked back at me.

'OK,' he said, 'what's the plan here?'

'Flash mob,' I told him. 'We all mingle with the crowd and then start singing. It will be streamed live on the internet as a protest against the sale of these properties to – um – to an unknown company. Plus you get a discount at Drusilla's.'

The policeman considered this.

'Where do I get a sheet of music?' he said, a grin spreading over his, suntanned face.

I gave him mine.

'Go and see Elvira: she'll run through the tune with you. And everyone else: mingle. We are on in ten.'

The singers and musicians obediently disappeared but the crowds that had been watching us didn't move.

'Go on,' I said, shooing them away with my arms, 'act natural.'

'No thanks,' said a lady with a large wicker shopping basket over one arm, 'I want to see them singers do that song again.'

I walked over to try and explain. 'It's a flash mob. The whole point is that the musicians look like normal members of the public who spontaneously burst into song.'

'Cool,' replied a young white man in a Rasta hat and a Che Guevara T-shirt, *they'll* look like members of the public and *we'll* watch them. It'll be awesome.'

'No,' I said, wondering what was conceptually difficult about this, 'if you do that, it absolutely *won't* be awesome. They need to mingle with *you*, that's the point! Try and look as though – as though – I don't know – you're walking along the street on your way out to dinner.'

'But I've had my dinner,' protested Basket Lady. 'I

had chicken and alfalfa sprouts and noodles and—'

'Then pretend' – I was begging now – '*pretend* you're going out for dinner and you are checking out the various eateries—'

'That one's not an eatery,' she replied, pointing at Doodles on Poodles, 'it's a dog parlour, and that one is a bar, and *that* one is a yoga place. They don't have any menus for me to check out.'

Jeez, what was this? State the bleeding obvious dot com?

I stifled a scream and dug my nails into the palm of my hand to stop me from committing actual bodily harm. I'd save that for later, I decided, once the police had pushed off.

'Listen, all of you,' I cried, 'just do as you're told and *move!*'

The onlookers shuffled uneasily to the left and then stopped.

I put my head in my hands: five minutes to go and the crowd didn't have a clue.

The policeman, who had wandered into the diner, stuck his head out of the door and wiped a dribble of cherry pie from the corner of his mouth.

'Just pretend you're going shopping, you jerks,' he shouted, 'or I'll arrest you for a section 43 violation of the Community Solidarity by-laws.'

'Is that a real offence?' a young man in an expensive-looking suit stepped forward and challenged him.

'Are you saying it's not?' The policeman stepped forward too, and put his hands on his hips.

'Come on, people!' I clapped my hands and waved my baton about frantically. 'Let's DO this! If you want to keep the heart in this community, we need to act. NOW.'

I wasn't sure whether it was me or the threat of a night in the cells that finally got the message through, but suddenly, and to my enormous relief, the crowd melted away and became a normal bunch of early-evening shoppers, diners and drinkers. The choir withdrew into the diner and, with a bit of help from the Hoodies, the Piano Man wheeled his instrument out of sight, and the horn section hid theirs behind a large refuse bin. The scene returned to one of an average, bustling, San Franciscan street.

Four minutes to go.

I once again scanned the available horizons and, to my intense relief, I spotted a dark head that seemed to be weaving and darting through the crowds towards me. Yes! There was definitely someone heading this way. I held my breath . . . the head rounded a corner and was temporarily lost from my view before reappearing and—

It wasn't Josh.

I let out a cry of frustration and anger. If he didn't turn up, this whole thing – everybody's time and effort, all the goodwill – would be for nothing. Although the logical, rational part of my brain refused to admit defeat, a growing pit of despair lurked deep in my stomach.

I pulled out my phone and checked for messages.

There weren't any.

I looked at my SuperConnect account.

Also zilch.

Finally, with my heart thumping and my face hot, I dialled his number but was immediately sent to voicemail.

'Josh,' I said, 'I need you here. I needed you here half an hour ago. Don't you *dare* let me down. Don't you dare.'

I rang off and stared at the phone, willing Josh, wherever he was, to pick up the message and come running.

'Is there a problem?'

The policeman, brushing pie crumbs from his uniform, stood in front of me.

'Yes,' I said, not having the energy to pretend anything different, 'the guy who was going to put this up on the internet isn't here.'

'He could be stuck in traffic,' said the policeman. 'Want me to go look for him? There was an accident down on Haight and Cole and everything's backed up.'

'Thanks,' I said, 'that would be great.'

Actually, I was just being polite: it would be pointless.

I had no idea where Josh was and, even if the police located him, once they'd brought him here and he'd set up, it would be far too late.

With a speed that belied his bulk, the policeman leapt into his patrol car, switched on the lights and sirens and eased his way into the stream of vehicles heading down - town. I fetched the laptop and booted it up.

'Anyone know anything about live streaming?' I called. 'Or even got a decent web cam?'

'I might,' called Bill, 'give me a mo.'

The problem was, we didn't have a mo. I looked at my watch. I didn't want to but my eyes were drawn there by some force I was powerless to resist: three minutes twenty seconds.

He wasn't bloody coming.

With a sick feeling in my stomach, I turned back towards the diner thinking I would have to go and break the news to Elvira that our cunning plan wasn't so cunning after all.

Or even much of a plan.

I would have to tell her that the last-ditch attempt to save her livelihood – and the livelihoods of all the other shopkeepers and traders in the neighbourhood – was over. That the big names with their wads of cash got to trample over the little guys yet again.

I picked up my sheet of music, my chopstick baton and walked towards the diner.

Then the screech of sirens and car tyres made me look round. A small red car with white go-faster stripes had pulled up beside me and right in front of it was the police patrol car.

I clapped my hand across my mouth as my heart leapt. He'd made it! He was here! But, crikey, he didn't have much time!

Josh leapt out of the passenger seat.

'Two minutes!' he yelled. 'Get to your places.'

The policeman took up the shout.

'Places! Places everyone!'

'And look natural!' I yelled, making particularly sure Basket Woman and Rasta-Hat Youth heard me.

In the mêlée, I turned to Josh. I was about to run to him and fling my grateful arms around him. However, there was a second person getting out of the car, a petite woman wearing skinny jeans and a clingy top that showed off her perfect figure. A woman with white, even teeth and a glowing tan, just like his.

Marty.

My stomach felt as though it had just been on the receiving end of a right hook from a heavyweight boxer.

Marty ran round after Josh, unrolling electrical cables and plugging things into adaptors. She looked perfectly happy and relaxed, although (I noticed) she didn't look me in the eye.

Not that I blamed her.

I took a deep breath and told myself to calm down. After all, what did Josh actually mean to me? He was a friend; a *good* friend; a friend without benefits but ultimately nothing more. I mean, what planet would I be living on if I thought Josh and I had any sort of future?

I turned back and watched as Josh set up the camera and then parked himself out of sight on the edge of the kerb. Meanwhile, Marty set up two hidden micro - phones and began fiddling with a set of switches on top of a small black box. Josh tapped at his laptop, leapt forward and adjusted the camera, then held up his hand and shouted:

'Everybody ready? Flora?'

I swallowed.

Hard.

Then I opened my mouth to speak, but no sound came out.

I nodded in lieu of speech and walked over to my designated starting position, which was looking at the price-list outside Doodles.

Then I turned round.

Josh was leaning over the computer, typing something in and, just at that moment, Marty came over to him and whispered something in his ear. They looked at each other, laughed and then he kissed her – a peck on the edge of her mouth – and tucked a strand of hair behind her ear.

It was a gesture of perfect intimacy, perfect understanding between two people who cared very much indeed for one another.

My stomach twisted and I looked away, my hand over my mouth and a prayer in my heart that I wouldn't barf live on air.

Josh, meanwhile, was grinning as though it was his birthday and Christmas all rolled into one. I put my hand in my pocket and it touched a crumpled ball of paper. I pulled it out. *My soul is like a dove*, it read, *soaring upwards on the wings of tranquillity*.

I screwed it up and threw it into the gutter.

'Then we're on in five, four, three—'

He mimed the remaining 'two' and 'one' with his fingers.

The crowd – thank you, God! – looked like a crowd. There was bustle and a low-level hubbub. Elvira came out of the diner with a broom and began to sweep the step. Then, at exactly the right moment, she took a deep breath and started to sing.

We were live on the internet.

# 20

The song finished on a powerful high of horn-blaring, piano-crashing, foot-stamping, drum-rolling, harmony-blending magic. The onlookers, who had now swelled into an enormous throng, paused for a moment and allowed the final note to hang magnificently in the air before breaking into thunderous applause – not to mention whooping, cheering, whistling, the honking of car horns and cries of 'encore!' Then Elvira, Sylvie, Bill, Drusilla, Brandi and two of the nuns stepped forward and Elvira said:

'We want some respect. We want it for ourselves and for our community. We want respect from the city, from the Mayor and from the planning authorities – and what we do *not* want are our businesses and livelihoods being sold down the river and the community we work so hard for being destroyed. We are special; San Francisco is special. Let's keep it that way and *save Hope Street*!

There was a huge echoing roar from the crowd: *Save Hope Street!* And everybody broke into applause once again.

Josh, hidden away with his laptop, flicked a switch and then held up his hands for calm.

'It's a wrap, everybody,' he cried. 'Fantastic. Awesome. *Beyond* fantastic. *Beyond* awesome.'

A surge of euphoria overtook both the performers and the spectators: people hugged and shook hands and kissed and wept. People who, half an hour earlier, had never met were embracing each other and congratulating themselves on the power of their performance. Business cards were exchanged, phones were pulled out and details programmed in. I imagine the take-up of SuperConnect soared by a couple of hundred per cent during those few minutes alone. Next to me, I could hear a newspaper reporter gabbling excitedly into his phone:

'Yeah, search for SuperConnect – all one word – and download it on to your cell *now*. It's massive; it's going to be the biggest thing ever. Then send it out to everyone in your in-box and tell them. I'm just going to get a quote from the guy who invented it and I'll be back for the half-seven bulletin.'

I looked round for Josh, but he was in the middle of a sea of people who all seemed intent on hugging him, slapping him on the back and wanting to know how they could get this new fabby SuperConnect thing that was about to take over the world. As I watched, Marty pushed through the crowd and made her way over to him. They looked at each other for a moment, before she took him in her arms and hugged him. He smiled, looked down at his feet, and then kissed her once again on the top of her head.

Did I need any more proof?

304

'The beers are on me!' yelled Bill. 'Any singers or musicians, come into the Lizard and claim your free one!'

There was a general cheer and a shout of gratitude went up from the performers, many of whom surged towards the bar. Sylvie too was busy, handing out glasses of juice to those whose taste did not run to the harder stuff. I felt an arm round my shoulders; it was Elvira.

'You want an iced tea, honey, or are you off with those other young people for a beer?'

I shook my head.

'Neither, thanks, Elvira. Actually, I need to go and ring Bella. Tell her it all went OK.'

Elvira hugged me tighter and rested her head on top of my own. There was something about her that was bringing back memories of my childhood. I inhaled deeply and realised that Elvira was wearing Granny's perfume.

I reached up and wiped a tear out of the corner of my eye. A sign? Maybe not, but another connection, nevertheless. We needed our pasts as well as our presents if we were going to make any sense at all of the future.

'You done us proud,' she said, 'you done us very proud indeed.'

'It still may not work.' I didn't want her to raise her hopes too high. 'Even if we got an audience on the net, it might not be enough. Stealth Holdings are very powerful.'

'But we did our best,' Elvira said. 'We stood up to them, we made our voice heard and we did our best. No one can ask any more of us than that.'

I leaned back against the circling comfort of her arm and closed my eyes, allowing myself, just for a moment, the luxury of hope. I had done my best – for Hope Street, for Bella, for myself. There was nothing I could reproach myself for.

'And that Josh of yours' – Elvira was grinning as she spoke – 'he done us proud too. He's a good boy, that one; make sure he don't go slipping through your fingers.'

I glanced over at Josh. He was standing beside Marty, both of them talking to the reporter.

Just like Barney, he had never really been mine to begin with.

I gave Elvira a huge hug, kissed her on the cheek and watched as she disappeared back inside the Apple Pie.

'You coming for a beer?' Bill called, holding out a bottle dripping with condensation.

I smiled and turned away, making my way through the crowds towards the junction with Hope Heights. Above the hubbub in the street, I thought I heard someone else call my name. It sounded like Josh, but I was not about to seek him out.

Instead, I fixed my face to the brow of the hill and walked back to Bella's house.

When I got there, I threw my keys on the kitchen table

and filled the kettle. I'd have a cup of tea, a scone (courtesy of Queen and Country) and then pop over to see how my cousin was doing. I had just put the tea bag in the mug and was looking in the fridge for the milk when my phone rang.

I checked the number to make sure it wasn't Josh and then picked up.

'Hello, Flora Fielding,' I said.

'Flora?' Mrs McMaster's voice came down the line. 'I need to talk to you.'

I remembered the last time she'd said she wanted to talk, which had led to me sitting around in her library doing sweet Fanny Adams apart from being yelled at by her husband. That was an hour of my life I wasn't going to get back.

'I'm afraid I'm rather busy at the moment,' I said, jamming the phone underneath my chin so that I could deal with my mug of tea.

'Flora, this is an *emergency*,' persisted Mrs McMaster. 'I insist that you come round.'

'That won't be possible, Mrs McMaster,' I said, pouring boiling water into my mug and wondering what exactly the 'emergency' entailed: Pugsy was off his food perhaps, and they needed me to pop out and trap a couple of rabbits for him? Or maybe the chauffeur had called in sick and I would be required to don a peaked hat and drive them to a society dinner in the centre of town?

'I'm sorry,' Mrs McMaster sounded puzzled, 'did you refuse my request?'

307

'Yes,' I said lightly, 'I did.'

I had less than a week before I was due back in the office and I intended to spend as much time with Bella and/or generally enjoying myself as I could before I had to go back to the grind and sort my life out. Pointless meetings with the McMasters did not come under either of these two headings.

There was the sound of a hand being placed over the receiver.

'Earl,' Mrs McMaster called to her husband, 'Earl, she won't come round.'

'Tell her she has to,' Mr McMaster's less-than-dulcet tones wafted over the ether. 'Tell her it's what we pay her for.'

The phone rustled again.

'I'm not coming,' I repeated, before Mrs McMaster could get a word in. 'I have other things to do. I will speak to you when I am back in the office next Monday.'

'Earl,' she yelled, not bothering to cover up the receiver this time and nearly deafening me with her screech. 'Earl, she won't do as she's told.'

Too right I won't, I thought mutinously. I had emailed Brenda to tell her about the acrimonious non-meeting and had also drawn her attention to the unpaid bills on the McMasters' account. I knew that unless they coughed up, I was under no obligation to keep them sweet.

'Give it here.' Mr McMaster was on the line: 'Here, you—'

He was so angry he had obviously forgotten the basics of social etiquette – like using my name, for example.

'Flora,' I reminded him pleasantly, 'I'm Flora Fielding. Employee of Relocation Wizards . . .'

*. . . who will be telling her boss about your appalling behaviour as soon as this call is over.*

'I don't care what the hell you are called or who the hell you work for, you just get your ass over here – now – or I'll bust you so hard you won't know what hit you.'

'Mr McMaster,' I replied calmly, 'are you threatening me?'

'You divulged confidential information about me over the internet,' he cried.

This took me aback. What the chuffing nora was he on about?

'No I didn't,' I said.

'Don't lie to me. You snooped round my office, helped yourself to confidential information and then broadcast it over the damn internet. I could sue you. In fact I *will* sue you, so help me.'

I thought about Drusilla plucking the name of Stealth Holdings from God knew where, but unless I'd blurted it out in a fit of madness, she hadn't got it from me. Even so, I felt sweat prick into the backs of my knees and my heart beat a little bit faster.

'Mr McMaster,' I said as firmly as I could manage, 'I have not snooped round your office, I have not "helped myself" to confidential business information and I have most certainly not put any of it on the internet.'

This was all true. I hadn't gone looking for any information – and even if I had, I wouldn't have done a loony thing like sticking it up on the web.

There was a noise on the other end of the line that could have been anything from a dying duck in a thunderstorm to Mr McMaster having a heart attack.

'IT. IS. THERE,' he shouted. 'IT. IS. UP. ON. THE. DAMN. WEB. I *SAW* IT.'

At that point, my fear left me. He was clearly mad. He had been so unpleasant and cantankerous for so long that his brain had finally given up and he'd cracked.

'Mr McMaster,' I said, 'are you feeling all right? You know, it might be best if you went and had a nice lie-down.'

'I don't want to lie down!' he thundered, 'I am going to talk to my lawyer and then to your boss and I am going to have you FIRED!'

Even though he was on the other side of town, that last word made me jump.

'And I am telling you', I replied, taking my courage in both hands and standing my ground, 'that I did not do anything!'

'Why you little—!'

But what Mr McMaster thought about me was never revealed, because at that moment, there came a loud 'clunk' noise, the sound of the phone being dropped and Mrs McMaster squealing:

'Earl? Are you all right, Earl? Earl! Talk to me!'

And the line went dead.

For a moment or two I just stared at the handset. What should I do? Call back and ask how he was? Ring an ambulance? Call Brenda and tell her I had killed one of her richest clients?

In the end I sent a text to Brenda along the lines of: 'Is everything OK with Mr McMaster?' Then I decided I'd better investigate his allegations, however far-fetched they might sound: if I was going to have to defend myself against a charge of industrial espionage, I needed to know what evidence there was against me.

I booted up Bella's laptop, put the details of the flash mob into a search engine and pressed 'go'.

Josh had done his stuff; the link was up there: first hit. I clicked and the web page opened up in front of me. There was Hope Street, full of people bustling round; there was I, clearly visible in the front of the shot; and there was Elvira, sweeping the front step of the Apple Pie. I watched the song unfold just as I knew it would: Elvira, then Sylvie, then the choir, then Melinda, then everyone else.

See, Mr McMaster? Why on earth were you getting your knickers in a twist?

And then I saw it.

Right at the back of the crowd, someone I didn't recognise was holding up a banner bearing the legend: 'Keep Stealth Holdings Out of Hope Street'. Whilst I was in full view, singing and swaying along, right in the middle of the front row.

I covered my face with my hands. The evidence was pretty much stacked against me, in Mr McMaster's eyes at least. I'd seen the letter that connected him to Stealth Holdings and which, in turn, linked Stealth Holdings to the sale of Hope Street – and there I was, fully visible to of anyone with an internet connection, protesting about that sale. Even if I hadn't actually leaked the information, it was all pretty damning.

Basically, I was stuffed.

My mind flicked back to the text I had just sent Brenda, now woefully inadequate. Even though she might be personally relieved to get the McMasters off her books (provided they paid their bills before they left) she would not be grateful for the accusations that would now be levelled at her company by Mr McMaster's legal team. I guessed that it wouldn't be long before she wanted to have words with me, and those words would probably include 'immediate', 'resignation' and 'P45'.

I glanced back at the picture, which had frozen right on the last 'hoorah' of applause and cheering. There, right at the bottom of the screen, almost out of shot, were Josh and Marty. He was leaning over and whispering something in her ear and she was grinning away like a Cheshire Cat that had just heard some very good news indeed.

My stomach lurched.

Given the choice, I knew that I would take a million Mr McMasters yelling abuse at me rather than spend one more second of my life looking at Josh and Marty, so obviously at ease with one another, so obviously happy.

Without even waiting to shut the computer down properly, I closed the lid. Then I locked the front door, left a message with the duty nurse for Bella, and switched off my phone, before climbing into bed fully clothed and pulling the duvet over my head.

As far as I was concerned, today was over.

The next day brought Bella's discharge from hospital.

At half past one, I drove with Toby in his ridiculously tiny car up to collect her, my heart heavy and my limbs like lead. Despite the warmth of the summer sun and the cheerfulness of the blue sky beaming down upon the answering glitter of the Bay, the image which kept dragging itself out of my memory and flashing across my brain was that of Josh and Marty: smiling, whispering.

Kissing.

And each time it dragged and flashed, my heart sank a little lower and my body felt even more burdensome and unwieldy.

'So, Toby,' I said, desperate for some happier news to distract me, 'have you been out on that date with Robbie yet?'

Toby shook his head sadly.

'But you promised,' I protested, 'and, what's more, you promised *Lisa*, or she was going to hijack the screen savers at work, remember? What went wrong?'

'I *did* ring him,' Toby admitted, sounding almost as miserable as I felt, 'and we fixed up a date and I booked the restaurant and everything; then Bella got

313

sick, and that threw me. Essentially, I lost my nerve and cancelled.'

'OK,' I replied, 'that's not the end of the world. I'm sure he'd understand if he knew the circumstances. Why don't you ring him up and reschedule?'

Toby's face was a picture of excruciating unhappiness.

'But what if he hates me for wasting his time? What if he thinks I'm a cowardly loser? What if—'

'What if he really likes you and is desperate to go on a date with you?'

'As *if*.' Toby pulled into a parking bay and turned off the engine. 'Anyway, we're here now and not a word to Bella. I don't want her rehospitalised because she yelled at me and burst her stitches.'

We found the woman herself, pale but pleased to see us, sitting on the edge of her bed with her belongings packed away in my suitcase on wheels.

'Are you hot to trot?' Toby took the case and helped her off the bed.

Bella grinned.

'Sadly, I'm not allowed any trotting for a few weeks, but I should be able to make it to the car all right. Thankfully it was only keyhole surgery and the doc says the stitches will dissolve as it all heals over. To be honest, the bloating is the worst. So they can see what they're doing they pump you full of gas and—'

Toby held up his hand.

'Too much information!' he shrieked, diva-like. 'If there's a gas situation going on, you keep all the windows open in the car. And if there is *any* mention of lady bits, the pair of you are walking home.'

Bella nudged him in the ribs with her elbow.

'Honestly, Toby, *lady bits*. What are you like?'

Suddenly, Toby's face crumpled. He put down the case and threw his arms round Bella.

'Thank God,' he said, burying his nose in the top of her head. 'Really and truly thank God that you are OK. I don't know what I'd have done if you . . . if you . . . you know.'

Bella's eyes closed and she held him tight and gave him a squeeze. Then she let him go and slapped him hard on the back.

'Oh, I'd have come back to haunt you all,' she said, 'you don't get rid of me as easily as that. And for your information, Toby, it wasn't as bad as it could have been. Sometimes they have to take out the whole fallopian tube and—'

'Lady bits!' trilled Toby, striding out into the corridor, pulling the suitcase behind him. 'I do not want to hear about the lady bits!'

There was a knock on the door and Joy-Anne entered. She put her arms round Bella and gave her a hug.

'So glad you are better,' she said, 'and I hope it all goes well at the inquiry. You know we're rooting for you, don't you?'

Bella nodded.

'I'll do my best,' she replied.

'You'll do better than that,' I replied. 'Now you can

remember what happened, especially about the herbal tablets, you've got a very strong case.'

Joy-Anne smiled enthusiastically and then indicated a beautiful bunch of roses sitting in a vase on Bella's night-stand.

'Do you want me to wrap those?' she asked.

'I don't know who they're from,' Bella replied. 'They arrived when I was in the shower this morning and there wasn't a card with them. In fact, I wonder if they were delivered here by mistake. Why don't you give them to someone who doesn't have any?'

Joy-Anne smiled and hugged her again.

'Take care,' she whispered.

And we made our way out into the corridor.

Despite her bravado, Bella couldn't walk very fast. In fact, by the time we stepped out into the car park, Toby had already stowed Bella's case on the back seat and was manically waving at us. We made our way slowly towards him, but for some reason he didn't stop waving. In fact, the nearer we got, the more he waved. Then he jumped in the air and shouted 'woo-hoo!' so loudly it made a couple of elderly ladies on Zimmer frames glare angrily in his direction.

'Look,' he whooped, waving his phone at us, 'just look at what the zippedy-doo-dah has happened!'

'Language, young man!' barked one of the ladies.

Toby grinned at her and waggled the phone in her direction.

'It's gone viral!' he yelled. 'It's only gone freaking viral!'

316

'Sounds like you need to get back inside the hospital, young man!' barked the other lady. 'We don't want you spreading your infections round here!'

'Not me!' trilled Toby. 'The video.'

He held his phone out towards them and they shrank away as though it was crawling with plague.

'Keep your germs to yourself!' they cried and shuffled off as fast as their Zimmer frames would allow.

We hurried across as fast as we dared given Bella's stitches, and Toby thrust the phone in our faces.

'Viral!' he shouted.

'What is?' Bella's face was a study in incomprehension. 'Viral? What are you talking about?'

Toby held the phone sideways so that we could see the screen, then he clicked on the SuperConnect icon and an image of Hope Street flashed into view. I saw bustling crowds . . . the policeman finishing off his slice of cherry pie . . . Basket Lady gazing in through the window of Doodles on Poodles and determinedly licking her lips. Elvira pretending to sweep the step . . . Elvira starting to sing . . .

'Bloody hell!' Bella clapped her hands to her face. 'They're doing my song – they are really doing my song! I mean, I knew they would, but even so . . .'

I looked at her, praying she would approve of what we had done with her work.

'Oh God.' She just stared at the screen. 'Oh. My. GOD.'

'Oh my God *good* or oh my God *bad*?' asked Toby.

Bella just shook her head in a non-comprehending manner.

'Just. Oh. My. God,' she said.

We watched, transfixed, as the choir joined in, clapping and swaying with the rhythm of the song; as Piano Guy was wheeled out of the diner by Mickey and Bill, playing as he went; as the horn section blasted their harmonies above the layers of melody and counter-melody; and as the customers of the Apple Pie unfurled a banner from the first-floor window that read 'Save Hope Street: A Piece of San Francisco History'.

I chose not to look at the other banner; the one naming and shaming Stealth Holdings. This was Bella's moment; I wasn't about to take it away from her.

We were joined by several other car-park users, drawn over to us by the music.

'This is *amazing*,' said a man behind me, getting his phone out. 'Where can I find it?'

'You'll find it on SuperConnect,' I said, a little smugly. 'Go to "my neighbourhood" and type in "Hope Street".'

The man did as he was told.

'Cool!' he declared, his head nodding in time to the beat. 'I'll put it on my home page and send the link to my buddies. Is it available as a download?'

I looked at Bella, but her eyes were fixed on the screen and she was barely breathing. She was away with the fairies – or at least away with the flash mob.

'Soon,' I said, taking matters into my own hands and answering for her, 'but spread the word.'

The man grinned at me and walked off, looking back down at the screen of his phone.

'Don't worry, I will,' he promised, nearly running smack into a lamp-post. 'This is *awesome*.'

With a rousing flourish of its horn and piano and gospel and soul finale, the song ended. The mob bowed to rapturous applause from the crowd of onlookers and the picture on Toby's phone screen froze.

Bella blinked and shook herself, as though she was waking up after a deep sleep. Then she glanced up at me and a single tear tracked its way down her cheek.

'Oh, Flo,' she whispered, 'it's amazing. I had no idea anything I'd written could ever sound as good as that. Who did the arrangement?'

'Mickey Ramirez,' I said, 'but he said it was easy because the underlying structure of the song was so strong.'

'It is amazing,' she said again, 'totally, amazingly amazing.'

I squeezed into the back of Toby's car with Bella's suitcase, whilst he helped her into the front seat and handed her the phone. We drove back to Hope Heights to the repeated musical accompaniment of the flash mob and Bella's murmurs of incredulity.

I settled Bella on the sofa with a throw, a couple of cushions and a mug of tea. Gently, I prised Toby's phone out of her hand and replaced it with her own. The SuperConnect icon on her screen was flashing manically at her, and I watched as she clicked on it and gasped.

'Over eight hundred messages,' she said, 'and over a million people have liked the song. *A million!*'

I grinned.

'You'd better watch out, missy, I have a feeling you are going to be famous.'

Uncertainty scuttled over Bella's face.

'I don't know about that,' she said, 'I'm not sure I want to be famous.'

'Might be too late to change your mind,' I replied. 'But think of the crowds you'll get in for Abbadabbatastic gigs.'

Bella nearly dropped her mug of tea.

'Shit!' she cried. 'The Battle of the Tribute Bands. It's tonight! I need to get down the Lizard and do the sound check.'

It was my turn to nearly drop my drink.

'Oh no you don't,' I said, sounding scarily like Granny, 'the doctor said you weren't allowed to exercise for at least another two weeks. You've had a major operation.'

'But it's not exercise' – Bella threw off her covers – 'it's singing. And it's the final. You're not seriously suggesting we miss the final?'

'And you're not seriously suggesting you get up on stage and rupture whatever it is that the surgeon has just fixed?' I countered. 'Get real, Bella. One trip to hospital cost us an arm and a leg. You can't risk another – we'll all be bankrupted.'

'But it's the final.' Bella was sounding desperate. 'It's my chance to actually *make* some money.'

'Listen.' I bent down and tucked the covers in tightly round her, as though this would somehow impede any plans she might have for escape. 'I will lend you as much as I can to cover the hospital fees but you have to work with me here. You are in no state to go parading round on stage.'

Bella's face was hot and red and I could see tears of frustration pricking in her eyes.

'But it's not for me,' she cried, 'it's for the others – well, not Toby, he can take care of himself – but the other two. They need this, they *really* need this. I have to do it.'

'No, you don't,' I replied, plumping up her cushions and putting the remote control by her side, 'it's not your problem. The others will manage somehow.'

Bella didn't look convinced, but laid obediently back against the cushions as I stroked her head.

I wasn't convinced either but I didn't want her to start worrying about the show; right now she had to put all her energy into getting better.

My cousin's eyes closed, her breath softened and she drifted off into sleep. I took the opportunity to steal out of the living room, pour myself another cup of tea and try to take stock of the situation:

1. Bella was alive – that was good.

2. The flash mob was going viral – that was excellent.

3. Bella could be the next big thing in songwriting – that was fabulous.

But, on the other hand—

4. There was no word yet on whether the flash mob had achieved its purpose – not good.

5. The Battle of the Tribute Bands was probably about to go up the wazoo for Abbadabbatastic – really bad.

6. Steve was still AWOL – even worse.

And I refused to even think about Josh.

I sipped my tea and helped myself to another Queen and Country scone. I was exhausted and hoped the combination of refined flour and processed sugar would give my brain the boost it needed to do some much-needed thinking. Then I checked my phone.

As well as a billion SuperConnect buzzes telling me how amazing the flash mob had been, there was a text from Auntie Stella saying that she would be arriving the day I left so that she could take over nursing duties and – oh, crikey! I dropped my scone into my tea – a missed call from Josh.

Before I could stop myself, almost as a reflex action, I had accessed my messages.

'Hey, Flo, Josh here. Look, I'm sorry not to catch you yesterday, you sort of disappeared; but, at the risk of repeating myself, I want to talk to you. It's really important. Ring me when you get this.'

I pressed 'delete'.

I already knew what he had to tell me, why did I

need to put myself through the pain of hearing him say the actual words?

I got a spoon from the drawer, fished the remains of my scone out of the mug and threw it in the bin. My appetite went with it.

To try and cheer myself up, I flicked through the congratulatory messages on SuperConnect, but it was worse than useless. SuperConnect made me think of Josh; the flash mob made me think of Josh; even Bella and the possibility that she could make some real money from her song made me think of Josh (who else was she going to ask to help her put it on the web as a download?). It felt as though everything I did and everywhere I went, there was Josh – and close behind him was always Marty.

My stomach twisted.

Although I felt torn over leaving Bella, really the sooner I left San Francisco the better; the whole place was marinated with Joshness.

I turned to my emails. There was one from Brenda. With my heart in my mouth, I opened it:

You might be interested to know that Relocation Wizards have just been fired by Mr McMaster. Apparently you have been reading his private papers and putting confidential information up on the internet. I also understand that when you denied this, he got so wound up that he passed out and hit his head on his desk.

Thank God! I wasn't a client-murderer at least.

Anyway, you will be pleased to know that I told him in no uncertain terms that none of my employees would stoop to such a thing and, assuming I am correct in that, I look forward to welcoming you back to the office next Monday.

I took a very deep breath. It was OK – for now, anyway. Mr McMaster was alive and I still had a job. Whether or not he wanted to sue me was still up for grabs, but I'd cross that bridge when I came to it. I had just emailed Brenda back to thank her for her support, when I heard a gentle knocking on the door. Thinking it was probably Toby or Lisa come to check up on Bella, I tiptoed across the hallway and undid the latch as quietly as I could.

To my utter astonishment, standing on the doorstep was Steve.

My initial shock at seeing him there was replaced almost immediately by a tidal wave of righteous anger.

'What the hell do you think you're doing?' I hissed, wishing I'd brought the frying pan with me so that I could give him a good clout across the head.

Steve looked at me nervously.

'I'd like to see Bella,' he said.

'Well, you can't,' I replied. 'You've had ages to see Bella. You should have turned up when she was in hospital.'

Steve's shoulders sagged. He was a stocky guy, but

324

he seemed to physically shrink before my eyes.

'I did visit,' he said. 'I really did.'

This was too much: first he couldn't be arsed to visit his sick girlfriend, now he was lying about it. I decided to let him have it with both barrels.

'Don't give me any crap, Steve,' I growled, keeping my voice as low as I could so as not to wake Bella, 'I know you didn't visit her – mainly because I *did*. And because I was there, on the ground, I can tell you categorically that at no point did you so much as stick your head round the door of her room, let alone spend any time with her.'

I looked into his face and got the shock of my life. His eyes had a strange, glassy quality to them that spoke of tears and the lids were red.

'I couldn't face speaking to her,' he mumbled, 'I only went in when she was asleep. I just sat there and held her hand. I – I couldn't get my head round it all.'

I hesitated. Was he telling the truth? Or did he just want to get into Bella's good books now she looked as though she might have a hit song on her hands?

'You guys,' he said, 'you and Lisa and Toby; you were always there. The last thing I wanted was a shouting match, that wouldn't have helped anyone.'

I thought back to the previous few days. Lisa and Toby and I had pretty much kept up a round-the-clock watch on her – within permitted visiting hours. It would have been hard for her and Steve to have had any time alone.

'I am so sorry for what happened that night,' Steve

continued, 'I really regret it. I went round the block to try and hail a cab because I thought it would be quicker than waiting for the ambulance, but when I came back, you'd gone. I suppose I should have followed you straight to the hospital, but the idea of Bella dying was so terrible that I sort of lost my nerve. After you called, I went and sat in a church for a while and then I wandered around downtown – I'm not really sure where. I couldn't believe what you'd just told me. It wasn't until a lot later that I pulled myself together and went to St Peter's; I spoke to Joy-Anne in reception and she told me they were doing everything they could and that you guys were with her. Like I said, I thought you all might be angry with me so I came back early the next morning and then again that night. Joy-Anne let me sneak in when there was no one else around. I thought it was for the best.'

There was a definite ring of truth to his words. My resolve softened.

'You'd better come in,' I said. 'She's asleep at the moment. Be prepared: she thinks you simply washed your hands of her.'

Steve stepped over the threshold and followed me into the kitchen. He looked even more awkward and nervous than he had done when I'd opened the door.

'I brought Bella some roses,' he said. 'I put them in a blue vase. I don't know whether she saw the card?'

I bit my lip. I remembered the flowers Bella had given away, but I had no idea where the card had gone.

Steve pulled up a chair and sat down.

'I've done my thinking, Flora,' he continued, 'and I've made some changes. Big changes. I want to ask her if we can start again.'

'Flo!' Bella's voice floated in from the living room. 'Flo, are you there?'

Gesturing for Steve to stay in the kitchen, I made my way into the living room to see what she wanted.

'Hey,' I said, reaching over to plump up her pillows, 'can I get you anything, sleepy-head? A cup of tea? Water? Juice?'

Bella struggled to sit up.

'My white sequinned jumpsuit and my silver platforms please,' she asked hopefully. 'I've got a gig to go to.'

I sighed.

'No,' I said, 'no no no no – oh, and *no*.' I sat down on the edge of the sofa and took her hand. 'There's a visitor for you.' I nodded my head in the direction of the kitchen. 'Now, I don't want you seeing anyone if you're not up to it, but if you do want to then—'

'Hi, Belle.' Steve was in the doorway. 'How are you feeling?'

Bella froze. Her mouth opened, but no sound came out. I could see Steve's awkwardness ratchet up by several thousand notches.

'If you don't want me here, I'll – I'll go,' he stammered. 'But before I do, I just – I just need to say that I love you and that I will do anything I can to try and make it work between us.'

You could have cut the atmosphere in the room with a plastic airline knife. Bella looked down at her hands and took her time before replying.

'I don't know, Steve; I really don't. You pretty much abandoned me. In my book, that's not how you show someone that you love them.'

'I came to see you,' he said, taking a couple of tentative steps into the middle of the room. 'I sat with you while you were asleep. Joy-Anne smuggled me in.'

Bella picked at a loose thread on the duvet cover.

'Why didn't you come when I was awake? Or answer any of my phone calls – or Flo's?' she said. 'I have every right to think you didn't care.'

Steve shuffled his way over to the sofa.

'I don't deny it,' he said, 'I behaved badly. But the bottom line is that I want us to be together, Bella. I want to make things good between us.'

Bella looked at him for a split second, then glanced away.

'Yeah, so that's why you took my gig money and threw it away on that stupid club in Oakland,' she said, 'to make things good between us.'

Steve shook his head.

'I pulled out,' he said. 'I went over the next day and got the money back. In fact . . .' He reached into his back pocket and took out his wallet. 'Here it is. Your share – and mine. Take it. And if Abbadabbatastic win tonight then everyone in the band wants you to take their winnings so that we can pay something to the hospital.'

He counted out the notes and handed them to her. Bella fingered them for a moment before turning her attention back to Steve.

'Don't you get it, Steve?' she said. 'It's not about the money. It's never been about the stupid money. It's about the fact you behave like a teenager: rushing about, making snap decisions and expecting me to bail you out. It has to stop.'

Steve took a deep breath.

'I know that too. And here's the thing: I've had an interview, for a job – a proper job – sourcing music for a local film company. It's only a very junior role but it's a regular wage and if I get it, I'm planning on taking out a bank loan to pay off your hospital bills.'

Bella stared.

'You're going to give up the music? Totally? Get a day job?'

Steve shook his head.

'Not totally, but I'll have to cut down on the bands. There are good opportunities for promotion in the job, but I'm going to have to work hard if I want to get one. You see . . .' He paused. 'You see, Bella, this made me realise . . . in the long term, this is what I want: you – and eventually another baby. I'm sorry it took me so long to figure it out, but this is where I want to be, with you.'

Bella rubbed her face. She looked as though she was having trouble taking it all in.

'You and me? You mean, like get married?'

Steve grinned.

'If you want to. We belong together; I knew it the moment I saw you, Belle. What do you say?'

'Give me a bit of time to think about it.' She smiled at him. 'It's all a bit sudden. My brain feels like a tornado's blown through it.'

'Of course,' he said. 'Have as long as you need. You have no idea how relieved I am that you didn't simply tell me to get lost before hearing me out.'

Bella shook her head.

'No,' she said firmly. 'I love you, Steve, I always have done. But love on its own isn't enough. I'm sad about losing the baby – really devastated – but if you're right and we can get our lives sorted, maybe some good will come out of it after all. That's the best we can hope for.'

She reached up, put her arms round his neck and kissed him.

It was so sweet, it made me want to cry.

'No promises,' she whispered, 'apart from to say that I really will think about it. I do love you, Steve.'

'Love you too, Belle,' he replied.

'Flo,' said Bella, 'you know that thing you need to do – the, um, the *thing*? Well, now it would be a really good time to do it.'

I smiled and, as silently as I could, I stepped out of the room and closed the door behind me.

# 21

I caught the cable car from the corner of Hope Street and made my way down to Fisherman's Wharf. The afternoon sun was warm and soothing, and I went straight over to my favourite ice-cream stall and bought myself another It's-It. A coach had just pulled up, disgorging its occupants, and the scene around me was bustling with tourists, meandering along the edge of the Bay, pointing at the sea lions and dodging the seagulls, who were intent on stealing any scraps of food they could get their webbed feet on. I settled myself on a seat that looked out across the water to Sausalito and remembered the promise I'd made to Bella in the back of the ambulance.

I lifted up my phone and took a picture of the view, shimmering blue in the summer heat haze. Then I uploaded it on to my SuperConnect page and sent a copy over to Bella. *Let's have that brunch before I go*, I wrote, *to celebrate your recovery*.

I could get the hang of this social-networking lark.

My phone rang. With my mind still on Bella, I took the call.

'Hey, you,' I said, 'do you need me to come back now or is Steve still with you?'

There was silence on the other end of the line.

'Bella,' I said, 'is that you?'

'Flora?' said Barney's voice in an accusatory tone. 'Who's Steve?'

I waited for the shakes, the uneasiness, the anger to come – but they didn't. Instead, I calmly ran my tongue under the bottom of my ice-cream to hoover up the drips. I really didn't want to talk to Barney. In fact, having a public bikini wax on Oxford Street during a busy Saturday afternoon would have been further up my list of preffered activities – but not because I felt upset; I simply had better things to do – like eat my It's-It and look out across the Bay to the blue-green shore beyond.

'Is this important?' I asked. 'Because if it isn't, I don't want to know. And when I say important I mean something along the lines of: a passing surgeon has offered to cut your head open and put a new brain inside and they need me to sign the consent form.'

'Flora . . .' there was another long pause. 'Flora, I owe you an apology.'

I took a bite of It's-It and considered this.

'Just the one, Barney?' I said through a mouthful of biscuity mush. 'I'd have thought you could have spent from now until Tuesday week apologising and you still wouldn't be finished.'

'I've made a terrible mistake, Flora and I'd like you to come home as soon as possible.'

I nibbled at the chocolate. I'd been caught out like this before.

'I'll be home soon enough, Barney, and I'll have my

332

stuff collected when it's convenient for me to do so. Until then you and Susan are just going to have to put up with it.'

'No,' said Barney, 'I mean come home. To the house to live. Sue and I are over.'

There was emotion in his voice. Or at least, there was a slightly whingey quality to it, which for Barney amounted to much the same thing. My surprise was so great that I gasped – and managed to inhale a large chunk of It's-It at the same time.

'Flora, Flora, can you hear me?' called Barney as I made a variety of coughing and choking sounds.

'What happened?' I said unsympathetically, finally dislodging the offending piece of biscuit. 'Did she find out what you were really like and dump you?'

'No.' He stopped. 'No, it was more complicated than that. It sounds weird, Flora, I know it does, but I found your sweatshirt – the red one with the fleecy lining – stuck down the back of one of the sofa cushions.'

I didn't like the sound of this. 'Barney, what happened? You're not a secret cross-dresser or some - thing, are you? You didn't put my clothes on and freak her out?'

'No, of course I didn't.' He sounded miserable. 'But inside the pocket was a folded-up paint chart – the one we'd been using to decide on colours for the hall – and I got to thinking about all the work we'd done together on the house; how generous you'd been over the renovations, how much fun we'd had planning everything.'

'I suppose we did,' I admitted cautiously.

'Anyway, Susan was insisting that I sell up. She doesn't like old houses; she says that too much work involved. But I don't want to sell, Flora – it's my home. And the more I thought about it, the more I realised that it's your home too. It belongs to both of us.'

I suddenly became suspicious. 'This isn't about the money, is it? You don't just want me to move back so that you can get out of paying what you owe me?'

'No,' he replied hurriedly, 'no – it's not that. I do miss you, I really do – and I've been thinking about what you said on the phone on Wednesday. You're right, we have been spending too much time at work and not enough with each other. In fact, I reckon if we could have a few weeks where we just concentrated on our relationship, we would soon be back to how we were.'

Funny how your perspective can change in a matter of days, isn't it?

'"How we were" was pretty crap, Barney.' I felt that at least one of us needed to keep a grasp on reality. '"How we were" involved you having an affair, remember? It's not somewhere I'm anxious to revisit.'

'Not like that – I mean *before* before. When we were happy.' He paused. 'Look, to show you how serious I am, I've decided to put your name on the deeds of the house. I mean, you've been paying the mortgage for long enough and a lot of your money went into the renovations and decorating. It really is your house as much as it is mine.'

The ice-cream middle from my It's-It dropped on to the floor and was swooped on by a pack of marauding seagulls.

I almost couldn't believe my ears. *My house. It would be my house?*

'I . . .' I said, all this unexpected goodwill and the promise of property ownership making my head spin, 'I . . . don't know what to say.'

'Hey! Flora!'

Someone nearby was calling my name.

There was the sound of running footsteps.

'Flora!'

But my mind was five thousand miles away, opening the front door of the little white house in Oxford, walking into the hallway, smelling the wax on the floorboards, hanging up my coat in the understairs cupboard . . . *My* house. It would really be *mine*.

*'Flora!'*

It was Josh.

I jumped in shock and the phone went crashing on to the floor.

'Oh shit!'

The grin vanished from his face and he was down on his knees picking it up. There was a large crack running diagonally across the screen.

'Oh my God, Flora, I am so sorry. I am *so* sorry.' He held the phone out to me.

Or rather, the remains of the phone.

'I'll get you another,' he said. 'I'll get you a better one. A friend of mine works at the Apple Store, I'll—'

I shook my head.

'It's fine, Josh. Really. I dropped it, it was my fault.'

'I was the one who made you jump.' He slumped down on the bench next to me. 'I shouldn't have been yelling at you, but I was just so pleased I'd finally tracked you down.'

'How did you know where I was?' I asked, gazing down sadly at the corpse of my brand-new smart phone and thinking of the conversation that had been torn asunder by its demise.

Josh raised an eyebrow.

'You just posted a picture of the view here on SuperConnect. It wasn't rocket science.'

We looked out over the Bay for a moment, the shock of Barney's suggestion slowly giving way to much more familiar (and unwelcome) feelings.

I turned towards him. 'You and Marty, that's why you came to find me, isn't it?'

'Well, yeah,' he said, 'sort of. I mean, I do but . . .' He pulled out his own phone. 'Although first I want to have a word about the message I sent. Have you read it yet?'

I looked down guiltily at my shoes and shook my head.

'Take my phone and go to your own in-box,' Josh instructed.

I did as I was told and, as I slid it out of his grasp, our fingers touched. I felt as though I'd thrown a toaster into a bath and jumped in after it.

I closed my eyes. Lucky Marty, I thought.

'Come on, Flora.' Josh was next to me, jiggling up and down with excitement.

With trembling fingers, I typed in the password for my email account. Then I scrolled down until I found Josh's message and opened it.

Out jumped a picture of my grandparents' house in Cornwall.

Only it wasn't the neat little cottage of my memory. This one had a garden wall that was starting to tumble down, and paint flaking off the front door. The interior shots showed peeling wallpaper and mould creeping its way round the window frames. There was even an alarming-looking hole in the roof.

I looked at Josh. What was he trying to do? Torture me?

'What's this?' I asked, rather brusquely. 'Well no, don't answer that. I know what it is. What I mean is: what is it doing in my in-box?'

'It's a present,' he said excitedly, 'a sort of gift. From me to you.'

I stared; first at him and then at the picture on my screen. It wasn't the sort of gift I'd give to anyone I wanted to like me after they'd opened it.

'It's for sale,' he added helpfully, pointing to the estate agent's details along the top of the screen.

'You're buying me a house?' I asked. 'But it's a real wreck. And you don't have any money – plus I wouldn't accept it even if you did.'

Josh shook his head.

'I thought you'd want to buy it yourself,' he said.

'You told me how much you love this place and what amazing memories you have of it. Now's your chance to have another slice of that happiness – and do the house a favour while you're about it. It looks like it could do with a bit of TLC.'

I stared again at the screen.

In my mind I wasn't looking at the crumbling brickwork, or the haphazard slates, or the hole in the roof next to the chimney pot; instead I could clearly see smooth, freshly painted walls, salvaged Victorian glass in the doors, quarry tiles in the newly fitted, handmade kitchen. I could smell bunches of fresh garden flowers standing on the whitewashed dresser in the hall, and hear the ripple of the bedroom curtains as they moved in the light summer breeze. And, as I stared, I felt a lump form in my throat and the corners of my eyes grow hot and prickly.

You see, the vision in my head wasn't my grandparents' house as it had been: this was my own creation.

It was my very own house.

I shook myself and clicked the button on the phone that closed the picture.

Josh frowned.

'What did you do that for?' he asked, puzzled. 'Don't you like it?'

I pinched the bridge of my nose and sent stern thoughts to my tear-ducts. There was no point in crying over spilt milk, and even less point in crying over milk you could never afford in a million years.

'No,' I said, forcing a smile on to my reluctant face, 'thank you. It was a kind thought. But I'm not in a place right now where I can do anything about it. I don't have the money for the deposit and I doubt if I could get a mortgage with it looking like that and – well, it's not going to happen, is it?'

Josh pulled a funny face.

'Well, no, it isn't, if you start thinking like that,' he said.

I sincerely hoped I wasn't about to be on the receiving end of a lecture on the American Dream and How Everyone Will Ultimately Achieve Their Heart's Desire. One thing I had learned was that life wasn't like that.

'Josh,' I said, 'with the greatest respect, just because you want something – dammit, just because you want something *really badly* – does not mean you will get it. There isn't some sort of cosmic pay-out system where, just because you wish hard enough, it all comes true. If that was the case, I'd be awash with L.K. Bennett handbags and Jimmy Choos, and you'd be Bill Gates.'

I glanced at him, hoping he wouldn't take the Bill Gates remark the wrong way. To my relief he grinned.

'And, *with the greatest respect*,' he countered, 'I have not yet given up on being Bill Gates – or at least a younger, better-looking and generally groovier San Francisco version. The point is, if you give up before you've even started, where does that leave you? At least if you *try*, you're in with a chance. It's not about wishing, it's about *making it happen*.'

I pointed to the price listed below the picture.

'Look, even if I could raise the deposit, even if my bank manager went mad and gave me a mortgage, even if I had the expertise to do the renovations, I couldn't afford to take six months off work to see it through. Look at it – it's not just a question of sticking up a bit of wallpaper and buying some new curtains, it needs serious repairs.'

But Josh didn't look at all disheartened.

'Even so, think about it. You might surprise yourself.' He grinned. It was a grin that started with his mouth and then spread over his entire face and lit up his eyes. 'You organised a flash mob,' he continued. 'That was amazing. If you can do that, you can work out how to get the money together to rebuild a house.'

The words 'flash mob' with their accompanying unpleasant memories thrust like a sword into my heart, but I steeled myself to act normally.

'Thanks,' I said. 'And I'm so grateful for what you did. It wouldn't have happened without you onside doing your techie bit. You and . . . Marty.'

I forced her name out of my mouth.

Josh shrugged modestly.

'One day computers will save the world,' he said. 'Until then, there's SuperConnect.'

I squinted at him through the glare of the afternoon sun. 'You really believe that, don't you?'

'I've got to,' he said, 'it's what gets me out of bed in the mornings. I wake up and think, "what can I do to make things better?"'

I handed him back his phone.

'You're lucky,' I said. 'You have a job where making people's lives better is a real possibility. All I have are a bunch of spoiled, wealthy clients who want me to arrange things just so that they can be spoiled and wealthy in a different part of the world.'

I looked at my battered handset: even the McMasters with their superhuman persistence wouldn't be able to get a connection on that one. I found a tissue and wrapped it round the phone, before placing it carefully back into my handbag.

'Flora.' Josh turned to me and looked into my eyes. My stomach did its now familiar (but pointless) somersaulting trick. 'This house: don't dismiss it out of hand. You've been wanting to go home since I met you. This could be your chance.'

I stood up and threw my bag over my shoulder.

'Thank you, Josh. Thank you for everything. Thank you for the flash mob and the beach and the picture of the house. It's been a bit of a rollercoaster, but thank you for being part of my tribe while I've been in San Francisco. I'm going to miss you.'

I bent over and kissed him on the top of the head.

'You and Marty . . .' I hesitated.

'Me and Marty?'

'I just wanted to say that I think I know what you're going to say and, for what it's worth, I reckon you've made the right decision. I hope it works out for you.'

The words felt like razor blades in my throat. I honestly don't know how I managed to get them out.

341

However, it was for the best; even though I couldn't have him, I very much wanted him to be happy. He deserved it.

Josh stared at me, a shocked expression on his lovely face. Then he shook himself and leapt to his feet.

'No, Flora,' he said, 'no, really, you've misunderstood. You see—'

But I had already turned away and was heading as fast as I could in the opposite direction.

'I'd better get back to check on Bella,' I called over my shoulder. 'I need to make sure she's not getting into her Abba costume and sneaking out to the Lizard Lounge. Thanks, Josh, and – I really mean this – have a good life, eh?'

And I hurried away, keeping my eyes deliberately focused on the road ahead.

## 22

By eight thirty that evening, the Lizard was completely heaving. In fact, 'heaving' was probably a gross understatement. The Battle of the Tribute Bands final, plus the extraordinary amount of publicity generated by the flash mob, meant that the whole of San Francisco was doing its best to squeeze in between the biking memorabilia and the squashy velvet sofas – or at least, that's what it felt like.

It wasn't a scene I'd thought I would experience first hand. When I'd got back from Fisherman's Wharf, I'd suggested to Bella that I should spend the evening with her. I'd thought I would rustle us up some supper and we'd spend a few hours quietly reminiscing over the good old days at Lavender Cottage. In reality it was nothing more than a vain attempt to distract my cousin from the fact that, had things turned out differently, she would have been up on stage singing her heart out that night. Bella, however, informed me that my babysitting services would not be required because Lisa had already asked if she could come for a girly night in involving black and white movies and a tub of Ben and Jerry's. Finding myself thus surplus to requirements, I decided I might as well go and see the final myself, so I put on my orange dress and golden heels and made my way down the hill to where it was all happening.

'Hey!' Bill flashed a delighted smile in my direction as soon as he saw me. 'Good work with the flash mob! You heard the latest?'

'No,' I said, unable to push my way through to the bar, peering at him round the broad, tanned shoulders of a couple of drag queens drinking bright pink cocktails.

'We had an email from the Mayor's office.' Bill was still grinning as though all his Christmases had come at once. 'The sell-off has been cancelled. The planning authority has put an embargo on any major building works in the Hope Street area for the next thirty years. Plus, they've registered all the buildings as being of historic interest. Anyway, I wanted to thank you – there's a bottle of champagne on your specially reserved table downstairs, but you'd better hurry because Lisa's already down there and I think she's got her drinking hat on.'

'Lisa's *here*?' I was puzzled.

Lisa was supposed to be on 'Distract Bella' duty.

'Well, unless it's her identical twin, and I don't think that even I could cope with multiple Lisas. And she's even in a good mood. She called me "sugar" twice – and that was before I'd put any alcohol in front of her.'

He couldn't have been happier if he'd won the lottery jackpot.

'Bill,' I said, 'I'm sorry if I'm being nosey, but what exactly do you see in her? I mean, all she ever does is insult you.'

344

Bill put down his cloth. He looked bashful to the point of being sheepish and there was the faintest hint of a blush spreading across his face.

'I can't help it, Flo. She's beautiful. She is simply perfect. I've known she was the one for me since she first walked through those doors and told me to mix her a gin martini with the emphasis on the gin and to hold the damn olives. I've never given up because I know she doesn't have anyone else – and you've only got to look at her to see how lonely she is.'

I nodded. I knew he was right because I'd seen it too: the wistful glances at other couples, the occasional sigh when she thought no one was listening. Lisa might pretend to have a heart of steel and an emotional dependency level of less than zero, but inside she was as human as the rest of us.

'So, is she downstairs?'

Bill nodded.

'And Robbie's there too. He was outside the door with his nose pressed up against the glass before we'd even opened. Didn't Lisa say that he and Toby were going on a date?'

'They'd planned to, but Toby cancelled,' I said, 'what with Bella being ill and Tobes wanting to spend time with her whilst she was in hospital.'

Bill frowned.

'Couldn't he have gone anyway – I mean, you and Lisa would have covered for him, wouldn't you?'

I nodded.

'Of course we would. I think it's got more to do with

him being his usual scaredy-cat self. Still' – a vague idea flickered into life in my head – 'if Robbie's here tonight, maybe we can sort something out. Leave it with me.'

Fighting my way as politely as possible through the crowds, I eventually made it downstairs. As I began to walk towards Lisa, whom I could see sitting alone at a table one row back from the stage, her head snapped round and she pointed accusingly at me.

'What the hell are you doing here? You're supposed to be with Bella,' she yelled over the hubbub.

'No,' I shouted back, 'that would be *you* spending the evening with her.'

'Nu-huh.' Lisa pursed her mouth into something resembling a cat's bottom. 'She texted me to say that you and she were having a night reminiscing about your girlhoods in Cornflake or some equally weird-sounding British place.'

'It's Corn*wall*, not Cornflake, and *she* told *me* that you were coming round to watch weepy movies and eat ice-cream,' I retorted, helping myself to a pistachio nut from a little dish in the middle of the table.

'Honey, when did I *ever* weep? Or eat for that matter.'

When indeed? I clapped my hands to my face.

'Oh Lordy,' I moaned, 'you don't think she's got us out of the way because she's planning on doing anything stupid, do you?'

'Like what? Get pregnant by Steve and nearly die?'

'No, I mean . . . Oh, I don't know what I mean.'

346

I pulled my phone out of my bag and rang Bella's number. It rang and rang and rang and then clicked on to voicemail.

'Could she be with Steve?' I asked. 'They've got a lot to talk about. That might be why she's not picking up.'

Lisa shook her head.

'Steve's not with Bella, he's around here someplace, I just saw him. Look, don't get your gussets in a twist over it, I expect she just wanted to rest. Leave it for a while and we'll try calling again later. I'm sure she's fine.' She hesitated before continuing: 'Although you did hear the news, didn't you? Abbadabbatastic are going to perform as a threesome.'

'Can they do that? Isn't it against the rules?'

'Tobes, Julia and Randall had a conflab and they're going to see if they can fly under the radar. If they win, the money goes towards Bella's hospital bill. Besides you can't imagine that Toby would let his adoring public down, do you? Uh-oh, speak of the devil.'

Toby appeared behind us and it was fair to say that he was not looking his best: his silver lamé catsuit was wrinkled, his hair was more Sid Vicious than Benny and Bjorn and he was limping because he only had one of his platform boots on.

'Bastards,' he hissed, waving the other boot at us, 'the total, utter, *beyond* bastard bastards.'

'Toby?' Lisa stood up and put her hands on her hips. 'Calm down and tell me what is going on.'

'The bastards over there – the Duran Duran Duran Duran Duran bastards.' Toby was so angry he added an extra 'Duran' by mistake. 'They've applied to have us disqualified.'

'How?' I was stunned. 'On what grounds? They're not even *in* the competition!'

'*I know!*' Toby stuffed his foot into his boot and yanked bad-temperedly at the zip. 'But Simon Le-fricking-Bon Bon is related to the guitarist in one of the other finalist groups and yadda yadda yadda they want us out. Bastards.'

I was genuinely appalled.

'So' – Lisa took a restorative draught of champagne – 'what are you going to do? Have you challenged it?'

'Of course we have.' Toby smoothed out the creases in his catsuit. 'Abbadabbatastic bring happiness, music and joy to the lives of the good people of this city. We're more of a public service than a band. It would be immoral for us to withdraw.' He paused and narrowed his eyes. 'Besides,' he growled, 'now I want to win just to *show* that crappy, fake-blond, eighties-throwback, tit-mouse asshole Le Bon-Bon. Steve's over there now, pleading our case with the management.'

'Go, Toby!' I patted him on the back. 'When the going gets tough, Toby pulls on a sequinned catsuit and platform heels!'

'Toby?' Randall tapped him on the shoulder. 'Bad news. Bill's checked the rule sheet and says it has to be the original line-up.'

'No!' I cried, leaping out of my seat and almost send - ing the bottle of champagne flying. 'That's not fair.'

The place was packed. If they won, Abbadabbatastic's share of the profits would make a decent dent in Bella's remaining medical bills. I looked up to see Bill himself pushing his way through the throng of spectators towards us. As he reached the table, we turned on him in a clamour of protest.

'Bill—'

'You can't *do* this!'

'Think about Bella!'

'I'm sorry,' he said, holding up his hands, 'but I've already bent the rules once for you guys. If you're not the original line-up, the band can't play.'

'But we *are* the original line-up,' Julie protested, 'it's just we're one short.'

'And the money is for Bella,' cried Toby, 'she's got whopping hospital fees that she can't pay. Can't you say it's a charity thing and let us through on a technicality?'

'I'm sorry.' Bill did indeed look deeply apologetic. 'I can't make an exception. Much as I'd like to.'

'And are the rules' – Lisa walked over to Bill and stroked a suggestive finger down his cheek – '*totally* sacred?'

Bill looked as though he was about to spontaneously combust. Lisa followed up the finger stroking with some seductive eyelash batting, but poor Bill just stared at his feet and looked miserable.

'You know they are,' he said. 'For pity's sake, you've signed them twice – which is once more than you should have done. Don't do this to me! If Bella is well enough to perform: fine. Otherwise you can't go on.'

'Come on,' I said to Lisa, 'it's not fair. You're putting Bill in an impossible position.'

'I'll put him in whatever position he likes if he'll let Abbadabbatastic play,' she purred.

But Bill was in the process of being dragged away by an impatient Simon Le Bon Bon and didn't hear her.

'OK,' Toby ran his hand through his hair, making it stick up even more in unattractive sweaty spikes. 'So the situation is this: we can't play, only we have to because otherwise we won't win.'

'Because if we don't win, we don't get the cash for Bella,' added Randall.

'And, almost as bad, Simon Le Pea-Brain Bon Bon gets away with it,' said Toby. 'Jeez, for two pins I'd go over *right now* and punch him so hard in his fat mouth that he'll need to put his toothbrush up his fat ass to clean his teeth.'

I'd never seen him so fired up. It was quite incredible. He was like a different man.

'That wouldn't help matters,' I reminded him, placing a restraining arm on his sleeve.

He narrowed his eyes. 'No, but it would make me *feel* a hell of a lot better.'

'So what do we do?' asked Julie.

'We go on,' said Toby, thumping the table manfully and making the champagne flutes jump. 'We just go on. Flo, put on Bella's costume.'

I stared at him as though he'd told me to harpoon a

blue whale and turn it into bite-sized, lemon-sprinkled goujons.

'Yes!' Lisa's face lit up. 'Brilliant idea, Toby! What are you waiting for, Flora?'

Had they all gone mad?

'No,' I said, trying to back away but finding all available exits blocked. 'I don't do stages and lights and stuff. Absolutely no. No way.'

Toby lowered his voice. 'Flo, this is serious. This is a shiny, platform-heeled, cheesy-disco *emergency*. We need you.'

'But I can't sing!' I hissed, hoping that Simon Le Bon Bon wasn't anywhere near with his ears flapping. 'And I'm a good few inches taller than Bella. If I put those boots on I'm going to be over six foot. How on *earth* do you think we're going to get away with it?'

'I don't know!' Toby flung his arms wildly in the air. 'Can't you *crouch* or something?'

'Yeah, right, because *that* wouldn't look weird!' I hissed.

'Or – or maybe bend your knees!' Toby demon - strated. 'Yes, like this!'

'And I will look indistinguishable from Bella because she *always* stands like a half-witted chimpanzee?' This was rapidly descending into madness. 'Look,' I said, doing my best to remain calm and not run screaming from the building, 'even if I agree *and* find a singing voice from somewhere *and* you can miraculously make the lyrics appear in my head *and* no one wonders why Bella is walking like a gorilla with a slipped disc – even if we get away with *all that*, do you realise this is fraud? We could get arrested. People take these competitions very seriously.'

Toby shook his head.

'We'll be fine. It's a local *band competition*, not international fine-art theft. Who's gonna care?'

'Do you care?' I replied.

'Of course I care.' His eyes narrowed again. 'Simon Le Butt Butt throws me out of the competition *over my dead body*.'

'Well, there you go,' I said. 'It's not something I want to get mixed up with.'

Lisa put her hand on my shoulder.

'I know,' she said softly, 'it's crazy, crazy stuff. But the bottom line is that Bella needs the money.'

I knew this. But I also knew that we'd find the money somehow: me, Auntie Stella, Steve, her colleagues at the hospital; we'd pull it together.

'Hey!'

We all looked round. Simon Le Bon Bon swaggered up to our table and helped himself to a handful of pistachio nuts.

'So,' he said, a grin spreading from the corners of his mouth to his cheap, highlighted hair, 'it seems Abbadabbatastic isn't so 'tastic after all. You see, I know what happened that night you knocked us out. I don't like being screwed over and I'm going to make damn sure you know what it feels like. So, so long, suckers. Oh, and Bathurst? Just so that you know, your ass *does* look big in that thing you're wearing. Not to mention stupid.'

'I'll give you stupid!' roared Toby, who looked as though he was just about to smack Simon in the face.

Lisa, Randall and I jumped on him and pinned him down in a chair.

'This is not the Wild West,' Lisa reminded him, 'and you are certainly not John Wayne. Now cool it.'

Toby turned to me with pleading eyes.

'You can't let him get away with that, you just can't.'

'Oh yes I can,' I contradicted. 'I don't want to go to prison for fraudulently impersonating a member of a Scandinavian pop band.'

'Hey! Abbadabbatastic!' Simon Le Bon Bon's voice floated over the noise of the crowd. 'Did you get your free beers? Oh, sorry, I forgot: they are only for people performing tonight. And did you know the whole of this evening's competition is being broadcast on KACMJ?'

'We *are* performing!' Toby yelled back. 'We're just waiting for Bella to get here, that's all.'

Simon smirked and melted back into the crowd.

It just got worse; now it wasn't only the fee for tonight that was in the balance, it was local radio airplay too.

'Where's Steve?' I asked. 'He's the manager, he should have the final say.'

'He went outside with Mickey Ramirez,' Julie chipped in. 'They said they wanted to talk business and it was too noisy to do it in here.'

'Oh, go on, Flora.' Toby's eyes were even more

pleading than before. 'Please. Pretty please. Please - pleasepleasepleasepleeeeeeease.'

I sat down at the table, poured myself a fluteful of champagne and drank it in one, huge gulp.

There was no way I was getting up on stage.

Absolutely no way.

Er . . .

'Which songs are you doing?' I asked.

'"Mamma Mia", "I Have a Dream" and "The Winner Takes It All",' replied Julie. 'Bella usually takes the vocal lead on the last two, but I will for tonight if you like. Can you do the harmonies or would it be easier for you to handle the main melody?'

Actually, I realised I could do either. Not only because Bella had been singing them round the flat for the past week and a half, but because she had been addicted to Abba more or less since she could talk and I'd spent year after year with the Swedish fab four as the soundtrack to my summer holidays.

Not that knowing the songs made any difference to anything. It was all still highly illegal.

'You can't let Le Bon Bon get away with this,' hissed Toby, 'you just can't.'

'Flora,' Lisa whispered, 'you *have* to do it. The honour of your family is at stake.'

'Not to mention the finances,' Toby chipped in. 'Think of the money we'll get from the airplay – and then think of Bella's twenty-grand hospital bill.'

I put my hands over my face. I really didn't have any choice, did I?

'I hate you,' I mumbled into my fingers. 'I hate the whole horrible lot of you. You are a bunch of bullies – and that includes you too, Julie. OK, I'll take Bella's place and I'll sing whatever it is that she sings.'

'Yessssss!' Toby punched the air in triumph. 'We have lift-off!'

With my hands still covering my visage, I allowed myself to be dragged towards the dressing room where I forced my reluctant body into Bella's costume. As well as being a couple of inches shorter, Bella was also a few pounds lighter and the Lycra bulged in an unhappy and unflattering manner round my midriff. This was not the sympathetic tailoring of Drusilla's beautiful vintage stock, this was a fashion nightmare from hell.

'Oh, God, *noooooo*,' I moaned softly, 'I look like the Michelin Man.'

Toby surveyed me critically.

'I'd say the Pilsbury Dough Boy,' he announced, a smirk flirting with his lips, 'after he's spent a weekend hitting the fried chicken and waffles in a big way.'

I turned on him and waggled an angry finger in his face.

'Don't push it, Bathurst,' I growled. 'When are we on? Do I have time to run home and grab my hold-it-all-in pants?'

'Sweetie,' drawled Toby, 'there isn't enough elastic in the universe.'

'Shudddup!' I elbowed him hard. 'One more fat joke and I walk.'

Suddenly, there were voices outside the velvet curtain that was all that separated us from the performance area. Toby blanched.

'Put your wig on and get out there.' Toby thrust a mass of unruly blondeness at me. 'That was the guitarist from one of the other bands. From this moment you need to be Bella, the whole Bella and nothing but the Bella, OK?'

I pulled the wig on and stared at myself in the mirror and was aghast to see my cousin's face staring back. I thought about how completely bizarre the genetic lottery was: once my red, unruly mop-top vanished, Bella and I were scarily similar. It was just a shame it didn't extend to the height or stomach departments.

'Whoa!' Toby looked suitably impressed. 'That's spooky.'

The curtain to the dressing room was pulled back and Lisa's head appeared.

'They're just about to announce the first act,' she hissed, 'are you coming? Oh my God – Flora, is that you?'

I nodded and then beckoned her inside.

'Bill,' I said. 'Back there when you were making certain suggestions to him: did you mean them?'

Lisa narrowed her eyes suspiciously.

'In what way?'

'I mean, would you say yes under other circumstances?' I elaborated. 'What do you really think of him?'

'He's nice,' Lisa admitted, glancing round before she replied to make sure no one else could hear. 'All right, he's more than nice – he's cute. And I like him. A lot. But that's my final offer.'

I threw up my hands in exasperation.

'So why don't you just go out with him?' I cried. 'You like him, he's nuts about you! What on earth is stopping you?'

Lisa's face clouded over and she stepped fully inside the velvet curtain, letting it swish closed behind her.

'Bill and I are good. We flirt; we banter; I insult the hell out of him and he looks admiringly at me and begs for more: it's how it's always been. I don't want to risk rocking the boat. I don't want it to go wrong.'

'Back at the hospital,' I said, remembering the night Bella was taken ill, 'you said you wanted to be loved. You said you didn't want to die without knowing what love is. You have to take a risk with love, Lisa. If you hide away from it like this, then you're never going to find it.'

'Like you and Josh?' she replied. 'Yeah, because you went all out to make sure you landed that particular catch, didn't you, honey?'

'That's different,' I snapped back, 'I'm certain that he's back with Marty. And . . .' I hesitated. I hadn't mentioned this to anyone else. 'I had a call from Barney, he wants me to move home.'

For the first time since I'd met her, Lisa was speech - less. She stared at me with her mouth open and her eyes wide.

'And you told him to shove his suggestion right up his proverbial, right?' she managed at last.

'Well, we kind of got cut off . . .'

Lisa shook her head.

'You shouldn't have even needed to think about it. And besides, I don't believe this crap about Josh and Marty, I just don't. The way Josh looks at you . . . No, no way.'

I was about to reply when the house lights dimmed. Then came the sound of a drum roll and Bill's footsteps as he made his way up the steps on to the stage.

'Come on' – Lisa tugged at my sleeve – 'there isn't any time for this. Sit down – and remember, *you're Bella.*'

## 23

It was only as the first band – a grunge-indie combo rejoicing in the name of Nevermind – began setting up on stage that the full meaning of what I had agreed to do sank in.

Within the next hour or so, I was going to have to stand up in front of several hundred people and make tuneful, coherent noises come out of my mouth. I suddenly felt very sick indeed. How Bella could do this sort of thing for pleasure was completely beyond me. And there was worse to come.

A movement out of the corner of my eye made me glance across the room – and my heart sank not just into my (platform) boots, but a considerable way below them; probably down into the subterranean depths of Bill's beer cellar.

Three tables away was Josh.

And standing next to him was Marty.

I felt even sicker.

'It's Josh,' I mumbled to Lisa who was sitting next to me, 'over there. No, don't look!'

'Coooo-eeeeee! Josh!' Lisa raised her hand and waved enthusiastically.

Marty noticed her, and nudged Josh, who squinted in our direction. When he saw it was Lisa, he gave a nervous grin and nodded in acknowledgement. His eyes rested on me for a moment and his brows drew together in a puzzled frown; then Marty spoke to him and he looked away.

As he did, Nevermind launched into a very loud version of 'Smells Like Teen Spirit', but I was too agitated to take any notice. Josh and Marty. Here. Now. Together.

'Hey!' Lisa summoned over one of the waitresses. 'That girl over there sitting next to the geek in the specs – who's she here with? Do you know?'

The waitress pulled a face.

'Well, I overheard her taking a call back up in the bar area and she said she was meeting a date. Is that any good?'

Lisa gave a brisk nod and then turned back to me.

'I'm sorry,' she said, 'I'm really, really sorry. I don't understand it, honey; mainly because I am *never* wrong on these matters. But listen: whoever he is going out with, that is not an excuse for you to hook back up with Boring, OK? Put the loser down; step away from the loser.'

She poured us both a drink and pushed the glass towards me but my stomach twisted and I pushed it back again.

But it wasn't Barney and his belated offer of the house that I was struggling with.

It was official. Marty was here on a night out with Josh. There was no way – *no way* – this could get any worse, was there?

Of course there was.

As I sat at the table, trying to keep my knees from knocking and praying that the zip on my catsuit wouldn't fail and reveal my muffin-top to the world, I became aware that someone was staring at me. You know that feeling you get when you can feel the weight of someone else's gaze upon you and all the tiny hairs on the back of your neck stand to attention in a slightly spooky way?

Well, I was getting it now.

I looked round, wondering if it was Josh – or, heaven forbid, Barney flying into SFO in a last-ditch attempt to save our relationship.

But it wasn't.

There, right at the far end of the room, squashed up against the staircase, were Steve and Mickey Ramirez – and they were staring right at me.

Oh monkeyfucklebutterchops.

I slid down into my seat as far as I could go and tilted the wig down over my face.

*Shit shit shit.*

Of all the people who could blow my cover sky high, it was those two. Steve of course knew Bella intimately; and Mickey knew the band, knew Bella's voice and knew her stage routines.

There was no way we were going to squeeze this past either of them.

'What are you *doing*?' Toby hissed at me, trying to readjust my wig.

I held on to it with both hands and pulled it down even further, so that it covered my eyes.

*If I couldn't see them, maybe that meant they weren't really there?*

'Steve,' I hissed back, 'over by the stairs. With Mickey. We're fucked, Tobes. Well and truly.'

'Steve wouldn't say anything, would he?' Toby whispered back, his eyes wide with fear. 'Tell me he wouldn't! We're doing this for Bella.'

'But Mickey doesn't know that,' I said. 'As far as he's concerned, Bella's sick. He sent her a bloody get-well card – I've seen it. What if he lets the cat out of the bag?'

As we looked, Simon Le Bon Bon sauntered over to Mickey and Steve. He said something, a nasty smile on his face, and pointed in our direction. As his eyes lighted on me, however, his smile lost some of its intensity and he turned back to Steve – presumably looking for an explanation.

'Oh my God.' Toby slid down in his chair too. 'What are we going to do? This is a nightmare. Think of the worst thing you can and then double it. No, quadruple it.'

'Come on, Steve,' I willed across the heaving room. 'Come on, Steve! Use your noddle and play along with us!'

Mickey continued to stare intently at me, but Steve – I heaved the most enormous sigh of relief – just shrugged and said something to Simon Le Bon Bon that looked as though it ended in 'off'.

I pushed the wig up from my face and heaved myself back into a sitting position. If I was going to make this work, I needed to get a grip.

'Hold up your compact mirror,' I hissed to Lisa, who obligingly got the article out of her handbag. 'I have to get my hair straight.'

I carefully rearranged the wig, tucking up any lurking strands of auburn underneath its platinum tresses. Nevermind played their last few grungy chords and bowed their shaggy heads before shuffling off the stage.

Bill walked past our table on his way to MC the changeover in the acts and caught sight of me. He stared as though he'd seen Elvis himself waiting to perform, then he hissed:

'I don't want to know. Whatever the hell crazy idea you have come up with, I am *not* a part of it, OK? If you are caught, on your own heads be it.' Then he bounded up the steps and grinned at the audience. 'And a huge hand for the first of this year's finalists: Nevermind!' he yelled as the applause once again rang out round the room.

Once it had subsided to the sort of level that would merely bend your eardrums, rather than make them bleed, he continued:

'Our next act is a favourite here at the Lizard Lounge. Their musical skill is legendary – as is their ability to dance and play musical instruments whilst wearing authentic seventies clothing. You've seen the rest, now meet the best: Abbadabbatastic!'

The audience's reaction was spectacular. Not only could I hear the sound of the people clapping and whooping as we made our way on to the stage, I could actually feel the sound vibrating up through my platform boots as I walked up the steps. I went to swallow, but noticed my mouth was doing a convincing impression of the Atacama Desert and there was nothing to swallow *with*. Then Toby bumped into me.

'Sorry,' he whispered in the semi-darkness before the lights went up, 'I'm just a bit anxious, what with Robbie in the audience. I know I should have gone and said hello, but I couldn't. I just couldn't.'

I turned to him. 'Toby, do you fancy him?'

'No,' replied Toby.

'No?' I whispered back aghast.

'I don't fancy him,' Toby continued, 'I worship him. I adore him. I think he's the best thing since granola-sprinkled-fat-free-black-cherry yogurt.'

'So *do* something about it then,' I hissed.

'I did,' he muttered, 'I asked him out, remember?'

'And then you cancelled – yes, I know. What you need to do now is stop moping around and ask him out again.'

Toby shook his head.

'I can't. I just can't, Flora. It was all I could do to call him first time round.'

I shook my head in despair. What was *wrong* with these people?

Then – suddenly – I found myself blinking in the glare of the spotlights.

The last time I'd been on stage had been twenty-five years ago when I'd played the Angel Gabriel in the school nativity. I'd been holding out for the part of the Virgin Mary, but that had gone to Justine Witherspoon and, when the time came for me to hand over the doll dressed as the Little Baby Jesus, I just couldn't do it. A tug-of-war ensued, ending only when the Little Baby Jesus' head parted with the rest of his plastic body, and sent me flying off the stage into the lap of a surprised-looking nun.

It had been my most humiliating moment to date, but one I was becoming increasingly sure I would now surpass.

I squinted into the glare of the stage lights but could only make out the first couple of rows of faces in the crowd. My heart was pounding and my stomach was doing its best to scramble out of my body via my oesophagus. All my ideas of cousinly solidarity were wiped from my mind by the sheer, holy terror of standing in front of a group of people wearing nothing but a straining silver catsuit and an unconvincing wig.

I looked round at Toby, hoping for some reassurance, but he was busy smiling and waving at the audience. Julie and Randall also seemed to be enjoying the experience, although how (or, indeed, why) they managed this was totally beyond me.

'Hello, Lizard Lounge!' Julie stepped forward to the microphone and the room erupted in the wildest of applause. 'We are Abbadabbatastic. We are live, we are hot and we are here to *rock this room*!'

The familiar plinky-plonky opening of 'Mamma Mia' started to stream out from the speakers and the crowd clapped and swayed in time to the music. Everybody was gearing up to party – everyone, that was, apart from me. In my head I was desperately trying to recall the lyrics to the first verse, but my mind had gone blanker than an unused cheque book. All I could think about was Meryl Streep in a pair of denim dungarees leaping around in a hayloft.

I closed my eyes and prayed very hard for something – anything – to happen so that I didn't have to sing.

And, just as I did so, there was a funny screeching noise and the music stopped.

I opened one eye, secretly impressed by the power of my thoughts, and saw Bill squeezing his way through the crowds towards one of the speakers.

'Slight technical hitch!' he called. 'Be fixed in a moment!'

A moment! I had a *whole* moment?

Surely I could come up with something in a moment?

Someone tapped my left foot. I looked down. It was Lisa.

'Say something,' she hissed, 'interact with the crowd. You look like someone just chipped you out of the Greenland ice-sheet.'

She was right: Bella would never have stood there on stage looking like a pole-axed lemon. Feeling as though I was taking my life in my hands, I stepped forward to the microphone, running my tongue round my teeth to loosen it up and willing inspiration to strike.

Thankfully, inspiration did.

'Hello, Lizard Lounge!' I cried, hoping that the genetic lottery had blessed me with my cousin's speaking voice as well as her bone-structure. 'Here at Abbadabbatastic, we are sticklers for romance. We are in love with being in love. So, whilst Bill fixes the sound system, we would like to introduce the new "date-o-matic" feature to our act.'

Toby, Julie and Randall were staring at me as though I'd gone mad and, frankly, I don't think they were too far off the mark. However, the good news was that my knees had stopped shaking and my heart was only beating half as loudly as before.

'So if you know of two people who are aching to get together but are letting circumstances keep them apart,' I went on, 'let us know and we will do our best to bring them together. Just to show you what I mean, we will begin with our own Bjorn here, otherwise known as Toby Bathurst. Now Toby, as you will see, is an attractive, successful man – in fact, pretty much your average San Franciscan sex god.'

Toby was torn between preening himself in the light of this description and staring at me as though I had a grenade in my hand and was threatening to take out the pin.

'Well,' I said, realising that I was beginning to sound more like Cilla Black from *Blind Date*, 'Toby is actually a lonely heart, ladies and gentlemen. He might look the part of a successful young professional who has it all but what he doesn't have is *love*, even though love is knocking on his door as we speak.'

A ripple of oohs and ahhs went round the crowd. Toby mouthed something at me and made a don't-you-dare motion with his hands.

I ignored him and turned my attention back to the audience. The few faces that I could see through the glare of the lights were fixed on me, their mouths slightly open and their eyes boggly with anticipation: they were hooked.

I felt a strange rush of power and my nerves vanished completely.

'Love came looking for Toby,' I recapped, the Cilla voice getting stronger and stronger, 'but Toby turned it away. Why did he do that, ladies and gentlemen? Why?' There was a gasp of anticipation from the audience. 'Because he is scared,' I replied, 'scared of getting hurt. But the thing is, if he doesn't take that chance, he will never know.'

I turned to Toby, who began to back away. There was, however, only limited room on the tiny stage to manoeuvre before he fell off the edge, so he stopped and glowered at me instead. If looks could kill, I would have been deader than a cremated dodo but, egged on by the crowd, I continued.

'Robbie,' I said, spying Toby's would-be date on one of the front tables, 'come up here a mo, would you?'

Robbie obediently bounded on to the stage.

'Robbie,' I asked, 'do you like Toby?'

'Yes,' said Robbie.

'Do you really, really like him?'

'I do,' said Robbie again.

It was starting to sound decidedly matrimonial. I turned to Toby.

'And do you like Robbie?' I asked.

Toby nodded his head.

'So then?' I asked the assembled multitudes. 'What should they do?'

'Date! Date! Date! Date!' the audience chanted in unison.

I turned back to the boys. Toby was smiling sheepishly at Robbie, who was smiling equally sheepishly back at him. It was unbearably sweet.

'When and where?' I threw the decision out into the throng.

'My brother owns the Orangery restaurant,' yelled someone from the crowd. 'Free dinner and drinks for the pair of them on Friday!'

Everyone clapped and cheered.

'You're done,' called Bill from the bottom of the stage. 'You're good to go!'

As he spoke, my newly-found confidence began trickling down my spine and exiting my body by way of my toes. Setting people up on dates was one thing, but singing Abba songs was quite another.

'Do you want another lonely-heart fix?' I yelled at the crowd.

'Yes!' came the roar of the response.

Conscious that I was only putting off the evil moment temporarily, but equally conscious that at least that meant I didn't have to encounter it *now*, I turned to Bill.

'Bill,' I said, playing for time, 'come here a minute.'

With a look of apprehension on his face, Bill hesitated for a moment before scrambling up the steps and joining me on the stage. He shielded his eyes as he looked out into the audience.

'Now Bill here is also in love, aren't you, Bill?'

Bill gave me an uneasy look but nodded his head.

'And you have been enamoured of this particular lady for a long time now, haven't you?'

Bill nodded again.

'Ever since she walked up to the bar three years ago and told me that I was a knucklehead without the first idea how to fix a decent martini,' he reminisced, a faraway look in his eyes and a smile on his lips.

'Awwwwwwwww!' said the crowd.

'And is the lady in question in the room now?' I asked.

'Yes,' said Bill, 'she's down there.'

He pointed at Lisa, who had the uncharacteristic expression of a rabbit caught in headlights plastered across her face.

'Lisa,' I said, 'will you join us?'

Lisa shook her head violently.

'Then go to her, Bill,' I urged. 'Go to her and tell her how you feel.'

Bill didn't need to be asked twice. He jumped off the stage and made his way through the throng, which parted before him like the Red Sea. Then he went down on one knee and took Lisa's hand in his.

I held my breath.

To my astonishment, she didn't pull her hand away.

Instead, something that might have been a blush – I couldn't quite tell, my vision was still compromised by the stage lighting – crept across her face.

Bill cleared his throat.

'Lisa,' he said, 'I love you. Please make me the happiest man in the world and tell me that I have a chance?'

This time it wasn't just me holding my breath – it was everyone in the entire room.

'Go on, Lisa, say yes!' someone called out from the back.

Lisa opened and closed her mouth a couple of times. Then she got out of her chair and pulled Bill to his feet. Despite the lights, I saw her eyes flash and noticed her sharp intake of breath.

I couldn't bear it.

None of us could.

Behind me, I could see Robbie and Toby clinging to each other as the tension mounted (although that could have been an excuse for a quick fondle).

Lisa let go of Bill and positioned herself with her hands on her hips. I had no idea if she was going to tell him she loved him or punch him in the face.

Then, with a little cry of abandon, she threw her arms round his neck and kissed him.

The crowd went wild.

Bill scooped Lisa up in his arms and kissed her again.

The crowd went even wilder.

'Lisa and I have a bit of lost time to catch up on,' said Bill, 'but, whilst we do, I give you Abbadabbatastic!'

He nodded at Randall and for the second time that evening the unmistakable sound of the 'Mamma Mia' introduction filled the room. Everyone clapped and cheered and jumped up and down. Robbie and Toby exchanged a quick peck on the lips, and Robbie – with a grin so dazzling you could have used it to guide aircraft in to land at night – trotted happily back down the steps to his table.

I listened to the familiar chords ring out from the speakers and waited for my nerves to return as they had done last time.

But they didn't.

My heart pounded and my stomach did a bit of jiggling, but it was more adrenalin than the terror that had paralysed me earlier. *I could do it!*

With a confidence I had never before felt, I stepped up to the microphone and unhooked it from its stand. The words of the song flowed easily through my brain and the harmonies I had heard Bella sing during the long, hot summer days in Cornwall flooded back. In my exuberance, I shook my head in the manner of a girl in a shampoo ad and then shook it again just for good measure and—

To my horror something dropped from underneath the wig on to my shoulders. Something that felt much like one of my own, auburn curls.

I continued to sing, keeping my head as still as possible.

But – plop! Another curl and then another followed the dictates of gravity and slithered out of place.

Still I sang on, trusting in the god of unwilling tribute-band performers to deliver me; however, I suspect he must have been on other duties that night because, as soon as the music for the first song ended, a puzzled voice from the back piped up:

'That's not the girl who's normally in that band!'

The words hit me like a punch to the solar plexus and I peered out into the glare of the lights to see where the voice was coming from.

It was bloody Rasta-Hat youth from the flash mob.

With the crowd murmuring their discontent, he continued:

'Bella Jones is blonde,' he said, 'and this one is a redhead. Look.'

Very slowly, I lifted up my hand to view the extent of the damage. Pretty much all of my natural hair had fallen down and quite a chunk of that was in full view round the edge of my face. Damn, damn, *damn*!

'She's the girl from the flash mob!' yelled someone else. 'Look, I've got the footage on my phone – it's definitely her. Anyone here with SuperConnect?'

Virtually everyone in the room said they were and a few hundred phones were taken out of pockets and bags and a few hundred SuperConnect apps were activated.

'She is, you know,' someone over to my left called out. 'She really is.'

'She's a cheat!' shouted Simon Le Bon Bon.

There were disgruntled murmurings amongst the crowd.

'She's not a cheat,' cried a familiar voice that I couldn't immediately place. 'She's Flora Fielding and she's a local hero.'

'She saved the Apple Pie!' called out a voice from the back which I recognised as Elvira's.

'And Drusilla's!' yelled the eponymous owner – whom I could just make out in the third row of the audience wearing a 1920s flapper outfit, rounded off with black lipstick and industrial quantities of eyeliner.

'And the Lizard Lounge!' shouted one of the waitresses. 'I'd be unemployed if it wasn't for her.'

Simon Le Bon Bon folded his arms.

'Well, she's still not part of the original band line-up – and I say this disqualifies them.' He stood at the foot of the stage like a malevolent, peroxided gnome, scowling at us. Then he began a slow handclap. 'Off! Off! Off! Off!'

'Listen.' There was nothing else for it. I raised my microphone to my lips. 'I'm not Bella, 'I'm her cousin Flora. Bella was desperate to be here tonight but she is recovering from a serious operation and is under doctor's orders not to perform. I thought I would be the next best thing. We do share twelve and a half per cent of each other's DNA, so on a molecular level I'm actually a pretty good substitute.'

A sympathetic murmur rippled through the crowd.

Simon Le Bon Bon, however, remained unmoved.

'The rules state you have to use your original line-up,' he replied, pointing at Toby, 'and whilst we're on the subject I've heard a couple of people muttering that you used to be Swedish, Bathurst. Are you an imposter as well?'

There were cries of 'get on with it' and 'I want the music'. The crowd were growing restless.

'Well,' I said, hoping that if I kept talking for long enough something miraculous might occur, 'well, I think it depends on what you mean by "line-up" . . .'

'For crying out loud,' yelled someone from the very back. 'Where's Bill? Get Bill to sort this out and let's get on with it!'

I shifted uneasily.

Simon Le Bon Bon fixed me with an inscrutable stare and began his slow handclap again.

'Off! Off! Off!'

'Listen!' I said. 'Bella is *ill*.'

'I'm sorry,' said Simon with faux sincerity, 'I think you are confusing me with someone who gives a damn!'

'She can't perform!' I cried again.

'Who says?'

I was so amazed, I dropped my microphone. My mouth swung open and I wanted to tug at my ears to make sure they were still there.

It couldn't be; it just couldn't be . . .

But it was.

A small blonde figure was pushing her way down the staircase. A small blonde figure wearing a white mini-skirt, a white top with huge bat-winged sleeves and white thigh-high boots.

I blinked and looked again – but it was still there.

Small, feisty and perfectly formed: it was Bella.

375

'You should be at home in bed,' I told her. 'You should be asleep.'

'And miss this?' Bella grinned and made her way across the room towards the stage. 'You underestimate me, coz. I wouldn't sit this one out for the world!'

Steve darted out of his seat, his eyes wide with concern, and murmured something in her ear. Bella, however, kissed him on the lips and then pushed him away before walking up the steps on to the stage. I could see that she was moving rather more slowly and stiffly than usual but apart from that, she was back to her normal indomitable self. She raised her arms to the crowd, who duly cheered, and then bent down slowly and picked up the fallen microphone.

'Mine, I think,' she told me, then turned to Randall: 'Let's get this show on the road. *Hello, Lizard Lounge!*'

The ensuing roar of welcome slowly subsided and Bella walked over to me and put an arm round my waist.

'This is my cousin Flora, everyone. When we were little, Flora was the big sister I never had – and she was brilliant at it. When I moved to San Francisco, we drifted apart, but now we are back together and I am never letting her go again. You've got to find your tribe, people – and when you find them, hold on to them tight.'

She turned to Simon who was standing at the foot of the stage glowering at us. If looks could kill, he would be up on a charge of multiple murder.

'OK, Simon, you win. We're not the original line-up, but so what? Music should be about entertaining people and having fun. So, Lizard Lounge, you have a choice. Now that Abbadabbatastic are officially out of the competition, do you want to hear something else? It's a little number I believe is doing quite well on the internet called "Respect Me".'

The crowd went nuts.

Mickey, grinning all over his face, plugged an iPod into one of the speakers and the opening piano intro of Bella's original composition flowed out across the room. Then Bella held her hand up and Mickey pressed pause.

'Hey, Elvira and Sylvie,' She called, 'you guys come up here. And Drusilla and Brandi . . .' She peered out into the darkness. 'In fact, anyone who wants to, come up here and sing. We're going to celebrate!'

There was a general scramble up on to the stage, some people I recognised, some I didn't. But none of that mattered.

Bella looked out into the crowd once again.

'There's one person missing,' she said, 'someone very important. Steve, come up here. Steve is the manager of Abbadabbatastic, everyone; but, more importantly, he is the man I've decided I want to spend the rest of my life with. So please, everyone, a big hand for Steve!'

And Steve, looking as though he didn't understand what was happening, came up on stage and was kissed again by Bella. The crowd cheered.

I glanced down into the small pool of visible faces at the front and saw Josh. He smiled at me – a small, hopeful smile – but I looked away.

Then Bella nodded at Mickey and the piano intro played once more. She put the microphone up to her lips and began to sing in a low, husky voice. Then, at the moment the harmony began, she nudged me, and I leaned in to share the mike, blending my voice with hers. It felt good. And it felt even better when the others joined in, and Piano Guy struck up from somewhere at the back of the stage and, eventually, the whole of the Lizard Lounge was swaying and waving their hands in the air in time to the music. It was a tribe – a huge, SuperConnected tribe – with Bella and myself at its heart. I may have arrived in San Francisco alone, but I would leave with a whole community of new friends. Friends who genuinely cared about me and about each other. And it was, as they say in California, *awesome*.

The only duff note – the only decidedly minor key – was, of course, Josh. But despite the lonely, Josh-shaped gap that lingered in my heart, I held my head up high and sang as loudly as I could. If he was not part of my tribe, then that meant there would be someone else. The universe was a big old place and, so long as I didn't lock myself away from its possibilities, I would find whoever it was I was meant to be with.

And that was definitely worth singing about.

# 24

The applause was thunderous. Any suggestion that Bella's song was not destined to be the stuff of legend was laughable. However, it had taken an awful lot out of her and, as she went to leave the stage, she stumbled. Steve caught her and swept her up into his arms. He carried her down the steps and across the room, the crowd standing aside to let him through.

Needing to know she was OK, I followed. As I walked through the throng, there was a tug on my sleeve. I looked round: it was Josh. My heart pulsed painfully for a moment or two, but I shook my head, remembered that he had never been mine to keep, and hurried after Steve and Bella.

Back up at street level, the air was cooler and fresher. Steve carried Bella to a plush, claret-coloured sofa and laid her down. I unzipped her boots and eased them off her legs, whilst Julie fetched her a glass of iced water. I crouched down next to her and smoothed her hair away from her face.

'Are you all right?' I asked. 'Do you need me to call a doctor?'

Bella shook her head.

'It doesn't hurt.' She adjusted her position and grimaced. 'Well, it doesn't hurt *much*. Nothing like it did.'

'Even so' – Toby was standing over her, putting extra cushions behind her back – 'you are still only a few days post-op, you need to be careful.'

'Bella,' I said, 'seriously, if you're not well, we will get a doctor. You mustn't worry about the cost. If you need it, we'll do it.'

Bella shook her head.

'Pass me my bag, I've got some painkillers in there. A couple of those and I'll be as right as rain.'

She duly located the bottle and swallowed a couple of white tablets. I dreaded to think how much they cost apiece and made a mental note to be grateful in future for the NHS.

The door behind the bar area opened and Bill and Lisa walked out. They both had the most enormous smiles on their faces and there was bright red lipstick smudged all over Bill's face.

Toby winked at her.

'Get a room,' he said.

Lisa grinned back.

'We already did,' she said. Then she caught sight of Bella. 'Holy laparoscopy, Bella-Boo, what are you doing here?'

Bella shrugged.

'Just couldn't stay away, I'm afraid. What's a girl supposed to do?'

'Stay at home and rest,' I said, squeezing her hand. 'That's with my bossy cousin hat on. My Abbadabbatastic fan hat, on the other hand, says go you and well done.'

'I'm sorry I missed it,' Lisa said before shooting a wicked glance at Bill. 'Well, when I say *sorry*, I actually mean *not that sorry*. I was having a rather good time.' She grinned sheepishly and smoothed the wrinkles in her silk dress.

Bill walked over to the till and pulled out a large wad of cash.

'Belle,' he said, 'I can't give you the winnings, obviously, but I'm going to give you this. It's my share of the door takings for tonight and I want you to have it and put it towards what you owe for your operation.'

Bella shook her head.

'No,' she said, 'it's a lovely gesture, Bill, and I appreciate it enormously, but I've had enough of living off other people's goodwill. This is yours, take it and use it to do something wonderful with Lisa.' She paused. 'One of the reasons why I wanted you, Flo, and you, Lisa, out of the way this evening was because I was planning to come down here and I knew you would both try and stop me – from the best of motives, naturally – but there was another: I'd arranged to have a meeting back at the apartment with Mickey. Now, Steve, you know all about that . . .'

Steve's eyes glowed with pride.

'Bella is going to be releasing "Respect Me" as a single. Mickey has agreed to produce it and we're arranging for it to be available as a download,' he said. 'It's going to be huge.'

'That's brilliant!' I cried, throwing my arms round her 'That's absolutely brilliant!'

381

Bella gave a timid smile.

'At the moment it's just the one song,' she said. 'I'm not giving up my medical career yet. I love nursing. It's all I ever wanted to do and I'd hate to feel I'd left because I was forced out, rather than because that was what I chose to do. But it's kind of like a Plan B, you know?'

'That's my girl,' said Steve proudly.

'And the other piece of news is that I'm planning to invest some of my earnings from the song in a spot of property development.'

'What are you talking about, Bella?' Toby frowned. 'You're not planning on buying up Hope Street and turning it into a giant shopping mall, are you?'

Bella laughed – and then grimaced.

'No, it's something much closer to my heart.'

She rummaged in her bag and pulled out her phone. After tapping a couple of buttons, she turned the screen round to face us. I caught my breath. It was the estate agent's photo of Granny's house.

Bella turned to me and frowned.

'Flo, are you all right? You look a bit peaky.'

'Yes,' I said, my brain adjusting slowly (and, I admit, a little unwillingly) to the idea that Bella, rather than myself, might be the new owner, 'I'm fine. I can't think of anyone else I would rather have living there.'

Bella went to laugh, but stopped herself just in time.

'Oh, you big old muppet,' she said. 'Think about it! I'm here in San Francisco. I can't be hopping over to

Cornwall every five minutes to oversee the renovations. And it looks as though there'll need to be a *lot* of renovations.'

It took a while for the meaning of her words to sink in.

'You mean you want *me* to project manage it for you?' I asked, still not entirely certain what was going on.

Bella nodded happily.

'Although I was thinking more along the lines of you being a co-owner,' she said. 'Josh forwarded the details to me. He said you'd dismissed the idea of buying it yourself, and he wondered if I could talk some sense into you.'

For a moment I couldn't speak.

'I don't want to step on your toes, Flo,' Bella continued. 'If you want the house, it's yours. But if you need a helping hand with the finances, I would be honoured to help you out as soon as I am solvent again.'

'You have more money than you think you do, Flora.' Lisa, who had been grooming hard whilst we'd been talking, put her lipstick away and snapped her compact mirror shut. 'You have the cash Barney is going to repay you for the contributions you made to *his* home. Remember, it wasn't just a few tins of paint you paid for. What you did must have pushed up the value of the place no end. He owes you for that.'

I thought back to the reclamation-yard bills, the builders' fees and the countless other things I'd stumped up for, even before the mortgage payments were taken into account. And I'd only done it because I'd believed him when he'd said it was my home as much as his. Lisa was right – he did owe me.

'And I'm paying the hospital bill now, remember?' added Steve.

'Flora,' asked Bella softly, 'what do you say?'

'I say "yes",' I replied. The idea of sharing the project with Bella was actually *more* perfect than doing it by myself. 'Of course I do.'

'Then it's settled.' Bella grinned. 'We'll use Barney's money as part of the deposit, and Toby's made some phone calls and it looks as though you will be eligible for a mortgage that covers a large chunk of the balance. We might have to wait a while for the money from the download to start coming through, so Mum has said that she'll lend us a bit in the meantime so that we can push forward. It's going to be a real family project!'

I nodded. Weekends spent down in Cornwall watching the house being pieced back together: it was a dream come true.

Suddenly, Bella gave a little gasp and all eyes were turned from me on to her. She had her phone in her lap and was staring at it.

'It's a text from Joy-Anne at the hospital,' she said. 'She's just finished her shift. She says there was a meeting this afternoon and the Hamptons have dropped their claim. There will still have to be an inquiry, but it will only be a formality. I told her about the herbal tranquillisers and they reran the toxicology tests and traces showed up in Jessie Hampton's blood. The hospital will be contacting me on Monday, but she says they want me back at work as soon as I'm fit. My pay and insurance and everything is going to be sorted out. Thank God. Thank God, thank God, thank God.' She buried her face in her hands and took a long, deep breath.

'We knew it wasn't your fault, honey.' Lisa smoothed her forehead. 'We always had faith in you.'

There was a moment of mutual, thankful silence. Then, from somewhere behind us, I heard someone respectfully clear his throat.

We all turned round.

Standing by the bar, and looking very nervous indeed, was Josh.

'I don't want to intrude,' he said, 'but if I could . . . Flora, a word . . . if it's not too much trouble?'

I opened my mouth to say that I was far too busy looking after my ailing cousin, but I felt a tugging at my sleeve and I realised that the same ailing cousin had different ideas.

'Dragons, Flora,' whispered Bella, 'you've got to face them. Go on. If I can do it, you can too.'

'Shall we' – Josh looked as though he was about to explode with bashfulness, 'shall we go somewhere else?'

I stood up.

'But what about Marty?' I asked, thinking this was strange behaviour for a man on a date.

'Oh,' he said airily, 'it's cool. Don't worry about her.'

This still didn't make sense, but I decided to let it pass until we were alone. Josh walked over to the door and held it open for me and, together, we stepped out into the San Franciscan twilight.

Hope Street looked as lovely as ever; the brightly painted shop-fronts as colourful and vibrant as a jarful of old-fashioned sweets. Music pulsed from the basement of the Lizard up through the pavement and into our feet; and, high above us, hung the same moon that had been watching over me since Ocean Beach. We walked along the road without a word passing between us, before crossing and making our way towards the park at the top of the hill. When we were nearly at the top, I stopped and looked back and saw San Francisco laid out like a fairy tale below us: street lights twinkling in the gloaming and, in the distance, the towers of the Golden Gate Bridge echoed back the very last rays of daylight across the inky expanse of the Bay. A thrill of belonging ran through me: I loved this city. I had felt more at home here, amongst the slightly mad group of people I had met during my stay, than I ever had in England – except, perhaps, for those summer days in a small house on a clifftop in Cornwall.

And the knowledge that I had, truly, found my tribe made me feel brave.

I took a deep breath and broke the silence. 'Josh, I know you came to the Lizard tonight with Marty as your date. One of the waitresses overheard her on the phone.'

Josh's features were a study in bewilderment.

'Marty wasn't my date,' he said.

I clenched my fists into little balls. *Why* was he trying to deny it?

'Josh,' I said as patiently as I could, considering that my heart was pounding so loudly my eardrums were in danger of perforating, 'I saw her kiss you – at the flash mob. I *know* how she feels about you.'

A very peculiar expression was creeping over his face.

'And you,' he said, 'how do *you* feel about me?'

I paused – but only for a moment. What was the point of pretending any longer?

'I really like you.' I stuck my chin out defiantly and looked him right in the eye. 'And I hate the fact that you chose her over me.'

At first, Josh looked shocked. Then he looked disbelieving. Then, to my annoyance, an enormous grin spread over his face.

'And what', I asked crossly, 'is so amusing about that?'

Josh's grin surged up a couple of thousand more volts; then, with a huge effort, he got his features back under control.

'Oh, Flora,' he said, 'you've got hold of the wrong end of the stick. In fact, you're so wrong you've managed to grab a completely different stick altogether.'

'I have?' I asked blankly.

Josh reached out and took my hand in his. It was warm and strong and comforting.

'Oh Lord, where to start?' he said. 'OK. Marty *did* have a date at the Lizard, only it wasn't me – it was someone from her regular work and she arranged to meet him there after the Battle of the Tribute Bands thing had finished. She had just come over to say hi when you saw her – she wasn't *with* me at all.'

I stared at him. My mouth may also have opened and closed a few times, but I wasn't really paying much attention.

'Now, as I have tried to tell you about a million bazillion times, Marty and I had a chat and I told her how I felt about you. She said that yes, it had been a nasty shock walking in on us, but she agreed it was time she and I got out of the rut we'd fallen into. She told me there was this guy, Graham, at work who she liked and we resolved that the benefits ended then and there. Talking to Marty was the easy bit; the difficulty has been getting *you* to listen.'

For a moment, hope flared up in my heart: Josh was in love with me! Then I quickly put my sensible head back on: at the end of the day, it didn't matter what Josh and I felt about each other. I lived in England and he had his whole life here in San Francisco – not to mention his business, which, by the looks of things was just about to go nuclear. The idea of us being together was pie in the sky.

Josh tugged at my hand and we slipped through the gates of the park.

'Do you know why I moved to San Francisco?' he asked.

I turned my head and looked at him. I could see his profile silhouetted against the darkening blue of the sky. My stomach did its usual trick of turning cartwheels, and this time I let it. Josh was worth turning cartwheels for – it was just a shame I only had twenty-four hours left to enjoy the sensation.

'No,' I said.

'Partly because I needed to be near the sea,' he said, pointing out across the Bay. 'I know all you hear about San Francisco is the fog and the mist, but isn't that glorious? A huge stretch of water leading out into the largest ocean in the world. This may sound a bit weird, but it's as if it gives me extra head-space. I can think, and imagine, and create, and there's no limit to what I can do.'

'But there are limits,' I replied, almost laughing at the ridiculousness of it all. 'I hate to rain on your parade, Josh, but it's true. My life is based in England and, even with the best will in the world, five thousand miles is too great a distance for us to try and make a relationship work.'

'I know.' Josh's grip on my hand tightened. 'But I'm ahead of you on that.'

He delved into his pocket and handed me a small, rectangular object. I squinted at it in the gathering gloom. It was a phone. A very nice one.

'Turn it on.' Josh sounded rather excited.

I did. The screen glowed in the darkness, illuminating a range of apps identical to my old phone.

I turned to Josh.

'I don't understand,' I said.

Josh put his arms round my shoulders, reached over and pressed the SuperConnect icon.

'This is your new cell – I mean mobile,' he said, 'to replace the one I broke. Except I've installed a free upgrade. This version of SuperConnect is the UK prototype. I've been in talks with a couple of manufacturers since the flash mob went viral and they are keen to roll out SuperConnect to the European market. I'm planning to come over for an extended visit in about six weeks' time and, if they like it, I'll be over for a lot longer than that.'

A shiver of excited anticipation flew up my spine.

Josh was coming to England!

Then my heart sank again.

'I'm not being picky,' I said, 'but six weeks – a *whole six weeks*.'

'Well,' said Josh, pulling his jacket round us both as a chilly breeze whipped in from the Bay, 'we've got a bit of time until you go.'

'Only one full day,' I said.

'You can do a lot in one day,' he informed me, 'including getting to know the girl you've fallen hopelessly in love with a lot better.'

I snuggled into the protective curve of his body to keep warm.

'Plus . . .' he pressed something else on the SuperConnect app and a little video camera icon popped up. 'This is for you. I took a bit of a liberty and customised your version. It's a live link that feeds in directly to my phone and my laptop. Wherever you are, whenever you want, press the button and I appear.'

I was stunned. This was my own little piece of SuperConnect technology – invented especially for me.

'And I will be counting every moment, until I get on that plane and see you for real in six weeks.'

I nodded. Then I took the phone from his hands and switched it off.

I felt Josh hesitate.

'Don't you like it?' he asked.

I turned round to face him and brushed my lips against his. He tasted even more delicious than he had done that Wednesday night on Ocean Beach.

'I love it,' I said. 'It's just that if I think about it too much, I'm going to cry – and I don't want to waste one single second of the next few hours being sad.'

Josh pulled me in close and buried his nose in my hair.

'There's no reason to be sad,' he said. 'So long as it's what we both want, we will find a way to be together. And you know you're coming back here, don't you? There are some people who just belong in SF, and the city never lets them go. You can live in Britain or Russia or even New Zealand if you like, but there will always be a little bit of San Fran lurking somewhere in your soul.'

I looked out over the cityscape, now just a bowl of twinkling lights against a black backdrop. I felt the certainty that I would return anchoring me to the earth beneath us.

Especially now I had Josh.

Not to mention Bella, and Lisa and Toby and Bill and Drusilla – yes, I was *definitely* coming back.

I kissed him again – just to make sure – and then, hand in hand, we walked back down the hill as the lights twinkled and the moonlit waters of the Bay gleamed before us.